MW01257985

SHIBBOLETH

Thomas Peermohamed Lambert

SHIBBOLETH

Europa
editions

Europa Editions
8 Blackstock Mews
London N4 2BT
www.europaeditions.co.uk

A catalogue record for this title is available from the British Library
ISBN 978-1-78770-555-5

Peermohamed Lambert, Thomas
Shibboleth

Cover design and illustration by Ginevra Rapisardi

The authorized representative in the EEA
is Edizioni e/o, via Gabriele Camozzi 1, 00192 Rome, Italy

Prepress by Grafica Punto Print – Rome

Printed and bound in Great Britain by Clays Ltd, Elcograf S.p.A

CONTENTS

For Wanda

SHIBBOLETH

PART 1
MICHAELMAS

Chapter 1

Stretching himself out on the edge of Oxford's least re-markable quad, Edward surveyed the little colonies that had sprung up since he arrived the previous week. There were precarious girls from North London on picnic blankets, floppy-haired boys meandering between them from croquet hoop to croquet hoop; there were footballers, netballers, rugby players; there was a troupe of rowers from the second boat grooming each other like apes; there were freshers with interesting new haircuts and postgraduates with interesting new political ideologies, and there was a man who looked too old to be doing a DPhil, wearing socks underneath his sandals and talking about something called, if Edward heard him correctly, 'the Baha'i Faith'; there were guitars, mandolins, banjos, bongos; there were amateur dramatists throwing around a foam stress ball and communicating in eloquent squawks to warm themselves up for Shakespeare; there were vegans; there were students with placards, loudly disavowing their parents, or their relationship to the means of production, or their genitals; there were students handing out badges asking their colleagues to *save* things—the children, the whales, the planet, Abdul's Kebab Van, themselves—and there was even a small circle of earnest Black nationalists, berets slouching in the late-September heat, though most of them, it had to be admitted, were white; there were picnic baskets; there were more vegans; there was a Korean girl silently watercolouring at a miniature easel; there were business school students talking about something called 'innovation' and mathematics students not talking at all; there were language students wittering on in their bad Spanish, and science students wittering on about various things they planned to explode. A few of the lawn's older inhabitants, he noticed, had acquired a new, slick, nervous quality since last year; they wore collared shirts and appeared to have combed their hair. Very occasionally, Edward heard new phrases drift over—talk of 'internships' and 'training contracts' and 'funding applications,' and, most disquietingly of all, 'the real world'— which was spoken with an undeniable sense of menace, but which would not unduly trouble them, he had it on good authority, until they had finished their exams.

Only after several minutes' observation did he notice the College porter. He was fairly typical, as porters went—a short, bald, anoraked creature who appeared to die a little with each breath, picking his way through the crowd, fending off 'This Sticker Ends Homelessness' stickers, growing redder and redder behind the pudgy authority of his forefinger as he tried to shoo the students away. No one seemed to be paying him much attention, and he was beginning, ever so slightly, to raise his voice.

'You need to vacate the main quad.'

He'd alighted on a scruffy-looking fresher, busy undraping a croquet mallet from his back and beginning to line up his next shot, grinning luridly at one of his friends.

'I said you need to vacate the main quad now. As in, right this minute.'

A bored flick of the hair. 'Yeah we're nearly done with our game.'

'I'm afraid the game will have to wait.'

'Yeah like five minutes. Ten max.'

'The quad is in use this afternoon for an external function.'

The fresher slid the croquet mallet off his shoulders and crossed his arms. 'Isn't it, like, for *our* use?'

'Not this afternoon.'

'As in, did the JCR Committee actually give permission for you to just take it over? Because there are lots of people who need the quad as a space for . . .'

'Look, I don't have time for this so just clear off.'

'Okay, so I'll be honest, this whole interaction is making me pretty anxious.'

The second fresher began to nod. 'He does have anxiety you know. It's diagnosed.'

'Exactly. Clinical. I have a letter and everything.'

'I really, really don't care if it's giving you a nervous breakdown, I just want you gone.'

'Yeah, well maybe you *should* care? Maybe you should care about the actual *students*. Like, I'm pretty sure we could file a . . .'

Edward began to gather up his things as he listened. Whatever was brewing, he wanted no part in it. Perhaps this aversion to trouble came naturally with having turned twenty-one, but, for some reason, what he was looking forward to most this term was the work—the tutorials with one of the dons already padding round the fringes of the green; sitting across from them in the armchairs as they nodded along in infinite indulgence to his essays. That, he supposed, was the *point* of second year; it was a time when people settled down after the furious jostling of the first, when they packed up their frenzied experiments in personality and affectation and succumbed to the simple inertia of who they were. He couldn't wait. Second year. The year everyone grew up.

'Edward?' The clap on his shoulder was enough to knock him off balance. 'Edward. It is you. Turn around at once. No, not like that—stand like a man, embrace me.'

'Youssef?' He squinted back up at the broad silhouette. 'I thought you were getting back tomorrow.'

'Precocious in all things Edward. He is come. The College may cease to hold its breath. No—no I won't, thank you.'

Youssef made a show of foregoing the cider he hadn't ac- tually been offered, but which he'd noticed, unopened, pro- truding from Edward's carrier bag. He had given up alcohol for Ramadan, he explained, and bowed his head in a way that made it clear that Edward was to admire this monk-like show of devotion. He had also shaved off last year's beard—a chinstrap for whose peculiar, patchy shape Youssef claimed to have found justification in three different hadiths—and without it, his face was rounder, bloated, presumably from all the fun he had over the summer.

'Job interviews,' Youssef explained, stroking his chin. 'Unsuccessful, alas. Goldman—bastards. Rothschilds—*bas- tards*. I'll grow it back, of course,' he added. 'My outward appearance will once again reflect my inner piety. But in the meantime, it's all a bit, well, "Death to the West."' He crouched down next to Edward and began to look him up and down. 'You look ill, Edward.'

'Why thank you.'

He nodded grimly. 'Fragile. Sick.'

'Yes, thank you, I'm glad you added two more adjectives.'

'Wilted. Impotent. Strangely effeminate, even. Where's that tan you white people are all meant to covet? What have I told you about venturing north of London during vacations? Have you been with that *family* of yours again? Edward. Edward, where are you going?'

'I was just leaving.'

'Well, now you are staying.' He began fumbling with his blazer. 'Now *my* vacation, of course, was rich and varied and full of important moral lessons.'

'Youssef . . .'

'Yes, I know you're desperate to hear about it, but there are dramatic considerations, many of which take time. Where shall Youssef begin? Where shall he pause for effect? Which of his many conquests will he relay in all their glory and which will he pass over in dignified silence?' He shrugged his blazer off his shoulders and laid it on the grass.

'What? No, don't sit down, Youssef. *Youssef.*'

'You really want to leave?' Youssef was smiling now, in the broad, uncomprehending way he always did when he wanted to make himself impossible to resist. 'And ruin our formidable demographic advantage? Come, Edward. Is this what the Prophet did at Badr?'

'I have absolutely no idea what the Prophet did at Badr.'

'I shall be honest with you, Edward: I, too, am hazy on the details. But I am told it was very impressive.'

Youssef was the first person Edward had met at Oxford, and the origin of their friendship, like those of most male friendships, had been strictly administrative. Last year's room ballot had placed Youssef in 33A, with its fireplace, its mezzanine, and the walk-in wardrobe that seemed so perfectly calibrated to house his treasury of crisp tweed blazers you could only assume that Allah himself had effected the allocation. Edward had been assigned 33B, a former priest hole with great wreaths of mould and plumbing that wailed like a call to prayer every morning at the break of dawn the moment Youssef cranked down the handle to commence one of his forty-minute showers. What Edward first noticed about him was not his immaculate suit, or his intimidating watch, or even the effortful way he adhered to his public-school accent, but the sheer *physicality* of him— the way his wide, boisterous, clumsy frame creaked floorboards as he approached; the way his suitcases dislodged blizzards of plaster from the corners of inconvenient walls as he hooted his vague, general greetings up the stairs. When he first pitched up on the landing, Edward had gone to shake his hand, only to be pulled into a long, pulverising embrace. While he politely tried to wriggle free, Youssef scolded him for being so *timid*, for letting Oxford turn him into one of those shy, useless little creatures of the written word it specialised in churning out as if this country needed more of them. His name, he said grandly, once Edward had finally been released, was Youssef Chamakh. What was his? Edward? Well, he couldn't be expected to remember *that*. What did he study, anyway? *English*? A grave mistake. 'I'd have assumed you spoke that already.' Youssef Chamakh, he explained as the two of them ambled down to face the single, wine-fogged night of socialising the members of their staircase undertook before forgetting about each other completely, didn't care about Shakespeare, or Milton, or any of those Englishmen of dubious sexuality whom Oxford would simply not let die. He had no need for such things, not because he was impervious to beauty, mind, or because he underestimated the contributions to human culture made by civilisations other than his own—which had occasionally been, he was prepared to admit, highly respectable—but because literature, he maintained, was for shy people with a hole inside of them, and Youssef was so full of life he might burst any second.

Apart from that, they had scarcely spoken in their first term, save for the odd grunt outside the bathroom, and perhaps a nod or two across the quadrangle. In November, Edward received a text in which Youssef wondered whether it might be prudent to separate a couple of fragile art students throwing glassware at each other down the corridor; in February, he and Youssef were forced to attend the same antiracist pottery class. But little more. If he did run into Youssef on the cramped landing they shared, Youssef would strike up a conversation—Edward, wasn't it? Had he gained weight? Had those glasses got thicker since last time or was it just his eyes?—only to break off suddenly, look impatiently over his shoulder, as though there had been something missing from Edward's reply, some set of manners or private code he had failed to observe. Perhaps it wasn't Edward's fault. He was learning that, when you'd been to a school as large and lavish and frankly indistinguishable from an Oxford college as Youssef's, you tended to stick to your own.

'He was from *where*?' Edward could still remember the moment he began to climb in Youssef's estimation. 'Zanzibar, Zanzibar—a Sultanate, no less. And African, too . . .'

It was last April. Quite by chance, Edward had taken his seat in the dining hall directly across from Youssef, and done his best to chisel his way into the conversation. As soon as he let the information slip, he felt Youssef's scrutiny through the row of tealights. He was leaning forward, scanning Edward excitedly, as though he were some rare exhibit you could only appreciate if you pressed your face right up to the glass. 'And now forgive me, Edward, I don't like to speak ill of the dead, but you are sure—you're *sure*—that your father was a Muslim?'

'Yes, but Youssef . . .'

'Who'd have *thought*!'

'But I've lost touch with the whole thing. The whole culture. I see them occasionally—a few uncles and cousins. But since he died . . .'

Youssef nodded gravely. 'No one to teach you where you come from. Yes, this explains your many deficiencies.'

'Right. Thank you.'

'Like the proud African baobab, upturned by the wind, its roots left to wither in the merciless sun.'

'Okay. Yes, sure. Whatever that means. But listen, Youssef . . .'

'. . . Now, you *must* come to IslamSoc, of course. And the al-Rifaaiya Sufi Discussion Group, and African Association, which should in turn, if you befriend the right people, get you into the Trinity Term Postcolonial Ball.'

'That's what I'm trying to say, Youssef. *African* is a stretch, too.' He sighed. 'Zanzibar isn't like Egypt. It's all a bit, well, *mixed*, genetically speaking. Persians, Indians, Africans—and you're never quite sure what you are, really.'

'Oh, but these are details,' said Youssef excitedly. '*Details*. Listen, I knew there must have been a reason we were put together.' He reached across the table and clasped his hand, studying the veins as if the blood belonged to both of them. Then, with a look on his face that suggested Edward had absolutely no choice in the matter, declared that he was to be followed, at once, to the college bar, where they would commence the first of many 'Don't tell *Allah*' bonding nights. The moment he settled on the creaking stool, Youssef began to pepper the conversation with Arabic, showing off:

'You will come to Islamic Society this Thursday?'

'We'll see.'

'You will, *Inshallah*. We'll bring you back into the fold eventually—into the *Ummah,* you see. One way or another. You know, you wouldn't think it, but this university is full of us.' He smiled. 'Well, not *full* of us—but there are plenty, enough to fend off the pig-eating hordes at any rate. Enough to avoid getting—what's the horrible word again?—*assimilated.*' He scanned Edward from head to toe as he accepted his third pint—very carefully, as though measuring him up for one of his tweed suits. 'Besides, I need someone to keep me company, make up the numbers against all those Arabs.'

'Excuse me?'

'All the Arabs. They look down on us you know. The way they look down on the Kaaba from their horrible skyscrapers.'

'Aren't *you* an Arab, Youssef?'

Youssef slammed down his pint; a great, yeasty sud rolled across the bar mat, which he summarily ignored. He was grinning in mock-exasperation, still friendly, but in a way that made Edward distinctly uncomfortable. 'How *dare* you Edward . . . An *Arab*? Me?' And so it was that Edward was introduced to the chaos—the great constellation of neurosis, invention, fear, pride—that Youssef had fashioned into an identity. Youssef was certainly not an Arab. He was a *Berber*, an indigenous North African, you understand. That was the first thing to get straight. Perhaps a little Nubian, too, or Ethiop—a splash of the Blue Nile in his veins—but an Arab? Never. They were simply a far older people, the Berbers: nobler, better established; they were in *Herodotus,* you know, who was Greek and reliable. Oh, and they were mystics—Sufis, not Salafists; that was *essential* for Edward to understand—and off he launched into one of his monologues, delivered in full 'imam voice,' as Edward had come to refer to it, thick with ancient scriptural quotations and peculiar grammatical constructions and little fragments of history that always seemed to go Youssef's way, somehow, as though all the triumphs and tragedies of the world had been perpetrated for his specific benefit.

'So you see . . .' He had finished now, and smiled sadly into his ale, watching it settle into two clear bands. 'They don't get it. They'll never get it. They think we're not real Muslims.'

'Yes, but—and I have said this coming up to six times now, Youssef—I'm *not* a real Muslim. I'm not even a fake Muslim.'

'Oh, but I'm afraid that's not something you get to choose.' Youssef held Edward's gaze for several seconds, very intently. 'Now . . .' his expression slackened into his usual grin, '. . . you know any Indonesians we could ask?'

Edward was finally dragged along to Islamic Society. He attended, with good grace, the al-Rifaaiya Sufi Discussion Group, the African Association, the Trinity term Postcolonial Ball—and the Marginalities Seminar, the Negritude Salon, the Oxford Circle for Friends and Allies of the Arab Nationalist Republics and the biannual benefit for the Home Counties Camel Sanctuary. The conversations, for the most part, were identical, varying only in length and contrivance depending on how much calvados Youssef had swigged on his frequent trips to the bathroom. This is my friend, he would gush upon returning. My friend from college. Have you met before? Have a samosa, Edward. No, his grandfather, actually. I know, very sad, but we're coping. Yes, he's handsome, in a way isn't he? That'll be the East African genes coming through. I mean, you have to imagine with a bit of a tan, you see, and some careful grooming. Yes, I'm trying, I'm trying. What? No, *Edward*. E—D—W. What comes next? O? Quite right, the prodigal son. No, Zanzibari actually. Or is it Zanzibarian? Here he is. The Zanzibarbarian . . . My friend, my friend—Edward could hear the insinuation, even if Youssef never spoke it—my drab, diluted friend, who has carelessly gone and lost his father, and would be alone in the world were it not for me.

'The thing about being a Muslim,' said Youssef, now firmly settled on the grass beside Edward 'as you and I are . . .'

'I'm not a Muslim.'

'Please, Edward, don't interrupt. The thing about being a Muslim—as you and I are—is that you instantly have a hook. I believe this is important, the world tending in the direction it is.'

'A hook?'

'A signature. A little kernel of interest around which to build your personality.'

'I think my personality is already firmly established.'

Youssef rolled his eyes. 'Come now, Edward. Be serious. I am trying to dispense advice.'

He reached forward without asking for a second can of cider, and launched into what was destined to become, the lilt in his voice made clear, another of his parables. Once upon a time, he explained, there was a young Egyptian prince. Yes, Edward, it had to be a prince; it gave the story a timeless quality. This prince's parents had built him a little oasis in the dusts of Cairo, a walled garden full of fountains and peacocks, enormous, syrupy dates and so many toys, that offered so many infinite narrative arcs of dragons and knights and damsels, that it was quite impossible to get lonely.

'It sounds blissful.'

'Oh.' Youssef's eyes had gone filmy. 'It was.'

One day, Youssef continued, the prince turned eleven, and was packed off to boarding school in a strange, rainy country where there were no palm trees and everything smelled of manure and no-one offered to sell you pyramid-themed keyrings whenever you stopped in the street. For three or four years, no one spoke to the poor little prince. He tried to play rugby, and fell on his face. He tried to talk to a few of the choicer students at the girls' boarding school with which his school was 'twinned' in what appeared to be some kind of covert eugenics programme, and was laughed at and told to try his luck on the Pakistani-laden council estate in the nearest county town.

'I know this part, Youssef.'

'Please, Edward. This is for your benefit.'

About four years into his exile, Youssef went on, a miracle occurred. A benevolent genie granted the girls their most fervent wish, which was to attend the grand old *madrasa* of Oxford, and they set about—and here Youssef paused for effect—*reinventing* themselves. They studied *Othello* for their A-levels and decided that they needed their own noble moor to drive into jealous rages; they took yoga classes and discovered deep affinities with the subtle religions of the East; they were cheated on by the pasty boyfriends who had controversially applied for Cambridge instead, and decided that the problem, in fact, lay in the entire edifice of Western culture and that it was incumbent on them to orchestrate a change. A few of the more enterprising among them, he continued, voyaged off into the dark continent on their gap years for various charitable initiatives, and discovered, while down there, the strange phenomenon of the *black* person, the *African*—the idea of him more than anything else, the way he bore so many sorrows and indignities without complaining and smiled his brilliant, nervous smile and looked so endearingly baffled when you told him you were interested in telling the world his story. When the girls returned to the rainy, manure-smelling country, everything was different. Everything, Edward. The sun glittered through the hedgerows, the butterflies danced in the ancient fields. The prince was treated like a prince at last.

Youssef settled back into the grass, staring up wistfully into the cloudless sky. 'You know a girl stopped me on Broad Street yesterday. One of the Wycombe Abbey houris. Phylloxera. Morton-Smythe. You must know her.'

'I definitely don't.'

'In harem trousers and everything. Supple. *Firm*. Fully recovered from the eating disorder. Anyway, she looks me up and down, and, apropos of nothing, you know what she says? She says "I'd love to learn more about your culture." Imagine it!'

'It sounds thrilling.'

'It *was* thrilling. Think about it, Edward. *Our* culture. Restored to the primacy not seen since the Abbasids erected their . . . Oh for goodness' sake, what is going *on* over there?'

He had turned towards the freshers, whose dispute with the porter had flared up once more.

The lead fresher was peering down his nose at the porter: 'See, even the phrasing's not great, is it. *I need you gone.*'

'Like we're going as quick as we can,' agreed the other fresher, nodding vigorously.

'You know we were literally in the final game phase.'

'Wait.' Youssef sat up fascinatedly on his elbows. 'Is that Monty?'

'I don't know. I don't know anyone called Monty.'

'It *is*. Montgomery Burton-Hogg. Durnford House captain. Honestly, Edward. You can't just go around *not knowing* people. It's embarrassing.'

He explained briskly, shaking his head as though disappointed that Edward hadn't been able to intuit the whole relationship by himself. He knew Monty, it turned out, from boarding school. And the other fresher had gone somewhere so similar, its social calendar and rugby fixtures and sexual assault hearings so intertwined with those of his own, he and Youssef were just as well acquainted. They were, he explained, gentry. Old money; sons of marquises, earls. Edward mustn't be fooled by their getup: this was what it was like now, you see; the faintly vagrant style of dress was a game, a lark, an excuse to trawl through the seedier parts of East London and feel the true depths of their pockets, just for a day. Yes, yes, they did look rather confident already didn't they? Standing there like that, croquet mallets draped jauntily over their shoulders. Quite right, Edward. As if they owned the place—and yet another sign, no doubt, of the institutional decline he had detected the moment he crossed the threshold at the beginning of term, in the unruly flowerbeds, the tracksuited freshers, the screw-capped wine bottles in the welcome dinner last Friday.

'And this is to say nothing, of course,' he continued, 'of the new crop of porters themselves. Look at this one. Grotesque.'

'I didn't know there were new ones.'

'There are always new ones. They breed them over the summer. Hatch them from test tubes in that horrible new godless Jewish biological sciences centre in North Oxford.'

'Yes, this seems highly plausible.'

'You haven't noticed them, Edward, because you are neutral, and are permitted to glide through the lodge like the angel Jibril. But with me they are different. Possessed of a cruelty known only to this country and its law enforcement.'

'And not Egypt, where the police are famously gentle and humane.'

Youssef took a final, long glance at the porter, who was just about giving up on his remonstrations, then turned, smiling sweetly, to Edward. 'Exactly,' he said. 'Now, enough of this. Pass me that book that you've been trying so hard to hide from me. You know I take a keen interest in your instruction. What is it, anyway? *Seas Incarnadine: Shakespeare, Macbeth and the Menstruating Body.*' He flicked it open. '"Chapter 1: Unsex me here." Goodness, Edward. Wonderful stuff, this. Potent. Timely. I can see why you think literature might just change the world.'

Edward had chosen to study English Literature not, like half of his course-mates, because he thought of himself as especially 'literary,' or even, like the other half, because he wanted a nice, clear proof of his own ability to read before surrendering to the cosmic inevitability of a law conversion course, but for the simple—and, he had since learned, slightly suspect reason—that he had liked it in school. In his first term at Oxford, he had attended every lecture and every seminar, and on the way back would run his fingers gleefully through chutes of ivy, patting the rain-weathered buildings as if the stone itself might leach some ancient secret directly into the skin. He roamed around the city in a haze of near-incredulity: he had done it, escaped from his old schoolmates with their mediocre grades and unimaginative dreams, and was *here*, surrounded by all these palaces of learning, all these bright, polished people with whom he would surely have long, meandering conversations about the dissociation of sensibility, and sprung rhythm, and tradition and the individual talent, deep into the night. They really *belonged*, these people; they already used all the right jargon, already knew all the best pubs, already felt in their bones which papers would condemn them to many tortuous evenings in the College library and which would allow them to cruise their way to a first if only they used the word 'hermeneutics' enough times. As the term progressed, however, he began to notice that very few of them seemed to feel the same way as he did. They were so *busy* all the time: after tutorials, his partners would zip off to the next workshop or JCR meeting, off to internships and interviews and somehow, before he had even noticed, autumn had rolled into winter and winter had rolled into spring without one of those long, meandering conversations ever actually materialising.

The first interaction that even came close had occurred in his second term. He had taken the Shakespeare paper that was still, despite the best efforts of the student body, compulsory, and had managed to lose himself beforehand in the warren of the College's old buildings. His tutorial partner was already seated when he arrived. She introduced herself as Rachel, and they exchanged the printed copies of the essays the tutor still expected them, in his old-fashioned way, to read aloud. From Germany, she added, and her dark brown eyes flickered in a way that looked almost embarrassed: English and Modern Languages, joint schools, so he would have to forgive the gaps in her knowledge. Her essay, which she read slowly in her slight accent, eyes moving back and forth like typewriter cartridges, was very, very good.

In the lamplit passage afterward, he found himself grinning: 'So?'

'So?'

'What did you think?'

She leaned thoughtfully against the stone. 'I liked him.'

'I meant my essay.'

'I liked that too.'

'It was terrible.'

'I enjoyed listening. You have a good reading voice.'

'I've been working on it. Trying to sound suitably posh.'

'Oh.'

'What?'

'You're not posh?'

'Me?' He laughed.

'Don't laugh. I can't tell these things. Are you joking?'

'No, Rachel, I'm not posh. I'm rough, actually, by Oxford standards.'

She wrinkled her nose in a smile. 'You don't seem very rough.'

'Well I am. Uncultivated. I'm surprised they let someone like me in the College at all actually.'

'Where are you from?'

Edward told her. She shook her head regretfully.

'Yeah, you wouldn't have heard of it.'

They talked for a while, leaning against opposite sides of the narrow stone passageway as the sky darkened outside. She was from Berlin, she said. Why Oxford? Well, because it was here, and it was beautiful. Come to think of it, she admitted, she hadn't chosen this entirely consciously—at least not with the hours of hair-tearing deliberation that you were meant to devote to these decisions. That was her secret, she supposed; that she didn't choose things so much as let them happen to her, and would doubtless end up with absolutely no money or prospects or job, or at least that was what her slightly staid German mother seemed to think when she mentioned that she would be studying Literature.

'What?' she said, when she saw his reaction. 'Why are you grinning like that?'

He shrugged. 'I can't imagine anyone *not* wanting their daughter to come here. In this country it's like—it's everything. I think when my mum found out I was coming to Oxford it was the best day of her life.'

'And your dad?'

'I think he would have liked it too. I don't know. He died before that was much of an issue.'

'Oh.' Rachel stared at him. 'Sorry.'

'It's okay. Honestly, it's fine. Hey, don't look so apologetic.'

'Right.'

'You're still looking apologetic.'

'I'm trying not to, I promise.'

A few noises had begun to drift into the passageway from

outside: voices, footsteps. Edward glanced over at the glowing windows, the line of students. 'Come to hall with me?'

'Now?'

'Yes.'

She shook her head. 'I can't,' she said.

'Next week then?'

'I'd like that.'

In hall that evening, he asked Youssef what he knew about Rachel. The two of them had only just begun to speak regularly, and Youssef was still in the first, manic flush of helpfulness that had attended the beginning of their friendship. Rachel? German Rachel, with the brown doe eyes and the surprisingly nice . . . Yes, he knew of her, in the way he knew of certain exotic illnesses and ambient species of mould. Why was he asking, anyway? Ah, so that was it. It was all becoming clear.

'What? No, nothing is becoming clear Youssef.'

'I see . . .'

'Nothing is . . .'

'Worry not, Edward. I shall ask around and see what I can find.'

By the time Youssef summoned him to the Common Room at the end of the week by means of a cryptic text message, he had amassed a great store of information. Rachel was an international student, with a scholarship from some foundation or other—'one of those foreigners they keep letting in,' as Youssef phrased it. He had been through what scant photos of her he could find online, and could, he had to admit, understand the appeal—in the interests of colonial reparation, if nothing else, given what the Germans had got up to in East Africa. This, after all, was the only possible reason for his unnatural penchant for all those pale-legged flat-posteriored birth-controlled English girls staggering up Headington Hill beneath their omelettes of make-up: Suez. But there was a problem, Edward. She had a boyfriend. Someone she'd known in Berlin and was now studying in one of the lesser colleges. It had been established, unfortunately, to a high degree of certainty and by all the proper scientific and exegetical methods: Rachel was taken.

'And you know what she's been saying about you, of course?'

'She's been saying things about me?'

'She has been slandering you, Edward.'

'What has she said?'

'She *said*'—Youssef shuddered—'that you're sweet. I quote directly: "He's sweet." Yes, I'm sorry to give such devastating news but there it is. Jemima has confirmed, and she is very reliable, at least for a woman. Her father is a judge, you know.'

'Sweet? That's not so bad.'

'What? No. Sweet is bad, Edward. Sweet is very bad. You know what else was sweet?'

'I don't know. Those raisins in the Qur'an you always talk about?'

'No, Edward. Be serious. I was going to say the poison fed to the Prophet by the treacherous Zaynab bint Al-Harinth. This is not a good thing.'

'Ah, I see.'

'The boyfriend: he is not sweet. He is older. You are not older. He is a highly accomplished political activist. You are not a highly accomplished political activist. He owns his own apartment. You will never own your own apartment.'

'Thank you, Youssef.'

'Better to give this up, Edward. Find yourself a nice East African girl, I say.'

Edward tried not to pay him any mind. Still, he tended to avoid Rachel in College from then on: he refrained from inviting her after their next tutorial, even though he had the strange sense, as she gazed across at him in the passageway, that she was waiting for him to do exactly that. They had four more tutorials together that term, and he spent most of them trying to say something of sufficient merit to get her to linger behind afterwards—or at least some joke funny enough make her stifle a laugh, or place the soft pink eraser of her pencil against her lips to stop herself from smiling, which, when it did happen, was a small victory all on its own. In the passageway after their final tutorial, he said goodbye, and said, without quite meeting her gaze, that he'd enjoyed it, that he'd enjoyed all of them, in fact, the tutorials, he meant, and that it was a shame they would be doing different papers next term—only to look up and catch, in her brown eyes, a look of amusement.

'Edward.'

'Mm?'

'Can I ask you something?'

'Yes. Sure.'

'Did you tell Youssef to ask about me?'

'What? No. Why?'

'It's okay, I don't mind.'

'I mean your name came up in conversation, maybe. But I wouldn't say . . .'

'What did you want to know?'

'Honestly Rachel, nothing . . .'

'Nothing?' She smiled. 'I'm almost disappointed.'

'Tell me, Edward,' said Youssef, adjusting a triangle of lower abdomen that had materialised at the bottom of his shirt as he wriggled into a more comfortable position on the grass, 'about your love life. Your conquests over the holidays. In these things, too, I take an interest.'

'There were no "conquests."'

'Ah, but there are incursions planned? Battle lines drawn for the new term?'

'This is very violent imagery Youssef.'

'Did you give up on the . . . well, you know.'

'I don't know.'

'How to put it politely... the German one?'

Measuredly: 'I don't know what you're talking about.'

'Yes you do. What happened after all those tutorials—some kind of liaison, I presume?'

'What? No, nothing like that. I didn't even see her. I was too busy going to Muslim things with you. Is that your *third* cider?'

'You should be bringing women *to* those Muslim things. You should be introducing them to *me* at the Muslim things. You should be explaining to them in great detail why they, too, should be going to the Muslim things, so as not to incur the wrath of the divine and be boiled for eternity in corrosive fluids.'

'I honestly can't think of anything worse.'

'How much did you like her anyway? Did you really really really like her? Surely not.'

'Surely not.'

'Are you blushing? Is this that feeble Caucasian sunburn thing I keep hearing about?'

'I don't want to talk about this.'

'Excellent. Because I have new prospects for you, anyway. There is, rumour has it, at this very college, a fresher . . .'

'Oh, good.'

'. . . who went to Cheltenham Ladies *and* is reported to be a highly skilled gymnast *and*—get this—is three-sixteenths Ottoman. *Imperial* Ottoman, Edward. I believe that, faced with the right suitor, she may well convert.'

'I'm not looking to *convert* anyone Youssef.'

'Well this leads me on to my major prospect then. She certainly will not convert for you, and is unlikely to mature into a model of wifely piety of the kind envisaged by the Surah An-Nisa, thirty-four. But rumour has it that she has become, for whatever reason, *ever* so slightly fascinated by exactly the region that you happen to come from, and with the right lack of scruple, could be induced to make an Edward-shaped mistake.'

'Lucky me. And who is she?'

Youssef shook his head. 'Not yet, Edward. Patience. You shall meet her, soon enough.'

Turquoise ocean, white sand, and a sky as blue as heaven itself. The Spice Islands conjure up exotic images of dhows, lateen sails against the dawn, whitewashed Arab houses curled like sleeping women in the spurs of the coast, and tall palm trees swaying on a warm tropical breeze redolent with the aroma of cloves and frangipani; the reality is . . .

'You coming, Edward?'

. . . Sumerians, Assyrians, Egyptians, Phoenicians, Indians, Chinese, Malays, Persians, Portuguese, Arabs, Dutch and—of course—the British: all have set foot on the island's white beaches, each leaving behind a different legacy, and each adding another layer of complexity to the question: what, exactly, is the 'real' Zanzibar?

The door rattled louder on its hinges. 'What are you waiting for, the *Mahdi*? We'll be late.'

Edward snapped shut *The Wayfarer's Zanzibar: Colour Edition, 1982*, a faded palm tree on the cover. 'One second Youssef.'

'Now, Edward.' Youssef occupied the entire doorframe. He leaned into the room, a hand on each pilaster, his grin muffled by the thick, woolly stubble that had sprung up in the three days since he had surprised Edward on the quad. 'The Cultural Sensitivity Workshop,' he continued, 'is the single most important moment in the academic year. Look what happens in the Middle East, where they have no such tradition. War, pestilence, rape. Barbarity beyond your wildest . . .' He had noticed the travel guide, and sauntered over. 'Brushing up on your Sub-Saharan credentials?'

'It was a gift from my dad.'

'Well, you shouldn't be shy about it. Here . . .' Youssef plucked the book off the table and flicked through the pages with interest. 'You should use this stuff,' he said. 'Tell the people the secrets of your insalubrious past.'

'Can you please put it down?'

'It would do you no end of good. Socially, I mean . . .'

'I asked you to put it down.'

'They're all terrified,' he went on, turning over the guide-book in his fingers and dog-earing the back cover in the process. 'Terrified of saying something wrong—accidentally summoning a djinn or contradicting someone's lived experience. And besides . . .' He leaned closer, his voice dipping to a conspiratorial whisper: 'I thought *Egypt* was exciting. But Zanzibar? The "Spice Islands"? All those "Z"s? You could be the king of this place if you tried.'

'That's enough, Youssef.' Edward snatched the book out of Youssef's hand, dropped it into his satchel, and pushed his way out into the passage.

Youssef followed, pulling the door shut after him. 'You want a programme?'

'Since when did these things have a programme?'

'Since the College allowed for one in its annual budget, Edward. Here.' He pulled open the lapel of his jacket and fished out a booklet from the inner pocket. 'Now,' he said, as he thrust the title-page—*Overcoming Whiteness: The Ally's Enchiridion*—into Edward's eyeline, 'you ought to know some of the Advisory Committee, which is useful in itself—a name to drop if they accuse you of touching up a fresher or denying a genocide or something. Page twelve, Edward. No, that's the list of corporate donors. That's a picture of the student welfare co-ordinator's dog. No, I'm not sure why either. There.'

He paused a second, eyes drifting down the list of exotic dou-
ble and triple-barrelled names. 'Well, I suppose you know
Hepzibah Coulson-von Ribbentrop at least.'

'I have no idea who that is.'

'Richard Ogedegbe? Harrow. With the sapphire mines?'

'Yeah, no.'

'Isabel Kramer, surely. Some of her ancestors are working-class, like you. She wrote a personal essay about it last year
in the *Cherwell*.'

'Astonishing as it may seem, no. And I'm not actually
working-class.'

'Francine Hogmanay-Pung?'

'I haven't heard of any of these people, Youssef.'

Youssef let out a little whimper of disappointment. 'I just
don't understand how you can spend so long in a college without actually *talking* to anyone.' They had reached the foyer of
their staircase now, and Youssef pushed open the heavy door
with his hip, stretching his fingers thoughtfully into the curtain
of rain. 'Well, it doesn't matter really. I suspect there's only one
name you need to worry about.'

Edward rolled his eyes. 'And whose name is that?'

'Look at your group. That's right. The table—between
the glossary and index of abbreviations. No, not *that* table—
that's . . . actually I'm not quite sure what that is. A kind of
Richter scale for hate crimes, I think. Next one?'

'Can you just tell me, Youssef?'

'*There* we go.' Youssef placed a triumphant finger at the
head of programme's forty-ninth page. 'Remember I told you
about a certain kind of posh girl, whom your ethnic credentials
will fascinate despite your basic lack of charisma? Well there
she is, Edward. Surely you know *her* at least.' He withdrew his
finger. *Group B:* read the curlicued heading, *To be chaired by
Angelica Mountbatten-Jones.*

Angelica Mountbatten-Jones was only a year older than Edward and Youssef by the calendar, but each time Edward had encountered her last year, she had given the distinct impression that the difference was far greater. Everything about her—the brisk, breathy voice, the expensive business attire, the subtle, foot-tapping impatience that undergirded every conversation—struck him as distinctly *grown-up*; it was easy, when she mounted whatever podium or barricade or soapbox she happened to be occupying that day, to imagine her commanding a large commercial enterprise, or perhaps a small nation. Angelica spent most of their first year playing up this maturity to any and every available audience: going on and on about how she'd lived an incredibly full life, full of *experiences*, you see, so it was only natural for her to exude a certain *je ne sais quoi*, a certain *authority* and *presence*, and that, quite as much as the vast gamut of qualifications she boasted on paper, was why everyone ought to vote for her for Common Room President. From what he could gather, these *experiences* seemed to consist mainly of the gap year she had undertaken in preparation for her Spanish degree, a Latin American extravaganza of the usual proportions attested by the Quechua charm bracelet that jangled round her ankle. 'It keeps me grounded,' she mused to Youssef the first and only time they had been involved in the same conversation—one afternoon last term, as she canvassed her way from college lawn to college lawn in one of her most diaphanous and persuasive summer dresses. 'Reminds me of my responsibilities to those less fortunate. Speaking of responsibilities, in fact . . .'

Edward watched her as she spoke. She had settled on the grass next to Youssef with such expert casualness he hardly noticed she'd done it, and was putting on quite a show: shaking back her sunburst of blonde hair and stretching out her slender legs, already tanned to perfection by what had been, he deduced from the fragments she relayed to Youssef, her third long-haul holiday that year. Some island called 'Bazaruto'—*stunning*, he just *had* to go before everyone else went and ruined it—with a safari on the East African mainland thrown in for good measure because her father was there on sabbatical and she had always found giraffes, in particular, very moving. Most of the conversation went by without her in any way inviting Edward to contribute: there was a lot about the new courses the College would be offering next year—the MSc in Sustainable Business and Management (good), the DPhil in Classics (bad)—and several disquieting minutes on English Literature, which Angelica, for some reason, took to be the most dangerous and bloodthirsty of all subjects, the handmaiden of a cruel white Empire. Unlike Spanish, of course, whose speakers were 'Hispanic, actually,' she explained when Youssef began to pipe up about the *Reconquista*, 'which is a totally different thing.' Then there were a few minutes about an ominous construction called 'the List' that Edward didn't quite understand, but which already contained the names of several of the older, greyer, more distinguished tutors. Then it was on to pleasantries: people they both knew, or people whom Youssef would soon know, if he played his cards right and replied to the frenzied messages of the schoolmate of Angelica's whom he had taken on that date. Every so often, Angelica's sundress would flutter up against her thigh in the breeze; she would smooth it back down without once breaking the flow of speech, tuck it beneath her on the grass so that Edward could see the full shape of her. He had the strange sense that these adjustments, when she made them, were very deliberate indeed.

'Youssef?' she said after a while. 'Could you do me a favour?'

Youssef drew himself up chivalrously. 'Why of course. I am your faithful vizier.'

'Could you tell me who this person is?' She didn't bother to look at Edward. 'Does he speak? Why doesn't he close his mouth properly?'

'This is Edward.'

'I see. Does he always stare like that?'

'Often, yes. But it's the way he was raised, I'm afraid.' He lowered his voice to a solemn whisper: 'State school, Ange.'

'Oh.'

'Single parent. *Upwardly mobile.*'

'Oh, I see.' When Angelica spoke, her voice was softened with pity: 'That's just awful. But good for you, I suppose, Edward.' She blinked her royal blue eyes and gazed at him. Slowly, she shook back her hair and turned up her face to the sun; as she leaned back, the summer dress rode farther up her legs and she pointed her toes, as though trying to expose as much skin as possible to the warm rays. 'I didn't mean what I said, you know,' she said, without turning to face him. 'About the staring. You can look at me, if you like.'

Youssef splashed his way quite happily down Park End Street to the Business School where the workshop was to be held. From time to time he stretched out his fingers beyond the province of his umbrella, as though even after his five years at a rural boarding school and one in Oxford, the rain was still a curiosity. To Edward, the enthusiasm came as something of a surprise. Youssef had long professed a deep hatred for the Business School, though he had, it was true, been there countless times in the service of his future career—to conventions and conferences, seminars and symposia: *Nurturing That Creative Spark*, *What Marcus Aurelius Can Teach You About Entrepreneurship*, *The Art of Trickling Down*.

'So you've mellowed, then, on the subject of the Business School?'

Youssef turned to face Edward, but kept moving backwards over the slick paving slabs. 'Mellowed?'

'You used to hate it.'

'I *do* hate it.'

'You should turn around, you almost hit that old lady.'

'I hate that hideous un-Islamic building by the train station for people who can't afford cars. And those . . . nooses they all wear around their necks—what are these called?'

'Lanyards?'

'And have you actually met a Business student, Edward?' he continued, still walking backwards. 'Have you spoken to one? Noticeably subnormal. Unable to eat solid food. They have to wear helmets when they go outside the lecture hall.'

'Right. Could you please turn around Youssef? You will get hit by a car and you will die.'

'And then, of course,' said Youssef, at last swivelling on his heel and teetering on the brink of the main road, 'there is the founder.'

Edward was familiar enough with this particular objection. Isaiah Levy was a wealthy Ukrainian Jew who had funded five libraries in Oxford, and whom Youssef despised with a quiet fury that seemed quite unmoored from anything he was actually supposed to have done. When the University slipped a place in the world rankings it was because Isaiah Levy had a niece applying to Cambridge. When the College cancelled its firework display it was because Isaiah Levy had a primary school in the West Bank to bomb and needed the gunpowder. When a last-minute recount of votes had robbed Angelica of the Common Room presidency, Youssef concocted a vast, blurry theory involving not only Isaiah Levy, but the FBI, the Babylonian Captivity and the moon—it was this aspersion, in fact, that he appeared to be recycling now, as he strolled obliviously through the honking traffic and rounded the final corner before the Business School's vast concourse.

As they meandered through the crude attempts at landscaping that led up to the great, glass entranceway, Edward listened with his usual indulgence. Youssef's litany, he had to admit, made him slightly uncomfortable: there was a definite *ethnic* tinge to the paranoia, affected and essentially humorous though it was almost certainly intended to be. Whatever the real source of the mistrust, Youssef did mention Isaiah Levy's Jewishness with remarkable frequency. Though perhaps, Edward reasoned as he trotted obediently up the shallow steps, this had been exaggerated for his benefit, laid on thick to impress the new recruit. Youssef was, after all, a Muslim, and Edward was pretty sure that a vague, instinctive suspicion of Jews was something you simply had to forgive in Muslims—that anything else would be some kind of failure of cosmopolitanism, a rejection of the hand of friendship that had been so graciously offered. He decided not to take it all too seriously. A lot of the more pointed references seemed to be going over his head, anyway: in truth, Edward wasn't even sure he knew any Jews, and they had certainly never been talked about when he was growing up; they seemed like one of those things that hadn't quite made it to his part of the country, like quinoa or Ayurvedic medicine, reserved for people who worked in law and finance and the editorial sections of all those literary magazines to which his course-mates had been given subscriptions for Christmas.

'You know, Youssef,' he said at the first available lull, when Youssef paused his speculation about Isaiah Levy's undue influence over medical research funding to scan his card at the door, 'I don't think they really have them where I'm from. At least not in the concentrations you seem to be describing.'

Youssef banged the door open with his hip. 'Stem cells?'

'Jews. Jewish people.'

'What do you mean you don't have Jews? Jews are everywhere, Edward. Scattered to the winds.'

'Well I've never met anyone who says they're a Jew. I've never met anyone who *I've* been able to identify as a Jew.'

'You know they don't wear the little hats all the time?'

'But it's not really something people talk about where I'm from. I don't know. Maybe there are Jews and they're too shy, or they just don't think it's worth bringing up. I mean, how do you know, when you meet one?'

'The names, usually. David. Adam. Jonathan. *Esther*.'

'Those just sound like normal names.'

'No, Edward. Youssef is a normal name. Abdulaziz is a normal name. Qudratullah-Waheed is a normal name. More normal than *Edward*, that's for sure.' He lowered his voice. 'Look here, are you sure you've never met any? What about the last time you were in Hampstead? Highgate?'

'I've never been to those places.'

He sprang back: 'Alas! Another poor Muslim boy robbed of his patrimony by the insatiable Jew.'

'Not so *loud*, Youssef. You can't say stuff like that.'

'I can say anything I like. I come from a marginalised group.'

'And you can't blame your upbringing either. Just because people are antisemitic in Egypt . . .'

'Now listen Edward,' he said, growing still all of a sudden, peering down his nose very gravely. 'There is absolutely no antisemitism whatsoever in Egypt. These are Israeli lies.'

'You see some might call *that* antisemitic . . .'

'No, no Edward. Antisemitism is when you think they're lizards. I just think they have a lot of money, which they do.'

'*You* have a lot of money.'

'Exactly. And this is why I must be considered an expert.'

At that, he flounced off, gliding through the Business School's immaculate foyer as though the journey had been programmed into him at birth. Edward followed reluctantly; he could see the other students from his college now, gathered densely at the back of the room beneath a strange, aluminium feature with no clear architectural purpose. Youssef emerged after a few seconds, brandishing three or four of the glossy leaflets, which he briefly flicked through himself, then offered to Edward, a look of disdain on his face. The leaflet on top was titled *Pocahontas's Feather: Or, Why We Should All Stick To Our*

Own Culture. There was a little photo of Angelica in the corner, in her business suit and Tanzanite earrings, lips stretched into their widest, most despotic smile.

'Now you'll need someone to keep an eye on you,' said Youssef. 'Whisk you out of danger should the need arise.'

'I didn't know there tended to be casualties at these things.'

'Oh, yes,' he said mock-seriously. 'Several each year.'

They were looking, Youssef explained as he piloted Edward through the crowd with a hand at the small of his back, for his friend Conrad—'from school' he added, with an approving little nod as though this were an unassailable assurance of good character. Now Conrad, he continued, was an aristocrat, a genuine one—not the spawn of one of those stupid life peers—with a coat of arms and a family history that could trace itself back to some truly virtuosic pillages: and whatever financial, sexual and other immoralities he may or may not be guilty of, they were entirely forgivable on account of his breeding. He was, however, unlike most aristocrats, literate, and would doubtless subject Edward to a small, informal test of his general cultural level— something Greek, most likely, given the aforementioned sexual proclivities—in order to work out whether Edward was educated enough to be worth his time. Not that there was any need to be nervous, of course. 'Here he is,' he said, guiding Edward forward. 'Yes, him, with the signet ring. Go on, Edward, don't be shy. Him. The tall one. For goodness' sake, Edward. Just put on your best, most irresistible Muslim smile and shake the man's hand.'

Edward sidled up to Conrad. He was tall, far taller than either of them, and so immaculately turned out in his long, waxed coat, studded with raindrops that looked as though laid there by his own personal jeweller.

'Edward, I presume,' said Conrad. He drew out his vowels in a way that somehow made every word seem like far, far more trouble than it was worth, looking him up and down in silent appraisal as he shook his hand. 'Yes, you were right Youssef. Skin suitably pasty. Eyes suitably blue. Posture suitably stooped and unimposing, with a vague sense of existential defeat emanating from every pore. He'll do nicely.'

'It's good to meet you too, Conrad.'

Conrad glanced at Youssef: 'He is aware of his sacrificial role, no?'

Youssef laughed and slapped Edward on the shoulder. 'He's only playing, Edward.' Then he turned to Conrad: 'Though he'd go willingly, I suspect. Edward here is more taken with Angelica than he'd like to admit.'

Conrad let out a doleful, cooing noise: 'She's got her claws into him already?'

'They have been introduced.'

'Warm evening, sundress, condescending tone?'

'Late afternoon,' said Youssef, before Edward had a chance to protest. 'But yes, in substance.'

'Did she like him?'

'She liked his debased social position.'

'Did she do that thing with her legs?'

'Of course.'

Conrad shuddered. 'That *is* a shame. I was almost starting to like you, Edward.'

Whatever Edward said in the three or four polite, excruciating minutes that followed, it didn't make much of an impression on Conrad. It occurred to him, in fact, that Conrad and Angelica had something in common: not a likeness, exactly, but a faint, sneering attitude you sensed lurked behind the crisp hairlines and unfollicled skin. At least Youssef was there to direct it. Until, that was, the doors clattered open and the students began to filter inside, and Conrad gave Edward his final, pregnant glance. 'Well, consider yourself warned,' he said, smoothing the front of his coat as he turned. 'There's a good chance she won't go for you of course. But if she does, *do* try and do everything she says. And watch out. Or you'll end up on that list of hers too.'

The moment Angelica Mountbatten-Jones appeared in the doorway and invited them inside in that famous, grown-up voice—calmly, please, and single file—the whole foyer fell silent. People were staring at her, involuntarily: the girls, with a kind of fear borne of experience; the boys, particularly the great hair-gelled expanse of the football team, with the kind of respectful admiration they usually reserved for graduate students or tutors or the actresses occasionally seen filming in some of the older, prettier colleges—women, in other words, who remained firmly out of reach. Angelica had certainly changed since last year. She had always been beautiful, always been poised and slim and authoritative from the moment Edward first saw her—but she had clearly looked after herself following the disappointments of her presidential campaign. She had let her hair grow longer; it fell against her shoulders now, and she seemed to have acquired a deft talent for flicking it attractively and breaking out into a disarming smile whenever she was on the verge of appearing too stern. She hadn't lost weight, exactly, but she seemed somehow reproportioned, her waist even more finely tapered, Edward's attention falling more naturally elsewhere, on the casual, matter-of-fact way she had left several buttons open on her soft, billowing, vaguely ethnic shirt. 'You can look at me if you like,' she had said on the lawn last term; as he passed her in the doorway, Edward tried his luck again.

'Just find a seat please,' she said flatly. There was no hint of recognition on her face: to Angelica, he realised, his was but a transient existence, liable to vanish as soon as unperceived, like in one of the dreary Buddhist proverbs she had begun to paste on the notice board every fortnight in a spirit of intercultural exchange.

As Edward let himself be ushered into the corner by Conrad,

Angelica took her seat at the head of the large, U-shaped conference table, and began to introduce her 'co-organisers'—distin-
guishable, if not from the bright cylinders of refreshment they
were permitted to keep on the desk and bang like gavels whenever they had something new to say, then from the way they
kept looking over at Angelica, nodding their heads, lowing and
burbling each time she said a word like 'hegemonic' or 'valid.'
To Angelica's left were Izzy K and Tilly F, art students with un-
necessary post-nominals conferred by the same north-London
prep school as Angelica, who, from the strange, yearning way
they shared a single reusable coffee cup, appeared to be in some
kind of relationship. To Angelica's right was Oscar, 'who was
actually in Peru with me,' and 'a really trustworthy and sensitive
person'; Anita (bangles, lime vitamin water, twenty-eight stone);
and finally, in the corner, 'Riz'—'a deserving beneficiary of the
new bursary scheme,' Angelica said proudly—who sported a
gold chain and a pouch of tropical-flavoured juice, and who
was also clearly on quite a number of drugs, though this last fact
was not mentioned in the introduction.

Conrad managed to enliven what looked to be turning into
a tedious business. His hand shot up at almost every opportunity (Edward counted twelve times in the first five minutes); his
face, whenever Edward glanced his way, was a mask of barely
concealed glee. The workshop's first topic of discussion—'discussion' was the favoured term, though Edward noticed very
little room for audience contribution, and indeed Oscar had
been equipped with a little bell, which he was to jingle any time
someone from the floor made a point that threatened the carefully crafted rubric—was something called 'culture.' 'Culture,'
Angelica informed them, glancing occasionally down at the programme, was just about the most precious commodity anyone
could have; it was found mainly among international students
and people who had at least one grandparent born overseas.
Culture—she checked her notes—was something that arose

spontaneously out of history, and was primarily the product of *struggle* and *suffering* and *resistance* and thus very difficult for anyone else to understand unless they had been through the requisite wars of decolonisation.

Tribal tattoos: that was culture. The non-nuclear family: that, too, was culture. Also, curry. For the rest of the student body, 'culture' could be accessed through a number of officially sanctioned channels: the Common Room's fortnightly 'Tell Us Where You Come From' evening, or the raft of society open days and events that would begin next spring with the Afro-Caribbean Professional Networking Mixer. The *problem*, she continued, on her feet now, programme discarded and her thumbs pressing themselves white into the desk, occurred when students decided they liked someone else's culture a little too much. Oh yes, she had seen it happen. They would go blundering in, twisting their hair into the most *awful* and *offensive* shapes and attempting to cook strange-smelling dishes full of spices they had not received the proper training to use, and which, if they were not careful, often sparked not just mild annoyance in the true proprietors, but grand, primordial emotions like *shame* and *dishonour* and *sacrilege* which most people here could not possibly appreciate, unless they had read a considerable amount of contemporary social theory and interned at several cutting-edge NGOs. 'And if in doubt,' she added, drawing herself up to her full, self-satisfied height, 'what you need to do is *ask* someone. If you could all just turn to page twenty-three of the pamphlet . . .'

Edward obliged. *Who can I ask?* read the title of the double-page spread.

'We've taken the time to put together a list of liaisons,' Angelica continued. 'Think of them as spokespeople, really, friendly faces inside the College who . . .'

Edward scanned the list of names below:

Black: Liberty Vanderbilt-Jackson
Asian (South): Hardipa Kaur
Asian (East): Asafoetida Wong
Latinx: Anita Primo de Rivera
Native American: [post as yet unfilled] . . .

Conrad, once again, had begun to snigger. He raised his hand, languidly as he could: 'Ange . . .'

'Now, I'm sure a lot of you'll be wondering where *you* fit into all of this,' Angelica went on, ignoring Conrad pointedly.

'*Angelica.*'

'Not now, Conrad.'

'I was wondering if I could be Native American liaison?'

'Well, you can't. You have to be Native American to be Native American liaison.'

'I am Native American. Spiritually.'

'No you're not.'

'I like body paint. I like feathers. I call this a spiritual affinity. Or do you think this is simply true of all gay men?'

'I don't think you realise how offensive this is.'

'I don't think *you* recognise how offensive this is. A proud, spiritually Native American man, told by a blonde privately-educated woman to skulk back to the dusty prairie whence he came.' He shook his head exasperatedly. 'I'm fully qualified. I like camping . . .'

'Can you sit down please? No, don't approach the desk . . .'

'You're not above stealing things from *my* culture when it suits you.'

'What's that supposed to mean?'

'My culture. As a gay man struggling to survive in this most conservative and unreconstructed of institutions. A member of the . . . what's the acronym these days?'

Tilly supplied the acronym; the room erupted in a brief moo of approval, until Angelica's glare silenced it.

'You see,' continued Conrad, facing the audience now and clearly enjoying himself, resting a starched, white sleeve on the back of an empty chair as though it were a despatch box, 'gay men have long had their pick of the bunch at Oxford. Boat club initiations, pederastic tutorials, All Souls dinners, that kind of thing. All in good fun.'

Angelica had begun to tear her pamphlet into little shreds. 'Yes, thank you Conrad, for sharing. But to return to the issue of culture . . .'

'Ever since they arrived at this institution in the 1920s, women have been chipping away at these time-honoured traditions.'

'This is not a debating society, there's no need to . . .'

'Women like you, Ange.'

'I don't know what you're talking about.'

To the audience again: 'We all know how she likes them, don't we? Rosy cheeks, floppy hair, a finger of tequila away from letting those delicious, boarding-school flirtations burgeon into an entire lifestyle. All those free, careless young men—locked up in the iron bonds of heterosexuality.'

'Conrad.'

'An ancient, noble culture, callously appropriated by . . .'

'For God's *sake* Conrad!' Angelica's chair skidded backward, scattering protective felt pads across the floor, and sending Izzy K and Tilly F into a frenzy of pacification. Riz, Edward noticed, had fallen off his chair. Even Conrad sat down, stunned into silence by the volume.

'Listen, everyone. I'm afraid I really need your co-operation today. Not only is "enthusiastic participation" a condition of our funding, but . . .' She glanced down once again, 'but Liberty's notes make it quite clear that this is meant to be a *dialectical* process.'

One of the football players raised his hand. 'What does dialectical mean?'

'Excuse me?'

'Dialectical. Like, the word.'

'Basically, it means . . . well it's like . . .' Angelica turned over another page of what remained of her pamphlet, then another, then flipped it over to its back cover. 'Right, so essentially it's when . . . Hang on. Sorry—Conrad, you don't need to stand up every time something pops into your head.'

Conrad ignored her. 'Doesn't it mean something like, I don't know, "relating to the logical discussion of multiple opposing ideas and opinions"?'

'What?'

'Rather than, I don't know: "restating the same shrill little orthodoxy over and over again in different voices."'

'I think it has something to do with Marxism, actually.'

'Do you ever remember what it was like, Angie, *before* you started reading all those blogs and subscribing to all those newsletters? When we talked in the normal rhythms of human conversation and spoke with words whose meanings we actually knew? You and I used to have such *lovely* conversations. But now, I fear, the faculty of language . . .'

'I know what it *means*, Conrad.' Angelica let out a short, sharp, astonishingly mirthless laugh. 'I was actually trying to bring in some opposing ideas before you hijacked everything.'

'Were you now . . .'

'Yes. We were going to hear from Oscar.'

'Oscar isn't a real person. He's a gap year with a nervous system. Sorry Oscar.'

'And I was going to go to the floor, actually.' Another laugh. 'Actually if you hadn't interrupted, we'd already *be* at the portion of the workshop set aside for diverse voices. So thank you very much for that.'

'Oh really? Who were you going to involve?'

'Everyone will get their turn.'

'They don't seem to have managed so far. Go on, Angelica, who were you going to ask for a contribution?'

'Well . . .' Angelica's gaze was roving round the room like a searchlight now, landing on each of them in turn. 'I'd like to involve . . .' and suddenly, without his quite realising, she was looking straight at Edward, completely motionless, content in her choice. 'Eric, was it?'

'Ed . . .' His voice came out hoarse, and he cleared his throat. 'It's Edward.'

He heard Conrad chuckle off to his side. 'No one is called Eric, Ange.'

'Ah yes, Edward. *Edward.*' She rolled around the syllables in her mouth, as though taking pains to impress some distinguished foreign dignitary. 'Now, Edward. As I'm sure you've noticed, some people, myself and Conrad included, tend to get rather, well, *passionate* about the issues expressed in these workshops. But sometimes . . . sometimes we ignore what everyone *else* thinks. You know, *ordinary* people. The man in the street.' Her smile retreated a fraction. 'So, I guess we were wondering, as someone who's from a more "conventional" background . . .' she scored the punctuation into the air with her forefingers '. . . well I'm just interested in what you have to say.'

'About what?'

'About the last twenty-five minutes of this talk. About everything. Did you agree with Conrad?'

'I guess,' he said, looking into his lap, 'it's just when I think about culture, I don't really see it a group of objects that are owned by distinct groups. Or at least, I just wonder if the language of private property is the best way to talk about whatever claims we all have on—a feather, was it?' He looked up; Angelica's face was blank and inexpressive. 'But that's just my perspective.'

'Well, there's quite a lot of literature to the contrary, Edward.'

'Yes, like I said I don't know.'

'Do you think it's fair to say that it's easier *not knowing* these things for, say, you and Conrad, compared to others in this room? Because of your background, perhaps?'

'Maybe, but . . .'

'Do you think that you might benefit from some time with one or more of the liaisons listed in the pamphlet?'

'Possibly, but . . .'

'There's no shame in it. It may not be ideal, but some people are simply born that way: white, male, heterosexual, English— what's important is how you grapple with that fact.'

They were all watching him now, every face in the audience peering over its shoulder in expectation. He looked from Angelica to Conrad, who was avoiding his eye now, staring at his face in his immaculately-polished brogues.

And suddenly, there it was: the middle way, the golden thread. Astonishing, really, that he had never had recourse to tell anyone before, while politely indulging garrulous Rhodes scholars on the quad; when introducing himself to Angelica the first time; or even in the interests of exculpation, when he walked in on a particularly militant graduate student the kitchen last year and made her spill a bag of huge, crocodilian-looking avocadoes that she'd bought from a minority-owned market. Astonishing that he'd never seen the *transactional* value of a secret like his, in a place like this. His relationship with Youssef was an anomaly: as far as the rest of the College was concerned, he realised, he was polite, shy, thoughtful, studious Edward, appearing occasionally at the fringes of the quad, like a snow-drop, soon to be forgotten or razed down to size. And yet, as he girded himself to reply, there rose in him a distinct feeling that all this was in some sense inevitable. He had never thought of himself as even having an *identity* before—that word used so extravagantly by Youssef, often with a misty, pious look in the eyes that reminded Edward of the one time he saw his school-mates take communion—but then again perhaps that was simply what identity was: something that slept inside you, until it was roused.

'Well, if I'm honest,' he said, 'I'm not sure I'm the best

person to ask.' He straightened up: 'Not that you'd know it to look at me—and I don't blame you, Angelica, for not asking—but most of my family isn't particularly white, or English, or Christian at all. They're East African-Indian. And Muslim.'

The change in Angelica was instantaneous. After the workshop (which was eventually put out of its misery around eleven forty-three), she trotted over: 'Edward, wasn't it? Do you have a moment? To talk?'

'Of course, Angelica.' he said.

She ushered him to the side of the room as the rest of her audience filed out. 'Which side was it? *Is* it?'

'I'm sorry?'

'Don't be sorry.' She had positioned them in a little alcove by the window, so that they stood artificially close together. He could smell her perfume, and see, when she leaned forward, the black strap of her bra inside her shirt. 'I meant which side of your family.'

'My father's. His father. But he came over years ago, and died before I was born . . .'

Angelica let out a little whimper of compassion. The room was fully empty now, but Angelica showed no sign of letting him leave. 'And your father?'

'Left when I was six, died when I was eleven. So I've always felt a little uncomf . . .'

'Ugh, of *course*.' Angelica squeezed his hand with an ostentatious quiver. 'So you gave up your name.'

'My name?'

'Your name. Your *Muslim* name.'

'I don't really . . .'

'It's okay, Edward. You can tell me.' She took a step closer, breathing heavily. 'What was it, his name? Do you know?'

It was a long time since anyone had asked. 'The family name was Zahir. Or al-Zahir, when you hear it in context.'

'Oh!' Angelica let go of his hand. 'Zahir. *Za-hir*. Such a beautiful name. Zahir. Za-*heer*. What does it mean?'

'I don't know really.'

'You don't?' She looked disappointed.

'Or at least it's hard to translate precisely,' he said, and she nodded as though she understood. Then another thought seized him: 'But I was told by a friend,' he said, 'that it's one of the ninety-nine names of God.'

Angelica let out a little gasp of disbelief. 'Oh, wow. God as in *Allah*, of course?'

'I mean I assume so.'

She nodded along solemnly. Then she raised her arms behind her and, not once breaking eye contact, pulled on her hairband and shook loose her hair.

'You know, Edward,' she said. 'I think you and I are going to be great friends.'

'Oh.'

She seemed to be waiting for something.

'I'd like that,' he added.

That appeared to satisfy her. They began to move towards the plexiglass door. 'Tell me what it's like,' she said, as they reached the threshold. 'Africa, I mean. Zanzibar. I'm a very empathetic person, you see, so I'm sure I can . . .'

He held the door open, watching her walk through as she spoke. 'Well,' he said, once he was sure she'd finished. 'You can probably imagine. Turquoise ocean, white sand . . .'

On the way back from the workshop, Angelica invited herself to dinner. As they walked, Edward recited a slew of made-up East African proverbs of the 'give a man a fish' variety, improvised the liturgies of several Islamic religious festivals, and concocted several extremely contentious opinions on African politics on which he hoped Angelica wouldn't press him. On this last subject, she seemed especially enthusiastic. Her latest project, she explained, involved lobbying to remove the statue of some monocled old colonialist on the College parapet. 'I can't imagine how *upsetting* it must be for you,' she'd said, foot tapping excitedly on the pavement as Edward tried to work out whether it was safe to cross the road. 'Samuel *Codringham,* Edward. I mean he owned plantations in *Kenya*—it's practically the same thing . . .' When he opened his mouth to protest, she stilled him with a touch on the forearm, which she somehow managed to charge with such depth, such suggestion, that for several seconds, neither of them said a word. Then she caught herself; she grew brisk, and flashed him a smile that looked almost sheepish: 'I know, I know. But we've tried everything already, I'm afraid. Eggs, rotten fruit. We even drenched the thing with red paint the other day.' She went quiet suddenly, staring off into the roadway, at the unending stream of traffic; Edward wondered what she was thinking. Part of him hoped it didn't involve him, part of him hoped it definitely did. Angelica blinked her wide, combed lashes. 'Now, this evening, Edward. I don't care if

Conrad will be there. I'm more interested in getting to know *you*.'

In the oak-panelled great hall they were tended to by the usual flock of waiters—a quiet, shy, uncomfortably-waistcoated bunch, most of whom would return to the council estate at the back end of College where they lived once they had put away all the silverware. Angelica greeted Edward with a kiss on the cheek, and took her place opposite him, smiling accommodatingly at Youssef, and even offering a nod to Conrad, who sat diagonally from her, invited by Youssef in gratitude for his efforts at what he referred to as 'babysitting.' Over the dinner table, and with a new, more intimate audience, Angelica came alive. Edward needn't have worried; she spoke fluently and without the need for interlocution, tracing, for the most part, the itinerary of her Latin American gap year: the three months building a mudbrick school for Bolivian children; the three weeks teaching in it; the six months at an Animal Rescue Centre in Cuzco, administering physiotherapy to condors that had flown into the glass walls of an eco-resort. That time she had been propositioned for marriage by an Araucanian chief, and he was so *charming* and so *polite* (though not, of course, in some stuffy bourgeois way) that she felt almost too guilty to refuse . . . Then it was on to her arresting spiritual insights: time is an illusion, existence is a spiral, all religions are really one religion, striving to make itself understood. For Conrad and Youssef, Edward sensed, the food couldn't have come soon enough. For himself, there was still something captivating about her, even when she was being ludicrous: the way she laughed authoritatively, flung her hair about her as she spoke. Whatever she said sounded like the kind of thing you ought to listen to.

The starter was some kind of broth, surrounded by little mangroves of feathered green. It smelled faintly iodinated. Angelica batted it away without a word to the waiter, then leaned across the table towards Edward, eyes starry before the candles, every so often raising her pale arm and running a finger back and forth over the lip of her glass. 'I'm glad we've finally had a chance to talk like this,' she said gently.

'Now, I understand the appeal of *doing* a gap year and everything, Ange. But choosing your whole degree based on a few doe-eyed Peruvians? *Really?*' Conrad was doing his best to hijack the conversation. He'd recovered from the workshop, and was now busy chipping away at Angelica's Spanish degree: 'It's just all the *same*, Ange—she-wolves with ambrosial breast-milk, five generations of shoemakers called Aurelio, some squat little Tiresias from a Buenos Aires slum . . .'

Edward felt almost sorry for her. Conrad, it seemed, had a way of implying that he knew everything already—that he'd read everything she had, everything any of them could ever *hope* to read, back in the mists of his infancy. Every time she looked about to collect herself, he would lace his fingers above his head in a self-satisfied stretch, and, enjoying how unsettled he had made her, make a grand new pronouncement that drove a stake through the heart of some cherished piece of culture: 'I've said it before and I'll say it again, Angie dear—Latin America is *such* a cliché these days. Magical realism is the lowest form of wit.'

Angelica took a sip of water. In her indignation she shrugged off her jacket to reveal a top, a dark, hoop-necked thing that showed off the little constellations of moles round her clavicles and was very different from what she was wearing earlier, lower-cut, not as careless or billowing; and for a brief, vertiginous moment, Edward wondered if she had chosen it with him in mind. It really did seem possible, too—Angelica struck him as the kind of person who would spend a lot of time in front of mirrors, appraising herself, holding clothes up against her slim body as if trying to work out whether they deserved her.

'Your problem, Conrad, is that you're obsessed with things being *canonical*. There are plenty of writers from, I don't know . . .' she smiled at Edward, amiably, but in a way that also seemed to demand him to sit up straighter, 'East Africa, for example—which is an area I'm increasingly interested in by the way—who make your *classics* look . . .'

'Name one,' said Conrad.

'That's not the p . . .'

'Name one, Angie. Go on. Give me the Somali Shakespeare. The Hutu Homer.'

Angelica laid her knife and fork to rest. 'I'm not getting drawn into this, Conrad,' she said. 'Edward understands what I mean.'

Edward stared across the tealights at Angelica. He wasn't sure he did understand. Angelica was just like Conrad, in her way; she had the same, unnerving habit—a way of presenting little fragments of knowledge, little pearls of history or literature that she had gathered over the course of her gap year, as pieces of profound, occult wisdom that he really ought to know too. *A Hundred Years of Solitude*. The Mexican muralists. The Malê Revolt. The shooting of Oscar Romero ('It means rosemary, you know,' she informed him solemnly, brushing her fingers over the back of his hand). And yet, even as Edward became aware of the technique, he was impressed by it, by this fund of reference, this horizon, hidden from view. 'The thing is, Angelica,' he said, 'I'm not sure I do. Understand, that is. Like I said before, I'm hardly even . . .'

'You see?' Conrad slammed a triumphant palm on the table, hard enough to make the cutlery jump. 'He's being polite, Ange. Truth is, he's fed up. Aren't you Edward?'

Edward glanced over at Angelica. Her brow was steepled, and she had begun to wring her crimson-nailed hands. 'I wouldn't say I was fed up,' he explained. 'Just that my relationship with all this is far more complicated . . .'

'Course he is,' Conrad continued. 'He's his own man.'

Youssef rose in his seat, smiling sweetly: 'If he's his own man, Conrad, then he doesn't need you to speak for him.'

'Quite right, Youssef,' says Angelica, nodding vigorously, then training her sympathy on Edward once more. 'Let's let Edward speak for once.'

'Well Edward?' said Youssef.

They were all staring at him now: Conrad and Youssef leaning back in their chairs, Angelica craning forward, chin propped expectantly on her fists.

'I guess . . .' Edward cleared his throat. 'I guess all I'd really say is that I don't *need* to have an opinion about everything. Sometimes it feels like that's all that's required of me. As if . . .' He stared down at his uneaten broth, hoping Angelica wouldn't assume he was addressing her and her alone.

'As if what?' said Angelica.

'Honestly, we can drop it.'

'No no. I have to hear it, Edward.' She nodded to herself stoically. 'It's important that I understand my own blind spots, too. That's the hardest thing, after all, isn't it? Self-examination.'

'I suspect the hardest thing,' said Conrad, 'might be selling that lovely old town house of yours and using the proceeds to . . .'

'Yes well I wasn't actually asking you, Conrad.' Slowly, she recomposed her face feature by feature, and turned back to him. 'Now, Edward, you were saying.'

'Was I?'

Firmly: 'You were.'

'I just . . .' He shrugged. 'I don't know.' They were all staring at him now. 'I just don't want to be someone people wheel out to prove a point.'

Angelica let out a little whimper of compassion. 'Oh Edward, I . . .' She stopped short, and pulled her hands into her lap as though worried what more damage she might do. 'I'm so sorry, I didn't mean—I didn't think.'

Conrad was grinning now, mopping away the last of his broth with a hunk of chalk-white bread. 'Dear me, Ange. Looks like you'll have to put *yourself* on the list.'

'You'll forgive me, Edward, won't you?'

Angelica was very solicitous after that, rallying herself with a burst of hair-smoothings and cutlery-straightenings and sycophantic laughs that made Edward question what it was he'd said that was so funny, interspersed with little barks at the waiters when she sensed their obedience waning: 'Yes, I certainly am done thank you. Do you think we could get some of these candles re-lit?' They had all begun to forage in their wallets, and one by one pulled out various dietary cards supplied by the College, Youssef with 'Halal,' Conrad with various food intolerances he blamed on the Hapsburg strand of his lineage, and Angelica with a whole five poker hand that covered her newfound veganism, her seasonal eating disorders, the little blacklist of additives she believed caused cancer. Once the set of rules stricter than any known creed that governed her body had been laid out, she stopped:

'Where's yours, Edward?'

'I don't have one.'

'They didn't give you one at the start of the year? Not even a 'Halal' card?'

'I didn't know it was an option.'

She sighed in frustration, and shook her head. 'Now that really is just *negligent* on their part.'

The waiter was summoned, harangued, and dispatched, rubbing the side of his pock-marked nose and muttering 'sorry' over and over until he was out of earshot. Eventually, Edward received four heat-lamped chicken nuggets ('Chicken: the greatest ecumenical invention known to man,' Youssef laughed) in a quivering tribute. Angelica, for her part at least, looked satisfied, launching off into dizzying new anecdotes and sociological observations that Youssef, nodding his head generously, seemed to be the only one following. She even accepted a glass of wine from Conrad, though only after thoroughly inspecting the label. Most unexpected of all, however, was the way she dealt with Edward. At first, he assumed she had simply grown bored of him. He'd been waiting for it, to tell the truth, to be rolled off into the background, part of the ever-moving scenery in Angelica's magnificent drama.

Then he felt it. First on his calf, very faint, the warmth of it rising slowly, as though drawing a line to the crook of his knee. He shifted in his seat, and felt her foot respond, the pressure redoubling itself against his leg. With his own foot, he could feel the arch of her high-heeled shoe lying flat on the floor, discarded. When he met her eye, he had the sense she'd been waiting for him to notice; she looked down bashfully, then slowly raised her eyes through her lashes, as if embarrassed.

'I really do think . . .' she carried on, her head snapping back round to Youssef and Conrad's side of the table, a little too briskly to be convincing, 'I really do think that they should make the food more *accessible*. Lots of people will be put off by all this fuss. I mean think of poor Edward.' She gave her toes a little squeeze. 'I mean, it's no trouble for *me* of course. I've done it all—roast llama brain, guinea pig fricassee, Brazilian blood stew. Yes, really, Conrad. That was the strangest of all, actually. It's pork blood. They use it as a thickener in this thing called *Sarapatel*. I always remember it, because one of the girls I was travelling with was called Sarah Patel—one of my *best* friends, yes, you've almost certainly met her, Youssef. Her dad's a barrister. No, no they moved. It's Dulwich now. Yes. Anyway, all I'm saying is that a lot of people, like Edward I should imagine . . .' She smiled, and charitably slid her foot up a few extra inches. 'A lot of people haven't had the *luxury* of growing up with food like this, and in any case couldn't eat it for religious reasons even if they had.' She sighed, and he felt her foot subside a second, briefly consumed by the injustices of the world. Then she straightened: 'But I want you to know, Edward, that it doesn't have to be like that with everyone. There are people here who care about you, people who . . .'

'Lucky Edward,' said Youssef.

'Look at them all,' said Angelica, not hearing, or at least pretending not to, and instead gesturing round the room, at the oak panels, the stern portraits, as though to conscript them into her argument. Her foot had drawn to a halt now, laid to rest on the inner slope of his thigh. She was, he had to admit, very skilled at not letting on, eyes trained on Youssef and Conrad, moving her hands as if trying to sculpt all her opinions out before them in a more solid, more irrefutable form. 'They're just *so* set in their ways. They didn't even *think* to ask whether Edward wanted a halal option too.'

'You do realise,' said Conrad, 'that he's not really . . .'

'Yes, yes I know. Culturally not doctrinally Muslim. But still . . .'

Edward wanted to say something. It would have been best, with hindsight, if he had corrected her there and then. Really, Angelica, I know what I said after the workshop, but I ought to make one thing clear . . . But when he opened his mouth to protest, he found he couldn't. He shuffled backward in his seat.

'It's okay, Edward, you don't need to explain.' Angelica squeezed his hand, as if it were a mute button. 'You don't *ever* need to explain yourself to them. Or anyone.' She gave another, sad, sympathetic smile; then with a brazen fidget, her foot crept the final distance into his lap.

'You okay Edward?' Youssef prodded at his food with his fork. 'Your face. You're starting to look like one of these little lumps of devotion we've been served.'

Conrad giggled. 'Dead and white and curiously devoid of shape?'

'Worse.' Youssef broke through the batter with a final, greasy crunch. 'Bloodless.'

Youssef ushered Edward away as the bottle of port was making its third trip around the table. Edward felt more comfortable the very moment the door opened to the musty room with its mahogany drinks cabinet, its hanging rail with Youssef's rainbow of smoking jackets, its general air of everything having been looted from a minor stately home after some fire or improbable earthquake—all of it left to marinate in the odour of sweet woods and dust mites, the windows never opened for fear of the treasures escaping.

Youssef was busy in the corner, liberating two fingers of calvados from a pomegranate-shaped decanter: 'It's after dark, Edward,' he explained: 'What are you, a *Talib*? Ramadan is nearly over, you do realise.'

There was a lull as he fumbled with the crystal stopper, and Edward sensed his chance. 'There's something I've been wondering, Youssef. This list—the one Angelica's always talking about . . .'

'Oh, *that*.' Youssef handed him a small plastic pot. 'I wouldn't pay that too much attention if I were you. It's for that magazine she edits—*Samizdat*. Every other week, lots of poetry. Yes, take it. It's a yoghurt pot—my cleaner has not yet deigned to wash the crystal glasses. It has been rinsed, worry not.'

Edward took the yoghurt pot. 'What kind of poetry?'

'Infidel poetry. Not the rightly-guided kind you and I read.'

'You don't read poetry.'

'I am a man of culture, Edward. I read. I recite.' Youssef gave a mysterious wink. 'Anyway, *Samizdat* is mainly poems, from what I am told, a few editorials, and these . . . line drawings, I suppose is the only way to describe them that does not verge in the obscene.' He shuddered. 'And most importantly of all, each month they publish a list of people who've upset them—racists, misogynists, patriarchs. That statue. But it's all for show, you see. The many blondes of the *Samizdat* letterhead are beautiful souls, quite removed from the grubby workings of the world. They'd never get actual blood on their hands.'

Edward nodded. He knew about *Samizdat*. How could he

not? Even if he had never actually *opened* it, it was unavoid-able, piled high on every flat surface of every common room in Oxford. The first issue had been published sometime in the seventies, a vast folio of pigment-leaching newsprint stuffed with multilingual poetry and clammy erotica; by now, however it had mellowed: the opinion pieces had become less openly revolutionary, and the line drawings had become less overtly gy-naecological. No one actually bought it, as far as he was aware, and most of its readers, he suspected, were simply contributors re-reading their own articles, but *Samizdat* was bigger than ever, ordered by the colleges themselves for ornamental reasons in forklift-tipping bulk, with Angelica proudly at its helm.

'She was strange at dinner. Angelica, I mean.'

'I noticed. I wondered why you were wriggling.'

'You saw the foot?'

Youssef nodded gravely. 'A classic.'

'You were right about her taking an interest.'

'Of course I was.' He aimed for the bin, and missed mag-nificently, then settled in an armchair as if preparing to read Edward a story. 'This, Edward, is the great conundrum of Angelica's life. The boyfriend question. Up till now, see, they've been pasty, floppy-haired, boarding-schooled. This is simply how she likes them. You remember Falconbridge?' Edward did remember Falconbridge: a rangy public schoolboy—first name never disclosed—with an inexhaustible cache of hand-rolled cigarettes and a vocal penchant for something called 'beagling,' which Edward gathered was some kind of sport, but also for some reason involved killing a rabbit. Youssef shook his head dismissively: 'But Angelica . . . Angelica also desires more, you see. Remember the gap year, Edward. The gap year explains all. Her friends are volunteering in the West Bank and Calais. Tilly is bedhopping from refugee to refugee. Izzy K got over *her* Falconbridge situation . . .'

'She had a Falconbridge situation?'

'They *all* had a Falconbridge situation. And she got over hers by falling head over lasciviously exposed ankle in love with a Tibetan monk, then a homeless man she believed needed rescuing, then someone at the University of *Hull*. *Hull* Edward!' He shook his head. 'They are simply all at it—saving the world one lonely young man at a time. And up till now, of course, Angelica had to choose.'

'I'm afraid I don't follow this at all.'

'A Falconbridge or a subaltern, Edward. A white knight or a swarthy Turk.' Youssef was staring at him now, as though at an inestimable jewel. 'And then you come along . . .' And he was off into his reverie, his mind dipped in the milk and honey of the night to come. He kept it going all through his preparations, which culminated in a green velvet smoking jacket which, he informed Edward as he slipped it on and barged out into the stairwell, cost more than his rent for the term. He continued talking all down the High Street, too, raising his voice a few notches to compete with the soundscape of the typical Oxford Saturday night—the screams, the broken glass, the slurred debates over whose college had more alumni in the Cabinet. As he walked, he swung his arms at his side; he seemed unusually excited, his nostrils flaring as he breathed in the fumes of the evening as though there were still a cup of calvados under his chin. Love was in the air, he explained. Youssef Chamakh was on a mission. Romance. Ensnarement. Conquest. Plunder.

'Gosh, it all sounds so consensual Youssef.'

Youssef rolled his eyes. '*She* is the one who shall be plundering *me*, Edward'

'I see.'

'Mercilessly, like the Qurayshites at Nakhla.'

'Ah, yes, thank you, that makes the image much clearer.'

Youssef, it eventually emerged, had his sights set on Lolly Bunton. Lolly, addressed variously as Lolly B, Lols or Bunty, was something of a legend in College by now. What she lacked in Angelica's poise and self-possession, Youssef reckoned, she made up for with a cornucopia of working-class gifts: the titanium liver; the huge, frank breasts; the rumoured ability to urinate while standing up. Sure, Lolly catered to mass tastes—the football team, the rugby team, the water polo team and other assorted wretched of the earth. 'But so did Nasser,' reasoned Youssef. 'And this is the appeal, anyway. This, to Youssef Chamakh, *is* exotic.'

'The ability to urinate while standing up?'

'Rumoured, Edward. And yes. This is what every handsome, ambitious Egyptian prince aspires to when he steps off the plane with his suspicious passport and promises of a proper English education: a real, authentic, fragrant, unwilted, English rose. With all her thorns.'

Edward paused at the kerb as he waited to cross the road over which Youssef had just waltzed without looking. 'I'm happy for you, Youssef.'

'And you, Edward,' he continued with an insinuating grin as they set off again round the corner of Cornmarket Street, 'You too shall have what is promised. You too shall pluck the living flower.'

'I'm not sure I know what that actually means.'

'The flower of womanhood, Edward. The succulent white raisins of Paradise.'

'Right, well in that case—and ignoring that second metaphor, which just raises more questions, frankly—I'm not altogether sure I want to.'

'What?' Youssef stopped in his tracks. 'What do you mean you're not sure you want to? You realise I'm talking about Angelica?'

'I'm just not sure I want to be . . . plundered by her, that's all.'

'Is there someone else?'

'No, it's just . . .'

'Of course. A stupid question really.' Youssef looked him up and down, unimpressed. 'So tell me, Edward, given that there's no one else, and that she is tall and blonde and aspirational, and you are none of these things; given that she went to an extremely reputable school and owns a house in Provence, and given that she is fully in support of the fine trajectory leading you back to the light of Allah on which I have set you—what, pray, is the problem? This is an *anomaly* Edward. A miracle.'

'How kind of you to say.'

'A violation of the laws of nature in favour of the wretched.'

'Yes, thank you for that.'

'Or would you prefer one of these *provincials*?' He gestured to a gaggle of freshers, all girls—a hockey team by the looks of the sticks with which they fired off crumpled beer cans down the road. Edward watched them pass. They weren't too different, he supposed, from the girls he had gone to school with, but here, beneath the perfect façades and spires and cupolas, they struck him as grotesque—the way they clattered over the shins of a nearby homeless man; the way their nipples peeped out of the front of their tiny dresses like rising suns. He glanced back at Youssef. He had lingered a few paces behind, and was kneeling down next to the nearest homeless man; he seemed to exchange a few words of apology with him, then slipped him something from his wallet. When he drew level, however, he was his old indignant self: 'No, no. Nonsense, Edward. You mustn't waste such a flattering opportunity. "Islam" means "submission," you know?'

They arrived at The George Inn with time to spare. The George Inn was not its real name—among the second-years, it was fashionable to refer to the various renovated pubs and bars and restaurants and organic fruit collectives that lined Oxford's more desirable postcodes as whatever they had been called a few years ago, so as to project a sense of worldliness and experience. The venue's *new* name, Youssef informed him, as they rounded the street-corner that housed it, was 'Favela.' Edward surveyed the lurid signage. *Favela—Cocktails, Small Plates, Memories.* He followed Youssef through the glowing entrance-way. Inside, the old wood-panelling and leather booths had been ripped out; in their place had been installed what struck Edward as a rather obvious attempt to ride the coattails of the gap-year craze. The walls were covered with painted humming-birds, the light fittings were slung with flower necklaces, and in the doorway of the toilets stood a distinctly Latin-American-looking woman who spritzed the air with a cheap, floral smell as they passed—then let out a meek little apology as a stocky first-fifteener barrelled past her and knocked whatever keyring or lollipop or dream she was selling out of her hand.

Angelica was there already. She greeted Edward and Youssef with a loud succession of squeals and screeches—'I'm so glad you both *made* it!'—as though trying to let the whole world know that he and Youssef were hers and hers alone. She seemed to have put a lot of thought into projecting a sense of informal-ity—as if to reassure everyone that, though she could be au-thoritative in the crucible of the workshop, she was not, in fact, above simply having a good time. She flicked her hair around as she spoke, making comments that in form at least resembled jokes, and quite soon Edward been handed a cocktail with a miniature umbrella, delivered of his coat, and whisked away into the nightclub's throbbing caverns.

'I really *am* glad you came,' she said as she led him along, leaning in and kissing him on the cheek.

'Oh.'

'Are you glad you came?'

'Yes.'

'You don't sound very glad.'

'I am. I'm very glad.'

She squeezed his arm. 'Well that makes me even more glad. Now, come, there are a few people I'd really like you to meet.'

Edward settled into the rhythms of polite conversation that Angelica maintained with her protégées and hangers-on: no, he hadn't been before, yes, he did love the theme. Yes, *very* exotic, he thought so too. Eventually, Angelica took off her coat—she was wearing an even smaller, sparklier, more inviting top now—and took his hand.

'Dance with me?'

Edward swallowed. 'Dance? Now?'

'Of course, Edward. Come on, don't be shy.' She shook back her hair. 'Come closer to me. Closer. That's it.'

'Like this?'

'You can put your hands round my waist.'

Edward obliged.

'My waist, Edward. That's the middle of my back.'

'Like this?' He moved his hands lower.

'Better.' Angelica took a deep breath, settling into the rhythm. 'I enjoyed dinner today,' she said, casually.

'I'm glad.'

'Did you enjoy it?'

'Yes.'

'What did you enjoy about it?'

'All of it, I guess.' He could feel her body moving against his.

'The conversation?'

'I found it hard to concentrate on the conversation.'

Angelica smiled. 'Me too,' she said, very softly, right in his ear.

The music changed to something faster, and he and Angelica drifted apart. Angelica, he soon came to realise, danced only in short bursts anyway; she was slightly too self-conscious to keep at it, and would interrupt herself periodically, canter off to talk to some minion with a bright, urgent phone screen, or else some long-lost acquaintance with an aristocratic-sounding name: 'I am sorry Edward but we *literally* grew up together. You understand, don't you?'

In the middle of one particularly long absence, Edward decided to slip outside. The courtyard was full of smokers, laughing jovially in little clusters. He cast around for a familiar face in
the orange lamplight, which was remarkably comforting after the
bright strobes indoors. Briefly, he considered asking someone for
a cigarette—it might at least help him strike up a conversation,
and even if not would justify his presence—but thought better
of it when he remembered Angelica, who almost certainly disap-
proved of such habits and had probably organised several re-ed-
ucation seminars for the purpose of its total social erasure.

When he saw Rachel, leaning against the fire escape where
Favela backed on to the street, he started off towards her without thinking. They hadn't spoken since last year, and to see her
here amid the wasp-faced posh girls and the Cologne-drenched
rugby players, sent a familiar, if half-forgotten feeling washing
over him.

Rachel seemed to be talking to someone. 'I don't see what
I've done . . .' she was saying. He didn't hear the response. 'And
she can't tell me this herself? Nothing, changes, does it?' Her
voice was slightly raised now, and Edward could see her interlocutor, a pinched girl he vaguely recognised from the year below 'Well, I won't. I won't do it, so just, leave me . . . Edward?'

The girl in the year below had turned too. She looked him
up and down through the boreholes in her make-up, but didn't
introduce herself.

'Sorry,' he said. 'I'm interrupting, I'll . . .'

'No. Tabitha was just going. Weren't you, Tabitha?'

They watched as the girl tottered away on her heels into the
pit of the nightclub.

'Are you okay?' he said when he was sure she had disappeared.

Rachel smiled. 'It's nice to see you.'

'Who was that?'

'It's fine. Just some drunk person with opinions. I'll be one
too, soon.'

'I doubt that. You look very put together.'

Rachel adjusted her hair self-consciously. 'I don't look put together, Edward.'

'Well, you look nice, then.'

'Thank you. She smiled at him, and he noticed her lipstick, dark red, carefully applied. 'It's nice to see you.'

'It's nice to see you. You've rescued my evening, actually.'

Rachel looked him up and down, and chuckled to herself, the tips of her teeth raking over her bottom lip. 'I can see that.'

'What?'

'Never mind, Edward.'

'Why are you smiling like that?'

'It's nothing.'

'It's not nothing.'

She smiled at him, almost pityingly. 'Your . . . on your face.'

'What's wrong with my face?'

Rachel didn't say anything—just held his gaze and slowly raised her fingers to her cheek. Instinctively, Edward's hand went up to his own, and when he removed his fingertips, they were smudged a deep, waxy red from where Angelica had kissed him. 'You've been claimed Edward,' she said. 'Branded.'

He could feel the brinks of his ears growing hot. 'Oh great. Is it noticeable?'

'A little, yes.'

'So is that how this looks to everyone? Like I'm a cow or a goat or something?'

'A lamb, maybe.'

'It was an accident. I certainly didn't ask for it.'

She kept smiling, but her eyes narrowed sceptically: 'I'm not sure that qualifies as an "accident," Edward.'

'I'm not sure it qualifies as being "branded" either.'

'She likes you.'

'Maybe.'

'She does. And as much as you insist that that little mark on your cheek is an accident, I suspect she left it there quite deliberately. No, don't protest, it's true. But it isn't my business.'

'No, it isn't, actually.'

'It suits you anyway. Makes you look very, I don't know . . . desired.'

'Now you're just making fun of me.'

'You're unfair to yourself. Haven't you noticed? Everyone's attracted to you all of a sudden.'

'Unlike last year, when I was literally invisible, apparently, because I hadn't been stamped with the right insignia and all anyone had to go on was my appearance and personality.'

'You weren't invisible, Edward.'

'I was. *You* forgot all about me.'

'You weren't invisible. And I didn't forget about you, by the way.'

'How come I never heard from you again?'

'I went home, for a while.'

'For a whole term?'

She nodded. 'Almost, yes. And then I came back and you were so friendly with Youssef, and . . . I don't know. I got the sense that you were quite happy as things were and wouldn't appreciate me intervening.'

'You suspected wrong.'

'I'm sorry.' She held his gaze for several seconds, then looked around; the smoking area was emptying now; the little huddles were dispersing or being broken up for the night. 'I missed our tutorials,' she said quietly.

'Me too.'

'In the second half of term I had this new partner—Montgomery something—and I swear he wouldn't stop talking about how he *felt* all the time. I couldn't get a word in. *Hamlet* was about this "identity crisis" he'd had when he was fifteen and his dad was away a lot on business trips. *Macbeth* was about how he had always had a complicated relationship with

Scotland, because it was where he and his dad used to go fly fishing. You were much better.'

'You certainly wouldn't catch me telling anyone how I felt.'

'I know. You're very English in that way.'

'I always suspected you were annoyed at me for not doing all the reading.'

'What? I wasn't annoyed with you, Edward.'

'You always ran off so quickly.'

'I had a language class. That's all.'

'Oh.'

'And I kept waiting for you to ask me to dinner again, but you didn't seem to want to, anymore. Or maybe you were too shy.'

'I'm not shy.'

'Aren't you?'

'No. Definitely not.'

Rachel smiled sympathetically. 'You are, Edward. Just a little bit. I don't mind. You blush a lot too.'

'For a Zanzibarian, maybe.'

She laughed. 'You're blushing now.'

'It's the light.'

Rolling her dark eyes: 'I see.'

He tried to smile, but it felt forced. 'My family always talks about that,' he said.

'About you blushing a lot?'

He nodded. 'And my being pale. And having freckles.'

'It's not a bad thing.'

'I hate them actually. The freckles, not the family. I honestly don't know the family at all.'

'I didn't think you'd be so self-conscious.'

'Yeah, well I didn't think my complexion would be seen as quite such a betrayal, but there we are. The freckles are the final straw. Youssef says they're where I've curdled into my constituent colours.'

She sighed to herself as though disappointed, but not surprised. 'I like Youssef,' she said. 'I do. But some things he says are incredibly stupid.' She looked him up and down one more time, then leaned forward close enough for him to smell her perfume. 'Here,' reaching into her into her purse and pulling out a stick of eyeliner. She turned the handle towards him in mock ceremony. 'Go on,' she said.

'Go on?'

'Go on.' She handed him the pen, then shut her eyes and wrinkled the skin on her nose.

'You want me to . . .'

She replied without opening her eyes: 'I want to try them out for myself.'

Edward glanced back towards the doorway. 'This is silly.'

'If you won't, I'll do it.'

There was another silence.

'All right,' said Edward. 'All right, just . . . Hold still.' He placed the pads of his fingers under her chin, and she craned her neck forward obligingly while he put the first dabs of eyeliner on her cheeks.

'You done yet?'

'I think so.'

Her eyes fluttered open.

'You look ridiculous,' he said.

'Good.'

CHAPTER 4

C ritical intelube please note following headcoming discourse antisemitic but whether Shylock or not sources unclear consensus etthat perhaps not man dialectic viewed unfavourably but also jews in government of Venice unquote whatsoever critical opinion interiorwards lawgeslation all but unintelligible . . .

Reading it over one more time, Edward began to suspect that much of the enthusiasm he had felt for his thesis at 3 A.M., having stumbled into his room full of serious, studious impulses he was sure would impress Rachel when he next ran into her, was premature. Not that he could concentrate now, either. He took one last look around the College's temporary library—a noisy, prefabricated affair which stood in for the famous gothic building that had been imprisoned in scaffolding since Edward arrived—and gathered up his things.

His garret was much further away from College this year, in a breeze-blocked building over the river called 'The Annexe,' about which Angelica had been briefly complimentary when he told her he was living there—'Oh how lovely, I must come and visit sometime'—before pressing her lips together in silent pity, as though adding it to her list of places she really ought to go and volunteer. He stole a glance up at her room as he passed through the main quad. Youssef had pointed it out the previous evening. Even from here, it looked opulent: the way the plane trees cast patterns against its large bay window, the velvet curtains, now drawn. For a second, he felt a pang of envy at being kept so far away, rather than in the centre of it all with Angelica and Youssef and Conrad, a few steps from the all-night toga parties, the croquet tournaments, the drunken thefts of ornamental carp. He had actually applied for something called the subsidised housing scheme at the end of last year—only to be rejected on the grounds that he 'did not occupy one of the recognised categories of disadvantage'. 'Not destitute enough,' sighed Youssef, during the ten or so seconds of commiseration he mustered before forgetting all about it. 'You could have at least faked a disability, couldn't you?'

'No, Youssef.'

'We could get you a wheelchair? It would suit you.'

'Right, I'm leaving now.'

To shave five minutes off the long walk back, Edward cut through the shopping centre. The complex was brand new, perched on the edge of the old city, and marked the beginning of a different kind of Oxford: the other Oxford, whose denizens were aware of the University—of the fancy round building in the centre and the swipes of perfect, forbidden green they sometimes glimpsed through the cracks in the college doors— but had never actually been allowed inside. He took his place on the escalator amid the shoppers. Townies, that was what they were called, at least in the student body's imagination: young men bruised from the brawls they picked with rugby teams on Wednesday nights, old women occluded to strange, purplish colours by the lines of plastic carrier bags they wore down their arms. 'Townies'—or 'provincials,' or 'chavs,' or 'sheep-farmers,' or 'bicycle-thieves,' or, once, by Conrad last night, 'The People of Gravy'—a nickname that he was sure didn't mean anything, and yet whose vague, impressionistic insult he somehow instantly understood.

Was that Conrad now? There was certainly someone who looked a lot like him striding through the automatic doors at the end of the concourse. Edward felt a throb of panic, as if he had been found out. It *was* Conrad—and he had seen him, too; he seemed to be having tremendous fun, showing off as he jostled his way forward through the herd of shoppers, drawling out little apologies like 'if you *would* excuse me,' and 'if you could just squeeze an *inch* in that direction, thank you *so* much,' and, to a small woman in a green and purple anorak, face too curled with worry and age to protest, 'Would you please fuck off out the way you little gargoyle that would be *marvellous.*' He cackled heartily as he muscled his way over. 'I didn't think you came to places like this,' looking Edward up and down.

'Oh. Well. Likewise, I suppose.'

'Heinous, I know, but what can you do?' Conrad shook his head pityingly. 'There really only is *one* decent place to get a watch repaired in Oxford. And they've put it here, in the Temple of the Scratch Card and the Family-Friendly Chain Restaurant. But this is immaterial. We have business to attend to.'

'Business?'

'Yes, Edward, business. I saw you with your lady friend last night.'

'Honestly, Angelica and I . . .'

'I'm not talking about *Angelica.*' Conrad almost sang her name in impatience, looking him up and down incredulously. He launched into a lecture so dense with carefully selected fact and hearsay, delivered in such a loud, airless drawl, that even if Edward *had* sensed he was allowed to respond (which he certainly wasn't), he could scarcely have managed to interrupt. Conrad was *talking,* he explained, about that winsome young thing whose face Edward was decorating last night. 'The *foreign* girl,' he said, insinuatingly. Well, half-foreign, anyway; not pure of blood like Conrad, in case he was interested.

'I know this, Conrad. She's German. We had tutorials together.'

Conrad raised an eyebrow. 'Is that what she told you?'

'What?'

'Nothing.'

'Wait . . . What do you mean?'

Conrad replied distractedly, gazing at a nearby advertisement, in which a photogenic mixed-race family received a city tour from a glossy teak punt. 'Nothing, Edward. Purge your pretty little quasi-Islamic head of worries. I had heard something else, that's all.'

'What had you heard?'

Conrad shrugged. 'Oh, just that she was Silesian or Moravian or some such—hence that surname, I supposed, all those 'y's and 'z's, like a differential equation. But names are not, as we ought to know, a failsafe indicator of the truth of the heart, are they, Mr. Zahir?' He turned, bored of the advertisement now, looked Edward up and down. 'And at least she's not called Izzy or Tilly or Lolly or Holly or Milly or Molly or any of those stupid little namelets they all seem to have these days. At least she's *different*. That's what people want now, isn't it? Difference for difference's sake.'

He swept off in the direction of the next escalator; stopping after a few paces, and jerking his head in a way that made it clear that Edward was expected to follow. As they walked, Conrad maintained a steady stream of hearsay on the subject of Rachel. She was an international student, he informed him, and reckoned by those luminaries whose schooling qualified them to reckon such things, to be a fairly typical specimen: she was passing through Oxford; she'd wake up in six months and find herself unsure where was home, and flutter off to the next university and the next valueless humanities degree and the next pasty little wretch with a story about palm trees to tell. 'So not a marriage prospect,' he said disapprovingly.

'Right. I don't think we're at that stage yet, Conrad.'

'You never know. Many women come to Oxford to find a nice, plausible, disease-free man destined for a job in financial services. This is what the place is for. It's in the charter.'

'Of course it is.'

'I'm quite serious. What did you think this university was for?'

'I don't know. Education, maybe?'

'What? No. Don't be ridiculous. Seriously, Edward when you say these things you sound extremely lower-class.' Conrad shook his head and resumed his old, didactic rhythm: there was little else to say, when it came down to it, on the subject of Rachel. There was the family: father in tech, mother in the home, all very traditional. Reports of some unwell relative, though everyone wanted an unwell relative these days—after all, one dead brother, one snivelling disabled sister could get you a scholarship to an American university. Rachel was clever, too, with a highly respectable mark in prelims—which was astonishing really, given the interest she had showed in Edward. She was pretty, obviously, in her bookish way—'That, presumably, is what you're interested in,' he added.

'Why do you keep assuming I'm interested?'

'Because it's obvious, Edward. She's made for you.'

'You really think so?'

'Yes. She likes Shakespeare. Unironically. She's foreign, and therefore won't understand what a crude, uncultivated yokel you are. What *is* that outfit by the way?'

'What? What's wrong with it?'

'She seems, moreover, to have escaped that first, psychotic intimation of their own sexual power all beautiful women get aged fifteen and which has all but ruined the likes of Angelica. She seems *normal,* Edward. And you, my friend, are as normal as it gets.'

'Thank you, Conrad.'

'There is just one, tiny problem.' Conrad smiled to himself and lowered his voice mischievously, burying his chin in his turtleneck. 'There is a boyfriend. S*worn* to be just a friend, of course—but half the rugby team swear *I* am just a friend, and I certainly retain a few spume-flecked memories to the contrary from the boarding-school showers.'

Edward felt his chest tighten. 'The one in Berlin?'

'In Oxford. The Berlin thing was a year abroad. Older, you see.'

'But Youssef said he was . . .'

'Youssef wants you to marry Angelica and convert her to an unusual form of Islam. He is not, I fear, dwelling entirely in the domain of universal reason. Now this boyfriend,' he continued, 'has the prior claim.'

'I'm not sure it works like that.'

'Of course it does. He knew her back when she was just a weird-accented nymph with an aptitude for English and German literature. They held each other's clammy hands. They made scarcely understood promises. Her first love, Edward. Advantage, him.'

'Great.'

'He's very good looking, and tanned, and from one of those exotic countries like you and Youssef where everyone has a lot of body hair.'

'Even better.'

'He got the top first in his year in prelims. He gets invited to lots of conferences.'

'Brilliant. Anything else I should know?'

Conrad thought for a second. 'He's six foot three.'

'Oh good.'

'And you're not.'

'Yes, I'm aware of this, Conrad.'

'But you mustn't give *up*, Edward. You have one distinct advantage. You've been chosen. You are one of the elect. You have cachet, and prestige, and attention, however undeserved. I saw how Angelica reacted to your little revelation in the workshop on Monday.'

'In order to make myself more attractive to Rachel I should

let Angelica adopt me or make me her pet or whatever it is she wants to do?'

Conrad had reached the foot of the escalator. He paused a moment, chin resting on a curled forefinger. 'That isn't all she wants to do though, is it?'

Once he was back amid the reassuring dilapidation of the Annexe, Edward headed to the laundry room. It was empty when he arrived, the air thick, almost tropical, and whirring with the sound of appliances. Sunday afternoon was always a quiet time of the week—free, thank goodness, of the Annexe's other inhabitants, the MBA students, the summer-schoolers, the rich kids from poor countries shipped over to study a master's degree in something like 'Development' to wave around when they returned home as though they had just stolen the crown jewels. He set down his basket, with the paperback of *The Merchant of Venice* he'd had in his pocket balanced on top, and crouched before the drum. Behind him, he heard the door open; he busied himself with the display, hoping not to get sucked into a conversation.

'Still on this?'

He recognised Rachel's voice at once.

'Yes, I can tell it's you, Edward, you can turn around.'

He shut the drum of the washing machine, and stood. Rachel had picked up his copy of *The Merchant of Venice* and had turned it over to the blurb. She wore a satiny blue robe, her hair was down, and her skin had that strange softness about it, as though she had just showered. 'It's for my thesis,' he said.

'Your *thesis*. I'm touched our tutorials meant so much to you. I wish my course involved a thesis.'

'What are you doing instead?'

'This term? It's just German, actually. One of the nineteenth and twentieth-century papers—Heine, Kafka, Schnitzler, Lasker-Schüler, Kraus.'

'I'm kind of envious. It sounds exotic.'

'You speak German?'

'Well, no, but . . .'

'But you like the idea of it.'

'Yeah.'

Wryly: 'I see.'

There was a silence. 'You should read Kafka,' she said suddenly. 'Have you read any?'

He shook his head.

She looked him up and down. 'You'd like him. They're young men's books, I think.'

'Do you recommend books to young men often?'

'No,' she said. 'Not that often.'

'So what will I like about it?'

'It's anxious and miserable and tortured. In a very beautiful way, I think.'

'I see. Just like me then.'

'Maybe.'

'You're smiling.'

'Yeah well I'm happy to see you.'

Another silence. One of the machines ticked over into the next phase of its cycle, and the whir was replaced with gentle, sloshing sounds. 'About last night . . .'

'Did you go home with her, by the way?'

'What?'

'Angelica.'

'Does it matter?'

'No, it doesn't matter. I was just asking.'

'Why are you pulling that face then?'

'This is just what I look like, Edward.'

'I didn't go home with her.'

'Really?' She softened, and then nodded to herself, taking the information in. 'But there is a specific script, you know,' she continued. 'She *will* try it on you soon.'

'A script?'

Rachel nodded. 'I know Angelica quite well by now, Edward. She'll find you somewhere. She sends out her helpers, and when one of them finds you, she'll act like it was just chance, the stars aligning. Then she'll curl up next to you . . .'

He gave a dry laugh. 'Right. And where are we exactly, in this scenario?'

'Somewhere public, for now. But there'll be a bench or something, or a picnic blanket, and if there isn't she'll just stand very close to you, and look up at you, and make herself seem much smaller and more vulnerable than she actually is, because she's very good at that too.'

'You know this for a fact, do you?'

Rachel nodded again. 'And *then*,' she said, 'she'll invite you up to her room—which is beautiful, by the way, far more beautiful than ours here—and she'll pour you a drink.'

'Angelica doesn't drink.'

'She will for you. And then she'll seduce you.'

Edward fiddled with his collar. *She'll seduce you.* The prospect of it of it made him feel almost sick—proud, too, of his own ascent, with a sense of having achieved something unusual and physical, like a respectable finish in a cross-country race—but sick nevertheless. Perhaps that was just desire he was feeling, something so total and overwhelming he couldn't even compute it. Everyone else seemed to think so.

'It'll be good, too. You'll like it. She's very accomplished.' Rachel said it matter-of-factly, staring him straight in the eye.

'Now that you definitely don't know.'

'You're blushing again.'

'Yes, thank you for pointing that out.'

'It doesn't matter, anyway. She'll find out what you like, whatever it is. If you've told Youssef, or Conrad, she'll know that too.'

'I don't talk to them about that kind of thing.'

'Are you sure?'

'Can we drop this now Rachel?'

Was that a flicker of guilt he saw? 'Sorry,' she said. She busied herself with her laundry, fishing out a crisp white chemise, suspending it from her fingers and thumbs, like a ghost of herself, before laying it gently in a separate pile. He had the distinct sense that he should make a joke, something to defuse whatever offence had been given, and taken.

'For what it's worth,' he said. 'I don't think I'm worth the effort. I'm not exactly widely accepted in those circles, am I?'

'Aren't you?'

'Or if I am, it won't last long. I'll do something to mess it up. I don't come from her world.'

Rachel put down the shirt she was holding. She leaned back against the drier and turned to face him, arms folded against the blue material of her dressing gown.

'Maybe that's what she likes about you,' she said.

CHAPTER 5

The term was just about to enter its fifth week when Youssef barrelled into the library, and peered disapprovingly at Edward's copy of *The Quality of Mercy is Not Stained: Shylock and the Poetics of Bodily Drainage*, and informed him, loudly, his lungs fortified by a week of Eid al-Fitr feasting, that Liberty was back.

'Liberty Vanderbilt-*Jackson*, Edward. She of the many hair beads. She of the many training contracts.'

'Right.'

'This is important.'

'No it isn't.'

'It is important because this is the first term of her presidency, and the whole Common Room is about to be purged and remade in her image.'

'Still waiting to hear how this is important . . .'

'It is important because she sits on several scholarship and bursary committees, which could benefit someone who comes from pure, gin-addled working-class destitution as you do.'

'I'm *not* working-class. I keep telling you this. Why is she back so late, anyway? It's fifth week.'

'She is busy, Edward. Irvine, California, I think it was this time. Liberty Vanderbilt-Jackson has duties, responsibilities, tasks.'

'*I* have duties, responsibilities, tasks.'

'Right. Well, whatever. Anyway, what I'm trying to convey to you is the importance of her arrival. And her arrival is important, most of all, because her deputy—the person who has to do all her little odd jobs, seething with resentment, envy, righteous indignation, and a host of other unbecoming womanly emotions—will be Angelica Mountbatten-Jones. It is important you appreciate the ambiguity of their relationship, should you wish to stand any chance at all of . . .'

'I'm trying to read, Youssef. Are you familiar with the concept? University. Work.'

'No. Work means toiling away to earn money and support a family. Work means chanting and whirling until you reach ecstatic unity with the divine. This . . .' He banged contemptuously at Edward's book-strewn desk, 'is a vile form of self-pleasure against which the Prophet strenuously warned.'

'Can you please . . .' He glanced round and lowered his voice. 'We're in a library. I have to show the first two-thousand words of my thesis to my tutor next Thursday, and I have nothing.'

'Did you hear what I *said*? Liberty. Back. In College. You'd better not be about to turn over another page . . .'

Liberty Vanderbilt-Jackson had been Edward's tutorial partner in the summer term of his first year in Oxford, and from the moment they first met, he had found her annoying. She was one of those American students who like to talk a lot about their advances in therapy and the precise ethnic makeup of their extended family before you've even had a chance to ask their names. In her case, there was a lot about West Africa, some distant yarn about female warriors and merchant ships, and a birthright in a place called 'Dahomey' whose legal standing seemed pretty tenuous to Edward, but which she pursued so energetically, with such furious invention, that before the term was out the invisible consensus that governed the College had awarded her a new nickname: 'Queen.' And Liberty, for her part, did everything she could to live up to it. She was behind the desk on every University committee, atop the barricades at every student protest. Her exploits at this year's Yale summer school were already legendary: the guided meditations on the quad; the hostile takeover of the English faculty; the public acquisition of a vast tattoo on her upper thigh. When asking for a week off to recuperate, she insisted that it 'symbolised her grandmother's struggle'; when Edward brought it up again without an audience, she dismissed his question with a pitying shake of the head: 'I'd rather not talk about it to you, if that's okay.'

In third week, he and Liberty had shared another tutorial together, and he had made the mistake of criticising 'Please Sir, Can I Have Some More: The Bulimic Challenge to Capitalism in Early Dickens'—which, it turned out, was written by Liberty's thesis supervisor over at Wadham and held to be something close to a sacred text. She never said anything in front of the tutor, but the moment they stepped outside she was upon him, about what, exactly, he had been thinking, and how could he presume to know everyone's *experience* like that, and had he not read, like, *Barthes*, for God's sake—and actually, come to think of it, why, in this country, which housed so many ancient universities with such gilded reputations, did everyone seem so *behind the curve*? Like, was Comparative Literature even a *thing* here? His ostracism was brief and swiftly forgotten, but for a few days, people he'd never met before were crossing the quad to avoid him—teasing him, as they passed, for his young, freckled face, his wayward hair, the way he walked, stooped as if the dark clouds that settled immovably over the city that May were closer to him than anyone else.

Only in late June did he venture to his first Common Room meeting, Youssef having assured him that it was worth going for the sheer fanfare of it, like something the Sultan himself would throw when he came riding back into town on his elephant or okapi or whatever they had in Zanzibar, and Liberty, in any case, would have long forgotten his little *faux pas*. It was hustings season, and the candidates had rallied around a new issue. For several weeks, a few of the junior lecturers had been flitting on and off strike; they were regularly to be found, as the evenings lengthened, huddled on Broad Street behind their placards demanding, in their quiet, university-lecturer way, something resembling dignity in employment. But though their placards attracted occasional honks of support from passing cars, from the students, Edward had observed, the typical response was more like that of Youssef's conquest, a stocky women's lacrosse player whose family owned an Armagnac distillery: 'Oh that's *nice*,' she cooed as she passed them on the way to College, with an approving little bob of the head as though she had just been shown a drawing by a child. 'I just hope it all gets resolved before my coursework is due.'

When Liberty took the stage in the Common Room meeting, dipping her bereted head to accept the storms of applause, the atmosphere changed abruptly. She strode up to the head of the Common Room, commandeered the notice board, and drew a vast, complicated grid that contained every possible species of human disadvantage, every line tending towards the conclusion that, actually, while the junior lecturers might *seem* hard done by, with their interesting dress sense and the angry red paint that dripped from their placards like the blood of the oppressed, they were, in fact, privileged. Highly privileged. *Terminally* privileged. Studies showed that very few of them were black, like Liberty, and there weren't even many brown ones to balance it out—like, did they even have Latinos here or what? Besides, other studies showed *very* few of them were 'non-conforming' in any way at all—a concept which Edward still didn't quite understand but suspected, based on a few empirical observations, had something to do with wearing dungarees. Indeed, she continued, up to forty-nine per cent, when her friend at the student union did a poll, identified as—she shuddered as she said it—*male*. What they really had to ask themselves, she reckoned, was where the *real* injustices lay. Oh, and Liberty knew all right. She had plans for the Common Room. Lions to tame and gorgons to slay. The lack of vegan options in the charity cake stall. The state of Israel. But first up—and here, she drew herself to her full, proud height, puffed with a whole continent's worth of slights and offences—first up was that *fucking* statue.

By the time Youssef had dragged Edward out of the library and into the Common Room, he was enthusiastic almost to the point of drunkenness, stirred by all the qualities that he believed make Liberty's presidency particularly noteworthy: Liberty's unassailable social pre-eminence, Liberty's ruthless Leninist efficiency. 'God, I wish *I* was black,' he said, stretching himself out in the gouged armchair opposite Edward. 'Think of what I could get *done*.'

'You are black Youssef.'

He snorted. 'I am, at best, brown.'

'I think most people would say you look black.'

'Anyone can *look* black.'

'Right. Well, you're from Africa.'

'This is the problem, Edward. My African-ness is what limits my capacity for blackness.'

'That I don't follow.'

'Now Liberty . . . *Liberty* is black.'

'Your skin is literally the same shade as Liberty's.'

'. . . American Black. *Prestige* Black. *Hollywood* Black. Whereas I . . .' he shook his head sadly '. . . am merely Maghrebi black. Carpet-salesman black. Lock-up-your-daughters black.'

'Youssef, this is deranged.'

'I'm surprised you haven't noticed this yet. It's exactly the same thing as is happening with you.'

'In what way is it like me?'

'Well, you're white.'

'Yes, I am aware.'

'But you're better than white—you're *prestige* white, despite your wretched upbringing. Hence your undeserved social ascent.'

'Why, thank you.'

'Because in a way you're also *not* white. You have the very thing that all white people crave, which is a little story about how you're not white, not really. Yes, you have absolutely no distinguishing physical features; yes, you dress like the teacher at my prep school who turned out to be a paedophile. I mean those *shoes*.' He shuddered. 'But this does not matter. You, my friend, are free.'

'Right. Well that makes absolutely no sense to me I'm afraid.'

'You've worked out a strategy, I take it?'

'For Angelica? You already . . .'

'For *Liberty*, Edward.' He grinned. 'No, I want to make sure you receive official sanction from the Queen herself. You will have to play up the Africa connection, of course—this is easy enough—but you'll need to pay attention, nonetheless. Now, tell me everything you know about her, Edward. Knowledge is power.'

Edward had very little to tell him. Youssef looked him up and down pityingly, then stretched out in the armchair, voice settling into full, sacerdotal flow as he dispensed all the wisdom he had gathered on the subject of Liberty since their first meeting—in a small crèche off to one side of a Fitzrovia cocktail party at the age of four when their respective fathers had brought the families along to London in order to elevate their business trips into holidays—helpfully distilled into a series of bullet points, which he emphasised by picking a new chunk of foam out of the upholstery with his fingernails when he reached a new number. One: Liberty was the Common Room's first *serious* president in some time, and had ended a rich dynasty of joke candidates—the ventriloquist's dummy, the vacuum cleaner—whose election she had excoriated in her acceptance speech as an insult to the noble institution of the Common Room. Two: even though she was studying English Literature, she considered herself somehow above it, and wrote a short column for *Samizdat* called 'Queering the Canon' by way of recompense, in which short passages from notable works of fiction (last month *Don Quixote*) were meticulously and sensitively interspersed with gay pornography, in a way that was generally accepted to be very radical. Three: she was, at least in theory, Angelica's best friend (their families owned adjacent villas in Provence). Four: she was possessed of an expansive and unconventional sexuality, a great web of desire that had caught up some of Oxford's most unpromising flies: a local drug dealer, several tutors, the timid cleaner of her staircase who was called in by management one day and never seen again. Five: the scholarship she was on was one her family had actually started. This was never to be mentioned.

'And then there's number six, of course.'

'What's number six?'

'Just the obvious.'

'Youssef, can you tell me please, rather than being cryptic?'

Youssef rolled his eyes. 'That which we all see. In all of them, all the committee ladies, behind the smiles and the attempts to end world poverty.'

'Right. What do we see, exactly?'

Youssef shrugged, and sighed, as though running up against the limits of his articulacy. 'Liberty is not . . . Well, she's not exactly *happy*, is she?'

And with that, Youssef threw back his head back, announced that he was hungry, and invited Edward to an impromptu feast at a pub he knew on Broad Street during which several Islamic dietary laws would be *severely* stretched. Edward declined as politely as he could. He pled tiredness, and trudged over to Abdul's Kebab's, Drink's and Food's.

Edward was fond of Abdul's Kebab's, Drink's and Food's. He enjoyed the insane colour scheme of the signage—the day-glo lettuce, the tomatoes red in tooth and claw—and the reassuring way the rickety old van had, since the first day he arrived, been parked outside of College every evening without fail, despite the tide of complaints and petitions launched by the porters. He enjoyed the little farces that played out in the Punch-and-Judy aperture while its patrons waited, and the veiled admission, in the crisp black and white sign, that Abdul's kebabs and the concept of 'food' could not be reconciled. He had even acquired a tolerance for Abdul himself—a grand old bear of a man from somewhere in the Middle East, who, while chopping onions and negotiating prices, berated passing homeless people with a venom few of the polite undergraduates in line would ever permit themselves to feel. Abdul took his order with his customary briskness; then, he settled into his trade, expression shifting from businesslike to murderous to unusually friendly in a way that compelled Edward to shrink his vocabulary down to polite little monosyllables as he collected his change.

Edward received his yellow carton and made his way back to College, settling on a bench in the main quad. The outdoor lights had not been switched on this evening. One of the alcoves in the building opposite him had been fenced off with orange road barriers, and gradually, as he peered at it, he understood why: three or four metres above, behind a makeshift chicken-wire cage, stood the statue—*the* statue, Codringham himself, features still blushing faintly red from last week's paint attack. He hadn't realised it was here, in College. True, he hadn't exactly concentrated during Angelica's breathless updates; true, he had heard the protestors in the quad this morning, the plasterboard walls of the temporary library proving no match for Liberty's megaphoned voice. But it had always seemed exotic, somehow, far-flung. Every so often, the University would put out statements in its defence that compounded the illusion; the

College's newsletters to donors were full of words like 'History' and 'Art' and 'Heritage' and 'Civilisation', plus something that one of the older history professors on Angelica's list referred to, bafflingly, as *Kultur*; its denunciations of the protests, meanwhile, were full of terms like 'threat' and 'intimidation' and 'regressive' and 'violent rhetoric' that made them sound like something he would have noticed. Combined, in fact, the furore had worked a kind of magic of transfiguration on the little, moss-covered statue. Samuel Codringham had become, in Edward's imagination, an impossible figure, a symbol of all that was grand and unanswerable about the University, at least thirty feet tall, cast in a whole colony's worth of stolen gold. The reality was so small and rain-weathered he couldn't help but be slightly disappointed. Samuel Codringham was a trinket, a decoration to enliven an alcove in Oxford's least remarkable College. No wonder Youssef and Conrad were so dismissive of the protestors. The whole saga was taking place right outside their rooms.

Edward's carton was empty, but he could not quite face the Annexe yet. Dimly, he remembered that in his satchel was the book he had taken out of the library, on a whim before Youssef bundled him away—a slim volume of aphorisms by Kafka that had seemed to call to him from the shelf. He opened the bag, pulled out the book; then let it flutter open to a haphazard middle page and began to read. *The Trees. For we are like tree trunks in the snow. In appearance they lie sleekly and a little push should be enough to set them rolling . . .* What on earth did that mean? A peal of laughter rang through the far archway, followed by a few voices, footsteps. His attention settled back into the book. *No, it can't be done, for they are firmly wedded to the ground. But see, even that is only appearance.*

'Edward?'

He looked up.

'It *is* you.' Angelica was halfway up the path already, striding very quickly, as if worried he might get away. She was dressed more conservatively than he had ever seen her, in a trench coat the colour of Oxford stone; her hair was loose, soft, as though it had been let down after a long day.

'I'm *so* glad I ran into you.' She slid on to the bench next to him. 'I've been wanting to tell you this for a while,' she says. 'How impressed I am.'

'Impressed?'

'Oh no need to be *shy*. Youssef's told me everything. And I wanted you to know I think it's superb.' She slipped closer, and Edward felt himself gathered into the jurisdiction of her perfume. She made as if to put her hand on his knee, then, at the last moment, hesitated, curling her fingers so that he could almost the feel her touch anyway, running up through him, into the pit of his stomach, like a flame creeping along a fuse. 'I didn't know you felt such—*solidarity,*' she said.

'Solidarity?'

'Yes, Edward. It's totally the right word—you needn't be scared of it.'

'I'm not scared, I just . . .'

'To outlast all the other protestors on the quad like this. To *refuse* to leave, even when it gets dark.'

'Oh, no.' He shook his head, trying his best to look disbelieving. 'Honestly I really haven't done much. I spent most of the day in the library.'

'You're so modest.' Her jacket, he noticed, had fallen open to reveal a white shirt collar, crisp and businesslike, though with one more button undone than was strictly necessary. She stared at him, then, smiling faintly to herself, glanced back up at up at the statue. 'I saw the way you were looking at Codringham just now. It really moved me, actually. I can't imagine what you must be feeling.'

Edward gave a self-effacing nod. He decided it was better not to correct her.

'Listen, Edward . . .' Angelica had placed the hand on his knee now, emboldened. He felt the brush of each finger: five warm pads. 'Do you want to come up to my room? It's not far—over in the next quad. It's really not far at all.'

Angelica's room was on the second floor, at the top of the most opulent staircase Edward had ever seen. She opened the door with a flourish and followed him inside, then stood next to him a moment, admiring the stoneware vases, the pruned pot plants, all of it conveying her own mastery over fixture and fitting. It looked, thought Edward, like something out of a catalogue. Even the floors were unusual: not the customary, scratchy carpet spotted with grey pads of trodden-in chewing gum, but polished oak, with a thick rug that looked like it was from the Middle East, and dotted with floor lamps which she flicked on in practised sequence after she had slipped off her shoes. When she turned to him again, her face was softened by the glow of all of them in concert; her skin even more perfect and blemishless than usual. Her eyes were softened by them too, and he felt them flit between his features, his eyes, his lips, his chest.

'This is me,' she said.

'It's beautiful.'

She shook back her hair modestly. 'It's not much.'

'I think we have very different ideas about what "not much" means.'

'Perhaps.' She said it thoughtfully, and as she did so let the coat fall from her shoulders. 'You can sit on the bed if you like.' He obeyed, and she padded over to a small refrigerator, tucked away under her desk. When she turned back to him, she was holding a pair of flutes and an impressive, low-shouldered bottle. 'I don't actually drink, of course. But I do make an exception for champagne, because—well, then it's a matter of appreciation, isn't it? It's cultural.' Their fingers touched on the stem as she handed him his glass.

'Tilt it. It makes it easier for me.'

'Like this?'

'A little more. That's it.'

Angelica settled on the bed next to him, very close, her legs in their sheer black tights crossed to one side. Edward started to feel breathless, almost queasy. The first sips of champagne were warming his throat now, prickling against his ribcage; he was aware of the meal he had just eaten, and realised, with a throb of panic, that if she asked him another question he would barely be able to reply. By way of distraction, he feigned interest in the bookshelves above her bed. The upper shelves were all Hispaniana from her course: *Venezuelan Ecocriticism: A Reader* and *Borges: An Overdue Denunciation* and *Anus Mirabilis: The Spirit of Freud in the Letters of San Juan de la Cruz*. The lower shelves, however, were more personal, more Angelica. There were a few self-help titles (*The Well-Tempered Spiral: An Ascent*), and a few fashionable novels set in Africa: *The Cry of the Elephant* and *We are all Children of the Kalahari Sun*. At the end of the shelf, he noticed, in pride of place, set apart from the rest bound in expensive-looking leather, was a Qur'an.

'It's like a window to the soul, isn't it? A bookshelf.'

He glanced at her. She was looking at the Qur'an with him, holding back a smile, as though impressed at her own cosmopolitanism.

'I'm doing the work, Edward. I really do want to learn.'

'You probably know more than me.'

'I doubt it.' She shook her head. 'Although actually,' she went on, enthused suddenly, 'I was looking into that name of yours—Zahir—and do you know what else it means?'

He did his best to say no through a gulp of champagne. 'I . . .'

'Of course, you do,' she sighed. 'Honestly, you should stop me if I'm being presumptuous.' She began to smooth her skirt, pressing it along her legs, half-sitting now, half-kneeling on the bed next to him. She rested a hand on her calf, then looked up at him, curious for a reaction. 'But it was so *interesting*. Za-*hir*. It means something like *outward* or *exterior*. But I guess you knew that already.'

'I really didn't.'

'You're sweet. Indulging me like this.'

'I'm not indulging you at all.'

'You must have all kinds of ideas about me.'

'Not really. Nothing bad, anyway.'

She considered that, for a moment. 'Do you think you can ever really know a person, Edward?'

He paused. 'I've never thought about it.'

'I've thought about it. I've thought about it a lot.'

Silence. 'But I mean,' he said, 'does it matter, really?'

'What do you mean?'

'Being known and understood. I think the world can function just fine without everyone knowing and understanding each other. I don't know if Youssef knows or understands me, for instance.'

She gave him a pitying look. 'We all like to be noticed once in a while, Edward. Even me.'

'I don't think that's something you need to worry about.'

'What do you mean?'

'You get noticed all the time. Every day, by everyone.'

'By you?'

'Sometimes.'

'We only just met each other.'

'I've known who you were since the beginning of last year.'

She was watching him closely now, taking in, it seemed, all the information she had been neglecting—the weight and shape of him, the cut of his clothes. 'What did you notice about me?'

'Well, I noticed the way everyone reacted to you. I don't know. I guess I was impressed by it.'

'How did people react to me?'

He shrugged. 'They were impressed by you, mostly. You seemed powerful. I certainly noticed that.'

'I'm not that powerful, Edward.' For a moment, she was thoughtful, staring down into her clasped hands. 'And physically? What did you notice?'

'I don't . . . It's embarrassing.'

'You have nothing to be embarrassed about. I'm just interested.'

'Well, I noticed your face, obviously. I mean, everyone knows you're pretty, so it's hardly going to surprise you.'

Quietly: 'And anything else?'

'I'm not sure . . .'

'I want to hear.'

He took a deep breath. 'Well remember when we were on the quad last year? The first time I met you—with Youssef.'

'I remember.'

'You were wearing this . . . this white dress.'

'I remember the dress.'

'And I guess, I don't know. When you stretched out on the lawn, and crossed your legs . . . I guess I noticed that too.'

Angelica's lips twitched into a half-smile. 'I think,' she said, 'if I remember correctly, I might have noticed you noticing.' She leaned back with her wrists on the bedspread, then uncrossed her legs, stretching the nearest one in front of her, as though fascinated by her own pointing toe. 'Interesting. It was the legs.' She smiled to herself again. 'What would you have done right then? In first week. If you knew.'

'Knew what?'

'If you knew you'd be sitting up here now. With me.'

'Oh, I . . .'

'Would you believe it?'

'I'm not sure.'

'Would you be scared?'

'Not scared. Nervous maybe.'

'You're all red.'

'It's warm in here.'

'It is.' She stood up. She was playing with the top button of her shirt now, sliding it back and forth indecisively through the slot with her finger and thumb. 'Would you mind if I took this off?'

He shook his head. She unbuttoned the shirt and shrugged it off her shoulders. Then took a few steps back from him, so he could see the whole sweep of her, and began to unzip her skirt.

'You know, Edward?' she said. 'I'm just a little bit nervous too.'

He couldn't sleep that night. He was too aware of her next to him, too aware of her breathing and the heat coming off her bare skin. He lay there, listening to the occasional footsteps in the adjacent quad, and the creak of the yew tree outside her window.

'Edward?'

It must have been one or two in the morning. 'Yeah.'

'You're awake.'

'Just about.'

'Your heart is beating really hard.'

'Sorry.'

She turned over to face him; she was speaking into his neck now, and he could feel her breath. 'It's not a problem. It's a good thing.'

'Right.'

A pause. 'Do I scare you, Edward?' For some reason, as he stared at her in the dark, he had the sense that she was smiling.

'Just a little,' he said.

'You don't need to be scared of me. I had a nice time.'

'Me too.'

'I enjoyed it. I want to do it again.'

'I certainly wouldn't stop you.'

She had slid down the bed now, and was resting her chin on his chest, looking up at him.

'You have a very hairless chest, you know.'

'Do I?'

'Yes. I don't know . . . I just assumed that someone with your parentage might have more.' She was running a finger absently down the side of his neck; then she stopped herself. 'Sorry. Is that offensive?'

'Probably.'

'Do you mind?'

'I kind of like it.'

She giggled. 'You like it when I'm offensive?'

'It just seems . . . I don't know. It just seems so unlike you.'

'And you like it when I'm unlike me?'

'No. No, I didn't mean it like that. Sorry.'

'Stop saying *sorry*, Edward. It's okay. I'm joking. And I like the lack of hair, actually. She kissed his chest again, once, twice, then looked up at him, watching. 'I can't sleep either, by the way.'

'Oh.'

'Mm.' Slowly, almost thoughtfully, she kissed his chest again, then, slowly, moved to kiss his stomach. 'You don't take hints very well, do you?

'What do you mean?'

'Lie back, Edward.'

Chapter 6

It had only been two weeks since Angelica first invited Edward up to her room, but in that time, she had made him her own. Every day she grew brisker, sterner, more authoritative; today had been her strangest performance yet. All afternoon she piloted him through Oxford's narrow streets and alleyways, an arm round his waist as though worried he might fall back into his old social position. His first real inkling that something was amiss, however, came at dinner, after they had curled themselves into a booth at what Angelica informed him was truly the most *charming* little diner on the Cowley Road that Liberty said was *just* like an American one and they just *had* to try out. Angelica ordered, tersely, for both of them, a strange, pressurised look spreading over her immaculately made-up face. Until the food came, she didn't say another word.

'It's not just an insult to everyone's hard work,' she burst out the moment the waiter had scurried off, 'but a *total* slap in the face. I mean think of what it looks like *politically . . .*'

He coaxed the infraction out of her eventually: he was not, thank God, the one who had committed it. Last night, Angelica informed him, the College rugby team had washed up in the Common Room as they always did, tired of vandalising curry houses and baiting the homeless. Most of the fallout was predictable—the forest of broken pool-cues, the capsized dustbins, the graffiti that, Liberty had sagely observed, *felt* racist even if no one could actually work out what it meant—'but then*,*' she said, her voice cracking in anguish, '*then* they found the pile of *Samizdats.*'

'How awful.'

'Yes, it would be awful even on its own. But that's not all, Edward. After they found them, they knocked them to the floor. The whole pile. A hundred copies.'

'I'm sorry. I know you worked really hard on them. Wait, the College ordered a *hundred* copies?'

'And then . . . then they . . .' Angelica's breathing had grown ragged. 'They . . .'

'It's okay. You don't need to . . .'

'They *urinated* on them, Edward.'

'Oh. Oh, I'm sorry.' A pause. 'Do you know which of them it was?'

'Does it *matter*?'

'No, not at all.'

'So why did you ask?'

'I have no idea. Sorry.'

'I'd have thought the urination itself was the thing, over and above who actually pulled the trigger. It's a metaphor, Edward, you don't need to look at me like that. But still, given, you know, how much *work* went into it, and how important the publication has become *culturally*, you'd expect a little respect, wouldn't you?'

'Yes, you're right.'

'I'd have thought you of all people would be incensed about this, given your background. You do realise that the main feature was an interview with a *real* Maasai tribeswoman?' She shook her head in exasperation. 'Such an exciting new voice. Silenced. By urine. So there's a clear racial angle to this, too, that's what I'm saying.'

'Yeah that's really bad.'

'Not that most people seem to get it, of course. Honestly, you should have heard Lolly Bunton going on and on and on and on trying to excuse it—as if she knows *anything*, as if someone from *Godalming*—I mean for God's sake Edward, *Godalming*— could have any idea about the sensitivities involved.'

Edward listened intently as Angelica detailed the blasphemy law she planned on tabling at the next Common Room meeting, occasionally nodding away the waiters who winced their way over to the table to check if everything was all right.

'I mean, it's not like I'd wish this on any other publication, either . . .'

'No, of course.'

'Because I'm very generous in that regard. Very giving.'

'Yes.'

'But I do wonder, sometimes, if it wouldn't have been better if they hadn't chosen a slightly newer publication. One with less *importance*—historically, I mean.'

'You mean to urinate on?'

'Precisely.'

So that was the problem. Edward was already aware of the new magazine in town, thanks to the invisible telemetry that transmitted these things round College weeks before any official announcement was made. He had hoped that Angelica would be somehow excluded from the revelation; she was not. Edited by none other than Liberty Vanderbilt-Jackson, *Gauche*, as the triumphant red lettering eventually proclaimed it in Liberty's annunciatory email, was a full thirty pages longer than *Samizdat*. At its centrefold was a glossy pull-out poster of a number of Cuban guerrillas. Inside its front cover was a complimentary sachet of cruelty-free lip balm. Rumour had it the next issue would feature an interview with a real, honest to God, Palestinian.

Edward listened as Angelica detailed *Gauche*'s inadequacies, its misguided ethos and murky funding, fork twitching back and forth as she spoke as though conducting an orchestra that only she could hear. 'But it's fine,' she was saying now. It was fine, because *Gauche* was not a competitor but an ally, and there was plenty of space in Oxford for two ferocious, uncompromising political magazines. Every Fidel needed his Ernesto. And anyway, Angelica was quite prepared to fight for her place in the popular imagination. She seemed to calm down as she explained her plans to him, her shoulders relaxing, her eyelids fluttering downwards as she applied her blood-red lipstick with the aid of the back of a knife. She stowed her knife and fork next to each other, paid, for both of them, and took him outside. And there, in the lamplight, she took his hand and stared up at him, and he caught again a glimpse of the rare, attentive, irresistible, vulnerable Angelica that still materialised from time to time after dark. She looked very beautiful. Whatever she had planned for the rest of the evening, Edward knew he could not refuse it.

They set off down the High Street, arm in arm. 'Aren't you excited, Edward?' she said, as she marched him along. 'It's a great event. And I guess, in a way it's kind of our debut.'

'Our debut? I think most people know already, don't they?'

'But we haven't *presented* ourselves, have we?'

'We've presented ourselves to Youssef. We've presented ourselves to Conrad. We've presented ourselves to Arabella and Fifi and . . . what was the other one's name? Mortadella?'

'We haven't presented ourselves to Liberty though.'

'I guess not.'

'But you'll try, won't you?'

'Sure.'

'I mean it, Edward.' He felt her tug at his arm, pulling to a halt. She was gazing at him now, imploring; she seemed shorter and slighter than usual, swamped by her heavy coat. 'Tell me you'll try.'

'I'll try, Angelica.'

And with that, the matter was closed. Deftly, Angelica began to steer the conversation towards the glittering promise of the event itself—VerboCity ('A night of poetry, dramatic mono-logue and musical accompaniment. Radicals only. Entry £10. See y'all there.')—once a regular fixture in the Favela calendar; now, she continued, voice hushed with insinuation, hastily re-housed. What was that? Oh, he hadn't heard? Favela was dead. Favela was done. Liberty had pronounced it first, but Angelica agreed: it was a bit *first* year, a bit *gap* year, and then there was that name, of course, which had struck her as highly problem-atic the moment she had first strode through the flower-draped door. But not to worry. There was a new venue now: something with a little more character, a little more *edge*. Something con-tinental. Liberty, it transpired, had spent a week at the Critical Theory Summer School at the Freie Universität, Berlin, and was now an aficionado of Schlachthaus '68—which was, Angelica breathlessly explained, a new club in a disused engine ware-house out by the train station, and really the only place in town for anyone who was anyone at all.

As they approached the venue, the scenery began to change. The reassuring façades of the colleges had been replaced by boxy new builds, the upper stories devoted to cheap gradu-ate accommodation, the ground floors housing shops, carpet showrooms, or vast, boarded-up spaces that housed nothing at all. The crowd that mingled on the pavement was certainly different from the one he had observed outside Favela. As he and Angelica passed, Edward felt himself eyed up by shabbily dressed patrons, leaning against drainpipes and smoking. By the entranceway was a couple of freshers, mouths locked vi-olently together; Edward could hear their nose rings clinking against each other, tender as wind chimes.

He nodded to the large, black, thoroughly bemused bouncer. Once inside, Angelica received the customary greetings and tributes as though they were long overdue, every so often tilting her head in Edward's direction in order to whisper someone's name or provenance in his ear. There was male Charlie, female Charlie, Charlie who could have been either, Charlie who was arguably both, and Flora, gushingly introduced to Edward as, 'the neighbour I told you about, from the Onslow Gardens days, pre-Hampstead, post-Holland Park, with the hairless cats,' as if that meant something. Last of all came a couple of freshers. They had the tall, lolloping, carefree look of public schoolboys, but they looked so white and malnourished, their new piercings so raw and swollen, that Edward assumed that Angelica must have branched out of her usual social circle in the direction of the Townies. Then it hit him. Of course: the quad, the first day of term. This was Monty, Angelica said proudly as the lead fresher put out his hand and lied that it was his pleasure, and this was Giles, who also nodded, but was mute.

'Listen, Ange,' drawled Monty, suavely flicking his disposable lighter and turning his back on Edward, 'I heard what happened to all those *Samizdat*s.'

'Awful,' said Giles.

'Yeah, despicable,' said Monty. 'Like, that poor Zulu woman, you know?'

'As if they hadn't suffered enough,' said Giles.

'Anyway, like, it doesn't *matter*, but Giles and I just wanted to make sure you knew we had nothing to do with it.'

Giles shook his head. 'Nothing.'

'Yeah, it really wasn't us'

Giles nodded. 'Yeah like, maybe a tiny bit was, but that we were caught up in the moment, you know?'

'It's a cultural problem, I reckon.'

'I mean, like literally a splash, Ange.'

Monty stroked his long, aristocratic chin. 'Like, I don't want to blame the other guys, but there's just such a gap in *upbringing* sometimes, you know? Education when it comes down to it.'

'Values,' agreed Giles.

'Anyway, Giles and I were wondering—and honestly tell us

if you think this would be a good idea—if you'd like us to put on . . . I don't know, like a workshop or something? We'd volunteer, of course. We could join the JCR Committee as liaisons.'

'Only if you think it'd be a good idea.'

Monty had finished rolling his cigarette now. He lit up, then opened the side of his mouth and blew out a wreath of smoke, right into Edward's face. 'What do you say, Angelica? Maybe you could have a word with Liberty?'

Angelica said she would, in a way that managed to be both very non-committal and very final. She bestowed a long, affectionate, lingering embrace, upon both Monty and Giles in turn, then turned, blinking, back to him.

'Oh. You're still here.'

'Yeah. Sorry. I can go.'

'No don't be silly, Edward.'

'I think I saw a friend of Youssef's over there, so . . .'

'Don't be *silly*, Edward. I'm glad you came. I'm sorry I didn't include you—it's just Monty and I have known each other for *such* a long time.' She was beaming up at him, the memory of why Edward was here restoring itself in her mind. 'You forgive me?'

'Of course.'

She kissed him on the cheek. 'Good. Let's go and find Liberty then, shall we?'

It didn't take long. Liberty was at the far end of the bar, surrounded by her own ring of nervous-looking acolytes. She glanced their way, half-smiling, just warmly enough for them to feel as though they were permitted to approach provided they made proper obeisance—then she turned back to her companion, a slender figure in a light blue smock with a short, aggressive haircut, and a look of grand, existential boredom mainly achieved by not looking anyone in the eye. Liberty introduced her promptly when they arrived—this was Minka, Minka was at Wadham but Liberty knew her via her friends from St. Paul's

Girls, Minka was Leninist and now Liberty was a Leninist too, Minka was a lesbian and now Liberty was a lesbian too.

'Anyway, it's good to see you, Angie. I barely heard from you this summer.'

'I messaged you,' said Angelica, as the pair embraced in a way that seemed essentially theoretical to Edward, forearms hovering over the other's necks without any actual contact.

'You did?'

'Yes. Several times. About the Committee makeup? And to approve the workshop calendar?'

'Ugh Sweetie I'm sorry. I guess I've just been so *busy*, what with . . .'

As Liberty ran through her list of excuses, Edward found it hard to pay attention. It was the first time he had been able to study Liberty this closely. She was just about the most polished person he had ever seen. Her teeth were perfect. Her *skin* was perfect. She was wearing an odd outfit, with large gold hoop earrings and particoloured beads in her hair—but she was so confident, so poised and black and cosmopolitan, that Edward had the sense that his failure to understand was his own deficiency, a symptom of not having spent enough time in New York and of reading Tennyson instead of keeping up with the latest fashions. She wasn't exactly *attractive* like Angelica—Liberty's efforts seemed concentrated on projecting power, serenity, poise, mastery over man and nature, like one of those neoclassical statues she enjoyed objecting to—but as he stared at her, he started to suspect that attractiveness was beside the point. If Liberty deviated at all from any given standard of beauty, then it was the standard of beauty that was wrong.

Pleasantries soon gave way to complaints—which Angelica and Liberty exchanged deftly, as though they had had a lot of practice. Angelica's litany he knew well enough: the desecration of *Samizdat*, the looming coursework, the fact that she had to read this old white guy 'Cervantes' who she was sure owned at least a few slaves. But Liberty's complaints were even more impressive. They came out in a great barrage, delivered with a briskness and bubbliness he had hitherto only heard in people who were happy: she was just so *busy* at the moment, with her new project, with studying with internships, with summer school applications. One of the experimental life-writing pieces she had dashed off last term had found a publisher, who thought she might just be a new 'voice'. And that was before Liberty even got started on all these *friends* of hers—so many people she'd love to see if she had time, but who barged needily into her inbox, with their little tributes and congratulations and favours to ask, and made her feel *crushingly* guilty when she inevitably had to postpone. God, it was hard to be so in demand. Honestly, she needed, like, a PA or whatever just to organise her personal life! And then there were the ambient stresses, the sheer, cultural insensitivity in this place—which was exhausting in its own right. 'Like, ex-*haust-ing*, you know?' She aspirated the 'h' the second time round, as though on the verge of physical collapse. People were just so *reserved* here, she lamented. They didn't say what they meant. And most tiring of all—she looked at Edward now, snubbing the hand he had extended—most tiring of all was the way that everyone in this country, from the porters to the administrators to the tutors, when presented with someone who looked like Liberty, would slather over their pastrami-pink faces that look of greasy, impermeable, English *politeness* that told you you'd never really be welcome here, no matter how hard you tried.

'So I'm Black, obviously Edward.' She had trained all her attention on him now.

'Right,' he said. 'Yes.'

'I mean that's very obvious here, I guess.'

'Here?'

'England. Britain. The United Kingdom.'

'Oh. Sure. I mean, it's kind of true everywhere though, isn't it?'

'What?'

'Never mind. I don't know.'

'No, Edward, it isn't equally obvious everywhere. You could only think it's equally obvious everywhere if you were pretty clueless about some pretty important things.' She glanced at Angelica. 'Haven't you taught him anything, Ange?'

'I have,' said Angelica. 'I promise. I think Edward just misspoke, didn't you, Edward?'

Edward nodded. 'Yeah.'

Liberty paid him no attention. 'The thing about identity, Edward, is that it's *situation dependent*. So actually, for a lot of people, things are *way* more obvious here than back home. I feel it all the time. I'm often walking down the High Street, and am just like—is everyone here just looking at me, you know?'

Edward tried his best to look polite and sympathetic. 'Yes. Of course.'

'No, Edward, you don't actually. You don't know. That's what I'm trying to say.'

'Right. Sorry.'

'And that's *okay*.'

'Right. Yes.'

'But you need to learn. You need to put in the time, and ask the right questions. Because otherwise it's not okay. Do you understand?'

'Yes.'

'Are you going to ask a question?'

'Now?'

'Yes. About my lived experience, or my culture, or my notion of "home," for instance.'

She was eyeing him with interest now, fist curled inquisitively under her chin.

'Yes, I am.' He paused, and studied Liberty's expression. 'What is your notion of home? Where is home?'

'Ugh, yeah, I mean that really is the question. Like where even to start?' Liberty rolled her eyes, as though it were faintly ridiculous that Edward hadn't yet heard, that she would have to repeat her spiel *again*. 'So I grew up in New York. Just a few blocks south of Harlem, I don't know how well you know the city. And my daddy's from DC and my mom grew up in Sacramento but actually she identifies pretty strongly as Akan these days, because she went I mean *deep* into the whole family history thing on her sabbatical. She was here too, you know. Econ. Behavioural. Very micro, very cutting-edge.'

'Liberty,' said Angelica, manoeuvring herself deftly into the triangle that Liberty had formed with him and the silent Minka, 'is specialising in African Literature.'

Liberty snorted. '*Africana*, Angie. Totally different thing— diasporic voices, hybrid identities.'

'Yes,' said Angelica. 'Africana Literature, sorry.'

'Africana Literature *and Culture*.'

'Africana Literature and Culture.'

'Because literature is just words, whereas I'm primarily interested in mythemes and paradigms. Units of culture rather than language. I'm sure you appreciate the difference.'

'Yes, sorry.' Angelica shifted her weight from foot to foot. 'Anyway,' she continued, turning back to Edward, 'the point is that Liberty is a real expert on the African continent and its people.'

'Yeah I don't really like that word "expert" sweetie . . .'

Soothingly: 'I'm just trying to tell Edward how much you know, Liberty.'

That seemed to pacify her. Liberty threw back her head and let out a short, luxuriant laugh. 'Yeah, I guess you could say that this is kind of my thing. What can I say? Sometimes I just get wind of something and just have to know everything about it. And yeah, the whole topic obsessed me. The whole idea of it, really. Guilty. Guilty as charged.' She glanced at Minka, who nodded her approval. 'I just think it's sad,' she went on, 'that, like, there's this continent with, what, three billion people on it? And in *this* country—your culture, guys—it's just . . . nothing. It's nowhere. It's nowhere in the mythemes and paradigms. Like, what's that even about?'

'Edward's got an Africana connection, too, Liberty.'

'Who has?'

'Edward.' Angelica installed herself at his side, arm winding into his. 'A pretty strong one actually.'

Liberty looked him up and down. Her lips were twitching in what looked like amusement. 'Sure. I get it.'

Angelica looked uncomfortable. 'No, Liberty . . .'

'It's okay, Ange. I understand. Say no more.'

'It's not what you think.'

'So tell me, Edward, where was it, then?'

Angelica was shaking her head. 'Liberty . . .'

'I'd like Edward to answer, Sweetie, if that's okay.' Liberty canted forward. 'Where was it Edward? We can guess if you like. It can be a game. Was it . . . Hmm let me see. Rhodesia?'

'No.'

'South Africa?'

'No.'

'Kenya?'

'No, Liberty, it's not . . .'

'Who was it, by the way?'

'What?'

'In your family. Which member has the Africana connection.'

'Oh.' My grandfather. But he wasn't . . .'

'I see.' Liberty chuckled. 'It's always the grandfather, isn't it? Honestly, I swear it's something about this country. Every single person has a grandfather who did something. It's like Germany or whatever. At least you admit it, Edward. Good for you, I say. But you're being shy.' She stared down her nose patronisingly. 'Come on, Edward, tell me—just how many of us did your great, great granddaddy own?

'No, I . . .'

'Honestly, it's okay. Like I said, it's this country, right? Everyone knows *someone*—kind of like in Germany or Rwanda or wherever. It's cool. I think the important thing is that you acknowledge it and then step aside when the time comes for new voices to be heard.' She giggled to herself. 'Like, just don't write a book or anything, you know?'

'They didn't own anyone, Liberty.'

He could feel Angelica pulling at his arm now. 'Tell her, Edward.'

He took a deep breath: 'My family are from Zanzibar. But they're not . . .'

Liberty raised an eyebrow. 'They're not?'

'They're not white'

'Oh.' Just for an instant, Liberty looked completely puzzled. 'Oh, right. Right, yeah of course. Zanzibar. I mean, I can see it now. So that's like—North Africa right?'

'East Africa. It's part of Tanzania.'

'Yeah, well that's what I mean. I mean it's north east. Like Kenya's east and it's just north of Kenya.'

'Yeah, maybe. I mean I think it's south of Kenya actually.'

'Ugh, well I guess map projections are so *colonial* anyway and everything's so distorted.' She crossed her arms, and said hastily: 'So where are your folks from exactly?

'Where in Zanzibar?'

'Like the city.'

Panic. He could conjure the pictures from his guidebook well enough—the corrugated roofs, the studs on the high mango-wood doors to ward off elephants—but place-names? 'Are there really *cities* in Zanzibar?' he said.

'Right, yeah of course. The town, I meant . . . The district. I just wanted to see if I'd heard of it.'

'Oh, well . . .' He shrugged modestly. 'They're from all over really. I mean if you can think of a town, we've probably got some relatives there.'

Liberty nodded. 'Sure, sure.'

'I mean feel free to say a town or a district, and I can tell you.'

'No, it's okay.'

'Seriously, try me.'

'I wouldn't want to get the pronunciation wrong. Have you read Chinua Achebe, by the way?'

'No, not yet.'

Liberty seemed relieved. 'You *should*.' Then she turned back to Angelica and Minka, the usual look of command settling once more over her perfect features. 'Africa,' she declaimed, 'has such a rich history, and it's like *totally* unexplored. And East Africa . . .' she sighed longingly. 'I mean Tanzania, Kenya—I think the region really carries with it its own unique historical experiences.'

Angelica, furious now, had looped her arm even more securely into his. 'Tell Liberty about the war, Edward. Against the British. And about how it makes you feel conflicted.'

'I mean there are lots of wars, Angelica.'

Liberty moaned sympathetically: 'Honestly, It's so *true*. I think that's one of the ways in which my eyes have been really opened by my research—the number of, well, everything really. Wars especially. Like, you've got the wars against the French, the wars against the British, the wars against the Dutch.'

'The wars against the Portuguese,' added Angelica. 'I was going through the Postcolonial Studies reading list and . . .'

Liberty rolled her eyes. 'Yes, thank you *so* much Ange. Nice of you to involve us in the curriculum.' She turned back to Edward: 'Which war was it, Edward?'

'It was the erm . . .' He swallowed. 'The Zanzibar War.'

'*Of?*'

'Well . . . Independence.'

'Ah sure,' said Liberty, nodding eagerly. 'I thought it probably was. I mean I was going to say that but I didn't want to interrupt.'

'You know it?'

'Oh, *sure*. It was kind of . . . kind of bloody, wasn't it? Or bloodless, one of the two.'

'Yes very bloody. On both sides.' He glanced at Angelica. 'On all the sides.'

Angelica cleared her throat: 'I've heard that the total number of casualties is estimated . . .'

'Maybe let the disenfranchised talk for a change?' Liberty shook her head patronisingly, then turned back to Edward: '*So* much blood in African history. It's so sad, because it's such a rich continent, and yet people know so little about it. Have you read Wole Soyinka?'

'No.' For good measure, he added: 'It's the fault of the curriculum, I suppose.'

'Right? It's the institutions in this country that are to blame, that's what I've always said. I mean, like, just step back for a second, maybe?' She was listing forward on her toes now, eyeing Edward with interest. 'You know what, Edward, it's really nice to meet someone who *knows* something about the period. Really encouraging. I guess the old white guys haven't totally killed Oxford yet.'

And with that, Liberty's heart appeared to be won. She ushered Edward over to a small booth in the corner and slid in next to him, with Minka, still silent and pinched as ever, installing herself on the other side. Angelica was forced to pull up a spare banana crate which Liberty assured her was *definitely* intended to be part of the furniture. Then she began her spiel. So this evening was pretty special, she explained; it wasn't just about *art* (art without clear social purpose was awfully reactionary, at least in her opinion; she didn't even *go* to things any more unless there was some kind of charity appeal hyperlinked in the online description of the event).

'No, it's about something *much* more important, Edward.'

'Oh.' He nodded, uncomprehendingly.

'*Money.*'

'Oh. Right. Yes that is important.'

'Did you know that many students really struggle to pay rent while they complete internships and spring vacation schemes? Like the ones we all did last summer. And we all know how screwed you are if you don't do one of *those*, right? I mean that's like your life—over.'

'No, I . . . Wait, we were supposed to be doing internships?'

'And did you know that this issue disproportionately affects students of colour? Because there are studies.'

'No, I didn't.'

'And did you know that only twenty-five per cent of boardroom members identified as female? In like literally every profession. The Big Four, the Big Six, the Magic Circle, the Gilded Eight.'

'Okay. That's a lot of professions. But Liberty, just on the subject of these internships . . .'

'Well, not for long, Edward. You see I'm of the opinion that writing—*good* writing I mean—is only really good writing if it changes the world.' She bobbed her head, impressed at her own aphorism. What she was driving at, she explained, was that this was a *charitable* initiative. There was to be a collection at the end of the evening, and the proceeds would go to five promising young 'creatives' hand-picked from Liberty's friendship circle—the word 'creative' was deployed often, Edward noticed, and always as a noun—and help make straight the way for them to train as the management consultants and lawyers and investment bankers and human resources professionals she believed they had it in themselves to become. This, Liberty promised, would benefit everyone. And they said progress was impossible.

Liberty seemed to slip in and out of self-awareness as she spoke: whole paragraphs of her monologue struck him as pre-rehearsed, ornamented with tics and gestures that had clearly worked before; occasionally, though, she would grow aware of their presence—if they failed to nod, or to titter sycophantically when she made a stab at a joke—and she would glare at them until they gave some sign to acknowledge what could only be, at least in Liberty's eyes, a shameful failure of attention.

'Edward?'

'Mm?'

'Did you agree with what I just said?'

'Um. Yes. Definitely.'

'What specific part?'

'Oh.' A pause. 'I mean, all of it. You're very hard to disagree with.'

Liberty looked him up and down. 'Good,' she said.

She paid Angelica most scrutiny of all. After Angelica's third infraction—a short breach in eye contact when someone at the bar dropped a glass—Liberty's face grew expressionless. When she finally spoke, to Edward again this time, her voice was cloying:

'So tell me,' she said, 'you guys are fucking, right?'

Edward spluttered on his drink. 'Excuse me?'

'Fucking. You guys.'

He glanced at Angelica. 'I mean, not right now.'

'But like, you have?'

'I don't really think . . .'

'Yes, Liberty,' Angelica interrupted. 'We have.'

'And it's, like, good?'

Angelica folded her arms. 'Great. Brilliant actually.'

Liberty made a little noise of patronising endearment. 'I love that word, "brilliant." It's so *English*. It sounds like you're talking about tea and crumpets.'

'Well, it is brilliant.' Angelica was still staring at Liberty. Not once did she look his way.

'Aw, sweetie. I'm so happy for you.'

'Of course.'

'And you, Edward?' She leaned back, surveyed him once, then gave an approving nod. 'And you know the important things about Angelica already, I suppose?'

'I'm not sure.'

'Because trust me, Edward, if there's one thing you need to know about me, it's that I really, really care about my friends. It's one of my qualities, I guess. I'm loyal.'

'That's great.'

'So trust me when I say that any man worth Angelica's time needs to know a few things.'

Angelica shifted in her seat: 'Liberty . . .'

'The thing about Ange, Edward, is that she's actually really shy.'

Edward glanced to his right. Angelica didn't meet his gaze. 'Yeah, I think she's a lot less shy than I am.'

'I wouldn't be so sure, Edward. Angelica's kind of an English prude when you get down to it.' She smirked. 'So you have to look after her, Edward. Because she really is my best, *best* friend. In Oxford, anyway. Can you do that?'

'I don't think Angelica needs my help with anything.'

Liberty pouted thoughtfully. 'Oh, I wouldn't be so sure.'

And then before he had time to respond, or even to assess the shifting topography of Angelica's face, Liberty was up on the stage, striding around purposefully in a way that made it quite clear that they were all expected to shut up and listen. She introduced a few people Edward had never heard of, then began to read out the rules: no phones, no cue cards, no logocentrism of any kind, and keep it tolerant, for God's sake, and civil, and resist the patriarchy, and yes, the bar would remain open throughout, but she had spoken to the organisers and if she at any point got the sense it had become a distraction from the important voices they were about to listen to—here she glanced at one of her black-shirts, poised in the wings with a buzzing earpiece—she would have no qualms about shutting the whole evening down. Really, she would. They had been warned. She had, for reasons opaque to Edward, donned a felt bowler hat to signal her role as compère, and adjusted it ostentatiously every few seconds.

Whenever she did so, Minka and Angelica broke out into lavish
burbles of approval, saying barely comprehensible things like 'So
chic' and 'So *Andro*' and 'So *populist*' and 'So *Weimar*.' Edward
did his best to join in, his arm draped hesitantly around Angelica,
his hand hovering a few inches from her waist: 'She's so . . .'

Angelica stiffened. 'So what, Edward?'

'So Weimar.'

'Actually, I didn't think that bit was particularly Weimar, did
you, Minka?'

Minka spoke through an impatient little yawn: 'No, not
really.'

'Never mind.'

Only when Liberty had vacated the stage did the applause
die down. Edward settled in his plastic chair. First up was a
gruesome little haikuist with an earlobe stretcher, clearing her
throat to recite 'Ode to a Sacred Gourd:'

'Sliced in half for dips.
Have I defeated you, or
made two cucumbers?'

He glanced around as the applause swelled again. He half
hoped to catch the eye of another dissenter, someone, anyone,
anyone whose expression might deviate from the glazed, con-
tented look they all shared, mouths parted as if poetry were less
an artform than a kind of salubrious vapour, one they had to
breathe in if they wanted to be good people.

'Argus died last week:
The best friend I ever had.
Now we have a cat.

The cat's name is . . .'

There was no one. Under the pretence of stretching, he peered behind him. There were a few faces from College, a few more from his lectures, but no one, except Angelica, who had ever blessed him with a conversation. The haikus were growing faster now, fierier:

'LGBTQ-
QIP2SAA:
Not nearly enough.'

At twenty past nine, a pair of postdocs crackled and groaned their way through 'Soundscape: First Movement'—a heady mix of owl hoots, car alarms, and storms of deliberate microphone feedback, descending into a competitive cough-ing fit that Liberty, strutting across the stage to collect the mi-crophone afterwards, dubbed 'an absurdist masterpiece.' At a quarter to ten, a tall, official-looking Ethiopian woman recited a lively slam poem called 'A Skin-Coloured Pencil.' There had been no male performers, of course—but then again, Edward had come to expect this by now. Among his fellow English Literature students, there were just two others, at least among the dwindling pool who still dragged themselves to lectures: one glitter-caked president of another college's JCR whose gender was so startlingly indiscernible that Edward was un-sure whether he even really counted, and one thin-faced, brooding boy from East Anglia who had a dirty beard and a National Union of Students membership and wasn't really invited to things. And that, as far as he could tell, was it. He glanced up at the latest girl on the stage, in her bobble hat and long plastic trench coat. Her face, when she stepped down into the aisle, was solemn and blissful, as though she had just received communion, or perhaps given confession—as though her poem, a sexually explicit epic poem she referred to as 'The Chlamidyad,' had been bearing on her with an inner pressure that demanded this public form of release so that she did not burst.

At nine thirty-four precisely, Minka took the stage. For the first seven or eight cantos of the work in progress named 'Love Beneath the Tractor' that she had chosen to recite, Edward sat attentively enough. By canto fifteen, he began to wonder how many more cantos there would be. At canto thirty-eight, he glanced over at Angelica: she had torn every paper napkin in sight to a fine snow, and even Liberty, so engrossed throughout the early cycles on Alexander II's 1861 emancipation reforms, had begun to slump in the seat to her left.

> 'The bodies shall be bled to pale
> beneath the combine's threshing flail;
> the bourgeoisie shall stop and quail . . .'

Phone screens flecked the darkness in the corner of the room. The audience was growing restive now, fiddling with the decor, dropping handbags and wallets, offering sibilant greetings to those they recognised.

> '. . . And with the kulaks bid adieu,
> We shall make the world anew
> Nor butch, nor fem, nor Greek, nor . . .'

The bar had begun to whir into life, too. Glancing back, Edward recognised a few faces from College—Monty, Giles, Lolly B, all now staggering—and one or two others he couldn't quite make out.

> 'Canto Thirty-Nine: The Execution of the Romanovs . . .'

Monty and Giles, inhibitions no doubt relaxed by their stint at the bar, began to clap. More joined in. Liberty and Angelica resisted at first, but soon the space was throbbing with applause—Monty on his feet, Giles whistling through his knuckles, eager to evade the horrors of Canto Thirty-Nine. Liberty, roused by the general change in ambience, looked over each shoulder; composing her face into her most conciliatory grin, she flipped on her bowler hat and began her stride down the aisle. She kissed Minka ostentatiously for seven or eight seconds. Gently but firmly, she took the microphone out of her hand.

'So I guess that's the *formal* part of the evening over,' said Liberty, giving her beaded hair an authoritative flick. 'But you're all so welcome to stay. In fact, lock the doors.' She laughed, and the audience sycophantically reciprocated, though Edward couldn't help but notice that one or two of them gave the exit a quick glance. 'And if anyone has anything they'd like to share—an original piece or a rendition of someone else's—remember, the mic is still open.'

Monty and Giles let out a few whoops.

'What do you say guys, shall I start?' says Liberty, and laughed with attempted modesty as the cheer of 'Yes! Yes Liberty! Go for it Queen!' ricocheted round the room. 'Aww you guys. All right, all right then. If you insist.' As Liberty slipped into a rousing delivery of something called 'Phenomenal Woman,' Edward trained his attention again on Angelica, whose pursed mouth, disapproving eyes, melted away the moment Minka approached. 'Oh Minka, it was *so* wonderful. Really—really moving, actually.'

Minka snorted. 'Gosh how disappointing. I was going for a *Verfremdungseffekt*. I thought that was clear.' She turned to Edward. 'And you? I suppose you hated it?'

Edward swallowed. 'No,' he said. 'I didn't hate it.'

'You were unsettled by it. Threatened.'

'No, I . . .'

'You probably thought it was too long.'

'I liked it, Minka.'

'Whatever.'

'I mean it. I actually thought it was very . . .' He glanced around: no clue, no reaction from Angelica. 'Very dialectical.'

And then Minka did something unexpected: she smiled. Not a leer or a smirk or a sardonic compression of the lips, but a wide, full beam, with a horseshoe of perfect white teeth that made her look almost feminine, just for a second. 'It *was* rather dialectical, wasn't it?' Without so much as another glance at Angelica, Minka stood and decamped to the chair directly next to him. 'I'm glad *someone* noticed.'

She began murmuring quite happily—all the way through not just 'Phenomenal Woman' but its two or three encores. Edward was treated, in sequence, to Minka's opinions on politics, Minka's opinions on aesthetics, Minka's opinions on her structuralist reading group, Minka's opinions on the cruel denigration of Lysenkoism, Minka's opinions on her cats, Minka's opinions on Israel, Minka's opinions on oil nationalisation, and Minka's opinions on the various films she and Liberty had walked out of. Edward hardly needed to say much: Minka did not so much listen to her interlocutors as pause to reload. Every so often, however, an unsettling shred of conversation would float over from the adjacent chairs, where Liberty had reinstalled herself next to Angelica and taken up once more her barrage of unsolicited advice.

'. . . I mean he's fine, Ange. Very cute. Very safe. And he has the Africana connection, if we take him at his word. But what *you* want . . .'

Minka chewed on a drinking straw '. . . I'm very into burning things down, actually. As an aesthetic statement. I mean, I've not actually burnt anything down yet, of course, but . . .'

'. . . Like, have you even talked about your preferences and ambitions? If there's one thing I can't stand it's people who just get in, like, a *relationship* or whatever and then have to make all these *sacrifices*. Does he know you could be in New York in a few years . . .'

'. . . I'm afraid, Edward, that Disney has really become untenable, too. If you think about it, it presents a highly revisionist . . .'

'. . . More like a *portfolio* of men, Angie. A roster. Different ones for different needs. Women have been silent about their needs for so long, you know. Are you aware that among the Tuareg people of the southern Sahara . . . ?'

'. . . And if push comes to shove, Edward, do we need the dresses? What's *wrong* with a set of overalls . . . ?'

'. . . I mean I haven't introduced you to Saïd yet. My friend from the West Bank. From Palestine. Back after Christmas.' At that, Edward felt the insecurity rise in his chest. Liberty was nodding now, excited: 'He's *gorgeous,* of course, and he's a bit more, well, you know . . .'

Over the course of the last week or so, Edward had been hearing the name 'Saïd' with remarkable frequency. Saïd, from what he understood, belonged to another college, far prettier and better kept and more munificent with scholarships than theirs, and had recently caused quite a stir when he attended a lavish reception Liberty had hosted for her friends in the College's rentable conference room. Edward also knew that Saïd was popular, and Palestinian, and that these two facts were possibly related; he had heard the rumours about Saïd's appearance: the tanned skin, the height, the easy confidence, the string of carved wooden beads he wore lazily round his neck to offset his muscles. He had confirmed it by looking at various photos of him online. But to hear the word 'gorgeous' applied to him, and in Angelica's presence no less, was a new low.

Part of the reason for his resentment, Edward suspected, was the fact that Saïd was a Palestinian. Edward was aware, by now, of the totemic status Palestinians had among people his age, the way the idea of Saïd's nationality combined with his deep brown molten eyes to make the girls in his year start making cooing noises and talking about things like 'moral complicity' and 'systemic change' whenever he came up in conversation—but, to his embarrassment, he knew next to nothing about Palestinians or Palestine, apart from the vague suspicion that it was something in which he, as a purported Muslim, was expected to take an interest. The topic of Middle Eastern politics had never come up when he was younger; people who *did* have opinions about these things were deemed to be putting on airs, showing off by feigning familiarity with something which everyone, deep down, knew was beyond all human comprehension.

Such matters were rather more frequently discussed in Oxford, of course: only last week at supper, Angelica had brushed him deftly on the arm and informed him that her heart beat not just for him but for his brothers and sisters of the Palestinian *ummah*:

'I'm serious, you know. I can't imagine what it's like. Just to sit back, and *exist* at all, when there's something like that going on.' She shook her head pityingly. 'I just want to make sure you know that I'm sympathetic to what you're going through.'

'Oh. Right.' Edward tried to look appreciative, gulping back the spicy East African food, all chickpeas and venom, that had just taken a layer of skin off the roof of his mouth, and smiling. 'Thank you.'

'I was talking to Youssef the other day. He was telling me about all you've done to raise awareness for this issue. I had no idea.'

'Oh. Wait, he did?'

Angelica nodded, her food still untouched. 'Yes. To say something like that—to a *police officer*, no less. I think it's very brave.'

Edward shifted in his seat. 'Oh.'

'Sorry. I'm making you uncomfortable. I'm still learning the etiquette. I'm sorry.'

'You don't need to be sorry. It's just . . . Honestly Angelica, the truth is I don't think about these things as much as you seem to think I do.'

'You're so *brave*, Edward. It's okay. You don't have to spare my feelings.' She leaned forward and squeezed his hand.

'Angelica. Angelica, listen. I think we need to talk about this. You seem to think that I'm some kind of . . .'

'Yes, you're quite right. I don't suppose I ever *can* really understand, can I? Listen, Edward. When we've done with Allegra and Jonty this evening, we'll go to back to my room, and I'll do my best to make it up to you.' He could feel her finger tracing a line along his thigh. 'I'll try very hard, I promise. How does that sound?'

Edward nodded dumbly. For that evening, at least, he was loyal to the cause.

'. . . Will you, Edward?' Liberty was waiting for a response, fluttering her false eyelashes so that Edward could see the lines of glue that held them on to her lids. They were all staring at him now—Angelica and Minka too, craning forward, faces bright with expectation.

Edward looked blankly at her. 'Sorry. Will I what?'

'Will you give us one?

'Yes. Right. Sorry, what am I giving you?'

'A *recitation*.' Liberty was on her feet now, ushering him to the stage. 'Come on Edward, don't be shy. Angie's been telling us all about those proverbs you used to win her over. Up and at 'em. Show us all your soul.'

And before he quite had time to register what was happening, Liberty had led him by the wrist up to the microphone, adjusted the posture of the stand, shoved him forward into the cold white light and the sea of faces upturned in anticipation.

'Whatever you like, Edward.'

Edward glanced back at the photo-plastered screen. What to choose? He had long forgotten the 'proverbs' he made up. He had never written a poem, not since his teenage years—but plenty of the contributors had recited other people's work. He was pretty sure Liberty had not come up with 'Phenomenal Woman.' Something from his course, then. He cleared his throat:

'The quality of mercy is not strained.
It droppeth as the gentle rain . . .

There was a sharp squeak from the microphone.

'. . . from heaven
Upon the place beneath. It is twice blessed
It blesseth him that gives and him that takes.
'Tis mightiest in the mightiest. It becomes
The thronèd monarch better than . . .'

He stopped when the lights in the audience faded up, and he saw the faces staring back, the faces sniggering in disbelief and frowning in disapproval, the faces rolling their eyes. Angelica was hurrying along the aisle towards him, mounting the stage; before he had time to protest she had reached out and covered the microphone's humid mesh with her hand. 'What are you *doing?*' she hissed. 'They don't want to hear this kind of thing. They . . .' She shook her head. 'Listen, just do one of the Zanzibari proverbs you told me, okay? Please, *please* don't embarrass me. Not in front of Liberty.'

She uncovered the microphone, and smiled out into the smudged audience. 'Sorry everyone,' she said. 'A misunderstanding. Edward's changed his mind. He's going to recite something very special. A Zanzibari proverb, passed down from his grandfather. Isn't that right Edward?' She stared at him: trying to look tender, though Edward sensed the expression was more for the audience's benefit than his own. 'And do stand a little closer, too. Don't be shy.'

Obediently, Edward advanced to the lip of the stage, scrambling all the while for combinations and recombinations of words that might satisfy her. He could see everyone from here now, just as Angelica had promised: Monty, Giles, Lolly B, Tilly C, anyone who was anyone who was anyone at all . . . Though no Youssef, he noticed. Or Conrad.

Then he stopped. Was that *Rachel*? He wouldn't have gone up had he known *she* were here; he had barely seen her at all since the Annexe; Angelica's ceaseless timetable of work, leisure and anthropological interrogation had just about expunged every other human relation from his mind.

'Please, Edward, the proverb. When you're ready.'

'Can I . . . ?'

'Whatever you like. Whatever pops into your head.'

He took a deep breath, and felt his feet on the floor. He had an idea. 'So there is this one proverb,' he said. 'From Zanzibar. It was told to me by a friend, actually. You'll have to forgive the translation.' He cleared his throat. *'For we are like tree trunks in the snow,'* he said. *'In appearance they lie sleekly and a little push should be enough to set them rolling. No, it can't be done, for they are firmly wedded to the ground. But see, even that is only appearance.'*

CHAPTER 7

When Angelica pushed open the door to her room, set down the vast, cuboid shopping bags she always accumulated when out for more than ten minutes, and saw Edward waiting, she treated him to a quick, disapproving scan from head to toe, as though he were some appliance she had left on by accident. It was the seventh week of term, and everything about her exuded a new impatience—for home, its improved living conditions and superior domestic service.

'You're here,' she said.

'You asked me to be here.'

'I did?'

'I can go . . .'

'No, it's fine.'

'I'll go.'

'Great. Abandon me then.'

'What?'

'Nothing. Forget it.'

'What does that mean? Is everything okay?'

'Yes, Edward, everything's fine. I'm going to work on the bed now, so would you mind migrating to the desk?'

She had been out with Liberty again. She had been out with Liberty a lot recently; the two of them had packed their calendars with schedules and appointments, and were often to be seen in the University Parks, squealing compliments back and forth at each other in tones that Edward suspected were too shrill to be genuine. Whenever Angelica returned, her mood would sink as soon as she padded across the Moroccan rug that marked the threshold; some problem would be discerned in Edward's behaviour—a lack of effusiveness in greeting, an inflection in his voice that betrayed his unsophisticated origins. She was sitting on the bed now, attention buried in her laptop, chewing her bottom lip.

'Angelica?'

'I'm working, Edward.'

'Right. Yes.'

She scarcely moved for over an hour. By the time she finally did stand, and stretch, her top lifting to reveal a band of her abdomen, the whole room was dark except for the bluish glow of the laptop. She padded over, switched on two or three of her favourite lamps, and kissed him absent-mindedly on the cheek.

'I'm ready for you now.'

It sounded bureaucratic, like something a receptionist might say.

'Angelica. Hey.' He closed the distance, and touched her tentatively on the arm. 'Angelica.'

'What are you doing?'

'Is everything all right?'

She turned her head reluctantly, but didn't reply.

'It's okay if you don't want me here.'

'Why do you keep saying that?'

'I just get the sense . . .'

'Are you bored?'

'What?'

'Bored of me. Of us.'

'Why would you think that?'

'Do you think I'm a boring white girl from North London with too much money and too much time on my hands?'

'Where is this coming from? Did Liberty say something?'

'Am I spontaneous?'

'What?'

'Spontaneous, Edward. Or do I plan things too much?'

'Angelica . . .'

'Kiss me.'

'What?'

'*Kiss* me.'

He did as he was told.

The following day, he requested a few hours with Youssef and Conrad—'I haven't seen them in a while,' he entreated, 'and I know you understand because I know how much you value friendship,' at which she nodded her understanding—and the three of them convened outside the All Souls gates at half past eleven. It was a crisp, cold morning full of trilling bicycles and quaintly bemused Chinese tourists. As Edward stared up over college rooftops at the stunningly, uncomplicatedly blue sky, he felt a rush of freedom, possibility. Angelica's mood had improved since yesterday: she had busied herself this morning with the occult customs of what she called 'self-care', all foil body wraps and volcanic mud masks and hours of listening to twangling Indian music with cucumber on her eyes, punctuated by short intervals of targeted benevolence during which she would will various positive humanitarian developments into existence with the power of her mind. She was primped and powdered and happy and occupied; before he left, she had even promised to spare a few moments of reflection for him.

'You've changed,' said Conrad, after he had handed him a steaming coffee. 'Kenyan blend. Terribly fashionable I hear, all this East African stuff.'

'I'm exactly the same, Conrad.'

'You're meeker, somehow. Conquered. Colonised.'

'Right.'

'I know, I didn't think it was *possible* for you to become meeker and less charismatic, but there we are. A miracle.'

'And let me guess, you've been suspecting this has something to do with my foreign ancestry, and Youssef thinks it has something to do with my lack of enthusiasm for Islam?'

Youssef chortled into his coffee. 'Maybe he's in love.'

Youssef spent much of the conversation talking about love. He was fresh from a short, unexpected liaison with Lolly B in Schlachthaus '68 ('That height. Those thighs. I mean, come on, Edward. She's practically *African* . . .') and now seemed obsessed with amorous relations in general, sniggering with Conrad about Edward's 'marriage prospects' and the encouraging signs of Angelica's father's extraordinary wealth—the château in the Luberon with its gold bath taps, the toilet paper made of purest mink, the waistcoated retainers who every so often had to be quietly killed. It was marvellous, just marvellous, Youssef reckoned, that he was getting on so well with Angelica.

'She has really raised our profile, you understand.'

'"Our" profile?'

'Yes, Edward. I have been propositioned several times.'

'Good for you.'

'Blouses have been unbuttoned in my presence. Legs crossed and uncrossed. This is very important for us.'

'Yes, it's nice to know the two of us are in this together. I had been labouring under the impression that it was just *me* going out with Angelica.'

Youssef rolled his eyes. 'Not the two of us, Edward. The *billion* of us.'

'Oh, I see: that's where you're going with this.'

'She's facing a threat, you know' said Conrad, tossing his empty coffee cup on the grassy verge. 'You mustn't *assume* anything—the billion of you that is.'

'A threat?' said Edward, just about level now. 'You should pick that up by the way.'

'To her pre-eminence,' said Conrad, ignoring him. 'Assailed from all sides. Slings and arrows and poisoned Amazonian darts. Surely she's spoken about it.'

'She's spoken to *me* about it,' said Youssef.

'What are you talking about?'

Youssef shook his head gravely. 'Diversitas, Edward. I'm surprised she hasn't mentioned anything.'

Edward was aware of the arrival of a company called Diversitas in Oxford—he had seen the vans with their strange, globe-like logo parked at the back of College—but he had no idea that they had anything to do with Angelica. Diversitas had been drafted in at the tail end of the junior lecturers' strike: instead of a pay rise, the University had suggested something called an 'Equality Reflection Programme,' a two-week frenzy of workshops and seminars that Diversitas sold off the shelf in one convenient bundle, and from which, the brochures that littered the common rooms assured everyone, a state of perfect social justice would ensue as surely as smoke from fire. Elderly dons had been rounded up and taken off for 'retraining.' A group of international students had been given a series of friendly lessons about what was and was not 'acceptable in the current climate.' Just that morning, a trio of leaflets had materialised in his pigeonhole, titled *Think Again* and *How to be a Race-Conscious Leader* and *Your Mind is Not Your Own.*

'But . . . wait. Youssef. Conrad,' he said, trotting to keep up with the pair of them, who seemed to walk more quickly when together, propelled by their shared history. 'What does Diversitas have to do with Angelica?'

'It's not Angelica,' said Conrad. 'Not directly, anyway.'

Youssef nodded. 'It's Liberty.'

'What does it have to do with Liberty? Can you slow down please?'

Youssef slowed, then stopped, leaning against the weathered stone of the All Souls outer wall. 'It's Liberty's *project*, Edward. She invited them. She lobbied for the funds. She'll be interning for them in the summer in the Cayman Islands office.'

Conrad cackled. 'Looks like dear old Ange is being cut out, Edward. You might want to reconsider your prospects. What about that other girl you have your eye on?'

'What?' Youssef had folded his arms. 'Who is this? Edward?'

'I don't know what he means.'

'Don't you?' Conrad was grinning mischievously.

'No. Definitely not.'

'Who is the other girl he has his eye on? Do I know her? Does she wear the veil, or will she have to be convinced?'

Conrad looked at Edward.

'Conrad?'

'It's nothing, Youssef,' said Conrad, without taking his eyes off Edward. 'Nothing at all. I must have made a mistake.'

That afternoon, he met Angelica in the Christ Church Meadow. She kissed him on each cheek and ran him through the highly-structured series of leisure activities to which he was now expected to devote the rest of his weekend, stopping, occasionally, to comment on how perfect the weather was, or how glad she was to be here, though various friends of hers had been quite sceptical about the relationship when they found out that she was giving up so much of her precious time to him. There was a lot about politics, and the efforts *Samizdat* was taking to maintain its pre-eminence. At the first available lull, he asked her, as tentatively as he could, about Diversitas.

'Hmm?'

'Diversitas. I think that's what Youssef said it was called. They run workshops?

'Yes, Edward, I know it. Look at that woman's outfit. Hideous. She looks like a tourist.'

'So you approve of it?'

'Of what, Edward?'

'Diversitas. You don't think this is all a bit like . . .'

'Like?'

'Draconian, maybe. I don't know.'

'No, Edward. I don't think it's draconian. Do you think it's draconian?'

'No, no.'

'Did Liberty ask you to talk to me about this?'

'What?'

'Because I'm going to sign up for one of their additional seminars, actually. It's only five pounds. Shall I sign you up?'

'Oh.' A pause. 'I mean, I'm quite busy. I have my thesis, and . . .'

'If you complete the full course you're a fully trained peer supporter.'

'Right. Sorry, a peer . . . what?'

'A peer supporter, Edward. People come to you with their problems, and you can talk to them and help solve them.'

'And can't you do that already?'

'What, if you're not trained?'

'I mean, I'd like to think my friends would be able to do that whether or not they'd received training.'

Angelica's arms stopped the brisk patters of gesticulations in which they had been engaged, and fell to her sides. She looked him up and down with interest. 'Your *friends*?'

'Youssef. Conrad.'

'*Oh*. Oh, I see.'

'What?'

'No, it's nothing.'

'What is it?'

'Nothing.' A smile. Then, gently: 'Peer supporters are necessary, Edward.'

'Right. Sorry.'

'Now, do me a favour and hold the bag.'

Angelica was never without her bag. She had acquired it during her gap year (she was convinced that the colourful woven Amerindian patterns had a particular cosmic significance).

These days, it contained the equipment for her newest and least convenient hobby: photography. 'Just one second,' she said as they strolled down the wide gravel promenade that led up from the river that Angelica chose, she said, because it reminded her of the Tuileries: 'This woman has *such* an aesthetic face.' She jogged over to what appeared to be one of the College cleaners, a slight woman in a rumpled purple headscarf. He heard little phrases drift over: 'I mean your *bone* structure' and 'Wow, amazing. Just amazing. That *septum*. You've modelled before, I take it?' and 'You know, we must have passed each other before, but I guess I never really *looked*.'

When it began to rain, the clouds heaping themselves up in endless reserve behind the train station, Angelica took him to the bookshop. Sensing him tend towards the cavernous basement where they kept the poetry, she took him by the elbow and escorted him up to the third floor where the photography books sat in vast, cellophaned slabs. Every so often, he would be called over and 'shown' something breathlessly—usually a gnarled washerwoman or child soldier—and nod along, trying not to let his gaze wander, as Angelica clucked through the next ten or so pages: 'Astonishing, isn't it? The *authenticity*. The *detail*. What do you think of this one?'

'Yeah. It's very . . . What are those things on their heads?'

'It's their culture, Edward.'

'I see.'

'Are you bored? You're bored.'

'No, not at all.'

'There's a *For Him* section just over there, you know? I can come and find you when I'm done.'

He threaded his way obediently past tables devoted to *The Mindful BBQ: Grill Your Way to a Healthy Mind* and *The Modern Stoic: Ten Lessons from Epictetus to Help you Succeed in Life, Love and Business*. Only when he rounded a particularly crammed case of military history did he stop. One of the tables was on its side, the books that had been piled up on its surface now strewn all over the floor. More than that: they had been vandalised, slashed up into little pieces, hardbacks ripped in half at the spine. There was a strange red pattern splattered over the pile. At first, Edward assumed it was a part of the cover, but as he drew closer, he realised the books had been doused in something—his first instinct was blood—though this, he soon realised with some relief, was unlikely, since the colour was too bright, and the smell artificial, more like dye or paint. Still, the sight of it seemed quite out of keeping with the wood-beamed charm of the bookshop. He could still hear the sales assistant talking to a customer about the DPhil she would begin the following autumn, and the coffee machine rasping out thick, expensive foam on the floor below.

He picked his way through the slashed-up pages over to the centre of the destruction. Someone had stretched a line of hazard tape from shelf to shelf to keep people away, but the glossy NEW RELEASE poster that had crowned the overturned table was still discernible. There was a photo of a stern, greying man in glasses, and a title: *Imperium*: *By Professor Roland Dyer.* Who was Roland Dyer? What had he done to deserve *this*?

'Admiring my work, I see?'

At the sound of Liberty's voice behind him, he composed his face into his best expression of indifference. He turned around: 'This was you?'

Liberty dipped her head in an uncharacteristic show of modesty. She was wearing a beret today, black and martial-looking. Tucked under her arms was what Edward suspected was the inaugural edition of *Gauche.*

'We did it. *Gauche*. Our intern, actually. You know Mandy Oyelowo, right? No? Do you know anyone?' Liberty drew back, and regarded her handiwork with a fond eye. 'The thing is Edward, I just couldn't let *Samizdat* have all the fun. What do you think, anyway? Impressive, right?'

'It's . . . good. I should get Angelica.'

'I'm surprised they've been so quiet about it. Just a few pieces of scotch tape? I'm kind of disappointed. Next time we'll go for something at the Ashmolean: hit them where it hurts. You know apparently they have this big hideous painting about hunting animals for sport. You know Hugo Fotherington-Wade at St. Catz? No? Well, he has an MFA in graffiti and related media. So we've got expertise, that's what I'm saying.'

'Right. Yeah.'

'You don't sound convinced.'

'No, I am convinced. It's just that Angelica . . .'

'You wanna know why we did it?'

Edward glanced about him. 'Erm, sure.'

'*Colonialism*, Edward.'

'Oh. Okay.'

Liberty shook her bereted head. 'Ugh, honestly Edward, if you're going to give me that miserable English "everyone's entitled to their own opinion" crap than I'll just leave. Is that what you're doing?'

'No, definitely not. Sorry.'

'Like, this is *Dyer* we're talking about.'

'Right. Sorry, Liberty, but I'm afraid I don't actually know who Dyer is.'

'Don't you know anything?' Liberty didn't bother turning from him, but angled her body so that the noise of her summons would carry: 'Angie? Angie. Come here a second. Don't you tell him anything? Like, he doesn't know who *Dyer* is.'

Professor Roland Dyer, Liberty explained while Angelica stared furiously at Edward behind her shoulder, was a professor at Oriel, who had made his name in the eighties with a searing essay for the *London Review of Books* titled 'The Classical Liberal and his Wisdom,' and had—save for a brief stint teaching something called 'Western Civilisation' at a private university in St. James's that no longer existed—been ensconced at

Oxford for forty-one years. He was ancient, stuffy; he would probably die here, get transubstantiated into a conference room or an essay prize.

'But what's wrong with him?'

'He's *evil* Edward,' cut in Angelica exasperatedly.

Liberty was nodding. 'Thank you, Ange.'

'He's an apologist. A revisionist. He has this *huge* new project with just *tons* of funding. Yes, Levy, I think. Or Schwartzman. "The Ethics of Empire" it's called—as if Empire could have an Ethics.'

'Basically he's one of those awful silvery old Englishmen who thinks the world would be better off if we all had the good sense to be born English,' said Liberty. 'Like, his new thing is that you guys set up *institutions* or whatever in Africa, and that made it all, like okay.'

'Oh.'

'Like, who needs institutions anyway? Totally overrated. Like, read some anarchism.'

'And there's the *domination* thing,' added Angelica.

'The domination thing?'

'Ugh yeah the *domination* thing,' said Liberty, lifting off her beret and using it to fan away her irritation. 'He's all like: the decolonised peoples of sub-Saharan Africa—that's us, Edward, I hope you realise—the decolonised peoples of sub-Saharan Africa can never be free. Can you believe it? Aren't you, like, offended?'

'Yes, he is,' said Angelica.

'Anyway,' continued Liberty, Dyer is all like: the term "nation" is a recent, nineteenth-century invention. He's all like: the nation deviates from the older imperial form of governance not because the people under it are somehow mystically represented in a new and better way, but because the new structures wear a cloak of racial legitimacy which obscures their essentially tyrannical structure. He's all like: the true consequence of decolonisation is to reify new fine-grained ethnic differences, thereby leading to new cycles of violence, brown on brown, black on black.' She shook her head. 'I know, right? What an asshole.'

'Just awful,' agreed Angelica. 'He tries to make out like either you have your own empire, or you're in someone else's. So everyone's colonised, he reckons. The Catalans. The *Welsh*.'

'I mean it's dumb, right?' said Liberty. 'Like, I've been to Wales, Edward. You know what it was like? Have you been there?'

'No.'

'It's awful. Like, the *food*.' She shuddered. 'Racist, too, that goes without saying.'

'I'm sure not everyone . . .'

'Whatever. You're so naïve.'

Angelica was beside him now; her fingers brushed proprietorially against his arm. 'We think it's great, Liberty,' she said. 'Such a message.'

'Aww, thank you sweetie. I mean, someone had to, right? Like *Samizdat* has been doing really well, don't get me wrong—fighting the fight—but these days it's such a legacy institution, you know? It's safe.'

'It's not "safe."'

'It's safe Ange.'

'How is it safe?'

'It's okay Sweetie. I get it. You're busy. And Edward here would disapprove if his nice English rose of a girlfriend got radicalised.'

Edward cleared his throat: 'I don't . . .'

'You sure Edward? You're looking queasy.'

'Oh, that's just how he looks,' said Angelica, hooking herself enthusiastically around his arm. 'Of *course* he approves. It's in his blood.'

'You know it's funny you say that,' said Liberty, still staring

at Edward, leaning in so he could see the little the spasms of focus round her eyes. 'Because if you're really on board with this
Edward—if you really want to make a difference, do something
that will be remembered—your blood's exactly what I need.'

Once Liberty had tactfully dispatched Angelica back to
College and given the lady at the bookshop's till a stern lecture on the historiography of the Mau Mau, she led Edward
up the High Street, promising over her shoulder that it would
all make sense when they got where they were going. It was a
typical weekday in the centre of Oxford: there were homeless
people strumming guitars, Muslims preaching from their per-
golas, Christians informing people through megaphones that
entry to the afterlife was far more competitive than they might
otherwise have thought; Edward, for his part, had to trot to
keep pace with Liberty, who strode purposefully through the
crowds, heels clacking on the ancient flagstones and cobbles.

'Liberty. *Liberty*, wait. Where are we going? I have an essay
due and I really can't be . . .'

'The Chamber, Edward. Why else would we be going this
way? You think I come here because I like it?' She dodged
someone handing out a charity leaflet. 'No, no thank you. What
is this? Guinea worm? Are you guys even accredited?'

'Liberty. Why does the Chamber need my blood?'

'Oh for God's sake, Edward,' she said, stopping in the middle of the street and turning to him, unimpressed. 'It's a *metaphor*. Your background. Your parentage. The Chamber is going
through a pretty rough patch—like it's having some problems,
if you must know, like *problems*—and I thought I could count
on you for your help.'

Edward knew about the Chamber, though when he had seen
the size of the monthly payment exacted for the privilege of
calling oneself a member, he had assumed he would never set
foot inside. What was nominally a debating society registered to

him, by now, as a kind of cult: it was said to have its own private languages, costumes, and rituals, not to mention a particularly Byzantine system of administrative elections that sent hordes of the pimpliest and most belligerent freshers into the streets every term in search of votes. There was, he knew, a clear *political* valency to the Chamber, too—it was whispered, with a frequency that could only suggest some degree of truth, that *six* former prime ministers had been its president, as well as the king of a small Arab nation—but its true commitment, he suspected, was to celebrity: every Thursday, the street outside would come alive with throngs of posh boys in black tie, queuing up outside great, red, gothic buildings in the hope of glimpsing whatever world leader, white-collar criminal or minor television personality had been invited this week. It was a place of reaction and pomposity, a place of self-congratulation and long disquisitions about how it had been operating uninterrupted since the eighteenth century, which was when most of its members seemed to wish they had been alive. Every term, a little flyer would appear in Edward's pigeonhole, opening with a few paragraphs on the Chamber's powerful social role, in these dark and uncertain and unprecedentedly censorious times: *Once again,* the last one had read, *the Chamber remains committed to free, fair and open debate, and this is why it will no longer tolerate . . .*

'So you know I'm acting President, right?' said Liberty as she buzzed open the iron gate and trafficked him through the courtyard, hand pressing athletically at the small of his back.

'I saw your speech. With all the . . . percentages.'

'No, not of the Common Room Edward. Honestly keep *up.* Of here. The Chamber. That's right, take a few minutes if you want. Neat, isn't it? Just about the only place in this city that doesn't make me want to tear it down.'

She filled him in as he looked around, open mouthed, at the neat squares of hedge-muffled lawn, the whispering fountain, the ancient yews with birdcalls ringing through them as though the city outside never even existed. There had been, she said, another scandal. He was familiar, she presumed, with the canonical scandals, the scandals of yesteryear that had made national news—the invitation of a troupe of Dutch neo-Nazis to debate the wearing of poppies on Remembrance Sunday, and of course that slavery-themed cocktail.

'But this last one was bad. Like, *bad*. Like, we're all kind of waiting for the papers to hear about it.'

'What happened?'

'Ugh, just the usual.' Liberty batted away the question with a flick of her ring-studded hand. 'I mean, it's unfortunate really. I think the wheelchair makes it look worse than it was, you know? In the video.'

'Oh. Right.'

'And how were they to know she was *blind*? Anyway, Edward, what I'm trying to say is that the Chamber kind of needs me right now. To steady the ship and convince anyone that it's moving in a more progressive direction.'

'Of course.'

'And it's an opportunity, isn't it? I mean, think how it'll look on my CV.' She turned her head up to the sun, basking for a moment. 'You know the last pres, Charles Stourbridge-Walker, already has a training contract at Sullivan Mengele Wright. Already, Edward. He's only twenty-one. And Bertie Beauchamp is at Goldman. And Miles von Ludendorff was *killing* it at Deutsche before the charges, and still, he'll be out in like two years, and the law surrounding those complex financial instruments is *so* unclear anyway, so it's really just a case of being in the wrong place at the wrong time . . . Edward? Yes, it's a fountain, I assume you've seen one of those before. Edward, *this* way. In here.'

She pushed open the door, and they found themselves in a hallway, very grand, with a brass chandelier and a mahogany staircase snaking up to a carpeted landing.

'So it'll help you too, is what I'm saying,' she continued. 'This is your opportunity to *be* someone. See, Edward, the thing about the Chamber is that it's run by *us*. The students. No administrators, no faculty, no *grown-ups* except for Terry the security guard. That's it, say hi to him. Give him a wave. He's an ex-cop, but, like, pretty reformed now—did all three levels of the 'From Enforcement to Empowerment' course at Diversitas, has a black nephew, decent guy. Anyway, what I'm really saying is we can do what we like, here. Your responsibilities are *responsibilities*, you know?'

'But Liberty. Wait . . .' He stopped her beside a vast felt notice board and caught a flash of the week's motions—'This house prefers Bordeaux to Burgundy,' 'This house would overthrow the government'—as he turned. 'What do you actually need me for? What am I doing here?'

'It's simple.'

'Simple how?'

'A workshop.'

'Like Angelica's? At the start of term?'

Liberty stroked her chin thoughtfully. 'Easier. Run more . . . professionally. You sit. You listen. You nod. And when the vote comes at the end—around 5 P.M. I guess—you vote to stop the speaker from coming.'

She kept tapping her foot briskly as she spoke, and her hand had already repositioned itself at the small of his back.

'Liberty, wait.' He shrugged his bag off his shoulder to try and anchor himself in place. 'Who actually is the speaker? Why am I doing this?'

'*Dyer,* Edward.' Liberty let out a strafe of tuts. 'Honestly, I thought you were *invested* in this stuff. I thought you wanted . . .' She shook her head. 'Listen, this is why I think the East African connection is so valuable, okay? In terms of optics, that is. Otherwise, I'd go with someone less . . .' she smiled, looked him up and down. 'Well, you know what I mean.'

'Liberty, *wait*.'

'Ugh what now.'

'I'm sorry. I really want to help. But all afternoon? My thesis . . .'

'Listen, Edward.' She had turned to face him now, arms crossed. 'I really appreciate that you're doing this. I'll *remember*.'

'Yeah, well it's not about remembering, it's about me not being kicked off my course. It's about . . .'

'I've not forgotten about last year, you know.'

That startled him. Liberty's voice seemed very cold, all of a sudden, her eyebrows raised as though impressed at her own capacity for threat. 'I never brought it up with Angelica, you know. No need. But no—don't think for a second, Edward, that I've forgotten.' She reached out her hand, and it took all his effort not to flinch; but the touch, when it came, was gentle. 'But I want you to know, Edward, that everything can change. Everything.' She stopped a moment, staring wistfully at the tall, oak door at the end of the passage. 'You know the best thing about this place, Edward? It's not the building, it's not the history. It's not that fountain you seemed to like so much—that's getting removed next year by the way. The best thing about this place is the *ambition*. Everyone here is going somewhere—going on to be popular, important—yeah, even rich, powerful, whatever. And it sweeps you up. If you let it, it sweeps you up.' She brightened: 'Besides,' she went on, 'If any *tutor* gives you trouble, you just do what I did.'

'What did you do?'

'Wrote a letter. To the undergraduate office, saying I wanted to change papers. Too many dead, old white men. Said I didn't feel *represented*.' Liberty giggled. 'They won't stop you. And after that proverb you recited, about how trees need roots to grow . . . well, now everyone knows how representative you are. Of course, for a moment I wondered why a Zanzibari proverb would involve *snow*, but Ange explained.

She hates the stuff, you know. Jets off to the Maldives every winter to avoid it.'

'She . . . what was her explanation?'

'That it stands for *whiteness*, of course. The hegemonic position. That however much we think we can break free of it, it keeps pulling us back in.'

The workshop began with Liberty introducing a speaker who seemed, if Edward heard correctly over the excited chatter about 'justice' emanating from the two Indian girls to his left, to go by the name 'Chlorophyll.' Chlorophyll had brought with her an instructional video of various 'scenarios' that could, she warned the room, arise when people like them set foot in a place as cruel and ancient and exclusionary as this. The first clip involved a conversation between two women during which one woman's name was repeatedly mispronounced by the other. The second clip involved two men in a shared kitchen or rec room, in which one man asked the other what he was cooking, because it smelled unusual. After about ten of these, Chlorophyll flicked off the projector and began her speech. The overarching message, so far as Edward could discern, was more metaphysical than anything else: no one, she explained, had the right to contradict anyone else's experiences or perceptions, to gainsay the delicate palaces of reason they had erected, to assail the truths they held most dear, especially if those truths related to something she kept referring to as their 'identity,' which they all had, she assured them, or they wouldn't have been chosen. Nor is there any such thing—and here she drew herself up to her full, self-satisfied height, her earrings jangling eloquently—nor was there any such thing as *objectivity*, at least not any more. That was very much out. Then it was time for a little game: up on the projector flashed the faces of different historical personages. It was their task, Chlorophyll continued, to decide which, if any of them the Chamber should invite to speak. One by one they voted. Henry VIII. Winston Churchill. Michelangelo. Aristotle. 'That's really great,' said Chlorophyll when the girl to Edward's left made the observation that Aristotle had probably never had to deal with lots of the challenges that she had, personally, to shoulder on a daily basis, and that perhaps it was time to put him aside for a while and make space for others. 'Just great. Seriously, thank you Parvati. I think we all learned something there.'

At last, they voted. The method was a show of hands, and the result was unanimous: they would recommend to the council that Dyer be disinvited immediately, and, if possible, publicly insulted in the upcoming newsletter. As Edward meandered his way down to the lobby, he passed Liberty, who was engrossed in what she clearly took to be a far more interesting conversation than the one she had shared with him, and who suggested, without even turning to him, that he run along and explore the Chamber a little while he was here, since who knew if he'd ever be asked in again.

He roamed around freely, peering round doorways and backing politely to one side when one of the herds of loafered Committee-members came cackling through the other way. He visited the new library, read the plaque about the famous Pre-Raphaelite paintings on its ceiling, and stole a glance through the plate of glass in the doorway of the debate chamber itself: the banks of red leather seats, the high oak gallery. His last stop was the bar, with its photographs of dinner-jacketed former presidents grinning next to cabinet members, celebrities, royals. He hadn't expected to see anyone he knew here, and it was a surprise when he spotted Rachel in the corner, at one of the high circular tables, surrounded by some people he had never seen before in College. There were about seven of them in all, with the open, slightly stilted look of international students. As he drew nearer, one of them made a joke; Rachel began to laugh and shake her head.

'Rachel?'

'Oh,' Her face fell a moment. She flashed her interlocutor an apologetic smile slipped down from the table.'

'Sorry I didn't mean to interrupt.'

'You're not interrupting.'

'Seriously, I just wanted to have a quick look at the bar before I left.'

'You should come and see the best part then.' She took him round the corner, a bay window and lower, leather seats. The light had begun to dip outside, and they stood side by side at the window staring out at the dark brick mass of the Chamber against the orange sky. He thought of Angelica waiting for him.

'I didn't know you came here,' she said.

'I don't, really. I'm not actually a member.'

'You're just here because you're following me then? I'm touched.'

'I didn't know *you* came here either.'

'That's because this is where I come to hide, Edward.'

'Well it's working. I've barely seen you since the start of term.'

'You saw me the other night. Before you got lost in the wisdom of your "proverb." Which was definitely some kind of appropriation of German language and culture, by the way, so I probably ought to be very offended.'

'Yeah. Sorry about that.'

'You could have at least said hello afterwards.'

'Yeah, well Angelica was there, so . . .'

'So?'

'I don't think it would have been a good moment, Rachel.'

'You know it puts me in a strange position, when you act like I'm some affair you have to keep secret from everyone?'

He didn't reply.

'What would she do if she found out about us talking here, now? You're blushing again, by the way.'

'Yeah, thanks.'

'Would she forbid you from seeing me?'

He could feel his ears growing hot. 'You know sometimes,' he said, 'people avoid upsetting others not because they're scared of them but because they actually like them.'

'So you like her then.'

'What?'

'You like her.'

'Yeah.' A pause. 'Yeah, I do actually. Does that bother you?'

'Yes, Edward,' she said, rolling her eyes and letting the arms she had unconsciously crossed fall to her sides. 'I have been weeping uncontrollably to myself in my room every night. I have a special ice-cream scoop to get me through the long evenings as I sit and wonder who, if anyone, will recognise the inner beauty I keep so thoroughly veiled.'

'That's not what I meant.'

'So is it Youssef's influence, this new high opinion you seem to have of yourself?'

'What are you talking about?'

'You know, Edward. All these women in your life you keep apart so we don't get jealous and start tearing shreds from each other. I mean, you *are* very popular now . . .'

'That's not what I meant, Rachel.'

'Are you sure?'

'I just know that you two haven't always got along, that's all.'

'How considerate. Angelica told you that, I suppose?'

'No one told me. It's obvious. I was kind of hoping someone would tell me what was going on.'

'You should ask Angelica about that.'

'Great. Another person who won't tell me.'

'For God's sake, Edward, you should ask Angelica because you're five weeks into a relationship with her, and normally people five weeks into a relationship feel like they can talk about these things. You know, when they *like* someone.'

'I don't know why you're being so hostile. It's not like I ever say this kind of thing about your boyfriend.'

'What?'

He stepped forward now, the indignation rising in his chest. 'Maybe I should. Maybe I should concoct a huge simmering feud with him, and make it quite clear in our interactions that I'm holding that feud against *you* in some unfathomable way, and then when asked about it refuse to tell you anything.'

'What are you talking about?'

'Your boyfriend, Rachel.'

'I don't have a boyfriend.'

'Yes you do.'

'Right. Well thank you for your opinion, but I suspect I know this better than you. Who told you I had a boyfriend?'

'*Everyone.* Conrad. Well, sort of, with Conrad. But Youssef unambiguously.'

'Well I don't, actually.'

His heart was beating very hard. 'You don't have a boyfriend,' he repeated.

'Oh, for goodness' sake . . .'

'So why did Youssef say you did?'

She paused a moment, lips pressed together in thought.

'Well that *is* obvious.'

'Is it? Not to me.'

'Isn't he your best friend?'

'Yeah.'

She shook her head, almost pityingly. 'You know Edward, sometimes I feel like you have absolutely no idea what's going on in your life. You've known Youssef for what—a year now? You're smart, I know *that* because we've been in tutorials together. Can you really not figure out why he might not like me?'

'Well I'm clearly not as smart as you thought, because like I said I have no idea. He doesn't know you.'

'He knows who I am.'

'Who are you then? What's this problem with you that everyone seems to know except me? Something they teach you at private school?'

Rachel looked him up and down, as though trying to work out whether or not to trust him with a reply. 'I'm Jewish,' she said.

CHAPTER 8

Angelica was out that evening, and the following one; in fact, it was a full three days before she and Edward saw each other again. Edward was summoned not by anything so undignified as an actual invitation, but with a single, declarative sentence, in the manner to which he had become accustomed: *I'm in my room.* She answered the door wearing a green silk robe, but the sash was pulled so tightly round her, the 'v' of the neckline so high and snug against her collarbones, that the whole outfit seemed more like a reminder of her own unattainability than anything else. The lamps, the fairy lights, had all been switched off.

'You can sit,' she said, and he obeyed. She sat at the desk, and took out a pot of nail polish, whose brush she began to run along the tip of her fingernail. 'Did you have a nice time at the Chamber the other night?'

'It was fine, I guess. Boring. She didn't really need me much.'

She spoke without looking up: 'Did you talk to anyone?'

'In the meeting? A few of Liberty's friends. The woman organising was called Chlorophyll, and she was pretty talkative.'

'And afterwards?'

'I don't know. I walked around. The bar looks nice. Lots of marble.'

'Meet anyone interesting?'

'Interesting?'

'Yes, Edward. Interesting.'

Did she know? She had started on the final nail now, and her face was all concentration as she curled the side of the brush along her cuticle far more carefully than it seemed to demand. 'No,' he said. 'No one interesting.' He thought for a moment. 'I mean there was Liberty, obviously.'

She looked at him for several seconds, then relaxed, as though she had made up her mind about something. 'Do you like Liberty?' she asked nonchalantly.

'She's . . . I mean she was very nice to me the other day.'

'She's very accomplished. You know she started her own charity last year?'

'Good for her.'

'Do you think she's pretty?'

Edward stared at her. She had stopped painting the first hand now, but rather than move on to the second, she screwed the lid back on the pot. 'Do you?' he asked measuredly.

'Yes. Very. She has beautiful features.'

'I'm not sure I really see it.'

'I wouldn't mind, you know. If you were attracted to her. I mean I'd understand it.

'But I'm not, so you don't need to.'

'I wish I looked like her sometimes.' She paused, and held her hand out in front of her, admiring her work. 'You know I once had this boyfriend called Charles—Charles Falconbridge. Did you ever meet him? I don't think so. There was this one evening after formal we were stood in front of a mirror, and he had this very pale skin and you could see all the veins in his shoulders, because he played rugby you see. Anyway, we were standing in front of the mirror and the sun was setting outside, and all I could think was how beautiful it would be if I had dark skin like Liberty. For the contrast, you understand. Aesthetically.'

'I like your skin.'

'Anyway, I wouldn't mind, is what I'm saying. I wouldn't mind because she's someone I respect. And maybe I feel an attraction to her, somewhere deep down. Or maybe it's envy: to be honest I've wondered ever since I was a girl if I could even tell them apart.' Slowly, almost primly, she picked herself up from the desk chair, and walked over to the bed. 'What I'm saying is I don't mind if, just this once, when you're with me, a thought runs through your head about someone else. I don't mind, okay? Just this once.'

'Angelica, this is ridiculous.'

'I'm very open minded, you know. It may not seem like it but I am. And I can be anyone you want me to be. Does that feel good?'

He didn't reply.

'Do you want me to stop?'

'No.'

'Would I be shorter? Would I wear different clothes? Tell me if you want me to stop.'

'No, don't stop.'

'What colour would my hair be? If I was someone else. It could be . . . black, like Liberty's. It could be dark brown.'

He could feel her fingernails on his scalp now, and smell her. He shut his eyes.

'Just this once, Edward. Anyone you like.'

Afterwards, she did none of the self-satisfied posing, none of the kittenish stretching in which she usually specialised. She sat up very straight in the bed, fixed her hair in a hairband lying in wait for her on the bedside table; then she pulled her robe tightly round her once again and sat on her phone in the armchair in the furthest possible corner of the room.

'Angelica,' he said. No answer. '*Angelica.*'

'It wasn't Liberty, was it?'

There was a long silence. 'No.'

She nodded, stoically, lips pressed tightly together. 'You can go now, Edward.'

'Can we maybe . . .'

'I said that's all.'

The following morning, Angelica stuffed all her quilted leather suitcases full to bursting and informed him, via a brisk, carefully worded text message that made no mention of the previous evening, that she was going home. Edward suggested, as casually as he could, that they meet. Angelica replied that yes, this might be a good idea, and that if he hurried over now, he could catch her while she waited in the rear quad for the car that had been arranged to ferry her to her leafy, pram-filled suburb.

'Really, Edward,' she said as he drew level, out of breath and flushed from the cold wind, 'there isn't much to say. I've decided to leave a week early. That's all.'

'I see.'

'Why are you looking at me like that? It's unsettling.'

'You sure it's not about us?'

'What?'

'Us, Angelica.'

'No, don't be silly.'

'Listen, about last night . . .'

'Oh look, that'll be the car.' Angelica shrugged her backpack over her shoulder and turned towards an expensive black car crunching up the gravel. 'I recognise the driver. My father's used him before, I think—he used to be a Gurkha.'

'*Angelica.*'

Angelica rolled her eyes. 'Listen, Edward. It's not about "us," I promise you. It's just something at home. Domestic disaster. I'd tell you the details, but you'd be bored.'

'I wouldn't be bored.'

'Edward.' She folded her arms, her foot grinding impatiently into the tiny stones. 'I am asking you not to make a big deal out of this. Are you going to make a big deal out of this?'

'No.'

'Good. Now kiss me goodbye, please.'

As he watched the car disappear through the gates, he decided to believe her. She would be back to her old, imperious self in no time—'domestic disasters' were hardly rare *chez* Angelica, anyway. There was always *something*, if not the exploded sourdough starter or the mildewed wine cellar, then the light-fingered housekeeper or the slipped disc on the family dachshund. By next week, the whole clan would be broiled and burnished on some tropical beach: 'A Christmas tradition,' she'd explained, almost guiltily, when he'd chanced upon the thousand-a-night villa on a tab she had left open, 'We *do* like to get away . . .'

Edward wasn't left alone for long. At lunch, Conrad swept him into his orbit, muscling in between the patiently queuing freshers with a sharp tilt of the head designed to convey to Edward that he, if he had any sense, ought to do the same. He was off early too, he informed him. He *needed* the extra week in Palermo or he was pretty sure he would die, the weather taking the turn it was, so if Edward wanted the benediction of his company then this was his last shot before Christmas: 'I certainly won't be keeping in touch, you see. In case you were thinking of dropping some wheedling little text message inviting me to spend New Year's Eve at your hovel. With all the animals.'

'Right. Thank you for letting me know in advance. You know we don't actually have livestock right? We live in a town.'

'I wasn't talking about livestock.'

'Oh. Thanks.'

Conrad dipped his head modestly as he pointed at the first trough of food for the dinner lady's benefit. 'You're quite, quite welcome Edward.'

On the subject of Angelica, he was typically unhelpful, loudly insisting, as they skidded their trays round the aluminium rails: 'You must tell me everything, Edward. I am an expert.'

'I see. Have you ever even had a girlfriend, Conrad?'

'Good heavens no. Disgusting. No, I come at the matter

unsullied, neutral,' he said, as he carved himself a cuboid from the tray of shepherd's pie.

'I see.'

'So she's gone off, has she?'

'She's gone home.'

Conrad nodded impassively, like a doctor forming a clinical opinion. 'Let me guess. Started acting all twitchy and uncertain and tortured? A sudden change in personality that cannot be accounted for.'

'I think she just needs some time.'

'I'm afraid this is what they do, Edward.'

'They?'

'Oxford girls. The occult glamour of the mental health wobble. Why be a normal human woman when you can be a precarious little autist trembling at the burden of her own embodiment?'

'Yeah, I don't know what that means.'

Conrad was enjoying himself now, plunging his hand into the fruit bowl beside the till. 'It's simple, Edward. Why fit in? Why *adjust,* when you can just trundle around between traumatic flashbacks about that time your parents forgot your birthday and that time your weird uncle gave you a bath? Why have a normal relationship when you can slap on a face mask of an evening and sit there stewing behind it, alone in your garret, writing strongly worded emails about all the horrible men in your life to the College Dean?'

'One second, Conrad.' Edward smiled apologetically at the hair-netted woman behind the till as he paid, and proceeded into the brightly lit hall. 'I think that's Youssef over there,' he said over his shoulder.

'Youssef will agree with me,' said Conrad, trotting past Edward. 'You must know these things. It's part of your education. If you're an ambitious young woman like Angelica, you need at least some personality disorder to make you interesting.'

'I'm going to go and sit with him.'

'Good idea. Youssef. *Youssef*! Conrad hooted across the hall: 'Make room, for goodness' sake. Kick those hideous freshers off the table and tell them to eat in the buttery. We're hearing about Edward's love life.'

Youssef shifted to his side as Edward slid in next to him. 'An excellent topic,' he said.

'A pressing topic,' agreed Conrad.

'Has he been invited to the house in St. Rémy yet? Has he had the family cheeses?'

'He's blown it,' said Conrad.

'What?'

'Blown it. Screwed it up. Set off a great improvised explosive device that has sent his relationship—if you *insist* on calling it that—flying apart in a million little pieces. Yes, I know, I know. It must be the Muslim in him.'

'I've not blown it,' protested Edward. 'She just needs some space, so she's gone back home a week early.'

'Oh you *have* blown it,' said Youssef.

Conrad nodded smugly. 'I told you.'

'How did you manage this, Edward? Wait.' Youssef paused, treated himself to another mouthful of the brick of halal lasagne in front of him, then spoke through it without swallowing: 'You didn't take her to see where you grew up or something did you?'

'No. What would be wrong with that anyway?'

'Did she meet your adopted family?'

'They're not adopted, Youssef. Some of them just happen not to be Muslim.'

'He sabotaged it, I reckon,' said Conrad gravely.

'I didn't sabotage it.'

'He has his eye on someone else, you see.'

Youssef sat up. 'What?'

'Edward here,' continued Conrad, 'has been spotted with

another woman. Several times. Leaning forward. Hair-touching. Clear amorous intent.'

'What are you talking about?'

'The Chamber bar, wasn't it, Ed? With a nice little fight with Angelica afterwards to commemorate the whole episode? Yes, Conrad does hear things.'

Youssef laid his cutlery carefully on the tabletop. 'And who, pray is this someone?'

Edward glanced at Conrad pleadingly. 'Leave it, please.'

Conrad had begun to giggle. 'Go on, Edward, tell him about your foray into the Promised Land.'

'It's nothing . . .'

But Conrad spoke only to Youssef now, drawing himself up in the chair to his full, smug height: 'Edward, it seems, has his eye on the Jewish girl. Don't you, Edward? What was her name?'

'Rachel,' he said unthinkingly. 'But we're not . . .'

'*That* girl?' Youssef had let go of his cutlery and folded his arms. 'I knew it. I had suspected as much. So you've taken a step backwards then, this is what you are saying? You have regressed.'

'What?'

'You could have had a nice Alhambra to yourself in the South of France with a nice blonde girlfriend—blonde, Edward, the prestige hair colour, like an angel—and instead you end up going after this Jew like it's 609 AD and the blessed visitation of the Jabal an-Nour hasn't even happened and no one knows any better.'

'Right well I'm sorry to disappoint, but I really don't think that's very important.'

'How Jewish even is she, anyway?'

'What's *that* supposed to mean?'

'How Jewish. It's a simple question.'

'It's a meaningless question.'

'Is she Jewish in the way I'm Muslim? Or Jewish in the way *you're* Muslim?'

'Do you mean is she only slightly Jewish, or is she *very* slightly Jewish?'

'Ah, yes, how amusing. You are quite Muslim enough when it suits you.'

'Honestly Youssef I'm really not in the mood for this—not from you.'

'Not from *me?*'

'You're the least devout Muslim I have ever met. You have a whisky decanter by your bed. You own those shares in that *ibérico* pig farm.'

'Not a *competition*, gentlemen.' Conrad gave a nervous laugh. 'I suggest we all kiss, make up, and find a new ethnicity to persecute. What about Armenians? Kurds?'

'You're welcome, by the way. After all the effort I have put into you . . .' said Youssef.

'Oh I'm sorry. I didn't realise "hating all Jews" was where this was all leading. I didn't realise that "hating all Jews" was the final step on the rightly guided spiritual path you keep talking about.'

'What about gypsies?' said Conrad.

'Not now, Conrad,' snapped Youssef.

'What even is your problem with Jews anyway?' said Edward.

'I don't have a problem.'

'Unless I happen, you know, to *talk* to one, in which case you do.'

Youssef sighed, frustrated. 'I simply want what's best for you Edward. You don't understand, because you grew up on a council estate where there were no books or newspapers or Muslims or sense of moral purpose and everyone had a dangerous dog.'

'How is this *best* for me? Also I didn't grow up on a council estate, I keep saying this.'

'You don't know what they are like.'

'What are "they" like?'

Conrad shifted in his seat. 'Gentlemen . . .'

'One second, Conrad. I want to be enlightened.'

Youssef threaded his fingers together, very serious. 'You really want to know?'

'Yes. I do.'

'Well for one thing, they whine.'

'Whine?'

'Want special privileges all the time. Want everyone to know they're different—oh, how our forefathers suffered!—and then become deeply offended when you point it out, or *dare* to suggest that occasionally the balance might tip the other way.'

'This is unlike you of course, who are entirely assimilationist, and never mention Egypt or Islam in conversation.'

'They *love* the idea of their own suffering, Edward. The Jew can be both aggressive and innocent, because he has suffered. It is a pathology I have observed elsewhere—in Benenden girls, in people from Scotland. But the Jew is, I am afraid, the worst of the lot.'

'Right. Well, we're not talking about 'The Jew,' I'm afraid. Or Benenden girls, whatever one of those is. We're talking about Rachel.'

'Have you asked her what she thinks of Israel?'

'What?'

'Has she spoken about the crimes of her people in Gaza? The West Bank? Lebanon?'

'No, Youssef. Funnily enough "the crimes of her people" hasn't come up. We were too busy talking about whether she has a boyfriend. Do you talk to Lolly B about the Suez Crisis?'

'No surprise there.'

'What?'

'No surprise it hasn't come up.' Youssef chuckled to himself knowingly. 'They rarely volunteer such information.'

'What are you talking about? You literally never speak about Israel, or Palestine, or Lebanon.'

'Not with *you*.'

'So, what, you think I should sit Rachel down and interrogate her? Make sure her allegiances are to me and not the Jewish state?'

'You're making it seem like this is a totally unreasonable request. I doubt Angelica would be going out with you if she was not labouring under the illusion—or the *lie*, I suppose you might say—you are some sort of pan-African Maoist or whatever she wants everyone to be this week.'

'I'm not going to do it. I shouldn't *have* to do it.'

'Why not? Why *shouldn't* people answer for what their countrymen do? Whenever some stupid illiterate camel-fancying Arab decides it would be a good idea to blow up a train, *I'm* the one who has to reassure people that, no, in fact, the Piccadilly Line is not mentioned in any of the Surahs, and that Islam is actually "a religion of peace," whatever this is supposed to mean.'

'I see. She's half-German, too—shall I check she isn't a Nazi?'

Youssef rolled his eyes. 'This seems unlikely, Edward. But if you have your doubts by all means check.'

'And if I find out that she doesn't have the same politics as you, what then?'

'It's not "politics," Edward. "Politics" is what you call things that don't really matter. Wealth redistribution. Women's rights. Luxuries. In Palestine people are being killed.'

'Rachel hasn't done anything to get anyone killed.'

'I might leave, gentlemen . . .' said Conrad.

'She won't be loyal to you.' Youssef sounded desperate now.

'Right, well I suspect your standards for this are very high. I'm not in the habit of calling women whores when they wear open-toed shoes.'

'She'll always have a suitcase packed, you know. However

long you're together. Half an eye on everything, conferring with her little Jew friends until one day they decide they don't feel safe and decide to fly away to Israel.'

'Gosh, I wonder why she might feel like that.'

'Are you ready for that, Edward? Are you ready to live in Israel? Then what? Your wife can buy genetically modified pipless oranges; your children can carry guns just like it says in the Torah?' Youssef shook his head, more in defeat than anything else. 'Are you ready to turn your back on everything? Everything I've taught you, everyone you've met. Are you *sure* you're ready to be the odd one out?'

How Jewish? All afternoon, in the silence of the library, Edward kept turning the phrase over in his mind. He was familiar enough with Youssef's general mistrust of Jews by now, but it had never come to a head like this, never actually intruded on his life in any tangible way. Isaiah Levy was one thing—he was inconsequential, abstract, like all the other Jewish people Youssef was convinced were in charge of all academic funding, or the 'cabal of devious Ashkenazim' at his father's banking firm who Youssef assured him had passed over a disproportionate number of Muslims for promotion at the annual review. But Rachel?

As he flicked through his notes in an attempt to prepare for his meeting with his tutor, he found himself growing more and more frustrated. What was he even *doing* this for anyway? He had resolved to take Liberty's advice and request a change of programme out of desperation more than anything else, thumbing his way into the depths of the English Literature course handbook, past 'Vegetarian Women's Writing,' past 'Beneath the Contemporary Australian Poem,' only making up his mind when he reached the last entry—a new course, convened by someone called Professor Lawrence Pfister whom Edward had never even heard of, with the unpromising title of 'Post-Human

Spheres.' He had filled out the online forms and waited for the switch to be brought into effect. Liberty had promised him it would be easy enough, that there were whole armies of administrators and functionaries, seething around their concrete bunker on Wellington Square, who existed for the sole purpose of helping out young, anxious, ethnically ambiguous students like him who couldn't make up their minds. It had been a shock, therefore, when at 8 A.M. that morning an email had shot into his inbox—not from Professor Pfister, but from the Shakespeare tutor, Professor Burgess, whom he had never even met—asking for 'a brief word in my office, if it's not too much trouble. I'd like to talk to you about your request to change topic.'

He shut his notebook and pulled up the course page for 'Post-Human Spheres' on the departmental website. Burgess would take the switch as some kind of slight, he knew—such was the way with these silver-haired old Oxford professors, with their pipes and anachronistic clothing, most of whom spoke about Shakespeare as if they had been close personal friends— and Edward wanted to find something to appease him, some text in which he could feign the kind of deep, eccentric, interest that an Oxford professor, of all people, would understand. The list of authors was hardly coherent. A week of Nietzsche, then a week on a group of people called 'the assemblage theorists,' then two weeks on something called 'the rhizome,' then a week on Artaud, then some cinema, all of it French. But the last entry on the list looked promising, for his purposes. He read it through once more, rehearsing the earnest expression he would wear when relaying it to Burgess: *In the last two weeks of term, we shall look at the works of Franz Kafka. We shall consider how Kafka modified the prevailing view of subjectivity and character in European writing, stripping away human predicates, qualities and characteristics until all that was left was a bare existential function. Alongside close readings of Kafka's most famous texts, including* The Metamorphosis *and* The Trial, *we will consider a number of critical attempts to parse the Kafkaesque, beginning with Professor Helmut Bawerk's ground-breaking article, 'Am I a Cockroach?'* Yes, he thought. *Am I a cockroach?* That just about covered it.

Ten minutes before the meeting was scheduled, Edward gathered up his things, dawdling a while at the edge of the quad so as not to arrive too early. Burgess's office was on the second floor; as he reached the lip of the final flight of stairs, he heard a strange, dim sound. He rounded the corner. Music, which grew louder as he proceeded down the passage, the melody now discernible. By the time he reached the door he could recognise the piece as something vaguely classical, though he could not place it beyond that, and felt incompetent as a result. He listened for a while, ear pressed to the cold lacquered wood; then, after checking that the hour had rolled round on his phone, he knocked.

For a while, nothing happened. The music carried on, confident and regular, and the door remained closed. Just as Edward raised his fist to knock again, the noise stopped.

'Come in.'

The voice was high pitched—not quite the gruff, pipe-smoking timbre he had come to expect from Oxford dons. Encouragingly, though, it seemed distracted, and certainly not angry or scandalised at the request to change course. He took a final, deep breath and pressed open the door.

The room Edward found himself entering was quite different from those in which his tutorials had taken place last year. A few of the architectural features were the same—the waist-high wooden panels, the floor lamps, the high dormer windows overlooking the quad—but it was darker, with a whole warren of antechambers and walk-in cupboards sprouting off on both sides. The room's contents were different, too. Ranged before him on the chipped wooden shelves was a collection that clearly belonged, not to a stuffy old professor of 'Shakespeare, Webster and the Metaphysicals' as Burgess's terse list of research interests indicated on his photo-less webpage, but of a highly distinguished orientalist. Across the shelves were Qur'ans and books on Mesopotamian history; feet of leather-bound exegesis of Islamic texts Edward had never even heard of. From the sides of the dormers hung Persian rugs, pictures of Moorish palaces rendered in fine pencil.

'Beautiful, aren't they?' The voice came from a far bay window, with thick, half-drawn velvet curtains.

Edward turned. In the window was a black, lacquered clavichord, and perched behind it on an adjustable piano stool was a small, rather elegant old woman. Her hair was short and silver, and her trouser suit was worn very precisely, buttoned at the waist. Despite the gloom, she wore thick, dark glasses.

'I'm . . .' Edward's voice gave an adolescent crack. 'I'm sorry. I was looking for Professor Burgess. You don't know where I could find him, do you?'

The woman smiled. 'I do indeed,' she said. The dark glasses made the smile seem intensely private.

Edward averted his eyes towards the nearest shelf, which was dominated by a great blue-and-white bowl, carefully polished and propped up on a delicate wire stand. 'Is he on this corridor?'

The woman followed his gaze. 'Safavid,' she said. 'A replica. And no. He isn't.'

Edward felt the tassels of another rug under his feet and took a guilty step backward, already regretting the intrusion.

'I'm afraid that *he* . . .' the woman continued, '. . . is here already. Sorry to disappoint.' The smile resurfaced now; the laughter lines grew heavier. 'And you must be Edward. At long last.'

Edward swallowed. 'Oh, I . . . I'm sorry. I didn't mean . . .'

She put a finger to her lips. 'No apology necessary. It's rather Shakespearean, is it not? Gender confusion.'

'It was just . . .' Edward tilted his head towards the shelves, 'the books. The objects.'

'An amateur interest, I'm afraid. When you get to my age . . .' she slid off the stool and put a hand on the clavichord to steady herself. 'When you get to my age,' she said, 'you realise that there's always more to learn. One tradition is never enough.'

'You don't get confused?'

'Oh, of course you get confused. I spend all my time confused these days.' She pushed the dark glasses up her nose. 'But this is how it should be. A word of advice, Edward. You should never be *too* sure of who or what you are. It isn't seemly.'

Edward nodded and turned back to the shelves. She seemed to approve of his interest, and for some reason, he found it easier than looking at her. He picked his way along: at the far end, beneath a mug of immaculate pencils, was a slim volume called *al-Zahir and al-Batin: Islam and the Problem of Immanence.*

'You can take it if you like.'

'Oh, no, I don't . . .'

'Take it. I shan't read it any time soon.'

'Thank you.'

There was a jingling noise, and Professor Burgess glanced behind her. 'I hope you don't mind Cyrus,' she said.

Around the clavichord's heavy stand trotted a large golden retriever, panting. It skirted the rug obediently and looked up at Edward, rubbing a velvet ear against his shin, and it was all he could manage not reach down and take it between his fingers.

'You can touch him,' she said. 'The truth is, I'm not sure I'm quite blind enough to need him. But I am blind enough to be entitled to him. And between you and me, I enjoy the company.' She smiled. 'I can still read, of course,' she continued. 'In case you were wondering. I can see most things if they're brought close enough. But that's it, I'm afraid. I live in details.'

Edward nodded sympathetically. 'And your collection?'

'The patterns, yes. But some of the larger objects . . .' She sighed. 'I can count the veins on a leaf, but I can't see the tree.' She removed her hand from the clavichord, and Cyrus led her over to a low sofa, and Edward took the armchair as invited.

'Now, about your request.' She slid a sheet of paper from her jacket and held it up tremulously, a few inches from her face. 'You want to give up Shakespeare, I see.'

'Yes. I guess.'

'May I ask why?'

Gathering himself, Edward began to recite the justification given to him by Liberty: intonation for intonation, word for word. It wasn't that he didn't enjoy Shakespeare, per se, but that he thought the canon needed to be expanded—democratised as it were—in order to accommodate other voices. He was sure she could understand. And he, Professor Burgess might not be aware, was actually of East African extraction himself. He had thought incredibly hard about the decision and believed he had the right to pursue whichever avenue of interest he pleased. And if he was honest . . . He looked down at his shoes . . . If he was honest he felt like it had all been said before, with Shakespeare, as if even to offer an interpretation was to be presumptuous, because surely everything that could be written about his work had been written already, and who was he, really, to hazard his own opinion?

He looked up. Professor Burgess was still smiling. 'Well,' she said, 'it seems like you've already made up your mind.' She turned over the paper and sighed. 'Remind me, Edward, what topic you'd like to change to.'

Edward shifted in his seat. 'It's a newer research area. A bit broader in scope.'

'Ah yes.' She placed a finger in the middle of a short paragraph before lowering the page in triumph. '"Post-Human Spheres." Well, it sounds fascinating.'

Edward stared at her—at his own face, flattened in the sunglasses. He was half-expecting a whisper of mockery, but none came. Professor Burgess kept smiling without judgement, one hand on the page, the other on Cyrus's muzzle.

'Am I allowed to change?'

'Of course you are, Edward.' She patted Cyrus's flank; he hopped down and began to lead her back towards the clavichord.

'I thought it was beautiful, by the way,' he said. 'Your playing. Before I came in.'

She said nothing but gave her head a modest tilt.

Edward turned to the door, lifting the brass latch with his thumb.

'Oh, and Edward?' She was back behind the clavichord now, stretching her hands over the keys as if he were never even here. 'Life is long, remember. You can study more than one thing. That's all Shakespeare really is, of course. That's what the canon is. Something you can always come back to when you're ready.'

PART 2
HILARY

L ying in his old bedsheets, listening to the storm outside his window that he had to repress all his literary training not to take as some kind of omen, Edward surrendered to the impulse to check what everyone else had been doing over the holidays: the impossibly exotic voyages they had been on, the highly competitive internships whose menial tasks they were 'thrilled' and 'proud' and 'humbled' to perform. If nothing else, he reasoned, it might help spare him the indignity of being the last to know when he returned to Oxford the following week.

He chose Angelica first: he brought up her profile and scrolled, in the dark, past the images of her lolling contentedly atop island after island, cove after cove, stretching out her legs on an icing-sugar beach, peering at a warthog through a pair of tiny binoculars that made her look like she was at the opera. He read her posts, too, in a recent salvo of which she detailed her favourite Christmas gift from Mummy and Daddy: a DNA ancestry test which revealed a mélange of different heritages—ten per cent Iberian, eight Silesian, seven Frisian and Belgic; and, most excitingly of all, Arabian, Turkic and East African, at one per cent apiece. On 1 January, he saw, she had published a short online dispatch declaring herself a 'born cosmopolitan,' a 'world citizen'; 'the rainbow,' announced the long, mystical conclusion, 'has unwoven itself before me. For the first time, I know exactly who I am.'

Youssef was next. Edward hadn't heard anything from him since December, apart from a quick text to ask him where he was going skiing this year, and in the meantime Youssef seemed to have spent several weeks and several years of a normal person's salary drifting through a glittering Emirate in the Middle East, every move documented in a separate, dedicated account that went by the name 'Youssef of Arabia.' Edward clicked obediently through the images: Youssef at the Palm, Youssef at the Burj, Youssef's legs stretched out in the bathtub next to those of a supine supermodel, Youssef pouring champagne at a sumptuous restaurant with its zodiac of Michelin stars. Conrad's pictures were equally sumptuous: Conrad at the ramshackle estate, with the hounds and the fireplaces, then Conrad in Naples, with a Panama hat and a faint whisper of a tan that made him look almost approachable. He flicked through a few more profiles: Lolly B, whose Christmas had comprised three weeks on a charity sports tour, selflessly bringing Zambians the gift of netball, followed by a surprise election upon her return to the presidency of the College's shadowy, all-female drinking society, the 'Hell's Belles'; and Liberty, who had embarked on a whirlwind disaster-relief tour of Haiti, financed by a concrete company owned by the family of her former professor.

He tried several times to glean some information about Rachel. She had an account, but hadn't posted any pictures for over a year. Scrolling through the list of people she knew, he started to feel anxious: they all looked so grown up, so *accomplished*, their pages littered with group photos from international scholars' programmes and holiday snaps from terracotta-coloured European cities. Rachel could be anywhere, with any of them. Somehow, the feeling of being passed over was even worse than it had been with Angelica; the silence stung far more than all the beaches and safaris and DNA tests in the world. Almost without thinking, Edward found Rachel's name in his phone, tapped a message out, and then, before he even had a chance to reconsider, pressed send.

— *hi*
Are you in London this Christmas?

Her reply came back five minutes later.
— *Christmas*
  Not really something I go in for Edward
— *Right.*
— *I'm offended*
— *Sorry*
— *(A joke. I do know what Christmas is.)*
  But I'm not, I'm afraid.
  In London that is.
— *Yeah no worries*
  Me neither
— *Why where you asking if I was then?*
— *Oh*
  nothing
  Was thinking of coming down for NYE
  Not many Oxford students willing to venture out here.
— *Where is here?*

He padded over to the window, pressed his phone up against the glass, and captured a photo of the street outside—the squat post-war houses with their plastic window frames, the overflowing plastic bins from the council—that had seemed quite welcoming before he started at Oxford, but now seemed like a caricature of deprivation.
— *Paris. Rive Gauche.*
— *wow it's changed since I was last there*
— *Yeah. There are more kebab shops now.*
— *I see*
— *Where are you?*

He opened the file she sent him to see a grainy picture of a riverbank in the dark, and beyond it, its green copper dome all lit up, its ironwork just about visible, a cathedral.
— *OK so you're actually somewhere cool*
— *Just Berlin*
— *Yeah like I said*

You're actually there now??
— *It's from earlier*
  Am in bed now
— *Early night . . .*
— *Yeah well I didn't have such a good day*
  despite the view
— *Ah, I'm sorry*
  You want to talk about it or . . .
— *No it's fine*
  family stuff
  I have a duvet and a phone to scroll mindlessly through so
  I'll be OK.
— *Shouldn't you be reading?*
— *probably*
— *If I were there I would insist that you read*
— *What would you make me read?*
— *Shakespeare.*
  (obviously)
— *Is that what you do when you're alone with girls in their*
  bedrooms? make them read Shakespeare?
— *Only if I really like them*
— *You're so English*

His heart was beating very fast as he replied.

— *I think Berlin has debauched you Rachel*
  You need to come back at once

She didn't respond. He kept staring at his phone for several minutes, then put it in his pocket and stared out the window. At last he felt it buzz.

Sorry just had to take a call
I'm back January 9th
flight already booked
You know where to find me

On 9 January, Edward was back in Oxford. He dragged

his disintegrating suitcase across the Annexe courtyard, now overgrown with chickweed and moss, its corners softened by piles of brown leaves, preparing himself for his garret. A group of third-years were loitering outside the laundry room at one end. They were clearly off to College to sit their mock-exams, dressed in black and white, with strange academic-looking tassels coming off them like herons; he felt their heads turn in unison as he passed, following, appraising him for several seconds before deciding, all at once, that he was not worth the interruption. 'No, it isn't . . .' he heard one of them hiss as he passed. 'I thought it was for a second. Anyway, you'll never guess what I saw at New Year . . .'

Rather than dealing with the exciting new configurations of mould and dust that seemed to have sprung up over the break, he decided to visit Rachel. He composed himself in the chipped bathroom mirror, pasting down his hair with a splash of water from the tap. As he rounded the corner of her staircase he heard voices. One of them was Rachel's; the other was deep, and sounded like it was making a helpful suggestion. The door was already ajar, propped open with a box full of overstuffed files, so he didn't bother knocking. Instead, he swung the door open: 'Hi,' he said, 'I thought maybe . . .' He stopped. Standing before him in a crisp white shirt, folded at the elbows, a heavy-looking box balanced on his forearms, was Saïd Abdelmassih. In the flesh, he was even more impressive than Edward had been led to believe, nearly a head taller than him, his skin still glowing from whatever warmer climate he had, until recently, inhabited.

'I didn't mean to interrupt,' he said. 'It's Saïd, right?'

Saïd beamed. He had deposited the box now, and the veins on his forearms were swollen from lifting.

'Not at all,' he said. 'I am delighted. The famous Edward.'

'Famous?' he said as he unfastened himself from Saïd's handshake.

Saïd gave a warm laugh. 'Rach has been telling me about you.'

He glanced over at Rachel. 'What's she said?'

'Oh.' Saïd swatted at the air. 'Just that you had tutorials together. And that she was excited to be studying Shakespeare with a real Englishman, in Oxford.'

'I'm glad I was an edifying cultural experience.'

'I didn't mean it like that Edward,' said Rachel. She had put down her box and positioned herself between them.

'But really, Edward,' continued Saïd, 'I have been hearing your name for far longer. And in such distinguished circles, too. I knew I had to meet you before too long. Obiora Adichie speaks very highly of you. He says he met you at the Biafran conflict gala. He said Angelica and you are very interested in West African peace processes.'

'Oh. Right, good.'

'I confess I know very little about these issues. I try to learn, of course, in the name of solidarity. I have bought Professor Nnamani's new book on the subject—I'm sure you've read it already—but I've just been so busy with conferences and papers. I suppose you will have this next year, too. Rachel tells me you're something of an academic superstar.'

'She's being flattering.'

'I'd been hoping,' said Saïd, 'to see you at the event in London.'

'The event?'

'Angelica's event.'

'Oh.' He glanced at Rachel; she was holding her wrist in her opposite hand, and staring at the floor.

'The soirée, after she got back from the Maldives. With the ice sculptures?'

He swallowed. 'Yeah, well . . .'

'It is a pity, you couldn't make it, Edward—I would have loved you to meet my friend, Iqbal al-Katib. He's the president of the Islamic Association, and a very fine conversationalist.'

'Yes, that is a pity. Remind me what the date was of it again?'

'The twenty-eighth of December, if I remember correctly.'

'Right. And remind me when she sent the invitations out?'

'Oh, I can't remember. Earlier that month, I think. As soon as we broke up for the vacation.'

'I see.' There was a pause.

Saïd was staring at him, his brow furrowed. 'She didn't tell you?'

Edward could feel his face growing flushed. 'No, no she did,' he said quickly. 'She did. It was just that I'd forgotten the dates. But yes, now you mention it, I already had other plans. You know—work, seeing my family. All my friends from home.'

Said looked sympathetic. 'Yes, of course.'

'I mean, to tell you the truth I think I needed a break.'

'Of course. It happens to me, too. Sometimes simply keeping up with people can become as onerous as one's degree.'

'Yes, it can.'

'Especially over the vacation, I find. I mean there are just so many things to *attend*.'

'Exactly. And besides,' he added hastily, 'I've been spending *so* much time with Angelica recently.' He tried not to meet Rachel's eye, instead training all his attention on Saïd.

'Of course,' said Saïd.

'You went I suppose?'

'Briefly. I had to stop in the city for a few nights,' he added. 'Just for a scholars' dinner at the Merchant Taylors' Hall. And of course, I wanted to see Liberty and Youssef.'

Edward felt his chest tighten. 'Youssef was there?'

Said nodded. 'Strange, I know. Given the travel schedule. But I suppose he was there for Conrad really.'

'Looks like I was the only one who *wasn't* there.'

'Well you were busy.'

'I know.'

Rachel rose from the desk where she had been propped, and began to busy herself with the next box. 'I'm sure it was probably for the best,' she said. 'I've been to those things. Edward, can you . . . ?'

'Perhaps I should have gone. It sounds like I missed out. I mean I didn't know there would be ice sculptures, for a start.'

She paused, stared at him, then laid the box back on the floor. 'Oh, I'm not sure.'

'I am.'

Saïd had taken up a box himself now, and was busy scanning the room for somewhere to put it, as though doing so might help reballast the whole conversation. 'Anyway,' he said brightly, 'I just wanted to let you know that, as far as I'm concerned, it doesn't prejudice me against you in any way. The whole Angelica business. I'm very glad to have met you.'

'Right. Sorry, why would it prejudice you against me?'

'Oh, I just . . . Rach and Angelica have something of a history, you know.'

'Okay . . .'

'And all I'm saying is that I've been talking to Rach, and just because of *our* history it doesn't mean you and I can't get along. I hear you're from Zanzibar. A wonderful island. I've been several times . . .'

'Yes. Wait, *your* history?'

'Yes, exactly. I suspect I'll be doing lots of work with *Samizdat* this term, and . . .'

Rachel was shaking her head. 'Saïd . . .'

Saïd glanced at her. 'But this was very long ago, of course,' he said, holding up his hands.

'Of course,' said Edward.

'Before Oxford, really. In Berlin.'

'You grew up in Berlin too?'

'I had a very international upbringing. My father is a

professor—international relations—and we simply followed his teaching positions.'

'Lucky you.'

Saïd shook his head sadly. 'Not so lucky, Edward.' There was a strained silence. Saïd rubbed the back of his strong neck, and brightened. 'I am simply saying that sometimes a new place, a new city or country or whatever, changes how one's relationships function. Yes, Rachel and I were involved with each other in Berlin. Yes, you and Angelica are clearly very close now. But one of the wonderful things about Oxford is . . .'

'*Saïd.*' Rachel was glaring at him. 'I really don't think we need to go into this now.'

'I am simply telling Edward how nice it is to meet him, and how he can consider me, should he see me around College, a friend.'

'He knows,' said Rachel. 'Don't you, Edward?'

Edward stared at her. 'Yeah,' he said. 'Thank you, Saïd.'

'I mean it.'

'Yeah, thank you.'

Something in Saïd's expression seemed to break at that. He looked at Rachel at length. 'But I suppose I should be going,' he said at last. 'It was nice to meet you, Edward.'

For a while after he was gone, Rachel failed to meet Edward's eye. She began to skim clothes off the surface of her suitcase, folding them carefully into the chest of drawers. Only now did Edward notice the little details that were beginning to take shape around her: the expensive-looking poster from the German art gallery—'Paul Klee,' it said—and the small basket of creams and perfumes balanced on the edge of her shelf. At last, she looked over at him. 'What?'

'Nothing.' He said it confidently, but then drew a breath, as if about to let slip something more.

'It's not nothing.'

He watched her. 'How do you know him?' he said at last.

She stiffened. 'International school.'

'You have a "history," apparently.'

'Sort of. Complicated.'

'Right.'

She stared at him. 'What?'

'Honestly, I've not come to litigate it.'

'Tell me, Edward.'

'I mean that's what people say, isn't it? People say "it's complicated" when what they actually mean is "I harbour a deep, and indeed previously consummated yearning for this extremely attractive young man."'

'Well that's not what I say.'

'You made it seem like Youssef had lied to me.'

'What?'

'You said you didn't have a boyfriend, and Youssef was lying. He and I had a fight about it actually.'

'He *had* lied to you.'

'I think that's pretty ungenerous.'

'He lied, Edward. Saïd is *not* my boyfriend, and I don't *want* him to be my boyfriend, and from the moment Youssef found out we were having tutorials together—and I'm sorry about this, I know he's your friend but I think you're being naïve—from the moment Youssef found out you and I were having tutorials together he has been trying to make it seem like I'm someone to avoid.' She shook her head. 'And you *know* why that is.'

'He just made an assumption.'

'He made his assumption very quickly.'

'You can't just expect people to come at you without making any judgements at all.'

'What does *that* mean?'

'Come *on* Rachel. You just expect people to have an infinitely open mind about every aspect of your life. I shouldn't assume you have a boyfriend. I shouldn't listen to what Youssef says about you. But then you don't actually come out and say anything about yourself.' He shook his head. 'I mean what am I supposed to do, other than listen to Youssef? No one tells me *anything* in this college.'

'I think you get told far more things than me, Edward. In this college.'

'Oh, sure.'

'You spent all of last term with Angelica. You got invited to the Chamber by Liberty. You got invited to the fancy party in North London, where you would no doubt have heard many more things if you'd been bothered to go.'

'I didn't get invited to the party.'

'What?'

'I didn't get invited.'

'You just said you did.'

'Yeah, well I didn't.'

'Oh.' She stared at him for several seconds. 'Why not?' she said, softly.

'I didn't even know it was happening.'

'Oh.' Rachel's face fell.

'So, yeah, I guess that's something you didn't know that I did.'

'I'm sorry Edward.'

He shrugged. 'It's fine.'

'She does this, you know. It's not you.'

'I said it's fine. Where do you want this anyway?' He nudged at one of the boxes with his foot, testing the give of the transparent plastic. 'Up there?'

'You don't have to.'

'I might as well. It looks heavy. And I've driven away your helper, and it will make me feel chivalrous and helpful after being lightly humiliated just now.'

'You weren't humiliated.'

'I said lightly.' He reached for the box.

'Just leave it.'

'Top shelf?'

'No, wait Edward. Edward. You . . .'

There was a snapping sound, and he felt a sharp pain across his fingers. The box clattered to the floor. 'I'm so sorry,' he said.

'Are you all right?' Rachel crouched next to him. 'It's okay, don't worry about it. Edward.'

'I didn't realise . . .'

'You're bleeding.'

'Oh.' He looked down.

'Here.' She took his hand and inspected the stripe where the handle had broken. He could feel her fingers soft against his palm. 'One sec,' she said. She disappeared into the bathroom, and returned with some tissues. 'Show me.'

'It's fine.'

'Keep pressing. Here.' She sat down next to him on the bed, and as she craned over his palm he could smell the shampoo in her hair. There was a silence.

'I don't think Angelica and I are together any more, you know.'

Rachel was very still. He could hear her breathing. 'Is that something you've decided, or something she has?'

'We haven't spoken since last term. Not even a message.'

'I'm sorry.'

'Like I said, I'm fine.'

'I'm here you know. You can actually talk to me.'

'There's nothing to talk about.'

She nodded and they sat in silence. The window opposite looked out over the riverbank, and Edward watched the movement of the willow tree back and forth over the black water. After a while, Rachel lifted the tissues from her hand to check underneath, then folded them and redoubled the pressure.

'Thank you,' he said.

'Do you like it here, Edward?

'Here?'

'As in Oxford.'

'I don't think it's about *liking* it.'

'What do you mean?'

He shrugged. 'It's a dream. Oxford is a dream. I mean, the number of people at my school who wanted to come here, and couldn't, or didn't try. Liking it seems beside the point, sometimes. I mean, do you like it here?'

'I like some things, yes. I like the idea of it.'

'But . . . ?'

'But . . . I don't know. I suppose there's something about this place that makes it very, very hard to get to know people. Maybe it's the country.'

'What's so different about it?'

She shook her head. 'Here people *lie*. They lie like nowhere I've ever been before. They'll make those squealing noises when you walk in the room, and tell you they *love* your terrible outfit. And God, if you've got some disadvantage or trauma, or *wound . . .*' she snorted mirthlessly, and gave his hand a little squeeze, 'well, then they just *love* that. But the following day they don't even look at you when they pass you in the street. I don't understand it. Okay you're looking at me like I'm crazy now.'

'You're not crazy.'

'Am I not?'

'You're not crazy.'

'What am I doing wrong?'

'You're not doing anything *wrong*.'

'Then why don't I feel at home here?'

'No one feels at home here. It's temporary. It has to be. You come and study Shakespeare, or Kafka or whatever for three years, just so you can earn the right to give it up. Become a banker or a consultant something. Get out into the "real world."'

'You're not going to do that.'

'Am I not?'

'No.'

'Well if that's true then it's only because I haven't ever seen the real world. So I take all this far too seriously.'

'What do you mean?'

'Come on, Rachel. You have Berlin. Liberty has the US, Youssef has Egypt, Angelica has *everywhere*. But Oxford is all I have.'

'You have Zanzibar.'

'I've never been to Zanzibar. I've never been anywhere.'

'You're here now, Edward. You could go to Berlin, if you liked.'

'Yeah, very funny.'

'What's stopping you?'

'I couldn't afford it, for one thing.'

'There's the College travel fund.'

'There's a College travel fund?'

'This is Oxford, Edward. Of course there's a travel fund. There's an ergonomic desk chair fund. There's a *falconry* fund.'

'They wouldn't fund me though. It'll be for people to do research for their degrees.'

'They funded Monty and Giles's trip to Thailand. Thailand, Edward. They study Classics. Besides, Liberty is in charge of allocation of funds, and you did her a favour.'

'I can't go to Berlin, Rachel.'

'You could go at Easter. The weather will be nice enough by then. I know this is important to English people.'

'I don't know anyone there.'

'You know me.'

'You'll be there?'

'I could be.'

'Well you won't want me hanging around you. Not with all your glamorous Berlin friends.'

'How do you know?'

'You're cross at me, remember?'

'Right,' she said. 'True. Well I suggest you try and win me back over this term.'

'How would one go about doing that?'

She wasn't smiling, exactly, but still Edward detected a faint twitch of amusement in her lips as she spoke. 'I'm sure you'll figure it out,' she said.

CHAPTER 10

On 13 January, an automated email arrived in Edward's inbox to inform him that he had been officially transferred to the undergraduate module named 'Post-Human Spheres,' convened by one Lawrence Pfister, Associate Professor, Departmental Welfare Czar, cognisant of ancestral and unceded land of the Chochenyo speaking Ohlone people, he/they. Edward skimmed the short text attached that was clearly designed to whet his academic appetite. Pfister, it briefed him, was fresh from a very prestigious position at Berkeley and highly qualified to induct a promising young beginner like Edward into the discipline of whatever 'Post-Human Spheres' turned out to be. Reading lists would follow.

Reading lists did not follow. Instead, on 17 January, Edward received a second email—not automated this time, but typed out with a multitude of spelling mistakes by a harried-seeming administrator who signed off 'K.' Due to the last-minute nature of Edward's switch, K informed him, 'Larry' had already been approved to take annual leave for the first week of term: he had volunteered to train as an Assistant Student Pastoral Support Liaison with Diversitas, so not the kind of commitment that could be shrugged off lightly—and could Edward please just have a flick through whatever books struck him as particularly post-human in the meantime?

Over the course of the next few days, Edward gathered what information he could about Larry. His departmental web-page showed him to be a surprisingly young, twinkly looking man—young, at least, for an associate professor—with a distinctly healthy, outdoorsy look that was quite unusual among Oxford dons. Undistinguished at first, his academic CV appeared to have taken off after he undertook a two-year-long postdoc on the American West Coast. From then on, his publications took a turn to the theoretical. Cyborgs. Rhizomes. The Anthropocene, which Edward had to look up, but was apparently something to do with literature. At lunch the day before his first tutorial, Conrad revealed a different side to Larry. He was famous, he said, for his indiscretions. He liked to sidle up to young male undergraduates in the glowing caverns of Favela, Schlachthaus, The Bunghole, Tiki Dream, and claim never to have met them when the College Dean called him into his office for a quiet word.

'He's particularly partial to Muslim boys, I hear,' said Conrad.

'Oh. Right. Good.'

Conrad chuckled. 'Worry not, Edward. Real Muslims only. Swarthy. Repressed. You, my pallid little friend, are safe.'

'I wasn't worried.'

'You look worried. But I suppose that's just how you look all the time, isn't it?' Conrad reached above his head into a long, languid stretch. 'Besides, he already has a favourite student, from what I hear. His protégé, his prince—all Platonic, in this case.'

'I'm glad.'

'You know him, I think.'

'Yeah, I don't think so.'

'You do indeed. You were spotted nattering with him in that horrible concentration camp you've chosen to live in. Saïd, his name is. Saïd Abdelmassih.'

On the day of his first tutorial, Edward found Professor Pfister's room easily enough, nestled in the warren of the

College's old buildings. He was encouraged by the warmth with which Pfister greeted him, springing up from the inflatable exercise ball he clearly believed was an adequate replacement for a chair and putting out his hand. Edward began just as Liberty had instructed him to: he thanked Pfister for accepting him as a student, and launched to the best of his ability into what, exactly, he hoped to get out of the course—the critical thinking, the mentorship, the transferable skills. It seemed like the kind of thing that Larry, as Pfister chucklingly decreed Edward must call him on pain of expulsion, would appreciate. When he looked up from his notes he saw a wry, mocking smile playing on Pfister's lips.

'Are you quite done Ed?'

'Sorry?'

'Done. With your soliloquy.'

'I just wanted to explain why I switched course.'

'I know why you're here, Eddie,' he said, looking him up and down, his lips pressed mischievously together. 'You're a smart guy. And you know as well as I do that as lovely as dear old Professor Burgess is—and she taught me back in the day, you know—she's on the way down.'

'Down?'

'Institutionally speaking, Ted. Did you read her last paper?'

'No, not yet.'

'Exactly. Nor did I. Nor did anyone. Her last paper wasn't a paper at all: it was a book, published four and a half years ago. People hate books, Ed.'

'Right. Wait, they do?'

'And being the smart guy that you are, you wanted to get out while you could, didn't you? Put all that money on a horse that might *win,* eh? I see you.'

'Erm, okay.'

'I *see* you.'

'Right. Yes.'

'I like your shirt. Vintage?'

'No, I don't think so.'

'Do you have an essay for me?'

Edward cleared his throat. 'I mean, yes. No. Sort of. I have two thousand words which I thought we could . . .'

'Throw it in here if so.' Pfister reached down and held out a mesh waste-paper basket, brimming with apple cores and collapsed energy-drink cans. 'That's right. Screw it up nice and tight. Tighter. Now, Ned. Sit down, and let's talk about your future.'

Larry's notion of Edward's 'future' was largely incomprehensible, and seemed mainly to involve cultivating a good relationship with something called the 'AHRC consortium,' 'demonstrating the ability to secure grants in order to secure grants.' 'The thing about academia, Edward,' he said as the grandfather clock in the corner ticked over into the next hour, 'is that it's a game. But you knew this already.'

'Oh. I didn't actually.'

'Well it is. Take this down. Do you have a pen? Are you paperless? That's it, good.' He drew himself up on his exercise ball: 'Academia is a game. There are rules, and objectives. There are skills that need to be cultivated, and strategies that need to be pursued. Do you play video games?'

'No, not really.'

'You look like you do. Anyway, the most important thing is working out what group you belong to. Now, from your change of course—an excellent decision by the way—I think we know where you stand on *that* issue.' Pfister nodded to himself. 'So the key is to stave off the other factions.'

'There are factions?'

'Are there factions? Are there factions?' Pfister looked around himself, incredulous. 'Of course there are factions, Ed. The Freudians. The digital humanities people. The affect theory lot. The textualists. The Comp-Litters. The people who work with the Department of Continuing Education. The old guys who are listed along with the buildings. There's nothing but factions in this place.'

'Oh.'

'Now Liberty's filled me in already,' he said, nodding to himself.

'You know Liberty?'

'Everyone knows Liberty, Eddie. You should *certainly* know Liberty if you want to go anywhere in this field.'

'Okay. Sorry, why would it matter if I knew Liberty?'

'. . . So I know about the Zanzibari angle, too,' continued Larry, not listening. 'Excellent, by the way very sellable.'

'Sellable?'

'Africa, Ned. Everyone *loves* Africa. It's having a moment. Did you read *We Are Children of the Kalahari Sun*? You could write on it if so.'

'Right. No, I didn't, I'm afraid.'

'Now the Muslim angle—and I know you're keen on this, and I really admire your religious commitment et cetera et cetera—the Muslim angle is a little problematic.'

'You mean for my essay? Because I'm not sure I really want to write about Islam. I actually chose the module because . . .'

'That stuff was popular ten years ago, Ed. But these days? Hardly any of that cohort got tenure in the end. Plus it's not current is it? I mean no one's flown a plane into any buildings for a while. Or have they? Have I missed something?'

'I don't think they have, no.'

'So it's settled then. Better to stick to Africa, I say. Famines. Elephants. Are there any Zanzibarian writers you could write about?'

'Presumably, but . . .'

'Or Kenyans? Sudanese? How close to your neck of the woods is Nigeria?'

'I mean it's not really that close.'

'Could it be *framed* as close? Two prongs or aspects of an essential pan-African unity? Marcus Garvey is pretty good on this.'

'It really isn't close at all.'

'Could you write on something like "conceptual Africas, past and present?" Then it wouldn't matter where you're from.'

'I don't think so. I mean, what would that actually involve?'

'Oh, we could work that out later. All we need to do is submit a title. You could write on "Transnational Africanities." I think that's a word now.'

'Shouldn't I just choose the writers I like?'

'What?'

'For my essay. Writers I like. Writers I think are good.'

'Oh *Edward.*' Pfister snorted. 'Whether they're any *good* doesn't come into it. Evaluative criticism is over. *Themes*—that's what you want. Ideas. Frameworks. Critical lenses. Between you and me . . .' He leaned forward, hands splaying out over his velvet-clad knees, 'it's almost *better* if the text is a little ropey. Then you can upset one of the old guard. Coax one of them into a rebuttal.' He made a mysterious, waggling gesture with his fingers. 'Controversy. *Citations.*'

'Oh.'

'Genius, right?'

'Yes, I suppose . . .'

'Say it's genius.'

'It's genius.'

'The key for you, Ed, will be *leveraging what you have.* You have a gift. Lucky you. Say "lucky me."'

'Do I really have to . . . ?'

'Now you need to be going to conferences. You need to be publishing. You need to be applying to the US. You *certainly* need to be talking to Saïd. You *certainly* need to be going to that talk Professor Dyer is giving tomorrow at the Chamber. Do you have any protests you can put on your CV?'

'I'm not sure I understand this.'

'For postdoc applications, Edward. Never too early to start thinking about this. Now Dyer is exactly the kind of person you can talk about in a Yale interview. There are plans to picket him, you know. Chants, animal blood, the works. '

'But Professor Pfister . . .'

'*Larry*, for God's sake.'

'Sorry. Larry.'

Professor Pfister rolled his eyes. 'Eduardo.'

'I . . .' Edward cleared his throat. In his animation, Pfister had trundled over to the fireplace and was busy fiddling with the stand of brooms and pokers that stood next to the grate. 'I'm grateful for the advice. Really, I am. But I'm not sure my interests . . .'

'Your interests? I'm sorry, Edward, but your *interests* don't really come into it. Do you know what year it is?'

'But that's why I . . .'

'You are not your interests, Ed. You are not a free agent, casting around for some object for your grand impartial intelligence to pluck from obscurity.'

'But what am I then?'

Pfister didn't reply. Instead, he took the long, black poker from the stand and held it into the unlit fireplace, turning it in his fingers as though trying to toast something on the end of it. After a few seconds he withdrew it, held it up to his face, and smiled—then, suddenly, he plunged it back down; he was holding it against the denim that clad his thigh now, pressing it in firmly, and writhing against it as though in agony, a strange, hissing noise—*ssshssshsssh*—coming from his lips. At last, he brightened. 'You see Edward?'

'Not at all.'

'Oh *come*, Ed.'

'I don't . . .'

'Think about it. The poker, the fireplace.' He leaned forward and peered over the brinks of his fashionable plastic spectacles. 'You're a *brand*.'

When Edward approached Youssef at the edge of the quad after lunch, with the intention of making fun of Larry as a means of chiselling his way into the conversation, he had the distinct sense that he was unwelcome. Youssef was already grumpy, having just found out, he explained, that the night porter had taken on extra shifts and would now be guarding the College, baton in hand, on the cherished Thursday evenings he devoted to the various societies of which he was a member.

'And now this,' he said, gesturing before him, at the group of students that was gathering, with a hum of anticipation, on the green.

'This? This isn't so bad.'

'What? This is bad, Edward. Look at all the white people. Observe how angry they are. This is very bad.'

'They're just protesting something. Aren't they always protesting something?'

'Yes, but *look* at them. Why are they all wearing berets? Is this a new stage in their evolution?' He ran his fingers through his beard. 'She hasn't even started *speaking* yet.'

'She?'

Youssef chuckled. 'Come now, Edward,' he said. 'Who do you think?'

As if on cue, Liberty stepped out of the crowd and began her speech. She was clad in a leather jacket and black beret that Izzy and Tilly and the twenty or so other onlookers clearly found very fetching, and waved her arms about wildly as she spoke, reminding all present of the efforts she had undertaken to prevent Dyer from speaking. She had organised workshops, she was saying, indicative votes. She had picketed the Chamber. She had nailed a florid *J'accuse* to the Common Room notice board. She had even participated in a piece of experimental performance art which involved standing around in the University Parks with the words 'I have the right to exist' painted across her forehead and shouting at anyone—mostly pensioners tottering their way over from the Wolvercote bus-stop—who looked as though they might disagree. When she finished, there was a hearty round of applause, and various chants—'Dyer, Dyer, pants on fire,' and something about de-colonisation that Edward didn't quite catch. Youssef turned his back on the protestors and sucked his teeth.

'Hideous.'

'I don't think they're doing anything wrong.'

'They are being disruptive. This is wrong. They are wearing berets. This is deeply wrong. And so close to my room, too.' He shook his head. 'A small squad of Egyptian police, this is what is needed. Where is this new night porter, anyway? Surely he of all people should be keen to drain such a foul swamp.'

'Right. I'm afraid we will have to disagree on this one.'

'You've become awfully wet and pliant and humanitarian recently Edward. Are you quite all right?'

'I'm not wet. Just because I'm not instantly agreeing with your pronouncements.'

'You sound very self-righteous. Perhaps that sun-cream I always tell you not to wear has seeped into your brain.'

'No, it hasn't, Youssef. Your views are just often quite extreme.'

'Is it the influence of the Jewish girl?'

'What?' Edward felt a lump in his throat.

'I hear you've been fraternising with her—against my wishes, but Youssef is merciful, Youssef is tolerant, Youssef is kind.'

'Right, I don't want to talk about this.'

'How is she, by the way?'

'She's still Jewish, if that's what you were wondering.'

'Is there any reason you're being like this?'

'I'm not being like anything.'

'Was there another terrorist attack while I was in Dubai? Did the Pope announce another crusade?'

'How was *your* fraternising, Youssef? If we're going to go into every little liaison each of us has had without the other, why don't we do it chronologically?'

'What are you talking about? And please stop making that expression, you look unhinged.'

'I'm talking about Angelica's party. Over the break. I'm sure she's an excellent host. You know, I'm surprised you didn't mention it before. I would have thought the whole experience would be rich and varied and full of moral lessons.'

'Ah, I see.' Youssef glanced back at the protestors, who were beginning to filter out of the quad towards the high street.

'Don't look at them, look at me. How was the party?'

'It was fine, Edward. Very sophisticated. You would have hated it—there was no home-brewed alcohol or formation dancing. Everyone there went to private school.'

'Conrad was there too, I hear.'

'It appears you've done your research already.'

'Saïd told me, actually. Turns out he's the only one in this college who is prepared to give me a straight answer about anything. Who'd have thought it?'

'Saïd the Palestinian?'

'Yes. Obviously. There are no other Saïds.'

'Since when did you know Saïd the Palestinian?'

'We were just talking the other day. He's very pleasant actually. And he doesn't go by "the Palestinian," by the way. A bit like how Rachel doesn't actually go by "the Jew."'

'Well that didn't take you long, did it?'

'What do you mean?'

Youssef shook his head. 'Saïd. He's been here—what is it now—ten days? But you just *had* to find a way to run into him. Did he tell you about the exchange programme he's setting up? Did he tell you about his people and their suffering?'

'You know he's a nice guy actually. Before you launch into whatever vague historical grudge is that you have against him. Do you worry he's more Muslim than you? Is that it?'

'You know what, Edward? I don't need to sit through this.'

'In fact, I think I'm going to ask him if he's going to the talk with Dyer tomorrow. If you won't be coming.'

'You do that. You ask him.'

'Maybe I'll ask him some questions about Islam. I've been starting to think that a lot of what you've taught me might benefit from exposure to a second opinion.'

'Go for it.'

'Like, for example, the idea that essentially the best way to express my piety is not, in fact, to abstain from sex or alcohol or pork, or to pray, or to ever even set *foot* in a mosque, but rather to act extremely weirdly around anyone who happens to have a Jewish grandparent. I wonder what Saïd will make of that?'

'He will say whatever you want him to say.'

'He's not like that.'

'He's a *fraud*, Edward!' Youssef's voice came out raised, loud enough to turn a pair of heads on the neighbouring bench. He gathered himself, and leaned over the table so Edward could hear his sharp whisper: 'He's a fraud. Wears his prayer beads round his neck like it's a fashion statement. Signs open letters— insane behaviour.'

'You know what's insane behaviour? Spending a whole term trying to get me close to Angelica, then not even bothering to tell me when she has a party and doesn't even think to ask me. *That* is insane behaviour.'

'But it is all for the best, Edward. Now you have a Palestinian friend to show for it. Lucky you. You have traded up.'

'Oh, honestly Youssef . . .'

'It's true. You've done it. Well done *you,* Edward. Look at what a good Muslim you've become.' Youssef drew himself up, buttoned his tweed jacket tightly round his midriff, and strode off through the protestors, doing his best to bump and elbow as many of them as possible as he passed.

As Edward made his way towards the Chamber, the High Street was in a state of minor civil war. He had to jostle people to make room: he had not invited Saïd to Dyer's talk in the end—the prospect seemed ludicrous the moment Youssef swept away—and he had the distinct feeling, as he neared the centre of town, of being the only sane person in Oxford, all alone in the murmuring, shuffling crowd. As well as the predictable pro-Dyer and anti-Dyer factions, Liberty had clearly managed to muster a healthy cohort of non-aligned opportunists: there were hippies trudging down from their North Oxford communes; there were Waldorf-schoolers with their stone-age pushchairs; there were various advocates of drug legalisation who seemed to show up at every protest, whatever the actual issue. At the centre of the mêlée was a large group of men with shaved heads proceeding in a stately column up St. Michael's Street, orange and red robes billowing behind them. The crowd slowed its surge towards the gates to make room for them. One or two students bowed their heads in respect.

'Buddhists,' he heard a posh-voiced girl whisper next to him, leaning across to a vacant-looking boy with long hair parted at the centre.

'Hmm?'

'*Buddhists*, Archie. From the local temple. I heard that Liberty had invited them, but no one knew whether they would show up because they're not very good with emails.'

'Gosh. Good for them for coming.'

'I've heard they're very sensitive to moral issues.'

'Yeah I bet.'

'I've heard that if they're really upset about it, they actually set themselves on fire.'

'Gosh.

'I know.'

'Like, how upset do they have to be?'

'Pretty upset, I think. But they can because they're so disciplined, you see. They're spiritual.'

'Gosh. That'd be pretty messed up, though. If they set themselves on fire.'

'Yes, I know. I hope they don't. But you have to admit, it would be great for the cause . . .'

By the time Edward managed to enter the Chamber, flashing his card at the red-faced security guard, the talk was just about to begin. He took his seat at the back, and was shocked by just how polite everyone seemed once inside, one or two of them even brandishing notebooks and pencils as Dyer strode down the aisle in his true-blue tie, as though whatever he was about to say might one day crop up in an exam.

Dyer took his place at the front of the Chamber and peered over his spectacles at the audience. The space was silent, now, except for a few coughs and rustles of programmes. The house lights had been dimmed slightly for the event, which was being filmed, and Dyer was surrounded by a ring of intense, white light, hemming him in like an arena. There was, Edward noticed, something very hostile in the atmosphere—a fact which Dyer, for his part, seemed to be enjoying, grinning out at his onlookers, as though daring them to make a scene.

Suddenly, from her designated spot in the front row, Liberty stood up. Edward could only see the back of her head, but her posture was clearly combative, her arms folded, her head raised defiantly. There were a few gasps. Next to her, a second figure stood; Edward could tell by the haircut that it was Minka. For several seconds, the two of them stared at Dyer. Neither of them spoke. In the spotlight, Edward could see Dyer's grin retreat, just a fraction. Then, just as wordlessly as she stood, Liberty turned on her heel and strode down the aisle. Minka followed her; there were whispers everywhere now; Edward watched the heads in front of him turn to their neighbours, people stare down into their phones.

'Is there anyone else?' said Dyer.

His voice came out loud from the microphone.

'Well? Is there anyone else?'

Even the whispers had died down now. The audience was sitting very still.

'No? This is your last chance now. Would you like to get up? Say your piece? Go on, don't be shy. Consider this an invitation.'

Silence. Edward stared into his programme.

'This is not,' said Dyer, 'how I envisaged beginning this evening. Perhaps I was naïve. But in a way, I'm glad this has happened.' He paused for effect, making eye contact with the Committee members in the front row. 'Because it shows, I suspect, two different approaches to disagreement. The first—which we have just witnessed—is a rather new procedure. It is popular, I'm afraid, among younger people—though I must say I am delighted to see so many young faces here, listening with respect and waiting their turn to express moderate, rational disagreement at the end. This is very encouraging. It is also popular among those who have lost contact with, or perhaps not been raised in, a certain Western tradition—of debate, and dialectic, and rational discussion.'

There were a few murmurs, and a few more uncomfortable rustles.

'A heretical opinion, I know. But I'm afraid we live in strange, inquisitorial times.' He stared smugly up to the light. 'And in such times, I suspect, it is only a heretic who can save us.'

At that, Dyer seemed to relax. He soon settled into the rhythms of his talk, which was polished and articulate, and, Edward could not help but think, ever so slightly disappointing. Dyer spoke about the desecrations of his book, and the works of Aleksandr Solzhenitsyn, and a small consultancy firm he had set up—'Agora'—whose job it was to advise people how to become 'free thinkers,' and which aimed to be running regular workshops in at least ten colleges by the beginning of next year. He used a lot of words like 'censorship' and 'liberty' and 'bastion.' The question-and-answer session at the end was equally predictable. Most of the contributions came either from sycophants in polyester suits ('Do you feel free to express your views?' 'Do you believe civilisation is under threat?) or angry-looking people with unusually coloured hair ('Is it true that twenty-three years ago you wrote . . . ?' 'How can you *live* with yourself when . . . ?'). Dyer's interlocutors seemed aware that the event was being filmed: they kept eyeing the camera which trundled around the Chamber on its runners, and correcting themselves when they realised they had offered a fact or piece of evidence that might be in danger of being checked.

Only once, in fact, did Dyer say anything of real interest. Someone asked him about the law in East Africa—how the British exported their courts, their judiciaries, and supplanted all kinds of local traditions and systems without right or title. Dyer stood still a while, pushing his glasses ruminatively into the bridge of his nose.

'Do you believe in rules?' he said.

The student looked confused. 'Excuse me?'

'Do you believe in rules? Laws. Statutes. The rules, say, under which this fine institution now labours regarding what I may or may not say, for fear of offending.'

'I believe in *those* rules.'

A yellowed smile. 'And who, pray, set up those rules?'

'The University set up those rules.'

'And is the University legitimate?'

'What do you mean?'

'Wasn't the University founded in an attempt to keep all thought under the watchful eye of the Church? Wasn't it expanded during the Wars of Religion, endowed by unelected monarchs? Are not all its colleges—as the student body *insists* on pointing out at every opportunity—funded by the toil of nameless slaves?'

'I guess, but . . .'

'*Legitimacy*,' continued Dyer, clearly enjoying himself, 'is something that comes about mysteriously, through the generations—not because of the Law's origins, but despite them.' He spoke to the audience now, grandly, one hand thrust emphatically into his jacket pocket. 'You must remember this, if you are going to deign to tell people what to do. You can trace authority back for thousands of years, but you will never find a title deed for the human soul.'

Five minutes ahead of schedule, and with a round of applause muted more by disappointment than any kind of disapproval, the audience began to file out and into the bar. The space was soon crammed with patrons, drinking, giggling, staring up at the walls, which were decked out with glossy posters advertising a new House Cocktail—something guava-pink called the 'Frida Kahlada.' Edward ordered one just to have something to hold, and immediately regretted it. He tried listening, through the three or four miniature umbrellas, to an adjacent conversation, hoping to worm his way in—'I guess what I identify with most in her,' a girl in a University rowing hoodie was saying, 'is her *pain*'—but couldn't make sense of it: no one seemed to be talking about Dyer, or East Africa, or even colonialism in the broad, abstract, thoroughly unmoored sense that these days was approaching a kind of default in Oxford, and into whose familiar patterns he often slipped with Angelica's friends, if only to reassure them that he, at least, was on their side.

He began to cast around for familiar faces. There was no sign of Youssef, or Conrad, or even of Angelica—she was still with her family, he had heard, having secured two weeks' leave from the term for vague, neurasthenic reasons she always pleaded when she couldn't be bothered to do something. He was surprised she had not made an effort to attend this evening, though. Perhaps her interest in East Africa was in the process of passing on to something else.

When he saw Rachel wave him over, smiling, ringed by friends from outside of College, he felt a throb of gratitude. She was surrounded by a group of her friends, all smiling with their ingenuous, international-student faces.

'Hi,' he said, raising his drink sheepishly as he approached.

'Edward,' said Rachel.

She introduced him politely to each of her friends in turn— Mihai from Romania, Callie from Greece, Johannes from Austria—and they asked him what he thought about Dyer, the talk, the questions; then about his course, his interests, all in a tone of polite interest. He, for his part, mainly asked them about where they were from.

'But Edward's got to come to Berlin first,' said Rachel at one point, when Johannes was talking about how absolutely necessary it was that he visit some lake whose mineral composition was supposed to have remarkable healing qualities.

'Yeah, maybe.'

'You should.'

'You should, Edward,' agreed Johannes.

'The College has funding,' explained Rachel.

'And I won't get it.'

'You *will*.'

'Oh, you have to try Edward,' said Johannes. 'You must try.'

'He's right, Edward. Promise you'll at least try?' She looked up at him, eyes hopeful in their dark make-up.

'I promise,' he said.

He and Rachel kept talking long after the others left. The bar was growing livelier, the pink cocktails phased out in favour of colourless, more potent-smelling mixtures, and the noise became a kind of cocoon, in which he could speak to her, at last, without being overheard. It didn't even matter *what* they were saying; he could be talking about anything: his holiday, Larry, even Kafka stories he had been plugging away at the week before Christmas. At one point, he made her laugh, and afterwards, as the glow of it drained from her face, she seemed to grow thoughtful.

'Why do I keep fighting with you, Edward?'

'We don't keep fighting. Not really.'

'We do. In my room, and last time we were here.'

'Maybe it's our deep religious differences.'

'Ah.' Her eyes were sparkling. 'Do you think we might be able to put them aside? For the new term?'

'I don't know. I'm very devout.'

She pursed her lips in mock-seriousness. 'Yes, of course. But do you think you could try?' She was standing very close to him now.

'I'll try if you will,' he said.

'Wow, you must *really* like me.'

He smiled at her. 'You know Rachel, since last term, I've just been thinking . . . Rachel?'

Rachel's face had fallen.

'What's wrong?'

'Just a second.'

It was then that Edward felt the businesslike tap on his shoulder. Something about the confidence of it, the heavy rings that rapped his collarbone, made him suspect who it was even before he heard the cawing American injunction to 'turn around for God's sake.'

He obliged. Liberty was swaying slightly. In her large, rower's hand was a double-ration of Frida Kahlada, and even with the leather jacket draped over her arm, she looked fearsome, leaner than last term, honed very fine by the thousands of miles she had flown from internship to internship over the break.

'So,' she said, folding her arms ostentatiously. 'This is what you do then, is it?'

'Excuse me?'

'The two of you. You sit across from each other and gaze into each other's eyes while talking about . . . lemme guess, Shakespeare? It's all very, like, quaint. Very *Oxford*.'

'I think you're reading quite a lot into this, Liberty.'

Liberty cocked her head to one side in interest, showing off the tiny quills of the hair she had recently buzzed down to her scalp. 'You're deflecting,' she said.

'You're interrupting,' said Rachel.

Liberty chuckled. 'Tell me, Rach. Have you had sex with him yet?'

Edward took a step forward. 'Liberty . . .'

Liberty paid him no heed: 'Because that's the plan, isn't it? Like, that's what this really is.'

'I don't think that's any of your business, Liberty,' said Rachel.

'You made it my business when you make me sit through *that*, Sweetie. In the middle of the bar, no less. It's so unsubtle.' She turned to Edward. 'You know what that means, right? When a girl looks up at you like that and touches her hair and giggles at all your little unfunny British jokes?'

Rachel folded her arms. 'Would you leave us please?'

Liberty ran her fingers thoughtfully over her scalp, smiling to herself. 'I mean does Angie know? Don't get me wrong, I think it's great whatever it is. Modern. Like, it's amazing that you're so open and non-possessive. But it didn't strike me as very *her*.'

At Angelica's name, he sensed Rachel stiffen. 'We haven't.' A pause. 'We're not.'

'You want to though, don't you? Have you guys kissed?' Her voice was singsong, mocking.

'Liberty . . .'

'Honestly why are people in this country so *closed off*?' She turned back to Rachel now, shaking her head derisively. 'You do know he's Muslim, right?'

'He's not Muslim. You've made him Muslim for your purposes.'

'Not round *you*. But around his buddies he is. And his new tutor. And with me he's African, aren't you Eddie?'

Edward rubbed the back of his neck. 'That's not fair.'

'He *is*.' Liberty had sidled up to Rachel now, and taken her arm in a way that would have almost caring if not for the leer stretching itself diligently over her face. 'You know what he said to Youssef? Said not to worry, that you *weren't very Jewish*. They laughed about it. They're always laughing about the Jewish thing. 'Cause that's just it, you see, with Edward. He's a very special, polite little kind of Englishman. He *gives people what they want*.'

Rachel had grown very still. Carefully, she laid her drink on the bar top, still half full.

Liberty was chuckling to herself. 'But it was just a joke right, Edward? Just a joke.'

'Rachel. Rachel, wait . . .' She was already gathering up her coat.

Pleadingly, he touched her arm. 'Do you want me to . . . ?'

'No, it's okay.'

'You sure? I can . . . ?'

'I said no, Edward.'

Liberty watched her leave with interest. Out of her bag, a charity piece printed with the command to SAY NO TO THE BIG 'R', she produced a cylinder of lipstick, and smeared it on her pursed lips. She seemed very pleased with herself. 'She's sensitive, isn't she?' she said, once she had snapped the lid back on.

'I think she had just had enough of the interrogation.'

Liberty rolled her eyes. 'She wasn't being interrogated, Edward.'

'Isn't that for her to decide?'

'Two words: Persecution Complex.'

There was a silence. 'I don't think that's fair,' he said, flatly.

'I think it's totally fair. Totally fair, and totally *predictable*, actually. If you get me.'

'Yeah, I don't, actually.'

'Ugh, don't act so dumb, Edward. She loves it. This is her *thing*.'

'I mean, it definitely isn't.'

'It fits.'

'Fits?'

A new look had started to sprout on Liberty's face—a smile, not just of amusement, but of mischief, as though finally giving into something she really ought not to say. She gave her cocktail a final slurp. 'I swear, it's like people in this country don't have a clue.'

'Don't have a clue about what?'

'Don't know any, don't know anything about them, very happy never to think about them at all. And then you mention that one little word. One word, three letters, and they all lose their minds.'

'What are you *talking* about?'

'You know.'

'I don't know. Everyone always says I know and I really, really don't.'

'*Jews*, Edward. Like you were saying to Youssef—like, it's okay. I'm not a Muslim, but I'm on your side. My Mom's been super into Nation of Islam stuff recently, and . . .'

'Liberty, wait. Wait.' What to say? His ears were hot, and he could felt his heart beating right up at the base of his throat. 'I really don't understand how that's relevant.'

'Of course you do, Edward.'

'I don't. And I think it's kind of concerning that you do.'

'Look, I get it. No, don't protest, I do get it. You like her. You probably think she's hot—and I get that too. I mean she's a little *obvious*, but you're a guy, and a British guy at that, so the more obvious the better, right? And God knows Angie hasn't been the most attentive girlfriend. I get that too. But don't act like you don't think her being a Jew, and your being a Muslim, is irrelevant, when they're literally the two most mutually relevant things in, like, all of history.'

'There's no "acting" required. It's very easy. And *all* of history?'

'Yeah, well trust me on this, it won't be easy for long. Have you even been following what's been going on over there?'

'"There"? Can you hear yourself? Rachel is half German and half English.'

Liberty batted the air in front of her. 'I'm from New York, Eddie. The Upper East Sid—which is, surprise surprise, not *that* far from the Upper West Side. I *know* Jews.'

'You can't just *know* Jews, as if all Jews are the same.'

Liberty made a scoffing noise. 'God, you're so *English*. Lemme guess, you think it's kind of uncouth having an identity, too, right?'

'I wouldn't go that far.'

'You think it's all stupid.'

'Maybe just a word people use when they want to be stupid. Or at least when they want to stop thinking.'

'Well guess what, Edward,' said Liberty, leaning forward, a dangerous glint in her eye. 'I'm not stupid, you know. Really, I'm not.'

'I know you're not stupid. I just think when you say things like "I know Jews," you sound stupid. *Worse* than stupid.'

'Look at Edward, putting on his suit of armour and wading into battle. Finally, a cause you care about. Nice of you to join the rest of us. Except . . .' She leaned forward, and he could smell the gin on her breath. 'You've picked the wrong issue, Eddie. This is not going to look good in a couple of years.'

'I'm not trying to pick a side in some great big conflict.'

'Oh, how admirable of you. Let me guess. You just want to judge people *as individuals*?'

'You're saying this like it would be the worst thing in the world.'

'Except we're not actually individuals, are we Edward?'

'Aren't we?'

'Maybe you are. Maybe you get to be. But look at me.'

'This is ridiculous.'

'*Look* at me.'

'I'm looking, Liberty.'

'What do you see?'

'I see someone who doesn't like Jews and is just deflecting. I see a beret.'

'Do you see an "individual"? Or do you see just another black woman? Be honest.'

'You know maybe people are reluctant to view you as an individual because you go on about being a black woman literally all the time.'

'Oh, *there* it is.'

'You don't need to keep saying it. I get it. We all get it. And I actually don't mind if you want to be the resident Africa expert, I'm happy to let that go—even though, by the way, you clearly had *no* idea where Zanzibar was and Angelica said you thought an okapi was a kind of food . . .'

'I don't need to keep saying it?' Liberty slammed down her empty glass on the counter. 'You *really* think this is all easy, that I should basically just shut up and accept that all the work that needs to be done has already been done.'

'Not all of it. But you have to admit that here—yes, maybe not anywhere else in the world, maybe not in New York or London or the West Bank or wherever but here, in Oxford— here, your skin colour has actually kind of helped you. Unlike, say, being Jewish, which from where I'm standing seems to help absolutely no one in no way at all.'

'You don't get it, do you?'

'Tell me what there is to get.'

'You know, Edward, I look around—here, in Oxford, not New York—and you know what I see? I see envy. For the first time in recorded history, I see all the white English girls look me up and down and think "God, I wish I was like her," or "God, I wish I had hair like hers," or "God, I wish I had skin like hers." So yeah, I'm proud of it, and I don't try and hide it. But you think that being envied by people is the same as actually being equal to them? Do you? Because when the English girls look at me with envy, they're not exactly wishing for the Middle Passage, are they? They're not thinking of Jim Crow, or burning crosses, or even just what it's actually like to be me, day after day, with all this expectation to meet, and to work so hard, and still—*still*—have some old guy in College take one look at you and decide what your grade's gonna be at the end of term.'

'Yes, I'm sorry you had to live through all those cross-burnings. It must have been really hard for you.'

'You think you're funny, don't you?' Liberty had lowered her voice to a threatening whisper. 'It's okay, I don't mind. I'm used to little English boys thinking they're funny. But it's true Edward. And you're not above it either, are you? Like, going on and on about Zanzibar and East Africa.'

'Angelica brought that up, not me. I never wanted . . .'

'Oh *sure*. You want a piece of it too. It's okay, I don't blame you. I'm just saying that everyone wants a piece of it—something to complain about, moan about, whatever. Actually, it's no wonder you're so taken with Rach. In my experience, if there's one group of people you can always count on to make a fuss whenever they feel threatened, to close ranks around an identity.'

'Yeah well maybe it's your *experience* that's the problem.'

'Maybe it's *your* experience that's the problem. You know I had such high hopes for you, Edward.'

'I'm sorry to disappoint.'

'I suppose it makes sense, doesn't it? You and Rach. You're both so determined to convince the world that you're not white. You want to scrub all that awful whiteness off your skin. Well guess what, Edward? It won't work. It won't.' She took another sip of her drink, and grew pensive. 'You know my grandmother lived in a tenement,' she said. 'Mom's side. In South Harlem— some slum apartment. She paid ninety-four dollars a month, which was a lot in those days. And the landlord was a Jew— God, you flinch every time I say it, don't you? What's all that about? Is that a British thing too? He was a Jew, Edward, and every day he walked out and got spat at by those nice white progressives he aspired to be like, and what did he do? He gave them discounts. Charged them seventy dollars, and jacked up my Grandma's to a hundred and five to make up for it. Wanted to be white, you see. Wanted to be *accepted*. And when there was mould, or rats, he would laugh and never do anything. And when there was a fire in one of his buildings he bribed the municipality to look the other way.'

'I'd better get Rachel to apologise.'

Liberty shook her head. She seemed almost defeated. 'Maybe she should, Edward. Maybe she should. Maybe the progressive thing to do is to admit one's responsibility for a change when you're part of a people that has done wrong.'

'Ah yes, the progressive option: blaming the Jews.'

'You know why sweet little Rach has gone off?'

'Because you *lied* to her, Liberty. And you humiliated her.'

'Bullshit. Because she's hiding some pretty reactionary opinions of her own, and she doesn't want me exposing them.'

'Oh sure. What's her problem? Did she vote against you in some meeting?'

'Not quite, Edward.' Liberty smiled, and shook her head. 'Tell you what,' she said at last, 'why don't you ask her. Ask her how she spent her vacation, and where. Ask her why she and Saïd broke up. Ask her. Ask the Jew girl.'

Chapter 11

Now that Liberty hated him, Rachel was upset with him, Youssef mistrusted him, Conrad barely even spoke to him—and, at long last, according to the pair of freshers dizzily discussing it a few desks over in the library this morning, Angelica Mountbatten-Jones was back in College having been excused from her first three weeks of tutorials with a flick of her psychotherapist's pen, Edward's social life had changed somewhat. He decided to go down to the College bar alone to soak up the Friday revelries as part of the collective, hitching himself to a drunken group of rugby players generous enough, or disorientated enough, to take one more. They left College soon after, sloshing their way through pint after pint at The Lamb and Lion, The Goat and Tricycle, The Spread Eagle. Edward looked on as they took horse tranquilisers at Lustmolch, dropped acid at The Bunghole, fought bouncers at Drench and locals in the tree-lined promenades of the University Parks. One or two even queued outside the twilit ruins of Favela. He drifted through the evening in a haze of polite introductions and slurred confessions, dodging the rugby players who bounced around like wrecking balls, weaving past the lofty, posh, unapproachable girls who swayed in blank unison like birches in the wind.

By 2 A.M., he was leaning against a drainpipe in the smoking area. It was there that he spied Lolly B—in full lacrosse regalia, sticks tucked under her humid arms.

'*Ed*ward!' To Edward's surprise, she lurched straight for

him, flinging herself into the embrace. 'What are you doing here?'

On her forehead was a plastic tiara; somewhere in the abyssal cleavage lurked a long, sleek sash, crimson, with the words *Hell's Belles* printed in proud black felt tip. From each arm straggled a male fresher, shirtless and clutching a bottle of fizzy red wine, torsos covered in lipstick.

'Lolly?'

'Do you like my freshers?'

'Erm. Sure. Are they okay?'

Lolly stabbed at the tiara with her forefinger, then swayed slightly, surprised at her own strength. 'I'm *Queen*, don't you see? Of the Belles.' Then over her shoulder: 'Stand up straight, boys.'

'Are *you* okay?'

'Read Freddie's chest.'

'What?'

'The words.'

'"Grape victim"?'

'It's a joke.' Lolly hiccupped.

'Right'

'It's funny.'

'He doesn't look very well. What's that stuff coming out of his mouth?'

'He's fine. Are you okay, Freddie?'

The fresher gave a groan.

'See?'

'Right. Well, have fun.'

Lolly was swaying now. 'You've changed, Edward. Since you started going out with Angelica. She's back, by the way. She looks very tanned and appealing.'

'I know she's back.'

'Why do we never speak any more, Edward? We spoke quite a lot last year.' Lolly gave another hiccup.

'We still speak, Lolly.'

'Oh, Edward.' Lolly smiled at him sadly. On each temple she placed a sturdy thumb; then slowly, ceremoniously, she looped them under the tiara, lifted it off her head and turned it to face her, the plastic gemstones lighting her face in strange patterns. 'Can't compete, I suppose. Not with Angelica. Not with any of them.'

'You're doing fine.'

'No, no I'm not really.'

'You're queen of the . . . whatever this is called. Sorry I've forgotten.'

'And they're horrible to me for it.'

'Who's horrible?'

'Liberty. Angelica.'

'They're horrible to everyone.'

'Even *Youssef's* bored of me.'

'Youssef's not bored of you.'

'He's not been messaging. Or he sent one, but I think he was drunk, judging by the way he spelled mosque. Also, what actually is a "thick-ankled woman of Jannah"?'

'I think it's a compliment. And he's not bored of you, he's just . . . busy. I don't know. Distracted.'

'You mean since the two of you fell out?'

'You know about that?'

'Everybody knows. Something religious, I heard.'

'That's one way of putting it.'

'It can't be easy for him though, can it?' She pouted through her make-up. 'Poor Youssef.'

'Poor *him*? What about me?'

'Think about it, Edward. He's come all the way from Egypt where no one's like him. And he must have felt lonely. *I'd* have felt lonely. And then, for a while, he had you. But now he doesn't.' Lolly smiled sadly. 'Look, I don't know Youssef as well as you do. But I suspect that whatever he's upset about, it might be worth talking about it. He isn't as bad as the others really. I mean it. He isn't.'

Edward let *Writing White: Franz Kafka and the Pan-African Imagination* topple shut and gazed around the emptying library. The term was entering its fifth week, and the day seemed to have finished before it even had a chance to begin: the strip-lights had blinked on, revealing the shadows of all the flies and spiders the tubes had sepulchred over the years. He swept three or four books into his satchel, stood, stretched, and traipsed over to the window—just to look outside, rest his eyes before it grew completely dark—only to realise, as he pressed his face up to the cold pane, that it was snowing.

That was the end of his scant resolve to work. Binding himself in his jacket, he trotted down the library steps and stowed himself in a cloister overlooking the quad. He stood there for several minutes, watching the whole scene fade to the same bright, blank colour as the sky, all the frills and brims on the old College buildings highlighted suddenly. It looked like one of the postcards they sold in the library gift shop, far too beautiful to be true. He padded to the edge of the cloister and stretched his hand past the threshold, feeling the cold flakes on his skin. He stayed there until all but the crudest features of the quad were obscured: there was no path now, or green, and even the fountain in the farthest corner was little more than a soft white lump, that looked as though it might be carried off by the wind, or melt into water, or be dismantled by a groundskeeper's shovel and remade in a different way.

It was nearly dark when his phone buzzed. He checked the screen. Rachel's name. She had sent him an image: a view of the Fellows' Garden from above, taken from a rooftop, or maybe through a window, with the flower beds all covered in snow, and in the corners three or four broad discs, where stumps of the old trees cleared for the library extension had not quite been submerged. His phone buzzed again.

— *Tree trunks*
in the snow.

He typed his response quickly.

— *Can we talk Rachel?*

— *Are you in College now?*

— *Yeah*

He watched his screen for several seconds, waiting for the message to come in.

— *Top floor*
rookery building

He followed her instructions: up the staircase, past 'the rookery,' whatever one of those was, up the stairs, along a creaking dormer, to a full-height window that someone had left ajar. He wrenched it up, and emerged out on to a short, slate promontory with limestone crenellations on either side. There she was, at the tip, in the last patch of sun.

'Worth it?' she asked.

Edward nodded as he folded himself in next to her. Down on the quad, the students had given way to the porters, now busy in the solemn ritual of clasping and locking and battening; spreading grit on the pathway.

'How did you find this place?' he said once he had settled.

'You're not going to like it.'

'Try me.'

'Saïd showed it to me.'

'You're right, I don't like it.'

'Last year. Someone in the year above told him. People seem to be in the habit of telling him all their secrets. I don't know why.'

Edward shrugged. 'I suppose I'm not in much of a position to be getting offended at the moment.'

She turned to face him, stern despite the snow catching in her eyelashes, 'No, you're not.'

'I'm sorry, you know.'

She nodded.

'Liberty was twisting things.'

'I know.'

'And I'm not . . .'

'I know, Edward.'

'She makes things up. She made things up about *you*, after you left.'

'Do I want to know?'

'You could guess, probably. Didn't like your political opinions, et cetera. I think the fact that you have family in Israel was part of it, obviously.' He took a deep breath. 'And she said I should ask you why you broke up with Saïd.'

Rachel pulled her coat around her. 'Not this again.'

'There is no "again" for me, Rachel. Everyone else seems to know this stuff instinctively—but I don't, so please, *please*, just tell me what's going on.'

'You really want to know? It isn't even very exciting.'

'I want to know.'

Rachel sighed. 'I met Saïd in Berlin, my Abitur year. That's like sixth form. He was doing a gap year for some international organisation, and he was going to Oxford, too. And, well, he was nice, and he upset my parents, which seemed very important at the time. And, and he was a year older than me. And he was very . . . very political. Very different from me really.'

'You fell out because of his politics then? Maybe that's why Liberty wants me to get away from you so much.'

'Oh I *loved* the politics. I went with him to things. It made me feel extremely distant from my family and culture in a way I found very, very exciting. It was like . . . like I was living with this guilt—always guilt, weighing on me quietly every day. And when I was with him I didn't need to feel it. He *told* me I didn't need to feel it.' She looked up into the night sky, faintly orange from the streetlamps which had begun to flicker on past the slate roofs. 'Anyway, in my final year there was a big demonstration in Neukölln. And Saïd was going, so I went too of course. There were these young Turkish men, three or four of them, and at one point they jumped up on this wall. One of them had a megaphone, and was screaming into it. Screaming "Fuck Israel!" over and over again. In English, funnily enough—perhaps he wanted to be international. And just like that—without even really thinking—the crowd shouted it back. "Fuck Israel!" And then at some point he switched: it was "Fuck the Zionists!" and the crowd repeated that too. And then you knew what was coming at that point. A whole crowd, hundreds of them, in unison: "Fuck the Jews!"'

'I'm sorry.'

'You know, it's funny but I really didn't care at the time. Or not enough, anyway; I didn't like it, but what could I have done? Should I have called the police? Should I have got the man on the wall thrown in prison—you can over there. Should I have found out where he worked and told his employer? I know that's what all the Oxford workshops tell us to do.'

'You could have done.'

Rachel let out a short, sardonic laugh. 'And that would have helped, would it? That would have changed their opinions, if I'd started complaining.' She shook her head. 'You know, Edward, what actually hurt most of all was the feeling that I had had my gift rejected. My little gift of solidarity and the assurance that I wasn't so very different from them after all. Isn't that strange?'

'It's not strange. Did Saïd find it strange?'

'No. No, he just rolled his eyes. I think he was proud of me, really; look how mature his girlfriend was, not making a fuss, not complaining or being dramatic—keeping focused on the task. Not being a Jew about it, in other words.' She smiled to herself, almost sadly. 'And I was impressed with myself too; I was so different to my parents, I didn't care about threats to my own person. I was *sophisticated*. And then, that evening, the strangest thing happened.'

'What happened?'

'I couldn't look at him. I went all . . . sour, and did that thing my mum does when she's angry and I never thought I would— all tight lips and sighs that people are meant to understand.'

'Did you not tell him how you felt?'

'It came out. But he didn't get it.'

'Did you try and explain it to him?'

'That's the problem, Edward. What is there to explain? I knew he was some idiot. I knew I wasn't in any imminent danger. And a lot of what I felt at that moment was a kind of distance, more than anything else. Like I'm not really all that Jewish when it comes down to it. I have family in Israel, and they're so brawny and ideological, and they're Jewish. And I have family in New York, and they're so intellectual and neurotic, and they're Jewish. And what am I? I'm nothing.' She sighed. 'But it doesn't matter. It doesn't matter because I'm my own person, and I have lots of languages and I study here in this beautiful place, and I'm an individual. At least that's what I half-believe.'

'What's so wrong with that?'

'Nothing. Nothing, until you come along and tell Youssef that I'm "not very Jewish." That made me feel wonderful, obviously.'

She was avoiding his eyes still, gazing down at the snow-covered lip of the turret. He turned to her, trying to find the appropriate level of solemnity in his voice. 'I'm sorry Rachel. I really am. All I meant was that he has a certain vision in his head of what a Jewish person, and that you don't conform to it. That's all.'

'See, even now I'm worried that I'm being Jewish about this. One of those windmill-tilting Jews who sees antisemitism everywhere, even in lovely liberal Oxford. Especially in lovely liberal Oxford.'

'I don't think you're one of those. I just think about Youssef, you're exaggerating. Most of it is just him repeating his parents, or trying to be funny.'

A roll of the eyes. 'Well, that's nice.'

'In general, though, you're not wrong.' He paused a second, rubbing his hands for warmth, unsure whether to continue. 'Liberty said something, after you left.'

'Do me a favour Edward. Just don't tell me about it.'

'You don't want to know?'

She shook her head firmly. 'No, I'd rather not, actually. I really would rather not give her the satisfaction.'

'But she won't change if no one says anything.'

'She won't change if people *do* say something. Liberty isn't innately antisemitic any more than she innately wears that beret or innately had her nipples pierced. No . . .' she shook her head firmly. 'She's doing it to be provocative, and because she has a vague sense that Jews are trying to steal something from her, some kind of credit for past persecution, and that this is somehow undeserved. And *that* would be fine, too, except we're in Oxford and we just happen to be surrounded by a load of people who don't seem to know anything but feel all these powerful, vague, directionless feelings and like nothing better than to sit around calling Liberty brave and me a coward on the grounds that, since I am a Jew, a private citizen is something I simply *do not get to be.*'

In her frustration she had turned away from him, and even in the twilight Edward could see her cheek was flushed against the cold. She blinked, regathering herself, as if taken aback at her own lack of composure.

'You could just forget them, you know. Forget Liberty, and Angelica.'

'I can't *forget* them, Edward. That's just it. I'm far too shallow. I basically just want to be liked.'

'I don't think that's true, either.'

'It is true. Listen, clearly you've built me up into some

impossible creature who's all aloof or serene or whatever. But all that's really going on is that Angelica and Liberty don't like me. That's it. That is the source of my mystique. I'm going to disappoint you.'

'Rachel.'

'I'll disappoint you, Edward.'

'Rachel. Look at me a second.'

She looked at him.

'I haven't built you up into anything.'

'Oh, of course you haven't.'

'And you couldn't disappoint me.'

'Okay, you can stop this now.'

'And actually, I think it's pretty obvious that I don't just like you because Liberty and Angelica don't.'

'Obvious? You think that's obvious? Nothing about you, or the way anyone talks to each other here for that matter—none of it is *obvious*.'

'What does that mean?'

Rachel gave a little groan of frustration. 'It means I've spent a whole term trying to work out what you think about me, and whether you even like me, what's going on with Angelica. And I don't find any of it obvious. Maybe it's me. Maybe it's a cultural thing. Is that it, Edward? Is this just how it works in England?'

'Is what how it works in England?'

'You come to me and complain about Angelica—as if you were a poor little lamb with absolutely no control over the situation at all. You come and meet me on a rooftop, in the snow, at sunset, and then somehow—and I don't actually know how this happens, but it does, every time—you get me to say something to you I really shouldn't say. And just, *just* when I've opened up, you tell me to look at you. And I look at you. And then . . . then you sit there.'

'You want me to do something different?'

'I don't know yet. There have been times I've wanted you to. Last term, for instance.'

'Why didn't you say?'

She shrugged. 'Because I don't want to be someone who asks, particularly. I know I know you're meant to these days, if you want to be an empowered woman or whatever. I know that's what Angelica does, and what Liberty acts like she does. But I can't, okay?'

'We were having an argument, Rachel. You were angry at me. You still are.'

'I'm not angry, Edward. This isn't anger.'

'Isn't it?'

At that, she just laughed. 'It's funny. All the time we've been having this conversation, which is clearly very meaningful and worthy, and supposedly gets to the heart of our respective identities, and is exactly the kind of thing people are meant to undertake in order to gain some grand, profound understanding of each other—all the time, you know what I've been thinking? I've been thinking: "I wish he would tell me to shut up. Seriously. I wish he would look at me, and laugh, and tell me to stop being so neurotic and overdramatic and frankly *Jewish* about everything, and come over here and kiss me."'

He kissed her. Afterwards, she stayed beside him, her head resting on his shoulder. Together they watched a breeze gathering in from the distance, the lines of treetops shivering one by one as it drew nearer, until it enfolded them. They were silent for a long time after it had passed.

'You need to talk to Angelica,' said Rachel suddenly.

'Where did that come from?'

'I just don't want you, or her, to think this is just some revenge, or whatever. Because it isn't.'

'I know that.'

She lifted her head from his shoulder and stared up at him. 'Did Angelica ever tell you about last year?'

'I didn't realise there was that much to tell.'

'It was right at the beginning. When everything felt . . . kind of fluid. Like everyone was looking around themselves all the time, waiting to be slotted into their given place. I was *always* nervous.' Rachel's hand had crept to her nape, and she rubbed it back and forth, nervously. 'Anyway, Angelica and I were friends, I think. Or at least, it seemed like that at the time. She found out I had a relative in Buenos Aires, and that was that. I felt myself getting gathered into that group, the entourage she always seems to have around her.'

'Yeah, I know them.'

'That's what she does, Angelica—she gathers people up. Took me to poetry readings, plays. There was this art exhibition where a girl in Keble would carry her mattress down the stairs every morning to the main quad, scream for five minutes, and then carry it back up. We went to that too, Angelica *insisted*. She said it reminded her of Marcel Duchamp.'

'Yeah, this sounds familiar.'

She smiled sadly. 'There was this one evening, towards the end of the first term. It was some *Samizdat* event. A dinner, starched white tablecloths, speeches. I really wanted to write for them, you see. Despite everything.' She sighed. 'Anyway,' she said. 'Liberty was there. The opposite side of the table. It was the first time I'd ever met her.'

'Lucky you.'

'She was even worse back then. She wasn't president of any-thing, and she hadn't had any of that media training they all get now, and she was just less . . . careful. Kept peering over at us with this contemptuous look on her face . . . And just like that, Angelica changed. That was it. Like the sun going in.'

She fell silent.

'Let's get down from here, Rachel.'

She nodded. He picked himself up and offered her his hand. As she folded herself back through the dormer, Edward took one last look over the rooftops, along the canyons of the streets, now bright with streetlamps, illuminated windows.

They took the long way back to the Annexe. Neither of them felt the need to say anything; they passed the great, snow-fretted arches, the shop-fronts with ferns of ice sprouting along their windows, peeling off after a while along the riverbank in easy step with each other. There was no sound except for the pontoon, lapping and creaking and covered in the dim shadows of geese, asleep now, bills stowed in between their soft shoulder blades, rising and falling. Slowly, almost imperceptibly, he felt Rachel loop her arm into his. He wondered what would happen when they arrived back at the Annexe. They would stand opposite each other in the gritted courtyard, smile at each other probably. But then what? It struck him that he should probably ask her back to his room, that this is what you did in such situations, if only to let her know what it still felt thrilling to be able to admit—that yes, he did desire her—and if only to give her the right to refuse, as she was supposed to in such situations. And if she didn't refuse? The thought made his heart beat very hard, and seemed to put him out of breath, though they were not walking fast. He glanced over at Rachel. He wanted to kiss her again.

As they turned the final corner before the Annexe, Rachel's arm grew rigid. 'Edward . . .' He let her ease him to a halt. 'Edward, maybe we should . . .'

Up ahead, framed in the bars of the Annexe's wrought iron gate, were two more figures. One was very tall, clearly male; the other looked female, and was now striding towards them, untroubled by the compacted snow on the riverbank—an unmistakable stride, rolling briskly and confidently from heel to toe, as if it were she who were stationary, and only the rest of the world turning under her feet. Dimly, he felt Rachel untwine herself from his arm. She had recognised her too.

'Well, would you look at that.' Angelica drew up before them and nodded at each of them in turn, her smile just a shade too friendly 'I was told you'd been spending time together, but *this . . .*' she gestured grandly at them, smile still untouched on her immaculately glossed lips, 'this really is just *perfect*.'

Edward's swallowed, his throat suddenly very dry. 'You didn't say you were back.'

'You could have checked. You've been to my room enough times. You know where it is.'

'I messaged you.'

'Oh, but you were clearly so *busy*.' Angelica was gazing at Rachel now, mouth still stretched wide in some vague attempt at hospitality, but the eyes cold. 'But that's just the place, I suppose. I mean we're all *so busy*, aren't we?' She let out a short, mirthless laugh, then pulled her long coat tight around her, and called back over her shoulder. 'Darling, are you coming?' She paused, then resumed a little louder. 'Darling? Come on, don't be shy. Saïd?'

By the time Saïd had marched up to them, awkwardly embraced Rachel, permitted Angelica to nestle cosily but determinedly against him, and, still yoked to her, put out his hand to Edward, so that to shake it would somehow involve both of them, Edward had assessed the various timelines and possibilities in his head. Whichever way you looked at it, Angelica had moved fast. She was certainly enjoying standing next to Saïd. Against the blank canvas of the snow the two of them shared a kind of mythical quality, he dark to her light, as though the universe had been split in two to fashion them.

Angelica, for her part, seemed rather unsettled. She had been studying them all with interest, looking first to Saïd, then to Rachel, then Edward, then back to Saïd again, calculating. She began to laugh. It was an unusual sound, more pitiful and high-pitched than doubtless was intended. 'Well, *well*,' she said, once she had finished. 'It looks like we all know each other already. Who'd have thought it?'

'Who'd have thought it,' said Rachel quietly.

'Beautiful, no?' said Saïd briskly, with an expansive gesture at the snowscape across the riverbank. 'We just came out to admire the snow.'

Edward stared at Angelica. 'To admire the snow? I thought you hated the snow.'

'I love snow, Edward.' She glanced at Saïd, then wound herself more tightly into his armpit. 'Saïd and I were talking about it the other day. We realised it's one of the many things we have in common.'

'I see.'

'And you two?'

'Us two?'

'You two were admiring the snow too, I suppose? It's nice that you have so much time for each other these days.'

Gently, Saïd uncoiled her from his arm. 'Perhaps we should . . .'

'Yes, you're right.' Angelica nodded to herself. 'I'm afraid Saïd and I are rather busy too.' She pulled at Saïd's arm as if to set off again, and as she pitched forward, her scarf fell loose. By the porchlight Edward could see a new charm at the tip of her necklace. The necklace had always been a repository for Angelica's new passions, home sequentially to a silver tapir from Paraguay, a pewter silhouette of Kilimanjaro, a little lozenge embossed with Arabic writing she seemed half-convinced Edward could understand. Now, however, there was only one pendant. It was silver, shaped like a blade; only gradually did Edward come to recognise it as a map. He didn't need to read the words etched across it to know where it was from.

Angelica had caught him staring. She didn't fix her scarf, but adjusted it smugly, making the patch of her neck even more obvious. 'We have things to organise,' she continued.

Rachel had her arms folded, and was glaring at Saïd. 'What things?'

Saïd spoke in a soft, conciliatory voice. 'Angelica is writing a feature in *Samizdat*. For the March edition. She wanted to interview . . .' He smiled at Angelica, who beamed back at him, '. . . well, me.' He turned back to the two of them. 'I hope you don't mind, Rachel.'

'I don't mind,' said Rachel flatly.

Angelica was craning forward with interest. 'Why would she mind, darling? She isn't in the habit of telling you whether or not you're allowed to speak, is she?'

'No,' said Saïd.

'Because that would be a little controlling.'

'I just said I don't mind, Angelica,' said Rachel.

'Good.' Angelica looked pleased with herself. 'It'll be a special issue,' she continued buoyantly. 'Full colour. Vouchers to the next VerboCity. I've been feeling for a while that *Samizdat* has lost touch with its radical roots.'

'What is it that you're planning on being so radical about?'

'Oh, plenty of things.' She looked pointedly at Rachel. 'Injustices are always interlinked, don't you find?'

Rachel shrugged. 'I think sometimes people find connections that aren't there.'

'And *sometimes*,' said Angelica, ostentatiously recoiling her scarf, 'people are wilfully blind. They sit around pretending like they don't have any connection to anything that's going on in the world. They don't *do the work*.'

'At least the blind don't jump to conclusions.'

'No. They don't, do they?' Angelica wheeled herself round, subjecting Edward to the full force of her disapproval. 'They're so intent on keeping an open mind that they end up repeating the mistakes the rest of us have already made.'

'Angelica, maybe . . .' Saïd seemed to have given up on diplomacy now, and rejoined Angelica at her side; delicately, he touched her wrist. Something in her seemed to defuse. He gazed at her a moment, then offered Edward and Rachel the same, apologetic smile.

'It was nice to run into you both,' he said, as he and Angelica set out along the riverbank.

'Likewise,' said Edward, before turning back, only to find Rachel had already disappeared, and that the Annexe gate was clanging after her, and that everything in the scene that now enfolded him—the wind, the desolate Annexe courtyard—conspired to deliver the same message: that the evening, and whatever he and Rachel had shared of it, was now over.

CHAPTER 12

E dward,' said Youssef, bursting into the library with his
customary disregard of its other inhabitants and their
looming end-of-term deadlines. '*Edward*. Yes, you. Do
you have a moment? Stop reading at once.'

Edward shut his book. 'Now? Why do you always wait till
I'm in the library to ambush me?'

'I shan't be long. Three or four hours should do the trick.'

'Oh, good.'

'Now get up. Dust yourself down. Quicker. You look sick
again. Are you taking your Vitamin D supplements like I told
you? Good.' Youssef took Edward by the shoulder and guided
him towards the library's exit. He was sorry, he said, he had
been possessed by the djinn of ill-temper the past few weeks,
but he was over it now: 'Besides,' he continued, 'we have much
to talk about. It has been, what, three weeks? You must have
been lonely, destitute.'

'Yeah I know. Listen, about our fight . . .'

'What? No, not that, Edward. I forgive you without reserva-
tion for your rudeness and lack of understanding. It's the way
you were raised.'

'How generous.'

Youssef nodded. 'You were not yourself. You were led into
temptation. These things happen. Even the Prophet had his sa-
tanic interlude.'

'I'm not actually apologising, Youssef.'

'It's too late, I have already accepted. Anyway, this is not
what I brought you here to talk to you about.'

'What *did* you bring me here to talk to me about? Are you going to ask me to check the spelling on another job application? Because I think five per term is a reasonable place to draw the line.'

'No, Edward. I am here because I *heard*. I heard everything. I heard that that fraud Saïd has pitched up and proceeded to occupy Angelica's territories. Scandal! We must not stand for this. I have plans to restore us to pre-eminence.'

Youssef continued to fill him in as he barged open the door of the Common Room, glared at the pair of freshers playing pool with broken cues until they scampered off, and settled creakingly into the gouged foam of the nearest armchair. Things had changed, he explained. Youssef had been thinking. And he had decided, after much deliberation, that he was going to be African now.

'African?'

'Yes Edward. The great big malarial mass between civilisation and the penguins. You may have heard of it?'

'Yes, but . . .'

'I have just as much right to call myself African as anyone else here, thank you very much. Especially,' he looked Edward wryly up and down, 'given what passes for African these days.'

'Right, so ignoring the obvious question of what *deciding to be African now* actually means, what has prompted this reappraisal?'

'Saïd. Obviously.'

'What does Saïd have to do with it?'

'We cannot compete with Saïd, Edward. Not as Muslims, not on that front. Not with a Palestinian. Have you seen the prayer beads?' He shuddered against the gouged armchair. 'Formidable.'

'I've seen the prayer beads, but I don't see why . . .'

'You know the more I consider it, Edward, the more I suspect that being a Muslim doesn't even count for all that much these days,' Youssef continued. 'Our stock is falling. No one wants us. I have woven subtle Islamic themes and imagery into several job applications—nothing. Not one response. Not even from the Aga Khan Foundation. Whereas Liberty . . .' he shook his head. 'Liberty has five job offers. Because she's *African*.'

'Do you think it might be because Liberty, unlike you, didn't get a third in her exams?'

'What? No. Of course not. It was an extremely high third. No, this awful discrepancy has arisen simply because she's African. Or African-American, which is somehow even *more* African.'

'I see.'

'I blame America, you see.'

'Right. I'm glad you added another geographical component to this immensely coherent theory.'

'It's not a "theory," Edward. It's a fact. Did they teach you anything at your school, or was it just stabbings? Let me explain . . .' Youssef nestled himself more irrevocably into the armchair and slipped into his imam voice. 'America is, as we know, considered to be prestigious. People in *this* country take their cues from it, worship it. They do, don't shake your head. Now, once upon a time in America, we Muslims—for whatever reason—were treated with some suspicion. You may remember it. Border guards reached for their weapons as we passed. White girls found us thrilling. Old ladies listened to us for ticking noises on the Tube.'

'Since when do you go on the Tube?'

'I have been on it twice, Edward. But this is not the point.'

'What actually is the point?'

'The point is that this period is over. In America, from where we get all our culture, we Muslims have gone back to being what we have always been, which over there is dentists, pharmacists, used car salesmen. Naturally pious. Community-minded. Charitable. Traditional.'

'Good for us.'

'Except what could be more boring for someone like Angelica? Conventionality, tradition: these are the very things she despises.'

'Oh, right. So the whole theory is about Angelica, actually. What a surprise. Does it come with a recommendation that I win her back too?'

Youssef swatted away the question with a flick of his hand. 'Angelica wants destitution, poverty, suffering. And we Muslims have none to offer her. Now the blacks . . .'

'Again, Youssef, you *are* black. And African. We have been over this.'

'Well yes, I am *now*. Honestly Edward, keep up, I implore you. Now the blacks, as we—you rightly point out—now are . . .'

'Youssef. I may just about be a Muslim but I am not black. That's just insane.'

'You're so *defeatist* about these things, Edward. Have you even tried? Now the blacks . . .'

'Please stop saying "the blacks" . . .'

'The blacks are glamorous. They have their rap music, they have their paternal absenteeism, they have their crime.'

'Oh, God.'

'Don't blaspheme, Edward. They have "soul"—are you familiar with this concept? I learned about it the other day from a music video. *Soul.* A marvellous Sufi word. A whole culture with immense social potential, ripe for us to exploit.' He stretched himself out in the armchair, suddenly very pleased with himself. 'Anyway, all I'm saying is that if you want to have any future in this college—which you do, I know you do—then it is into this portion of your wonderfully incoherent heritage that you must lean.'

Over the course of the afternoon, Youssef managed to convince him that he had repaired not only their friendship, but Edward's standing in the great, dizzying hierarchy of the College. He had already worked his magic on Liberty, he

234 · THOMAS PEERMOHAMED LAMBERT

promised: she was feeling slightly embarrassed about her little indiscretion at the Chamber—several of the publishers to whom she had submitted the first volume of her memoirs, it transpired, were Jewish—and had sent her people out to make amends. The olive branch had been extended, via Youssef, to Edward. He had applied for a travel grant from the College, had he not? To go to Berlin or some other Turk-riddled hellhole. Well, he'd be pleased to know it had been approved. In exchange for his silence, it had been approved.

For several seconds, Edward simply stood there. It was all he could manage. Image after image was flashing before him: cobblestones, cathedrals, promenades by the river, art galleries with white walls and black-and-white photographs, road signs in other languages—and best of all, Rachel standing right there with him, her arm looped around his.

'Thank you, Youssef. Seriously.'

Youssef blew dismissively through his teeth. 'Oh, come now. Anyone would think you've never been on holiday before.'

'I don't think you realise how big this is for me.'

Youssef shrugged modestly. 'Well, it isn't guaranteed yet. The College still needs to approve it. You'll need the bursar to sign off. But provided you don't do anything controversial or upset the porters or anything—and let us be quite honest, Edward, when have you ever done anything remotely controversial?—you will be fine. Now, are you coming along this evening?'

'I didn't know anything was happening this evening.'

'The first event of spring, Edward. *Rabi al-Awwal.* Here . . .' He reached behind a lapel, took out a crumpled flyer, and handed it over, coloured ink smudging on his fingers. 'Something to get you out of Angelica's sphere of influence, and a venue for you to try out your new African credentials.' Edward unfurled the paper. 'The Mixed Heritage Society. For people just like you.' He grinned. 'The more diluted, the better.'

Youssef permitted him forty-five minutes to jog back to the Annexe and change his clothes to something less embarrassing. Once he had been greeted, criticised for his choice, and told where they were going, they set off towards the High Street. Edward had to strain to keep pace as Youssef glided along in his swift, easy lope, dropping a note into a homeless man's hat without even breaking his stride. He kept up the pace of his oration, scarcely even looking at Edward, features alive with the thoughts and implications that never ceased to burst into his head. The most prevalent topic of all was Liberty.

'I'm glad you have something concrete to hold over her,' Youssef mused. 'This will come in useful. And it might help keep her in check—all this "Queen" business—I believe she may start to think she actually has the power to declare war.'

'I thought she was your new ally. Especially now that you're black.'

'For the purposes of convenience, she is.'

'You don't like her?'

Youssef chuckled to himself. 'I have known Liberty a long time, Edward.'

'You have?'

'Since we were twelve. Her father did a couple of years at the Goldman branch in London. Overlapping circles. I suspect in due course half of her friends will end up married to half of my friends, if the institution of marriage has not been completely undermined by then by this decadent pornographic culture you lot have concocted in this country. Anyway . . .' His face fell slightly. 'You know what she was like back then? You know what she spent her time doing?'

'I don't know. Going on hunger strike. Volunteering in the Sudan.'

'Just "Sudan," Edward. The "the" makes you sound like some horrible Englishman.'

'Right. Sorry. How awful. Volunteering in "Sudan"?'

'Not quite.' Youssef's pace, he noticed, had slowed. 'She used to walk up and down the lunch hall at school—arrived early, with her entourage. Flagella. Annabel. Pip. Godolphin, I think—with the lazy eye? You must know *her* at least. Oh for goodness' sake. Anyway, all the while, Liberty would be scouting, searching, casting around for someone awkward, or spotty, or overweight. Someone weak, you see. Like you. And when she found her target, she would walk right up to her—tower over her, because she was very tall in those days—and say: "You shouldn't be eating that. You're disgusting enough as it is. I'm just looking out for you, because I *care*." And then she'd take the horrible English food off the poor wretch's tray and throw it on the floor.'

'I . . . I didn't know'

'She doesn't like to publicise it. It does not quite fit her personal brand.' He stared down at the pavement, with its patches of blackened gum, as if trying to work out whether to proceed. 'I suppose,' he said, 'you can guess who her *favourite* victim was.'

'How would I know? I wasn't at that school. I don't know anyone who went to that school, or your school, or any of these schools which . . .'

'You do, Edward.'

'Who?'

Youssef drew to a halt. He gave Edward a sad, knowing smile, that seemed designed to convey just how impossibly naïve he was about the ways of the world. 'Angelica, of course,' he said.

Edward scarcely noticed they'd arrived at the venue. The city hall where the event was to be held looked unremarkable from the outside, distinguished only by a bouncer whom Edward vaguely recognised from Favela, neatly repackaged in a cheap suit and tie, who ushered them in after a wave of Youssef's card. Inside was a long folding table, banked with labels that you could peel off the surface and stick on to your lapel, manned by a brisk, rangy girl in a sari. Edward scanned the first column of stickers: *Acehnese, Afrikaner, Akan, Albanian, Amhara, Apache, Arab . . .*

'So basically,' said the girl in the sari, 'I give you a wristband, and then, well . . .' She gestured down at the table, '. . . you take as many as you like.'

. . . *Guaraní, Gujarati, Han Chinese, Hausa, Hawaiian . . .*

'It's just so we know where you're from, you see,' she added, gesturing to the banner above her head, printed with the words MIXED HERITAGE SOCIETY, and a strange, two-dimensional picture of a woman whose skin had been painted a diplomatic blue. 'Who you're representing. So we can place you. It's a conversation starter.'

'Marvellous,' said Youssef. He had prised away the pea-green *Berber* sticker with his fingernails, and was now searching for another line of ancestry to fabricate. He appeared for a moment slightly tempted by *Belarusian.*

'Yes, it is marvellous actually,' said the girl, her hands tending automatically to the next attendee in the queue. She kept looking back at Edward, with what seemed just a shade of suspicion. 'Everyone's guessing about us the whole time, aren't they? Where's *she* from? What is *he*? Well, now they know.'

Youssef, however, seemed not to be listening to her, his entire focus poured into the bank of stickers. He was enjoying himself. *Berber* had been joined by a smattering of other African ethnicities (*Balanta, Dogon*) that Edward at least would never have the temerity to question—but also, improbably, *Samoan*, and, in a final moment of daring as he turned to face Edward, *Cherokee.* 'How are you getting on?' he asked.

Edward shook his head. He started well—*English* was conveniently close to *Egyptian*—but soon faltered. What else *was* he? He looked in vain among the 'Z's, there was no *Zanzibari* sticker. By now, several other groups had appeared behind them; all of them, it seemed, were tipped over into a state of childlike excitement by the stickers, thrilled to have their ethnicities appear on the list in front of them. '*There* I am,' buzzed a girl over to his left, prising off her sticker, and pasting it proudly to her collarbone. All Edward could think of, was the guidebook still gathering dust on the shelf in his cold Annexe room: *Sumerians, Assyrians, Egyptians, Phoenicians, Indians, Chinese, Malays, Persians, Portuguese, Arabs, Dutch* . . .

'Here, Edward. I have the perfect one for you.'

Youssef peeled off the sticker—a drab, greyish mauve—and pressed it into Edward's lapel, finishing it off with a couple of pats that almost knocked him off balance.

Edward glanced down. It read, simply: *Other.*

'I can't just . . .'

'Of course you can. Now come with me and behold the wide-eyed houris of Paradise.'

And with that, they were inside, winding their way towards the bandstand under the makeshift *Mix it Up!* banner, Youssef already on the trail of a shapely postgraduate whose black lace gown was adorned with a heady mixture of *Uzbek, Filipino,* and, most tantalisingly of all, *French.* As soon as Youssef crossed the threshold, his face lit up. Over the course of the next hour, Edward was bundled off to meet, in sequence, Fatima, who was Iranian-Irish and whose branch of Islam was complicatedly different from Youssef's and discussed at some length; Precious, who was Nigerian-Swiss and whose gluteal muscles, Youssef whispered, were said to resemble prize marrows; and Thomas, whom Youssef seemed in a hurry to get rid of, and whose only distinction seemed to be that that he was the only other attendee who was as pasty and awkward as Edward.

He almost didn't feel it when Youssef tugged at his sleeve: 'Looks like there's someone who wants to meet you.' He was already fixing his clothing and waving in his next visitor—large and sturdy, with inquisitive eyes and curtains of grey-flecked beard. 'Oh, and Edward,' he added quietly. 'Act Muslim.'

'What does that mean? What would that involve?'

'Piety. Sincerity. Grace.'

'But I thought . . .'

'Not *now*.' He plastered his features into a smile. 'Look who it is,' he drawled. 'This is Edward, by the way.'

'A pleasure, Edward.' Edward felt the visitor's judgement wandering across his face, as he shook his hand. 'I have heard plenty about you.'

'You have?'

'Of course I have. I am great friends with Saïd Abdelmassih. He speaks very highly of you.'

'Oh, right. Yes. Wait, he does?' Edward glanced at Youssef.

'He does indeed. My name is Iqbal, by the way.' The visitor drew himself up. 'I am the President of the University Islamic Association. I am studying for my doctorate in Islamic studies—the exegetical works of Ibn Tamiyya, you might be interested to know—though I am a lawyer by training.'

Youssef let out a faint groan.

'What was that, Youssef?'

'No, nothing. Nothing at all.'

'Are you unwell?'

'I was just enjoying your oratory. It was very moving.'

'Youssef has always been slightly put off by those with credentials to their names.' Iqbal's eyes remained fixed on Edward. 'Now Saïd,' he continued, 'bears no such prejudice. He really is a fine young man—I suggest you cultivate your acquaintance with him Edward. Knows exactly where he stands, and always conducts himself with such grace.'

Youssef rolled his eyes. 'Iqbal is a fellow Egyptian, Edward. We have known each other for many years, unfortunately. Though you're not a fan of Sufis, are you Iqbal?'

'Youssef believed that, because I am a student of the *Salaf*, I am therefore unreasonable and literal minded.'

'. . . or Berbers for that matter.'

'This, Edward, is simply not true.'

'It *is*.' Youssef put his hand to his mouth in a mock aside. 'He prefers his Arab brothers, you see.'

'All men are my brothers.'

'Do you see what I have to deal with, Edward? This is why we are going to have to become Africans . . .'

Iqbal raised an eyebrow. 'I was *told* . . .' he says slowly, 'that you'd grown up a little, Youssef. Saïd was very complimentary about you too.'

'Oh, how lucky I am. Long have I craved ratification from a real, genuine, certified, Palestinian.'

'I see now,' continued Iqbal, straightening up so that Youssef suddenly seemed very short before him, ungainly, 'that Saïd is perhaps not such a flawless judge of character as I thought.' He turned to Edward: 'You know Youssef used to be very diligent in his way. Before that public school of his debauched him.' He shook his head, more in apology than anything else. 'He would sit up all night reading the Sufi poets. Yes, you did Youssef, so there is no point shaking your head like that. He was an excellent student, Edward. Rumi, Hafiz, Faruddin Attar. *The Conference of the Birds*, this was his favourite. The illustrated version, of course, but admirable, nevertheless.'

Youssef had his arms crossed. 'I don't know what you're talking about.'

'He wanted to be a poet, before that school convinced him that Economics and Management was a far finer prospect.' He turned back to Youssef. 'Why don't you leave us alone,' he said. 'Chase after young women. This seems to be all you're interested in.'

Youssef held his gaze for several seconds, as if about to respond; then, gradually, seemed to wilt in the glare of Iqbal's disappointment, as though his head had all of a sudden grown very heavy.

The moment he was gone, Iqbal appeared satisfied. 'Now

tell me, Edward,' he said, 'about your family. About your heritage. Tell me everything. I've always found that what you are and where you come from are essentially the same question.'

Edward tried his best. He began, in fact, with remarkable fluency. He spoke first of his grandfather, of Zanzibar; he sprinkled in a few vague references to Islam and 'spirituality' of the kind that always impressed Angelica. When the time came to pronounce the name 'al-Zahir,' he made one of the strange, baroque noises with his throat that he had heard Youssef attempt while riffing on his favourite themes, like the promises of the *Surah ar-Rahman* and 'Islamic finance' and the assorted bra sizes of the maidens Allah had promised to the pious ('And you know what Bukhari said of them of course? *The marrow of the bones of their legs will be seen through the bones and the flesh.* Hot stuff!'). As he spoke, he grew more and more confident: it didn't sound so bad, this improvisation; perhaps it was the proximity with Youssef that had changed things, or the term spent with Angelica, but for the first time he felt almost comfortable with the material, like the whole mass of tradition and law and catechism was something he could simply slip on, like something as light and loose as Iqbal's robes.

When he looked up, however, Iqbal was unimpressed. 'I don't understand,' he said. 'You say your grandfather was a Muslim. Fine. Good. *Alhamdullilah*. But are *you*?'

'What do you mean?'

'A Muslim.'

'I mean my family are Muslims.'

'You seem to have misunderstood the question.'

'No, no . . . I get what you mean. I just think it's complicated.'

'Most Muslims do not think it's particularly complicated.'

'Well I do, I guess.'

'Forgive me, Edward, but this is an extremely strange response, and is quite at odds with what Saïd and Youssef, and *you* had led me to believe.'

Edward took a deep breath. 'Look,' he said, 'I didn't actually grow up as a Muslim, Iqbal. I'm sorry if I made it seem like I did, just now. This is quite new to me. But I also have a lot of respect for . . .'

'Oh good heavens, please do not give me this "I have a lot of respect for it" nonsense. Why are white people always saying these ridiculous things? "I have a lot of respect for your culture." "I have a lot of respect for your beliefs." What does this even mean?'

'I was just trying to tell you what *kind* of Muslim I am. Isn't that what you wanted to know?'

'I see. Now, I ask you again—no, don't look for Youssef, he's gone—I ask you again what kind of Muslim *are* you, Edward? Start with the family, if you must. We shall proceed genealogically if it helps. From the roots upward.'

'I . . .' Edward's throat felt dry. 'I don't know how to answer that.'

'You don't know? But you *must* know. You must know where you're from, Edward, in a place like this.' Iqbal motioned round the room: at the technicolor spangles, the sputtering band. 'Let us begin with something basic,' he continued. 'The grandfather. He was a Muslim, Youssef tells me. Was he a Sunni Muslim or a Shia Muslim?'

'I . . .' He could feel the anxiety rising. 'I don't know.'

'How can you not *know*? You *have* to know. Do you think that your grandfather, God rest his soul, thought it was acceptable *not to know* these things? Do you think your illustrious family, in Zanzibar, under the Sultanate, said things like "I don't really know very much about my faith, but I have a lot of respect for it?" Come on Edward. Be serious. If you wish to coast through this institution on Muslim goodwill then you at least ought to have *something* to offer a friendly enquirer like me. Were they Sufis, perhaps? Mystics, like Youssef?'

'No. At least . . .'

'Right. At last. This is something. And you must know the juridical school, too. The *madhab*. For how can a family be known except by the way it orders its affairs? Hanafi? Hanbali, like the Saudis?' Iqbal took a step forward, white hem swishing aggressively over the floor. 'Or Shafi'i? Maliki? Jafari? Were they *Zahiri*?'

Edward wiped a hand over his brow. 'Does it really matter?'

'Does it *matter*?' Iqbal laughed, very loud. 'Of course it *matters*. Everywhere in the world, Edward, it matters what you are and who you are. Everywhere except here, that is. Here we all get along—one big happy family, shoulder to shoulder. One big rainbow.' He drew himself as tall as he could muster, making little, didactic circles with his knuckle and his thumb. 'But this is an anomaly, Edward. Only here in Oxford. Only here and in Paradise.'

Edward glanced round once more.

'I said don't look to Youssef.'

'I'm not looking to Youssef. I'm just looking around and thinking that what you're asking seems pretty against the spirit of this . . . whatever this is. And there are plenty of places where people coexist, quite happily. Take Zanzibar, for instance— Sumerians, Assyrians, Egyptians, Phoenicians . . .'

'Ah, so you have been?'

'Excuse me?'

'Have you *been* there, Edward?'

'To Zanzibar?'

'Or even to Africa. To any Muslim country?'

'My family never . . .'

'Because if you had, you'd know that for those who live there, knowing who and what you are isn't just a choice. But you don't, do you?'

'I . . .'

'Pure ignorance.' Iqbal shook his head, defeated for a moment, before another wave of indignation overcame him: 'An

Arab? One of the Omanis? Or an Indian perhaps—a Khoja? I mean, look at you . . . you are white as clay. Your family could be *Portuguese* for all I can tell.'

There was no use remonstrating. Edward stared down into his cup. The ice had nearly melted and sat in little glassy beads at the base.

'You know what I think?' continued Iqbal. 'You are no different from any other of the other undergraduates who come to Islamic Society because they once went to the Alhambra and decided they were Muslims. You are *not*—this is abundantly clear to me—interested in Islam. *Difference itself*—this what you are chasing. A taste of the exotic. A pinch of spice.' Iqbal's face was very red now, the skin taut. 'Is that all we are to you?' he said, turning on his heels, but not without calling back over his shoulder on more, incredulous time. 'A product? A commodity? Something you can sell to the world when you want it to give you something?'

Youssef was conciliatory as he and Edward traipsed back down the high street towards College, dodging the broken glass the various itinerant sports teams had left in their wakes: he oughtn't to worry about Iqbal, he reckoned; that was just him, one of those grand old Arabs who thinks he's the Cosmic Qutb just because he went to a few Stop The War protests as a teenager and his uncle once sold a car to a Saudi prince. 'A hypocrite, Edward. A liar, like all Arabs. Nothing to worry about.'

'Can I ask you a question, Youssef?'

Youssef inclined his head distractedly. 'Always, Edward. Youssef Chamakh is an open book.'

'What's *The Conference of the Birds*?'

'Oh . . .' Youssef turned, his smile creeping down a fraction. 'This is nothing.'

'Iqbal said it was your favourite when you were young.'

'It's a poem, Edward.'

'I didn't know you read poetry.'

'I don't. Poetry is for people who have lots of time and no chest hair.'

'What's it about?'

'Look at this woman's thighs. Shot-put, would be my guess.'

'I want to hear about the poem, Youssef.'

Youssef stared at him. 'You really want to know?'

'I really do.'

Youssef frowned. 'One day,' he said, 'all the birds of the earth gather together. Like you, they are listless and timid, and they desire rule by a powerful sovereign. They decide to look for this bird called the Simurgh.'

'The what? Say it again.'

'The Simurgh. It's Persian for "You should learn proper languages rather than studying English like some immigrant." Now, like me, the Simurgh is possessed of a powerful natural authority that makes all the other birds go out in search of him. Every bird. The hoopoe. The parrot. The peacock. The *duck*—a truly elite bird. Proper Muslim avian stock, Edward—not like these useless little homosexual pigeons you have in this country. Anyway, eventually they reach the mountain where the Simurgh is meant to live. Except when they get there, they perceive that *they* are the Simurgh, and that the Simurgh is each one of them and all of them, et cetera, et cetera, profundity, wisdom, *Allahu Akbar,* the end.'

'How come you never told me about this before?'

Youssef shrugged. 'I didn't want you to dribble it out at one of Liberty's poetry readings.'

Edward did not push further. Youssef was buoyant again, and it seemed a shame to upset his mood—the way he bounded up to Abdul's Kebab's, Drink's and Food's the moment they rounded the final corner before College and gazed at the newly unwrapped doner rotating like a dervish above the counter, beaming all the while. Abdul, without his helpers today, saw him, trotted down the steps, subjected Youssef to an elaborate handshake that must have lasted ten or fifteen seconds.

'Anything today my brother?' said Abdul.

'Not today.'

'Being good, are we?'

Youssef grinned. 'Never.'

Edward left them to it. The pair of them were laughing now, real laughter, hands on their bellies. What were they even laughing about? He watched as Abdul unhooked his apron and slung it casually over his shoulder. Youssef, too, had changed: his voice seemed to reach a new, deeper register as Edward crept away.

The night porter was already installed in the lodge. He was hunched over, concentrating intently on a little plastic model he was gluing together—a figurine that looked looked vaguely Napoleonic to Edward. He spoke without looking up:

'Edward, wasn't it?'

Edward stopped in the archway. 'Sorry?'

'I recognise you. You're Edward, aren't you?'

'Oh. Yes, I am.'

The night porter began to laugh. 'No need to look so guilty— you've not got something to be guilty about, have you?'

'No.'

'Well then, you have nothing to worry about.' He shrugged. 'Nah, I just recognised you from all the time you spent clinging on to Angie Mountbatten-Jones last term. Not that I blame you.' His eyes narrowed slightly.

'Oh.'

'I got asked about you. By the grant-awarding committee. Don't worry, it's standard procedure.' He nodded to himself. 'Thing is, Ed, it's the porters who have the best idea what everyone's *really* like in this place. You can't hide from a porter, can you? We know who the troublemakers are.' He grinned. 'No need to make that face, though. You're not a troublemaker, I know that. Berlin, wasn't it?'

'Yeah.'

The night porter's eyes misted over slightly. 'Marvellous city, Berlin. Very historical.'

'Right.'

'Some really fascinating battles. And the Stasi Museum, of course. Wonderful stuff.'

'Right.'

'Anyway, I'll be sure to approve your application. You're *not* a troublemaker, are you?'

'No.'

'Good.' A cackle.

Edward began to turn.

'Oh and Edward?'

'Mm?'

'Don't make me regret it.'

This, the night porter seemed to find extremely funny. He was still chortling as Edward crossed the dark front quad, to the bench at the chapel where Angelica had ambushed him last term. He had planned on waiting for Youssef nearer the lodge—but something about the night porter's demeanour made him want to get away: he could still see the stone archway from here, and would know when Youssef entered.

It didn't take long. Youssef seemed even more cheerful as he swept in, as though the conversation with Abdul had diffused through his whole being, into his gait, as he ducked through the doorway, rapping the transom jauntily with his knuckles.

'Excuse me young man. Excuse me? Stop right there.'

If Youssef had heard it, he didn't let on.

'Stop right there. What do you think you're doing?' The night porter was on his feet now. Youssef was swaying slightly. How much had he drunk this evening, Edward wondered?

The night porter creaked himself out of his chair and ambled over to Youssef. His anorak was unbuttoned, and his fists sank into the girdle of flesh above his hips. 'What do you think you're doing young man?'

'Me?'

'Yes, you. Course I'm talking to you. Who else would I be talking to?'

Youssef rolled his eyes. 'Of course. Excellent.' He swore under his breath in Arabic. 'Now tell me, are we really going to have this *again*? Aren't you lot simply meant to carry up our suitcases and leave it at that?' He couldn't have seen Edward yet, and made his way across the lodge petulantly, sneer turned up to the porchlight. 'What do *you* think I think I'm doing? Coming to rob you? Blow you up? Carry off half the netball squad for my harem?'

'I'm going to need to see some identification.'

'Of course you are.' Youssef began to pat his pockets. 'And tell me, good Sir, will a student card do? Or do you need a fingerprint? A strand of hair? Will you be wanting a blood sample this evening?'

The night porter looked unimpressed. Without taking his eyes off Youssef, he began to unfasten the anorak's cuffs, jerking them down over his thick wrists. For a moment, Edward considered going over—but it would hardly help the situation, he reasoned, and could only hurt his own prospects, if Youssef was right and the night porter really did have sovereign power over the travel grants. In any case, Youssef could handle himself. He was patting harder now; at a distance the frantic movements seemed like a kind of dance. His face had fallen. He ran one hand through his beard, then pulled open his jacket and inserted his whole hand, extracting receipts, banknotes, credit cards—faster now, not caring where they fell. He shook his head, exasperated.

'Listen, I thought . . .' For the first time, Edward noted a hint of panic in his voice.

The night porter raised a triumphant finger in the direction of the door. 'No card, no entry.'

Youssef snorted. 'Oh for goodness' sake, you know who I am.'

'No need for that kind of language.'

'For *what* kind of language?'

'Please don't make a scene, Sir.' The night porter's face remained impassive; his mouth gave away small tic of pleasure.

'What, you expect me to sleep out in the cold?' Youssef's voice echoed off the stone. 'I *live* here. I come in every day. Can't you just . . . ?' He had taken out his phone, jamming his fingers into the buttons, but the screen wouldn't illuminate.

And suddenly—without Edward quite understanding why, or how, or who started it—both of them were shouting. The night porter's hand clasped Youssef at the lapel; Youssef tried to swat it off, and stumbled. 'What are you . . . ?' Youssef was looking around; he let out a yelp of discomfort, followed by a strange, almost incredulous laugh. 'You can't just . . . Is anyone seeing . . . ? Hello? Anyone? Edward?'

At the sound of his name, Edward started forward in the direction of the lodge. He began skirting the quad on the designated path, then corrected himself and cut straight over the grass. 'Youssef? What are you . . . ?' He felt the words swallowed by the wind as soon as they left his lips, and tried again, louder: '*Youssef*? Wait, I can explain . . .' Neither had noticed. Youssef was still struggling, the night porter had the better of him now; he was dragging Youssef back across the floor of the lodge, towards the door, all the while his eyes shining with pleasure.

'Oi!'

At this new voice, the night porter relaxed his grasp. It was enough. Youssef wriggled free, and began to dust himself down.

'Oi. That's right, you.'

Striding through the high oak doorway, lambs' blood spattered on his apron, was Abdul. Edward was nearly at the lodge now, and Abdul seemed larger than ever, no longer hemmed in by the aluminium counter and the great mangers of plastic-covered food. His face was a few inches from night porter's, reddish, flushed with some new emotion, deeply felt, quite different from the polite, transactional smiles he usually dispensed. With his forefinger, he stabbed the night porter once, twice, in his flabby chest.

'You leave the poor boy alone,' said Abdul.

The porter was fixing his anorak, embarrassed. 'What are you doing here? You have no right . . .'

'Now. Leave him.'

'Listen, this is an internal College issue, and I'd be grateful if you didn't butt in.'

'I would be grateful if you didn't assault my friends.'

'Your *friends*? Don't you work in that van?'

Abdul was still tense. 'Should be ashamed of yourself . . .' For a moment, it looked to Edward as if he was going to throw a punch: he loomed up over the night porter, shoulders forward, hands in fists at his sides. Then he exhaled. 'Just let him go,' he said. 'Let him go.'

And the night porter did. He lowered his head, zipped his anorak meekly to the chin. He opened his mouth to deliver a parting shot to Youssef, then closed it again.

Edward had reached the lodge. 'Youssef,' he said, 'are you . . . ?'

But Youssef strode past, eyes fixed on the paving slabs ahead of him, the hand over his brow not quite masking the brilliance of his tears.

CHAPTER 13

F*or months, we at* Gauche *have regarded our colleagues over at* Samizdat *not as competition, but as fellow travellers, comrades, even friends. Many of you will have attended the free events our respective editorial teams have jointly staged: last term's multiracial ice-skating initiative, for instance, or the now famous 'Women with a Y' lecture series. It is with a heavy heart, then, that the* Gauche *editorial team must now disavow this longstanding association. Though mild forms of revisionism are of course to be tolerated . . .*

'Exciting, isn't it?' said Conrad from the depths of the Common Room's plushest armchair, gathering himself forward to peer over Edward's Easter edition of *Gauche,* published last Monday, which was, as Liberty's 'Note from the Editor' gleefully reminded everyone, the final Monday of term before Liberty and her masthead jetted off to their newest round of charitable engagements. 'I *do* love a good old-fashioned schism.' Conrad fished up the remains of a broken pool-cue and began to trace vague, lazy shapes in the air. 'Besides, Edward, it was about time someone gave them a shot in the arm. There's only so much a reader can take. Only so many line drawings of genitals. Only so many poems about black women's hair . . . Are you done? May I have it?'

'I'm still reading. There's a pile just over there.'

'This is old news, Edward. Hand it over.'

'Not to me.'

'Well, everything's new to you, because you are obtuse.'

Edward flicked over another page of Liberty's editorial. 'You think they'll take her side? They'll believe her?'

'Do I think who'll believe her?'

'College. Everyone.'

Conrad spoke without looking up: 'That hardly matters, does it?'

'I think whether people believe Liberty matters a lot.'

'No, no.' Conrad let the magazine fall shut on his knee. 'What *matters*,' he said, 'is what people *do*. Listen, Edward. You think all those little goblins who trot around after Liberty *believe* her?' he chuckled to himself. 'You think Youssef *really* believes that little black rock will wipe his soul clean? You think your Israeli girl-friend really believes that if she just gets a goat to bugger off into the desert that she's absolved from whatever it is her people are supposed to have done wrong? Murdering children and so forth?'

'Oh, she doesn't . . .'

'Of course not, Edward. But it works all the same.' He shook his head wisely. 'Beliefs can exist without believers. This whole university relies on it.'

'I think people do believe some of the things they say. Even here.'

Conrad rolled his eyes. 'This is because you went to a state school and you don't understand people and you probably have foetal alcohol syndrome or something.'

'I think Angelica believes the things she says.'

'I see. Have you spoken to her yet?'

'What?'

'Spoken to her Edward. It would be a good idea, before jetti-soning her completely in favour of your new Semitic squeeze—out with the old, in with the Jew and all that—to *talk to her*. Not least because she's rather fond of revenge, is dear old Angelica, especially on ex-boyfriends.'

'I'm just not sure she even wants to hear from me. I don't know. I have no idea with her.'

'And have you spoken to Youssef?'

'What?'

'Youssef. I trust you remember him. There have been rumours that he was appallingly victimised by that strange little man who lives in the lodge. And I would have thought that you, as his best friend, might have met him at some point to commiserate, pray, sacrifice a small sheep, or whatever it is you lot do when left alone.'

'I'm not his best friend, Conrad.'

'Of course you are. Why do you think he keeps inviting you along to all these little events? I suspect it's not because he fancies you.'

'Aren't *you* his best friend?'

'What? No. Ridiculous. Youssef and I were cordial enough in school and have ended up in the same dreadful chav-filled College. But you, dear Edward, are the chosen one. You are his protégé. Anyway, you're avoiding the question. Did you speak to him?'

'Yeah, I spoke to him.'

'Because he seemed rather irritated with you last time I saw him. And not just on account of the usual things like your dress sense and inability to close your mouth like normal people. Yes, close it, that's better.'

'I just said I spoke to him.'

'And did it go well? Did it end in a nice, teary rapprochement with lots of gruff, embarrassed heterosexual hugging?'

'He was very . . . cold. He didn't even talk about Islam.'

'Interesting. Very interesting.' Conrad stroked his long, aristocratic chin. 'Did he talk about various devotional practices you perhaps don't associate with Islam on account of their being too obscure? Camels? Raisins? Did he talk about the Ottoman Empire, perhaps?'

'No. He just nodded politely and thanked me for showing up.'

'Good Lord. It's worse than I thought. He must be incredibly angry at you.'

'I don't think he's *angry*. Yes, I was slow to intervene. But I was a long way away, and it was dark, and Abdul was there first.'

'Did you apologise?'

'I didn't need to apologise.'

'Sometimes you need to apologise for things you didn't do, Edward. This is England, after all.'

'Can we drop this?'

'We can indeed, Edward. I shall be going soon, anyway because I am tired and I have to pack for Barbados.' He smiled sweetly. 'But I'd advise you not to keep rebuffing *everyone* when they show an interest in you. Because from where I'm standing, you don't have an awful lot of people left.'

As Conrad snapped together his leather briefcase and smoothed his expensive clothing, he dispensed what would be, he promised, his last jewel of advice before the end of term. Edward, he said, would have to fend for himself. He really ought to man up, have that conciliatory word with Angelica, then judiciously disappear: accept his travel grant with fawning good grace, grovel at length to the College Dean, and then book a plane ticket—to somewhere actually good like Paris or Florence if he had any sense about him (the Uffizi wouldn't be *too* heaving if he sorted himself out in the next few days)—and to Berlin if he didn't, and he *really* thought that statues of Karl Marx and people taking heroin and cheap Polish fireworks and ugly Soviet buildings marred with graffiti and ugly German people marred with tattoos constituted *culture*, and he *really* believed his raw masculine energy was so intoxicating that that Rachel girl might actually be waiting for him when he stepped off the plane.

Edward took his advice, and set off for Angelica's ivy-covered building that afternoon. As he drew up to her staircase, he began to feel short of breath. The sun had gone in, and the sky was white and featureless above the turrets. When Angelica opened the door to him, he was surprised at how polite and nonchalant she seemed. The initial pleasantries were scrupulously well executed: he nodded cordially and asked 'May I come in?'; she made courteous attempts at conversation, offered him a seat on the bed, even made an insincere suggestion of a cup of tea, which he declined. Everything she said was suffused with a sense of quiet anticipation. After a couple of minutes, she grew quiet. Slowly, deliberately, she walked over to her chest of drawers pulled out her a hairband—scarlet, with an African-looking pattern—and wordlessly began to truss her hair back behind her neck, very tight. She turned. The smile had disappeared from her lips.

'How dare you,' she said slowly.

'Angelica . . .'

'How *dare* you.'

'Angelica, let's just . . .'

'How *dare* you!'

'Okay, I don't see what I've . . .'

'You don't *see*? You don't *see*? You disappear off the face of the earth over Christmas. You *know* I'm having a miserable time. But do you message? Do you contact me at all?'

'If you'd wanted to see me you could have invited me to the party.'

'Oh the *party*, the *party*. Is that what this is about? Honestly Edward there were maybe five people there—my oldest and closest friends, Izzy K, Francine Hogmanay-Pung, Sarah Patel.'

'Oh, good, so even the blood stew girl was there. Great.'

'I didn't invite you because I thought you would *hate* it. Because you always, always hate things that I bring you to. Always! You always sit there and roll your eyes and make fun of my friends—yes, my *friends* Edward, whom I've known for years and can't just abandon because you don't approve of them. And yes, a few other people turned up later, but it wasn't *my* fault.'

'Can you see why it might not be particularly pleasant not to be invited?'

'Can you see why it might not be particularly pleasant to turn up in Oxford—after seven weeks of absolute radio silence I might add . . .'

'I was waiting for you to message me.'

'Oh, right. I see. So I have to do *everything*, it seems. Good to know. God, you're so *passive,* aren't you?'

'I'm not passive. I just didn't want to . . .'

'You didn't want to what? Talk to me? Ask me if I was okay? You weren't passive when it came to *her,* were you. How do you think that feels? To come back to Oxford only to find you've replaced me? With that absolute, total, unbridled, irredeemable, disrespectful, foreign *bitch* whom you know I cannot stand? Can you see why *that* might be unpleasant?'

'Angelica, I didn't . . .'

'Have you kissed her yet?'

'Angelica, please.'

'Have you fucked her yet?'

'I'm not going to get drawn into this.'

'You're already drawn into this. That's what happens when you have a relationship with someone, Edward. I can't believe I need to explain this. You get *drawn into things.* No, don't shake your head.'

'I don't think it's fair for you to act like this is only my fault. Like I ditched you unceremoniously without exactly the same thing happening the other way.'

'What are you talking about?'

'*Saïd*, Angelica. How long was it, in the end? Three days? Four?'

'That was after I had come back and found that my boyfriend had "ditched" me. I was *humiliated.*'

'You've had your eye on him since last term.'

'What? He wasn't even *here* last term, Edward.'

'I heard you and Liberty going on and on about him at the poetry reading. I was right there. How do you think that made me feel?'

'That was *Liberty*, not me. Did you hear what I said in response to her? Did you? Or were you too busy making up proverbs?'

'No, but . . .'

'I said that I didn't want to be with Saïd. In fact, Liberty and I actually had something of a fight, the following day. We did. I said I didn't appreciate her interfering in every aspect of my love life, that I was a big girl and quite capable of deciding whom I wanted to go out with without her intervention. She called me a counter-revolutionary. She called me a Zionist. It was very upsetting.'

'I'm sorry. I didn't know.'

'No, you didn't. You saw me as essentially the same as her, with absolutely no capacity to form thoughts or opinions of my own. But that's a description of *you,* as it happens.'

'Look, I'm sorry. But fighting isn't going to help anything.'

'Gosh, how big of you.' Angelica shook her head in disbelief. 'Maybe I want to fight, Edward. I certainly have a lot to say to you. For instance: wasn't it enough to run away for the vacation? Couldn't you have pulled yourself together when you got here? Did you *have* to go after her too? You had everything you wanted, Edward. Liberty approved of you. She helped you change your course; she gave you money.' She shook her head despairingly. 'Or was it Saïd? Maybe that was it. You were clearly obsessed with him *long* before I ever even spoke to him, that's clear now. You couldn't *bear* the thought that there was someone in College who was more glamorous and fashionable than you, could you?'

'You don't understand, Angelica. Honestly, you're acting like this was all planned out, like everything that happens is some huge conspiracy that directly relates to you, but . . .'

'No of course. No one understands you, do they? Well guess what, Edward—I *refuse* to understand.'

'I didn't mean . . .'

'You didn't *mean*? You didn't mean what? That's just it. You never *mean* anything at all.' Angelica was standing over him now. 'You just sit there, all quiet and neutral, and we're all meant to assume that you're the better for it—that . . . that you're the one who sees the world as it really is. I've seen boys do this before—Conrad does it. Falconbridge did it. I suppose it makes you feel so superior.'

'I don't think that's fair, Angelica.'

She drew herself up triumphantly. 'But you'll never get close to people, Edward. Not like that. Not to me, not to anyone.' She was breathing very heavily now, gathering her strength before the next swell of anger reeled her back round. She was scarcely even talking to him any more: she had lifted her gaze to the ceiling, with a desperate, imploring look crumpling her brow. 'Anyway, Edward, you'll be pleased to know you've won, by all accounts.'

'What?'

'You've won, Edward. I'm nothing. Not only have I been humiliated by you, but I've been defeated in the project that matters most to me. Doesn't that give you a little glow of satisfaction when you think about it?'

'No, of course it doesn't. What are you even talking about?'

'*Samizdat* was my one thing, Edward. It was mine . . .'

Tentatively, Edward pushed himself up from the bed.

'Stay there. Don't come *near* me.'

'Okay. Okay.' There was a silence. 'Angelica,' he said gently, holding his hands up as pacifyingly as he could manage. 'Don't you think this is a little bit out of proportion? The *Gauche* thing, I mean. Forget about the other things for a second.'

'Out of *proportion*?'

'So what if they printed one bad article about you? I mean, it's *Gauche*—they do it for everyone.'

'Oh, they do, do they? Is this something you've *noticed*?'

'In your next issue, you can . . .'

'Just stop, Edward. Don't pretend. Just this once. Don't pretend.' She had begun to wring her hands, and suddenly Edward noticed how small they looked, how pale. 'It's over,' she said quietly. 'They stopped it. They stopped the whole thing.'

The news came out eventually. The coup had been carried out yesterday, and was now universally recognised, whispered around College from ear to prurient ear. It was remarkable that Edward *hadn't* heard, in fact—a testament, said Angelica, to his utter obliviousness when it came to the truly important things in life. Liberty, she continued between ragged breaths, had made a move to take over *Samizdat*. The immediate catalyst was Angelica's absence: 'While our thoughts and prayers are with poor Ange,' Liberty had declaimed to the Committee, 'such a vibrant and dynamic publication as *Samizdat* cannot—*must* not—tolerate a government in exile.' Angelica just shook her head, as though wearied by the effort of memory. Liberty had already studied the rules, of course, the arcana that governed impeachment, dismissal, transfer of power that someone had written down on a back of a napkin thirty or forty years ago and not thought about since. The handover hearing was to take place in the Business School. Diversitas would mediate, for a small fee.

Defeatedly, Angelica settled in one of the armchairs at the far end of her room. She looked very fragile there, contorted awkwardly against the seatback, the space around her unusually untidy. He walked over and crouched before the armchair. Angelica's head was pressed into her hands now, her hair falling through her fingers. 'It's okay,' he said softly. 'Hey. Look at me. It's all right.'

'It's not all right.'

'Liberty will have forgotten soon enough, and then . . .'

'Don't you see, Edward?' She looked up pleadingly. 'This is a *punishment*. It's a punishment for what *you* did.'

'I didn't do anything, Angelica.'

'That's not what she said. She told me the pair of you had a nice long chat in the Chamber.'

'She picked the fight.'

'You picked the fight. You abandoned literally her best friend for literally her worst enemy and you expected her not to say anything. She was drunk. She was upset by Dyer. You were oversensitive, and you picked a fight.' She took a deep breath, then another. On the third breath, she made an odd, ragged movement with her shoulders. Edward took a tentative step forward, and only now he was close to her did he realise—and the thought of it was something so unexpected, so at odds with the image she had cultivated that for several seconds he found himself completely at a loss for what to say—that Angelica Mountbatten-Jones was about to cry.

'I know you think you're somehow above it all,' she sobbed. 'That you're somehow enlightened—that you see past the way we all style ourselves. But your behaviour . . . it never changes. Never. All Zahir, no Batin. Just like Youssef said . . .' She wiped her eyes with the back of her wrist. 'Not that you've treated him particularly well, either. No, it appears to be the case that if you want dear, sweet, considerate Edward to treat you like a human being, it's not enough simply to be his best friend, or his lover. There is a list of special requirements. You need to have big brown doe eyes and stupid curly hair. You need to read Shakespeare. You need to be *Jewish*, apparently.'

'Right. Well I'm afraid that's not fair at all. I saw Youssef. I spoke to him.'

'For all of five minutes, by the sound of it.'

'Who told you that? Youssef?'

'He's not *just* a cartoon character you know. He has feelings.'

'You weren't there, Angelica. Honestly, I've never seen him like that, even when he's been angry with me in the past. He was so quiet, and cold.'

'Of course he was *cold*, Edward. He had just been racially abused, in public. Do you have any idea how that might feel? You know what? I'm not even going to recommend any literature to you on this—although there is a literature, a sizeable one—because you'll just sneer at it. And you don't actually need it. He's your friend, allegedly. You should *know* how he feels.'

'I didn't . . .'

'What? What is it now? What are you saying?'

'I didn't . . .' Edward sighed. 'I didn't think it was my place,' he said meekly.

'Your place? Oh, but it *was* your place to storm up to Liberty and put her in a bad mood, was it? It was your place to assume that I wanted nothing to do with you and that you could start fawning over Rachel and that I wouldn't even care? *That* was your place?' He started forward, but she pulled away, talking once more up towards the ceiling: 'What did I do wrong? I did *everything*. Everything I was supposed to . . . That's all I ever do. I really tried with you, Edward. I did. I tried to learn about your family, about where you're from.' She sighed.

'You didn't try. You didn't even like me.'

'I *did* like you. Do you think I would have . . . ?' She tailed off. 'I liked you from the moment I first met you.'

'Oh, sure . . .'

'I liked the way you blushed. I did. It made me feel like you desired me, and that you were someone whom I could be perfect for. And I liked your eyes, and . . .'

'You were only interested in me because you found me exotic.'

'Is *that* what you think?'

'Isn't it the truth?'

'Are you sure you're not just interested in Rachel because you find *her* exotic?'

'What are you talking about?'

'I suppose it makes you feel very sophisticated, and enlightened, and progressive, and free of your origins. Maybe you're reinventing yourself, now you're at Oxford. You can, you know. It's not like anyone else here went to your school.'

'Honestly, Angelica, as I've said hundreds and hundreds of times, my "origins" don't come into it. And Rachel's Jewishness, that doesn't come into it either. Because I assume that's what you're talking about here—which is itself interesting given how much "being opposed to racism"—which literally everyone in Oxford is, by the way—seems to be the main feature of your personality.'

'Oh, good. Now you're offended. Just what I need. Edward in his tetchy, self-righteous incarnation. That really is *everyone's* favourite.'

'Why does everyone have such a problem with her being Jewish?'

'Why don't *you*? Really, Edward you are *so* obtuse sometimes. Surely it isn't news to you that Jews and Muslims do not always get along. No, wait—I'm not saying that Jews and Muslims can never be friends, or lovers, or close to each other. But I think that it often requires the Jewish person to hold their hands up and *acknowledge their complicity* in some way. And listen to me, Edward. I have known Rachel longer than you, and I'm clearly a better judge of character than you. And I can promise you that this is something Rachel has never, ever done.'

'Listen to *me*, Angelica. No, listen. I am not a Muslim, and I do not care about this. Okay? I have not been wronged. Look I'll say it again. I. Am. Not. A. Muslim. I know everyone thinks I am; I know I may have implied as much sometimes. But I'm not.'

'Your father was a Muslim, though.'

'What?'

'Your father.'

'I don't want to talk about him right now.'

'Of course you don't. You never do.'

'What are you talking about?'

'You expect me to believe you just don't think about him? Come *on*.'

'He really isn't relevant. Why do you always want to know about him, anyway? He wasn't nearly as exciting or exotic as you're hoping. He was a car salesman. He had a bad heart. That's it.'

'Did it ever occur to you, Edward, that all my questions were real? That I actually *was* interested—that Zanzibar was a way to him—to *you*—and not the other way round? I know you think that it's all a joke—stupid Angelica, hysterical Angelica—but did you ever stop and wonder if maybe it wasn't? At least to me?' She exhaled through her nose. 'You'd given up on me before we even started. That's the truth. It's not you who wasn't special enough. It was *me*.'

With that, she had finished. Effortfully, almost drowsily, she pushed herself up from the wall with one hand and trudged over to the door. Edward had the distinct impression that she was showing him out of her room, not just for the evening, or even two or three days that remained of the term, but for the rest of her life.

PART 3
TRINITY

CHAPTER 14

Edward was standing in just about the most beautiful apartment he had ever seen. He looked around in disbelief at the thick curtains, the high cornicing. He felt light, everything suffused with the same sense of unreality as the rest of his trip to Berlin; his legs ached pleasantly from walking through the park, and the drinks he had bought for himself and Rachel beside the Landwehr Canal under the pretext of thanking her for showing him around the city had begun to go to his head.

'Rachel. This place.' He shook his head in disbelief.

'I know.'

'These windows. These *ceilings*.'

I know,' said Rachel, as she stooped to turn on a lamp.

'Whose is it?'

'My aunt's.'

'Is she here?'

'It's just us.' She smiled, and reached behind her neck to let down her hair. 'This took so long, didn't it?'

'Honestly, I can't remember the last time I saw you, one on one, without there being some great controversy that we had to defuse.'

'Why didn't we manage, do you think?'

'Because here people seem to care about absolutely nothing. And in Oxford they seem to care about absolutely everything.'

'I wish you weren't flying back so soon.'

'Me too.'

Rachel smiled sadly. 'Shall we just stay here? We could stay, and have breakfast on the balcony every morning, and not go back. We could get jobs as English teachers.'

'You shouldn't joke about these things. I'll take them literally, and then you'll never get rid of me.'

'I wouldn't mind.'

'You wouldn't?'

She shook her head 'You have to go back though, Edward. It's your dream remember?'

He shrugged. 'I don't know. My horizons are much wider now. I'm cultured.'

Rachel chuckled, and slipped past him to a wood-panelled kitchenette that seemed far too small for the rest of the room. From the cupboard she took out a bottle of wine, and two glasses. 'Oh, are you now?

'Yes. I'm standing in a beautiful Berlin apartment with a beautiful continental girl, who's just poured me a glass of wine. I think that makes me cultured. Thank you, by the way.' She handed him glass, and there was a long silence. 'What?'

'You've never called me beautiful before.'

'I have.'

'No, you haven't. You've called Angelica beautiful. You've called the *snow* beautiful.'

'You're beautiful. Sorry. I thought that was a given.'

She had closed the distance now, and was standing right before him. She had left her glass on the counter. 'You mean that?'

'You're beautiful, Rachel.'

He could feel her breath on his neck. He leaned in and kissed her.

Rachel was smiling when he pulled away. 'I'm glad you came here, Edward.'

'I'm glad they gave me that grant.'

'Do you think this is what they had in mind? Back in Oxford? On the Committee?

'Definitely.'

'Weren't you meant to go to museums or something?'

'This is much more cultural.'

'It is?' She draped her arms round his neck.

'Very.'

'I see.' She pushed herself up on her tiptoes and kissed him again. 'Light the burner? I'll be one minute.'

He found the matches, and within a few seconds had the burner blazing up behind its little window, the warmth of it flushing his face, and the orange colour filling the apartment. He heard the door click behind him, stood, and turned.

'You look . . .'

'Come here, Edward.'

The following morning, after they woken up and looked across each other in the light that pooled through Rachel's aunt's shutters, and after he had kissed her again, and they had had sex again, and he had thought to himself that this, *this* was what it was like to be at Oxford, securing travel grants and flying off to foreign cities and spending the night with beautiful foreign girls, kissing them in grand old apartments in the evening and watching them pad away barefoot to make you coffee in the morning; and that maybe this was what it *would* be like from now on, not so much the end of his education as the beginning of his life—he pulled out his phone, flicked through the notifications that had arrived overnight, and saw, in the very first line of the very first page of the bulletin that flashed up on his screen, that war had broken out in Israel.

On the first day of term, Rachel phoned to say that she was going to spend some more time in Germany with her family, and would not arrive in Oxford until the following week. On the second day, realising he was essentially alone in College, Edward spent breakfast in the great hall flicking through the papers and trying to assimilate what news he could. *The Times*:

'Many readers have responded to the use of "disproportionate" in yesterday's editorial on the Israeli response to Friday's terrorist attack.' *The Guardian*: 'Many readers have responded to the use of the word "terrorist" in yesterday's editorial on the events leading up to Israel's disproportionate reaction.' On the third day, when Rachel didn't respond to his messages, he checked the news from Berlin, and found an article from *Die Zeit Online* reporting that, following previous unrest in Neukölln, Berlin police had arrested forty protesters from an Orthodox Jewish group called Neturei Karta, whose idiosyncratic interpretation of the Talmud had led them to begin a public chant to 'dismantle the Zionist state.' A statement from the *Bundespolizei* read as follows: 'Given historical considerations, Germany must not tolerate antisemitism in any form. According to the most recent definitions of both the IHRA and the European Commission, it was determined that the Spandauer Vorstadt protests fell under such a definition and therefore officers were mobilised.' On the fourth day, as he scrolled absently through the news during his first lecture, he found a report from the BBC offering 'a little glimmer of hope amid the chaos': while administering emergency medical care in Gaza, UN aid workers came across a dog, miraculously emerged from the rubble, who didn't leave their side. Journalists christened her 'Salma'—the Arabic word for 'peace.' At 3:36 P.M., the Associated Press reported that Salma had been killed by a rocket attack. On the fifth day, *The Daily Mail* reported that several major supermarket chains had ceased to stock Kosher food out of fear of Islamist reprisals. In response, the Conservative MP for Witney and West Oxfordshire went on Sky News to denounce the 'moral cowardice of the UK retail sector.' A supermarket spokesman: 'The absence of Kosher products from our shelves is entirely the result of local supply chain difficulties, and should not be interpreted as a political statement.' On the sixth day, a number of diplomatic responses started to appear. The Egyptian ambassador: 'Given the increasing humanitarian pressure on the region, Egypt can no longer guarantee the integrity of Israeli restrictions on vehicles entering Gaza.' The Saudi ambassador: 'Saudi Arabia will no longer pursue normalisation of relations with Israel in the foreseeable future.' The Israeli ambassador: 'International invocations of "humanity" are cynical attempts to expunge the word "terrorism" from the discourse.' The US ambassador: 'The US remains unwavering in its support of Israel. At the same time, the international reaction, and the unprecedented unification of the Muslim world around this issue, offer an opportunity for policymakers to reassess the geopolitical logic by which they understand the region.' The British ambassador: 'The UK remains committed to its allies during this conflict.' A spokesman for Hamas: 'We are called a nation of martyrs, and we are proud to sacrifice many more martyrs in the weeks, months, and years to come. On the long march towards victory, there will be blood.'

On the seventh day, after a number of focus groups, meetings with two PR firms, and lengthy consultations with its list of Tier A donors, the University of Oxford put out its statement. Edward was in bed when the email swooped in, but clicked on it at once, as his phone loaded up the dark, solemn blue of the University webpage:

In light of the impact of the appalling attacks and hostage-taking by terrorist groups, and the terrible wider effects the conflict has had on the entire region, we express our profoundest sympathy with all those affected. We acknowledge that many of our staff and students have family and friends who are directly threatened by the ongoing hostilities. Many others in our community share the pain of those who are suffering.

In a vibrant academic institution such as ours, [a link to the most recent QS world rankings] *it is inevitable that our*

staff and students will hold a range of views about the conflict.
The University must remain a place where all members of our
community are supported and welcomed, and where diverse
voices and perspectives are tolerated and respected, within the
limits of the law. We ask that all of our members engage each
other with civility and respect.

However, it has become regrettably clear that some of our
students and staff have experienced or witnessed antisemitic
and Islamophobic behaviour within Oxford. As a university,
we will not tolerate any form of discrimination or harassment.
Advice for staff and students who have experienced harass-
ment, including how to make a complaint, can be found below.

On the first day of the second week of term, bright and early,
and by all the usual channels—emails, flyers in pigeonholes, a
hastily bought megaphone on the quad, her back to an ancient
rhododendron bush in order that she might seem more dramatic—Liberty called a meeting in the Common Room. Edward
arrived with several minutes to spare, dragged along by Conrad,
who claimed to be attending purely in the hope that someone
might get maimed or killed and thereby furnish him with an exciting story to tell his real friends in London. Liberty strode in at
eight o'clock exactly, in her finest Cultural Revolution overalls,
shoes loud as gunshots against the Common Room parquet.

'Gosh, I've missed her, haven't you?' Conrad leaned over
chortlingly. 'Makes you want to guillotine someone. Wouldn't
even matter whom.'

Edward took one last look around as Liberty girded herself
to speak. Youssef, he noticed, was still absent: he had barely
heard anything about him since the end of last term; his usual
bi-weekly salvos of holiday posts had not been forthcoming, and
it was rumoured that, when approached by the usual troupe of
loafered old schoolfriends, he hadn't even had the energy to ski.
Angelica, however, was present, skilfully avoiding his eye in a

chair at the front of the room. She spent the whole of Liberty's opening address hunched over a small yellow notepad, pencil in hand—murmuring, minuting, occasionally glancing up to hurl an earnest frown into the back of the Common Room when she noticed some of the freshers beginning to flag.

'. . . Now the first item for discussion . . .' said Liberty (*discussion*, Edward was learning, was a word whose meaning Liberty interpreted flexibly) '. . . is—and I don't want to exaggerate, folks, but it's true—is a matter of life or death. Do I have everyone's undivided attention? Well? Do I?'

Liberty spoke at length, voice switching seamlessly back and forth between righteous fury and a softer, breathier register that Edward assumed was meant to denote pastoral concern. By now, she said, she was sure *everyone* was aware of the situation in the Middle East. The horrors. The turmoil. She shook her head. 'So I'd just like us all to take a moment—silence, please, that includes you Giles—to examine our own complicity. And to reflect on the fact that some groups of people are disproportionately affected by this. Women, for example. And people of colour. Oh, and Palestinians, obviously.' She looked around the room imperiously. 'Now,' she continued once she was satisfied everyone agreed, 'unfortunately, the College statutes prevent me from acting unilaterally in my capacity as President. Yeah I know, it's pretty fascist, and I'll sure see what I can do in the upcoming constitutional review next term. But in the meantime, folks, there's something that we can all be doing. It's probably the most important thing you *can* be doing, under the circumstances. Can you guess? That's right, guys. You can *put out a statement*.' She paused, to let a round of applause flutter across the Common Room. 'Now there is a catch. Sadly—and this is really sad folks, but it's true—sadly I can't put out a statement myself. You guys understand right? What with me being on the Fulbright programme, and a first-generation immigrant, and a certified black community leader, et cetera et cetera. It would jeopardise my funding, for sure and probably my visa, because this country is pretty messed up when it comes to this kind of thing. Like, just let people in, am I right? I'm a vulnerable person, basically. But I want you all to know that I'm very keen to organise, administer, *manage* other people's activist efforts. I've already organised a symposium at the Chamber to debate the issue, at which I'd really welcome some strident activist voices, outside and inside, if you catch my drift. But beyond that, guys, I want you to know that, if you're the kind of person who feels able to make a bit of a scene, then you should go for it. Anything. I'm talking Liberated Zones. Sit-ins. Graffiti. You have my full support, and I'll do everything in my power to make sure you get rewarded. Seriously folks. Favours can be granted. Strings can be pulled.'

Perhaps it was just Edward's fancy, but he could have sworn that Liberty, as she spoke, was looking straight at Angelica.

'. . . If I could have your attention please . . .' Liberty rapped her heel against the floor. '. . . the *second* item for discussion is a little bit different. Something . . . Giles?' Liberty asphyxiated a conversation in the back row with her gaze. 'As I was saying, the second item for today is especially pressing. One of our number—you all know Youssef Chamakh, I take it?' A few nods. 'Youssef, I'm afraid, has been targeted. It happened towards the end of last term. There was an altercation with one of the porters, which, with hindsight, looks to be clearly related to the wider developments in the Middle East. Youssef is from *Egypt*, you know.' There were a few murmurs; in the passageway outside, one of the doors banged loudly. 'So,' continued Liberty, 'It has been decided, in conjunction with the College administrators—who, it must be said, were *very* apologetic and keen for this not to escalate into something it doesn't need to be—that we, as a college, will set up a body—a separate, independent, *student-run* body—to deal with this kind of thing going forward. To give the students a voice.' Another ripple of applause, another modest wave of the hand. 'Now, I've been talking to our friends at Diversitas. Because one thing's clear—we need professionals looking after us. Trained Human Resources people. No more *porters*.' The she uttered the word with a burst of saliva-flecks. '. . . Isobel? Are you ready? Send him in now, if you don't mind.'

Obediently, Izzy K stood, trotted over to the brink of the doorway, peered round it, then, with a proud clang of the latch, swing the door open on its hinges and began to clap. Liberty joined in, then Angelica. Soon the whole Common Room was on its feet, and in—nodding almost apologetically, first at Conrad, then Liberty, then Angelica—strode Youssef. He seemed uneasy, hand massaging the back of his neck; when he reached the chair designated for him he lingered, as though checking it for traps.

'Sit down, Youssef,' said Liberty warmly. 'Please, join us.'

Youssef obeyed. They were still clapping him—or not him, exactly, but the idea of him, the impression of him. Eventually it died down, and Youssef settled in his chair. At Edward he didn't throw so much as a glance.

The rest of the meeting was taken up with more mundane items. There were the usual calls for a new DVD player; the motion to reinstate the split infinitives that had been removed from the Common Room constitution; the amendment to the College's bathroom antifungal policy; the statement on Dyer; the statement on Cuba; the statement on the plight of the Yangtze river dolphin; and the resolution that the words 'he' and 'she' were to be phased out by all Committee-members and replaced by a single, utilitarian, lawyer-approved 'they'—all ratified solemnly, if briskly, by Liberty. There were a few more scraps of news, too: Lolly B, Liberty declared, was to stripped of the premiership of the Hell's Belles, on account of an accusation of groping by a young male fresher, and a new leader was to be elected. At this, Angelica sat up a little straighter. The other piece of news concerned the rugby team. On the advice of Montgomery von Hardenberg-Buffer—and following the *horrific* desecration of the one of the leading voices in student journalism last term (soon to be subsumed by the *Gauche* masthead)—it had been decided that all men's rugby, football, hockey, basketball and water polo teams were to attend a compulsory workshop, provisionally named *Caging the Beast: Masculinity and its Acceptable Forms*, that Diversitas was offering at half price as part of its 'Spring Cleaning' sale.

Youssef slipped out the moment Liberty closed her mouth on the final syllable of the word 'dismissed'; Edward tried to follow, but was caught up in the sports teams ambling over to the richly stocked snack table. For a moment, he just stood there, the broad shoulders streaming round him, jostling him.

'Edward,' said Liberty behind him. 'Can I have a word?'

He did not protest as Liberty ushered him out of the Common Room into the adjacent corridor, where the Committee kept its cache of wine. 'Stop. Here will do.'

As she stood across from him in the passage, he wondered what Liberty was actually planning. Was she going to shout? He glanced warily at her right hand, studded with dense, African-looking rings. Would she try and *hit* him? Liberty was always canvassing that sort of thing, political assassinations and the like, but usually targeted remote, abstracted figures—governors of colonial provinces, authors of books she'd read about online.

'Now, Edward. This won't take a minute.'

He steeled himself. The wall of the corridor felt cold and unforgiving against his back.

'I just wanted to check you were, like, okay.'

A pause. 'Sorry. What?'

'I wanted to check you were okay. I know you're particularly affected by this. Your relationship, especially.'

'Are you serious?'

Liberty was shaking her head, brow steepled in commiseration. 'It must be awful. But I suppose you choose, don't you? And you did the right thing, Edward. You chose your roots.'

'I'm not sure I did, really . . .'

'It's *okay*, Edward. You can open up to me. I've been fully trained by Diversitas on ethno-religious sensitivity. I have the certificate at home and everything.'

'Right. Well, that's good for you. But I don't see why . . .'

'I know what happened. You left Berlin early. I saw on the travel grant form you said you'd be there for twelve days, and Izzy K saw you back in Oxford after eleven.'

'Oh.'

'Rachel made you, right? I guess she showed where her allegiances lie, too, no?'

'That wasn't . . .'

'It's *okay*, Edward. Saïd explained it all to me. Like, I'll be honest, I was pretty annoyed at you when term started. I kind of went off on a rant at Saïd the other night, about how you're all reserved and neutral and goddamn *English* about everything. But yeah, he explained where you're coming from pretty well. So it's good now. We're good.'

'Oh. Right.'

'I didn't realise you guys were such close friends.'

'Yeah, well, I suppose we're reasonably good friends.'

'I guess you guys bonded over the issues, right?'

'What?'

'The issues. You guys.'

'Yeah, maybe.'

'You know,' continued Liberty, leaning in, as though disclosing something she really ought not to, 'you and Saïd have had much the same experiences with Rach, from what I hear. Like, don't get me wrong, I don't dislike the girl—really, I don't. I don't hate her. She's . . . well she's fine, I guess. But in times like *these . . . ?* It's impossible. You and her.' She tailed off into a sigh. 'Angelica's confirmed it too. You know she and Saïd are together now, right?'

He swallowed. 'I had suspected, yeah.'

'But that's fine, right, since you guys are buddies?'

'Yes. It's fine.'

'Like I'd be okay if you weren't fine with it. To be honest I find it kind of obvious that all you guys want to go out with Angelica anyway. Sorry, I don't mean you guys in an offensive way. I just mean that she's, like very *pretty*, and very *polished*, and very *blonde* and *blue-eyed*. But is she a radical?'

'Yeah, like I said. I'm fine with it.'

'I suppose Ange and Saïd are together in a pretty loose sense, anyway. I don't want to put words in their mouths. And I know she's very taken with him—but I just know Saïd, and I have a sense he'll end up with someone a bit more, like, *serious*, you know? Sorry, you probably think I'm being a bitch.'

'No.'

'Tell me if you think I'm being a bitch. I love Ange, really I do.'

'You're not being a bitch.'

'Anyway, the point is, we've all been talking, me and Saïd and the whole Committee, and we all know what you're going through.' She leaned forward, very close, voice softening: 'Do you have family there?'

'There?'

'In Palestine.'

'No, Liberty I don't have family there. I'm from Zanzibar.'

'Right, right. Well, anyway . . .'

'Honestly Liberty most of my family in Zanzibar are dead, or moved abroad.'

'Oh *Edward*.' Liberty made a tutting sound. 'Of course. I guess there are reprisals. It's such a global conflict. I mean I worry about my family too.'

'You worry about your family?'

'Of course. In many ways I feel very personally affected by everything that's going on.'

'Of course you do.'

Liberty stared at him in interest, her mouth hardening, ever so slightly. 'And you do too, don't you?'

He stared back at her. Her arms were folded. 'Yes, Liberty,' he said.

'Thank you, Edward.' Liberty's smile re-established itself. She stepped back and made space for him to return to the Common Room. 'You know,' she said, 'It's good to have you back.'

E dward effortfully avoided the gaze of Liberty, waving at him from the high table, and instead slotted his tray into the one free space at the farthest end of the hall. It was strange to survey the familiar landscape of the College dining room, with its loud groupings and factions pressed up beside one another, without the reassuring presence of Youssef behind him, exhorting him to pick a spot and turf away any nearby freshers he deemed to be too close. He settled into a gap in the middle of a bench. He was surrounded by braying members of the year below, all boys, whose self-administered haircuts and strange, grunting rhythms of conversation suggested to him that together, they constituted some kind of sports team.

'Edward, right? Friend of Youssef's.'

It took Edward several seconds to recognise Giles. His piercings had mostly been removed, and he looked surprisingly conventional, in his frayed College rugby shirt, cheek bulging as he politely pasted a wad of gum into it with his tongue.

'So basically, Ed,' said Giles, unprompted, 'here's the situation. *Monty* . . .' he spat out the name with surprising venom. 'Monty is off organising all these workshops now.'

'Fucking Monty,' muttered the mud-caked creature next to him.

'Yes, *fucking* Monty.' Giles sighed. 'He's just Liberty's pet now. All independence gone. He's running workshops now— deranged behaviour. And Trev is out with a broken ulna.'

'Fucking Trev.'

'Yes, *fucking* Trev . . .' Giles shook his head. 'And anyway, long story short, we're a couple of men down . . .'

A sorrowful noise drifted out of the mud-caked creature.

'So what do you say, Ed?' Giles was grinning now, torso rocking back and forth, one hand stowed expectantly in his armpit. 'Do us a favour? Join the team?'

'Yeah, I'm really sorry, but . . .'

'C'mon Ed, we need you.'

'You have no idea how useless I'll be.'

'No, we have a pretty good idea,' said the mud-caked creature.

'It's just about numbers,' said Giles, nodding.

'It's an *experience*,' said the mud-caked creature.

'No. Sorry, but no.'

'You'll meet some new people,' offered Giles, hopefully.

'I don't want to meet new people.'

'Course you do.' Giles glanced behind him, and leaned forward. 'Listen, Ed. I know what's happened with your friends. Youssef. Ange. Terrible luck. Happened to me too, in a way, with Monty. Did a silent meditation retreat. Started reading social theory. He keeps threatening to make me use *pronouns*. Pronouns, Edward! But the guys on the team are a nice bunch. And actually, for the privilege of having a group of people who don't ask too many questions and don't care what religion you are and won't have you executed for using the wrong word for a disabled person, getting bashed around on a muddy pitch once a fortnight really isn't too much of a price to pay.'

Edward stared at him. His face was bright and earnest, his thick, stodgy brow furrowing up in anticipation.

'Okay,' he said at last.

'Okay?'

'Okay. Just once.'

The mud-caked creature let out a small cheer.

They dragged him along to celebrate, despite his protestations.

Giles had rented a local curry house, paying the owner hand-somely for the right to perform what were described, in hushed, reverent, allusive tones, as 'traditions.' Edward sat through the drunken excursus on 'manhood,' the coins hurled into pint pots, the vodka-soaked samosas, the shy fresher forced to drink out of his own footwear. He sat through almost enough rounds of 'Chug the Slug' to work out the rules, and, to his dismay, one of a game called 'Zulu Zulu Zulu.' He sat through the impromptu drumming circle, and the ceremonial ranking of female freshers according to an opaque metric referred to simply, mysteriously, as 'diameter'. It was only, in fact, when they were deep into the second course of the second meal of the evening, and the conversation turned to Angelica, that he began to fidget.

'. . . I mean you *would*, obviously Ed. I'm not blaming you.' Giles was slumped forward against the tabletop, brow fur-rowed, trundling a pakora back and forth along the rim of his plate. 'But you have to admit, she's . . . I mean, they're all . . .'

'They're all what?'

Giles sighed. 'I'm just glad you got free of her, that's all. Glad you're back with us now. Where you belong.' He propped his head against his fist as he spoke; his cheek looked soft and childlike against his hand. 'Anyway, what I'm saying, Ed,' he continued hiccupingly, 'is that there's no room any more. Not for guys like us. I know you know what I mean. I mean, Dad's right, isn't he? I'm going to *have* to get that first. I'm going to *have* to do that law conversion. I'm going to *have* to . . .' he trailed off into incomprehensible muttering. Beside him, the mud-caked creature, now mercifully sponged down, was slowly taking apart an onion bhaji sinew by sinew. Edward surveyed all of them, in turn. It was an astonishingly sorry sight, he thought; all of them looked defunct, somehow, left behind, like the army of an empire that no longer existed.

The rest of the night was predictable: the slow plod from

venue to venue, defusing fights, scraping swooners off the tarmac, peeling off in splinter groups to the emergency room, and erupting, when they reached the empty patch of cobbles where Abdul's Kebab's Drink's and Food's used to stand proud, in a shared little groan. Giles filled him in as they rounded the corner. It was a vendetta, he reckoned, a hit job. College had stepped up its objections over the vacation, you see: letters to the council, petitions from staff, accusations of *verbal abuse*, *trespassing*, even *assault*. Exhibit A, the extra porter—a new hire, with a fur-lined raincoat that the mud-caked creature thought made him look like a ponce. Exhibit B, that laminated sign up there on the wood: ALL STUDENTS SHOULD HAVE ID READY UPON ENTRY.

Parked a little further down the street, as though out of respect to Abdul's, was a new, smaller truck, clad in reclaimed wood, and great, childish letters proclaiming *Comida do Brasil Muito Yum Yum!* in primary colours from its rooftop. Slung over the light fittings were little flower necklaces, in a manner that vaguely reminded Edward of Favela. He stayed a while, even after Giles and the rest of the team had slunk back into College for their salubrious three hours' sleep. The truck was staffed by just one person, an exhausted-looking young man, flitting deftly between piles of taco shells in cellophane bags, reservoirs of hot sauce, vats of stews and beans, stopping every so often to score open a cardboard box or smoke a cigarette. Edward watched him with interest from the far side of the street. Now he looked, closer, he could *swear* it was one of the young men from Favela—yes, one of the barmen, he was certain now. He was busy packing boxes—each of them labelled with the bright, exotic names of dishes Edward didn't immediately recognise: *Feijoada, Moqueca de Camarão, Acarajé, Sarapatel.*

'Edward?'

Edward turned to see Angelica gliding over the cobbles towards him, very fast. She was tanned, as she was after every vacation, and was adorned with a remarkable amount of old gap-year paraphernalia: the hair-ties, the woven backpack, which looked very full today, no doubt with newer, heavier camera equipment now she had a more physically imposing boyfriend to cart it around. She looked flushed with purpose, her clothing crisp and carefully thought out, as though she were about to put on some workshop.

'What are you doing here?' she said.

'Oh. Nothing. I was with the rugby team.'

'Were you talking to Álvaro?'

'What? No. I was with . . .' He gestured uselessly at the empty street.

'What were you talking about?'

'We genuinely weren't talking, Angelica.'

Eyes still narrow with suspicion, she said a few words to the man in a foreign language, who laughed.

'I didn't know you spoke Portuguese.'

'I don't. That was Spanish. You're not very observant, are you?'

'Isn't this a Brazilian truck?'

'Yes, but Álvaro here is actually from Ecuador, aren't you Álvaro? Most people here don't know the difference.' She kept studying him as she spoke, eyes flitting up and down his rumpled outfit, and the dark stains that the evening had deposited down his front.

'So you weren't talking?' she said at last.

'No.'

'No?'

'I promise.' Edward sighed, and softened his voice. 'Listen, Angelica. I don't know what you've been hearing about Rachel, but . . .'

'I'm sorry, but I don't have time for this.'

'You wanted to talk about it last term. You wanted to talk about it at length.'

'Yes, well I was in a difficult place.'

'Yes, it must have been so hard for you.'

Angelica glanced apologetically up at the food truck's counter. 'Could you just give us one minute, Álvaro. Sorry. *Discúlpanos*. Yes, Edward. I was in a difficult place. I was actually very upset, for a number of reasons—thank you for asking after them by the way, for checking in on me. Anyway, it had been one of those weeks, and Rachel was the final straw.'

'What was so difficult then?'

She rolled her eyes. 'Oh *now* you want to know . . .'

'I do, actually.'

'You do?'

He nodded.

Angelica stared at him, very intently. She took a breath, which came out ragged. When at last she spoke, it was matter-of-factly, with a little shrug of defeat. 'It was my father.'

'What was your father?'

The brims of Angelica's eyes had begun to shine. 'At the end of last term. He left. He's . . . he's living in a flat now, with some twenty-seven-year-old. Honestly, it's such a cliché. But for my mum . . .' She wiped her eyes with the back of her wrist, and gave a humourless laugh. 'That's what I spent my Christmas doing, Edward. And I know it's not the most original or exciting disaster. And it's hardly the biggest surprise. But it's . . . it's like what I tried to tell Youssef. Getting used to something isn't the same as it no longer hurting.'

Edward stared at her. The tears were gathering freely now, smudging her carefully drawn eyeliner.

'Why didn't you say anything?' he said.

'You didn't ask.'

'You could have . . .'

'Could I? Could I really?' She let out a strange, ragged sound: half-laugh, half-sob. 'How could I have mentioned my father when you've never even *mentioned* yours? Or your family, or your childhood . . . When all you talk about is how you're from a country you've never even visited? No, don't look at me like that. Don't act like you weren't being evasive.'

'I thought that's what you wanted.'

'I wanted it, Edward, if it was true. But I never wanted you to feel like you had to make it all up. Like I wanted some story. That's your wish. Your dream—a different story for each of us. It *is*. Tell me I'm wrong—Youssef, Conrad, Liberty, me. And a different story for Rachel, no doubt. What does she think you are, I wonder? What version of yourself are you with her?'

'I'm sorry about your father. But I didn't . . .'

Angelica shook her head: 'I don't actually need your sympathy, you know. I never asked for it, not once. My story isn't very good, anyway.' She shrugged the backpack over her shoulder again, then stood there, arms at her sides, exposed. 'Besides,' she said, 'I know what I am in yours.'

'In mine?'

'In your story. The one you tell yourself when you're feeling all smug for leaving me and going off to Berlin or wherever. How was that by the way? Was it nice?'

'I don't . . .'

'You do. And I know in it, I'm ridiculous. The madwoman, the bitch. The joke . . . Because of my little projects. my protests, my politics. Because I *care* about things. But have you ever asked yourself why you think of me like that, Edward? There's so much misery in the world. That's why we do all this stuff— Liberty, me . . . You'd see it, if only you stopped wondering how it all relates to you. Why don't you take us seriously for once?' She was holding her wrist in front of her now, as though worried what her hands might decide to do. 'Go on,' she said. 'Why not try it? Maybe it'll change things, in that little story of yours. Maybe this'll be the chapter where things stop being funny.'

When she turned from him, blinking back her tears and beaming up at Álvaro with great effort, it was clear that his presence was no longer welcome. Álvaro said something to console her, and before long the two of them were chatting freely, the foreign syllables bright and carefree once more in Angelica's immaculately lipsticked mouth. Edward turned to leave. He couldn't understand what they were saying, but she seemed happier without him—and despite it all, it felt reassuring to see her slip back to her old confidence in the new language. He did catch one word, though. Before he strayed out of range, over and over again, maybe five or six times, used by both of them. A word he recognised, even in his general ignorance, and remained on his mind, too, even when he was woken up at 7 A.M. sharp by Giles banging on his door and telling him to chuck on his rugby kit and take a swig of gin and come and meet his maker: '*Sangre.*'

'Welcome to the gas chamber, Eddie.'

Edward kept his head down as Giles led him further into the stinking changing room, skirting the piles of rugby boots piled up like peat bricks in the corner, the genitalia that peeped blearily through gaps in towels. He pulled on the kit he had been handed, still smeared with the residue of last week's forty or fifty-nil defeat, then clicked out on his studs to the touchline. At least there wouldn't be too many witnesses. Rachel was flying back tomorrow, Youssef considered rugby un-Islamic, and Liberty and Angelica had recused their support from all College sporting events until every team had caught up on the requisite canon of workshops, not that they would have attended anyway. There were only a few Millies and Mollies and Tillies and Hollies, gambolling up and down quite happily, and one or two stalwarts of the club with broken arms and legs, who looked secretly glad they weren't playing.

'Oh, brilliant. Bloody brilliant.' Giles's face crumpled into a frown as he scanned the far end of the pitch. 'So he actually came.'

Jogging brightly over, silhouetted by the pale sun, stretching eagerly first his calves, then his thighs, then his hips, came Saïd.

'Why does he look like that all the time?'

'Like what?' said Edward.

'That. So . . . *healthy*. Oh, stop smiling, you git.'

Edward squinted through the sunlight as Saïd sank down into a round of press-ups. 'He wasn't there last night.'

'Doesn't drink, does he? Palestinian and all that.' Giles rolled his eyes, and when he turned back to Edward it was with a new fondness, like a father appreciating a child for the first time: 'I'm glad you don't go for all that stuff, Ed. Glad you take it *à la carte*. Oi! Saïd!' He cupped his hand to his mouth and called louder: 'Saïd, mate. Listen, really sorry about this, but Corpus haven't got enough players. And I think it's only right you volunteer. Seeing as you weren't there at the initiations, yesterday.'

Saïd rose on to his knees, nonplussed. 'Me? But you asked . . .'

'Yeah really sorry mate. You understand, don't you?'

'Fair's fair,' called a mud-caked creature from the halfway line.

'Get this shirt on,' said Giles, 'then off you pop.'

Defeatedly, Saïd began to change his shirt. As soon as he peeled it off, there were whoops from the touchline. Edward's stomach sank: Saïd's torso was not only tanned, it seemed, but covered in lines and striations that he'd never actually believed real people could have. The whole effect seemed like something Youssef had in mind, when lecturing him about 'the superior vigour of the marauding Turk' and 'the rough-hewn oriental who makes the desert bloom,' and the 'unmistakable pheno-type of the Rightly Guided seed.' Saïd was trotting his way over now, between the doughy, pasty, freezing bodies desperately trying to warm themselves up on the halfway line. To Edward's surprise, he installed himself opposite Edward, clapping him warmly on the shoulder before stepping back into his position on the other team. 'I didn't know you played,' he said, then began twisting at the waist, grabbing his ankles behind his back and stretching out his thighs.

'I don't play. I don't know why I'm here.'

Saïd laughed. 'Well, then this makes two of us.'

'Why did you come then?'

Saïd let go of his ankle, and shrugged. 'I wanted to help. Show my allegiance. And I heard you were playing, and I thought that this would be an excellent way to get to know you.'

'And now we're opponents.'

'It appears so, yes. But friendly ones, nonetheless, no?'

'Very friendly.'

'Is everything all right, Edward.'

'Yes. I'm cold.'

'Jog around, perhaps?'

'This shirt was damp when I put it on for some reason. I'm trying to work out what this stain is.'

'Perhaps we could have a little chat?'

'We're about to kick off, Saïd.'

'No, I am aware of this. I meant afterwards.'

'I'm busy afterwards. Aren't you busy afterwards?'

'It's a Saturday.'

'Angelica usually has plans on Saturdays.'

'Well Angelica's plans can wait, Edward. I would like to talk to you, because I suspect that you and I have a lot in common, and I keep missing you. You weren't at the Two-State Soirée. Youssef was there.'

'Yeah well Youssef didn't invite me this time. Perhaps my stock is declining, who knows.'

'This afternoon?'

'Sure, okay. We'll find a time.'

'I'm sorry about what happened with Rachel, you know.'

'What?'

'I heard. You flew back early, and she stayed. Because of what happened. Something like this has occurred with me, too. When I was on my year abroad in Berlin.'

'Did Angelica put you up to this? I know she's determined to make an issue out of this, but I'd really rather you weren't involved.'

'Angelica has nothing to do with it. I wanted to talk to you.'

'I left because I wanted to give her space, that's all. I know she has family affected, and I was staying at her aunt's house. It has nothing to do with how "what happened" interacts with our respective identities, if that's what you, like everyone else, is implying.'

'So you two are still . . . ?'

'*Yes.*'

'I see. Forgive me. I was under a misapprehension.' Saïd frowned. 'But Edward . . .'

'But what?'

'Have you spoken to her about the issue?'

'The issue?'

'Does she know your position?'

'Yes, insofar as I have one.'

'Does her family know about where you come from? They're not all like her, you know.'

'I don't know. I don't care.'

'And does *your* family know about where *she* comes from?'

'It's private. In fact, I don't particularly care about what our families think.'

'Forgive me, Edward, but this is the kind of thing people only say in England. "It's private."'

'It *is* private.'

'Well this is your decision, of course.'

'Yes, it is my decision.'

Saïd held up his hands. 'I'm not trying to fight you, Edward.'

'Yes but when you said it's my decision it sounded like you meant precisely the opposite.'

'I'm just looking out for you. This has happened to me before.'

'Well I don't particularly want you looking out for me.'

'I think you may be underestimating how difficult these things can be.'

'Right.'

'I want to help you, Edward.'

'Don't bother.'

'Edward . . .'

'I said don't bother, Saïd.'

At last, a coin was procured for the toss, which they lost, and Saïd jogged away to the other side of the pitch. Edward was bundled into position by a prop forward, burly, thick legged, his body held in check strips of black electrical tape, and a thick white band masking the twin horrors of his ears. 'Right, this way . . .' The prop's face was gathering into a look of fierce concentration; before Edward even had time to register his surroundings, he had been steered into position with a hand on the shoulder. Saïd was only a few yards away now, kicking up clods of grass with his studs.

'You ready?'

'No, I'm not ready. What do I even do?'

'Isn't it obvious?'

'No, it isn't obvious. Nothing is obvious. Why are they all lined up like that?'

'It's a simple game,' said the prop. 'It's about territory.'

'Right. What do I do?'

'You know what the ball is?'

'Yes, of course I know what the ball is.'

'Well,' said the prop, running up and down on the spot with surprising nimbleness. 'If the ball comes to you, you catch it. And if you catch it, you run.'

The whistle sounded, followed by a muffled, leathery thud. Edward felt all the energy drain out of him. What was he *doing*

292 · THOMAS PEERMOHAMED LAMBERT

here? Never in his life had he been attracted to this sort of thing. Never once had he even been *tempted*. He was overwhelmed, in fact, by a distinct feeling that this absurd ritual, which had been so unremarkable during his school years, so ever-present in the culture, was simply not *for* him—that he ought to be somehow exempt from it, that he ought to hold up his hands to the great oncoming rush and inform them that there had been a grave, grave mistake. He was *different*, he wanted to shout. He was from Zanzibar, and had a Muslim best friend, and had been Angelica's paramour, and was simply not built to take the indignity of being wrenched out of bed and dressed up in this damp uniform and corralled into position in front of fifteen snarling wads of muscle and anxiety and ill-founded college pride. This was a madness, he wanted to shout. For some, unknown reason, it seemed like all the other English boys in the College had given up on using their minds, on reading and culture and thought, and consented to become creatures of the body, lining up obediently to clatter into each other every Saturday morning, kicking up clods of grass with their studs. But not him! Not Edward, not yet.

'Yours, Eddie' shouted the prop, '*yours!*'

Edward looked up.

'*Yours*, Ed!'

The ball was arcing towards him, slow and lazy, as though still making up its mind whether or not to land. Vaguely, he was aware of the onrush, the shouts, the boots landing heavily against the grass; he remembered a comment Youssef once made: 'Europeans get weaker as they get older,' he said: 'they go all grey and frail. But we *Africans*, Edward . . . We Africans just keep getting bigger. Bigger and stronger. A grown man from Zanzibar is something to be reckoned with. When I'm ninety, my footsteps will make the earth quake.' There was a burst of sun from behind the cloud, and for a second the ball was extinguished; he could see Saïd bearing down on him, the whole team at his flanks. And suddenly he had caught it; he was running forward blindly into the throng; and there was a brief sheet of lightning, a shot of pain; and then nothing—nothing but darkness, the sound of his own pulse beating on in his ears.

Edward's first thought, as he ventured into the botanical garden, now steady enough on his crutches after a week and a half, was that if paradise did exist, it would look a little like this. He had been to the botanical garden before last year, but never at this time of year, on the cusp of May, and never with Rachel. He could hear the creak of oars in their brass rowlocks at the riverbend, and the paddles disappearing into the water; he could hear the frogs on the great, waxy lily pads and the feet of peacock ticking over the warm stone. It really was perfect. The sun was out, and Rachel had turned her face up to it, eyes closed.

'This is nice,' she said, over the sound of the bees in the lavender beds.

'It is.'

'You want to stop a second?'

Edward laid his crutches against a wooden arbour, and let her fold herself in next to him. She had been with him a lot in the last week, always accompanying him when he left the library for the light exercise the doctor had recommended, enjoying, he suspected, the excuse to get away from the fractiousness of College, if only for an hour or so. She looked him up and down, mouth bunched in the mixture of amusement and disapproval she always adopted when she thought about his involvement in the rugby game. Her dress was thin and summery, pale blue. She looked very attractive.

'I like your dress.'

'I can tell.'

'I thought I was being subtle.'

She laughed. 'No, Edward. You weren't being subtle.'

'Sorry.'

'You can look at me. It's allowed.'

She leaned over and kissed him on the cheek, then stretched out contentedly in the arbour.

'I think I was harsh on Oxford,' he said. 'This isn't so bad. Maybe we were right to come back.'

'This isn't Oxford, really. It's just us.'

'Well I like it when it's just us.'

Rachel took a deep breath. She was playing with the hem of her dress, and looked uncomfortable.

'What?'

'Edward,' she said, without meeting his eye. 'I have something to tell you. Or at least, something I want to run by you, and you're probably not going to like it, but I want to talk to you about it anyway, because it matters.'

'What is it?'

She explained briskly, not lingering on the details, seeming to intuit that if she slowed down, it might give him a chance to lodge an objection. It was the Symposium, she said. The one Liberty was organising later this week in the Chamber. She had seen the call for speakers—very meticulously worded, she thought—and seen the list so far. She did not approve.

'What's wrong with them?'

Rachel rubbed the back of her neck. 'I know some of these people, Edward. If you're a Jewish student you do actually end up knowing all the other Jewish students.'

'You sound like Youssef.'

'Yeah, well.'

'And what? You don't like these other students?'

'I like a lot of them. The problem is that the portion of them I *don't* like and the portion of them who got invited to speak at the Symposium are pretty much one and the same.'

'So don't go then.'

'That's the thing. I think I have to go. I hate the thought of it happening without me, Liberty just setting it all up for these people to embarrass us like that, and no one even registering an objection. Why are you looking at me like that?'

'I'm not looking at you like anything. I'm just wondering why you care so much all of a sudden.'

'Because the speakers they've chosen are the *worst*, Edward. They're Jewish in the way Liberty is black. Really, really obsessed with race, and blood, and Israel, and all the things I try not to think about on account of the fact they make everyone crazy. They organise societies around being Jewish, and speed-dating nights and hideous little mixers around being Jewish, and, well, they're not particularly the people I want representing me. Not that I want *anyone* representing me, really, but that seems like too much to ask these days.'

'Can't you just ignore them? You're good at ignoring Angelica—since last year at least. You've managed to ignore everyone else, so why don't you just ignore them too?'

Rachel shook her head. 'You don't get it, Edward. There's this one boy, for example, who basically wants to be a politician in the Knesset by the time he's twenty-five. And so he needs some issue to campaign about while he's at Oxford, because that's what you do, if you want to be a politician by the time you're twenty-five. And his big thing is that we Jews should be afforded all the special treatment that all the other ethnicities get. How inspiring! He stands up at the Chamber every week. He writes open letters, asking for "Jew" to be added as a category in the annual Diversitas survey.'

'I understand that it's annoying. But it seems harmless, Rachel. I wouldn't get drawn into it.'

'You know, Edward, call me old-fashioned but I don't particularly *want* a survey circulating every term where I have to tick a box marked "Jew." This doesn't strike me as very enlightened.'

'But isn't standing up and asking a question "as a Jew"— at the Chamber, I might add, which is not a particularly sane place—isn't that pretty much the same thing?'

'Not if I *choose* to do it. It's Jews I want to speak to anyway, as much as anyone else. Honestly, Edward, you have no idea what it's been like this week. It's almost made me think I *was* a little harsh on Youssef last term. Turns out there are actually some Jewish people—Americans, mainly—here who are a pretty bit weird about me going out with *you*. Not Saïd, *you*.'

'They do know I'm not actually a Muslim, right? You can tell them. I really don't care.'

'It doesn't make any difference, Edward. People aren't really interested in seeing someone like you as "not a Muslim." Not since what happened. In fact it's as if some of them have been waiting patiently all their lives for an excuse to see you as nothing but one.'

'But you want to try to convince them anyway? That doesn't make much sense either.'

'Maybe it doesn't. Anyway, I feel like I really can't win because I make the small point that, for example, and allowing for a fact that I don't have some stupid MA in international relations, I suspect killing *everyone* in the occupied territories might not be an excellent long-term strategy for Jews in Israel or abroad—I make this point and then I'm an outcast, an apologist, self-hating, not a real Jew, et cetera. Fine. Whatever. But then I go to the other side and say, for example, that there may be some people in Israel who are *not* bloodthirsty warlords and might be permitted to remain where they are—my ninety-year-old grandmother, for example, who was a Tolstoyan anarchist and uses a breathing tube, or my cousin, who is four—I am an apologist, a racist, a coloniser. I just feel like everyone has gone mad. It makes me want to go home. But where even is home, now?'

'I'm sorry. But I just think you're expecting too much from these people. I mean why do you talk to them? It'll blow over. We've been so *happy* this week, Rachel.'

'I've been happy with you. But you can't just be happy with one person, it's not enough.'

'Why is it not enough? It's enough for me.'

'But not for me. You know I walked past the encampment yesterday. Sorry, the "Liberated Zone." Outside the science library. Anyway, I saw a girl from my Goethe paper, and cut across to go and say hi. And they stopped me. Actually grabbed me, Edward. You know what they wanted me to say? They wanted me to say "I declare I'm not a Zionist, and I commit to keeping this encampment Zionist-free."'

'Okay. That's bad, I get it. But you're not a Zionist though. At least based on what you said in Berlin. So how much does it actually affect you?'

'But the declaration seems rather stronger than my actual feelings, doesn't it? I mean, they weren't leaving me an option to say "I am not a Zionist if Zionism is identified as the actions of the most recent string of Israeli governments, though I do retain a sense that maybe expelling all Jews by force and setting up an Arab nationalist state—because we all know how well those tend to turn out—might not be the best idea either." For some reason, there doesn't really seem to be a way for someone like me to say something like *that*.'

'So, what? You're going to stand up in the Chamber and ask a question then? Like that'll fix it all? I don't know why I'm even asking, since it sounds like you've made up your mind already.'

'No, Edward, you're not getting it.' Rachel paused, looked down at her hands, which she was wringing. 'Not a question. I want to sign up as one of the speakers.'

Quietly, Edward said: 'No.'

'What?'

'No, Rachel.' He felt his chest rising in indignation. 'What are you, insane?' He made to stand, but found himself too weak to haul himself up on to his crutches. 'We've finally, finally carved out a little space here. No one is bothering us, no one seems to care much about us, and you want to go in front of four or five hundred of the actual worst people on the planet—yes, they are the worst people—and give them another reason to hate us?'

'Edward . . .'

'It's a terrible idea, Rachel. Terrible. What, you think if you just get up and say something reasonable people will just go: "Oh, well then, yes, I guess that settles it."'

'Maybe, yes.'

'It won't happen. I promise. It doesn't work like that any more, not here not anywhere.' He shook his head. 'Where's this even coming from anyway?'

'I was talking to Saïd, and . . .'

'Oh, *great*. I see. Since when was Saïd someone to listen to on this? You know how close he is with Angelica.'

'*You* were close with Angelica.'

'That's different.'

Rachel had raised her voice now: 'He isn't some monster, Edward. He's very reasonable, actually. In fact, it's in his interests for everyone not to go and lose their minds over this, too.'

'He's setting us up. This is exactly what he wants.'

He tried again to approach her, but she pulled away from him, arms folded. 'You know I'm not actually asking, Edward. I'm going to do this. I just wanted to ask if you'd look at my speech.'

Edward was growing desperate. 'Rachel, look around.' He gestured around, at the perfect flowerbeds, the shivering trees. 'Look at this. This is paradise. Garden of Eden, whatever. And you want throw it away.'

'You could at least try to understand where I'm coming from.'

'You could at least try to understand where *I'm* coming from. Listen, Rachel. I *know* this place. I know this country. It *will* blow over. People will get bored. It'll go back to the way it always has been, provided you don't make too much of a fuss, and don't offend anyone, and try not to set yourself up as some kind of martyr. I promise.'

Rachel's mouth hardened. 'I want to show you something, Edward.'

'What?'

'This way.'

She stepped down from the arbour and set off along the path.

'Where are you taking me?'

'Just wait.'

'You're walking too fast.'

'Sorry. One second. Here.'

At the end of the path, tucked into a space between two hedges, was a small, brassy plaque.

'Read it,' she said.

'Read what?'

'The plaque.'

Still indignant, Edward shrugged his crutches up his arms and hobbled forward towards the smudged brass, which bore a large inscription in an alphabet he didn't recognise.

'Yeah, I don't speak Greek, Rachel.'

'Underneath that. And it's not Greek.'

Edward peered forward at the small, etched letters beneath. THIS STONE MARKS THE PLACE OF THE OXFORD JEWISH CEMETERY UNTIL 1290. MAY THEIR MEMORY BE BLESSED.

'Zikhronám liv'rakhá,' said Rachel. 'Sometimes it's worth remembering that history didn't just happen in Berlin. Or in Jerusalem, or in Babylon, or even in Zanzibar. It happened here, too.'

'I don't understand . . .'

'They used to bury Jews here. It wasn't allowed inside the city walls. But in the twelfth century the Jews of Oxford got together and bought a water meadow—right here, by the river.' Rachel nodded down the path, to where the garden fell away into a jade-green expanse of water boatmen and flies. 'But it didn't last. They started making accusations, the gentiles. Blood libels. Every Jew, all over the country. Always something to do with blood—draining it, drinking it. There was a massacre in York . . .'

'But *Oxford*?

'It happened everywhere, Edward. Everywhere the Jews were—Norwich and Lincoln, London and Winchester. Oxford. A few years later, the Jews were expelled. Every last one of them. And the land was passed over to the hospital for gentiles. That's what the plaque is for.'

'Oh.'

'I know. You'd never guess would you?' She shrugged, and watched a white butterfly disappear down the path. 'But anyway, it's something I think about sometimes. And you probably think I'm being terribly oversensitive for doing so, or unsophisticated, or naïve, or just foreign and obtuse. But it's true. If this were the Garden of Eden, we wouldn't be standing on people's bones.'

It was just about impossible that afternoon to do any work. The afternoon sun streamed mercilessly through the makeshift library's cheap glazing; in a desperate attempt to seem relevant, the librarian spent several hours rattling together a display of books that dealt with 'Borders' on the ground floor. Edward knew he needed to do something to impress Larry. He had been all but uncontactable since last term; every request Edward had typed out with scrupulous politeness—for reading lists, essay titles, clarifications as to what, exactly, the 'spheres' in 'Post-Human Spheres' actually referred to—had gone unanswered. With a twinge of despair, Edward even embarked on one of Pfister's own writings—one of his earliest publications, before he decided that "books" were the scourge of academe. The title of the volume, *Subjective Transformations: Thoughts, Marginalities, Narratives, Perspectives*, struck Edward as so vague as to be largely meaningless, and it was a surprise, flicking through the index, to see that there were at least twenty entries under 'Kafka, Franz.'

One of sub-entries, he saw, was for 'Kafka, broken bones.' He couldn't resist. Carefully, he flicked back to the relevant entry:

Despite all the ink that has been spilled over the creature in Kafka's most famous story, no one seems to know quite what that creature is. Into what does Gregor Samsa transform? A cockroach, a louse? 'Vermin'—the most popular translation—seems vague, but the German is even more so. Das Ungeziefer *comes from the old High German word for any animal that is unfit for sacrifice. It is worth remembering this, as we are plunged into the fever dream of Kafka's prose: for a while, Gregor could be anything that falls afoul of one of the ancient priestly codes—a cow blinded in one eye, a goat insufficiently drained of its blood, a lamb with a broken bone.*

What does the Ungeziefer *represent? The tortured saint? The tyrannised son? The Jew? As always in Kafka, the story seems to resist exegesis. There is something pre-interpretative about the story, something nameless and impossible about the anxiety it relays. Above all else, perhaps, the creature stands for the strange state where the individual ceases to believe fully in himself. Lionel Trilling, himself a Jew, points out that the essential difference between Kafka and, say, Shakespeare, is that 'the captains and kings and lovers and clowns of Shakespeare are alive and complete before they die,' while characters in Kafka are 'stripped of all that is becoming to a man except his abstract humanity.'*

We pad ourselves with attributes, predicates, statements of identity. I am a man or a woman; a student or a professional; a Christian, a Muslim or a Jew. But what is the existential kernel to which these designations cling? 'Abstract humanity' is never quite satisfying, somehow. For a certain kind of existentialist—a Sartre, a Camus—this revelation of nothingness lays the potential for great freedom. For Kafka, however, it is something monstrous in this interruption, this void, this hole at the centre of things. And nature abhors a vacuum. The void must be extinguished. The unfit animal must be driven out into the desert. The existential skeleton is not adequate to support the weight of the world.

He must have read the passage over three times. In prose, Larry's voice was so different, so free of the usual twangs of informality and ingratiation, that it was a great effort to convince himself that he had even written it. When the time approached for their scheduled meeting, he actually checked the book out and stowed it in his bag: *this* was what he wanted to write about, he decided, this feeling of rejecting categories and yet somehow needing them, of chafing against the very thing that holds you up. Who knew, perhaps it might help him express the very things he had tried, and failed, to say to Rachel—make her reconsider her decision to speak in the chamber, or at least help him understand why that was not an option. Yes, he would ask Larry. This, after all, was what education was for, was it not? To make one's life, however fleetingly, make sense.

Edward barged into Pfister's office, without knocking, just as Larry insisted, bursting with ideas: he would write on Kafka, he had decided, but it was okay, because Kafka was precisely the writer you should choose, if you had a parentage like his, a background like his, all mixed and jumbled and incoherent— because he had been thinking, you see, and had realised Kafka was the only writer he had ever read who managed to articulate what it was like to be him, to stagger through life, crushed by all these abstract things you were supposed to care about and then finally, against all the odds, meet someone, make some connection you had dreamed since you were a boy, only to be told . . . He stopped. Pfister was nowhere to be seen. The room had been stripped of the posters, the picture frames that used to teem with the ghosts of kayaking holidays past. In the corner of the room, in an armchair where Larry's exercise ball used to be, her trouser-suit freshly pressed and the great, soft mound of Cyrus rising and falling at her feet, was Professor Burgess. When she saw him—an operation that involved several seconds of peering over the frame of her glasses—she gathered herself to her feet and offered him her armchair: 'Oh, you poor thing. What *happened*? Here . . .' She settled on the stool opposite. Cyrus padded after her. She *was* sorry, she said. She knew it must come as something of a disappointment, to have one's tutorials discontinued like this. But Professor Pfister . . . Lawrence had decided to take some time out from his teaching obligations. He'd be transferring to Amherst in the autumn. She didn't expect he'd be back for some time. As she spoke, she moved her hands with brisk efficiency; but her brow, Edward noticed, remained furrowed in what looked like disapproval.

'He's transferring in the middle of the term?' he asked. 'Is that normal?'

'I'm afraid, Edward,' said Professor Burgess, 'that this wasn't entirely by choice.'

'Can you tell me what happened?'

'I'm afraid there are various arcane rules which require me not to. But I think you can probably guess. I trust the rumours haven't escaped you?'

'Oh.'

'Yes.' She was silent a while, her whole face still and impassive. Then she brightened: 'But we oughtn't pass sentence on him too eagerly. One oughtn't to pass sentence on anyone too easily, even oneself.'

'So what will happen with the thesis?'

'I shall be taking you for the rest of the term. If you don't mind, that is.'

'I don't mind.'

'Lawrence mentioned you've taken to Kafka.'

Edward nodded.

She smiled, twisted her fingers through the crests of hair on

Cyrus's neck: 'You know, I take it, about the other Professor Burgess? The one you mistook me for, in your little nod to Shakespeare?'

'I didn't know there was another Professor Burgess.'

She smiled sadly. 'My late husband. There's no reason why you should have known him, of course. Some students went to the funeral in College in Michaelmas term this year, but they were mostly graduate students. Anyway, I only mention him because he happened to run a course on Kafka.'

'I'm sorry, I didn't know any of this.'

'There was no reason for you to know,' she said, shaking her head soothingly. 'There is something, though, isn't there, about very bright young men and Kafka? Something about all that anxiety wound up with all that ambition. Professor Burgess certainly had a streak of it too, when he was young.'

'And later, from the sounds of it.'

'Well, he always read Kafka, and taught him. But I suspect the fascination was most potent when he was—well around the age you are now.' She took off her glasses, and wiped them absent-mindedly with a tissue. 'I know nothing about this, of course, and I'm aware this is a rather unfashionable thing to say, but I've always suspected it's rather difficult to be a young man.'

Edward said nothing. He could feel a lump in his throat.

She spoke very gently. 'Are you all right, Edward?'

'Professor Burgess?'

'Yes?'

'Does it get easier?'

'Does what get easier, Edward?'

'I just . . .' He swallowed. 'I don't know. All my life, I thought that if I could just get here, come to Oxford, then . . .' He sighed, impotently.

'I am afraid people *do* tend to build this place up into all kinds of things. I suspect the trick is not to take one's expectations too seriously.'

'I thought if I just *came* here, I would become the kind of person who has answers, and I'd be able to get the things I wanted, or even know what I wanted at all. But now I'm here, it's just more complicated than ever, and the people here are more difficult to understand than ever.'

'Ah, yes. This is all too common too, I'm afraid.'

'I guess I'm just wondering if that's what it's going to be, from now on? The more educated you become, the harder it gets to . . . just . . . live.'

'Well, that's a very large question.'

'I know. Sorry. You don't need to answer it.'

'But I think it needs to be taken seriously. Look, Edward. I'm not sure about getting answers, or getting exactly what you want. But I suspect that's not really what you're asking me.'

'That's the problem, I'm not sure what I'm asking, really.'

'You're asking whether education will take you inexorably away from people, or bring you closer to them. Might that be right?'

'Maybe, yes.'

Professor Burgess leaned back thoughtfully in the armchair. 'Well then, for what it's worth—and please keep in mind that this is just the opinion of a rather short-sighted old lady who's certainly not as *au fait* with what it's like to be twenty as she once was—but I rather think you can. There's a certain strand of writing out there that will tell you otherwise, of course—Kafka is perhaps its laureate. But I suspect you really can learn, and think, your way towards other people. Whoever this other person is—yes, Edward I'm afraid I can tell—whoever this person is, he, or she . . .'

'She.'

Burgess smiled behind her glasses. 'I'd bet the two of you really could make it work for yourselves, if you tried.

CHAPTER 16

At the beginning of fifth week, Liberty sent out her first mass email under the subject line 'RE: Justice'. It was addressed to all College undergraduates, graduates, professors, maintenance staff, alumni, and several local and national newspapers, and stated that, effective immediately, the JCR would consider itself to be in a state of emergency. Soon, several 'working groups' composed of people Edward had never met had been set up with the expressed aim of working out a statement on which the Common Room would eventually vote. To oversee the process, Liberty announced in a second, more hastily-drafted email, she had appointed her most trusted deputy: Angelica Mountbatten-Jones.

When the statement eventually did materialise, its main demand, from what Edward could work out, was that the College put out a statement itself. This, Angelica remarked in her lengthy email after several paragraphs' musings on *honour* and *gratitude* and *responsibility*, was the only way it could expiate the guilt it had accrued over the years of systemic discrimination of students and murky investments in East African agriculture. In response, the College did indeed put out a statement—whose main purpose, it seemed, was to explain that it was an educational institution and 'putting out statements' was not part of its pedagogic remit. Angelica then responded by pointing out that 'not putting out a statement' was tantamount to complicity, and that it had put out plenty of statements on other political matters like Pride Month and Remembrance

Sunday, and had, for a whole week last year, lit up all its buildings with the national colours of Ukraine. The College then replied that, if it put out a statement, *some* students (though it
did not mention which kind of students) might feel 'unsafe.' At
this, Angelica and a few friends camped out on the quad. The
College threatened to call the police. Angelica made a strate-
gic retreat from the quad to the bastion of her room and sent
another email, again addressed to all College undergraduates,
graduates, professors, maintenance staff, alumni, and several
local and national newspapers, that said she was shocked at the
College's heavy-handedness, especially given the record of law
enforcement among people of colour like the camp's newly appointed superintendent, Asafoetida Wong (for good measure,
links to several of Liberty's essays in *Gauche* were included).
The College replied that several of its staff (though it did not
mention which staff) had complained to them that Angelica's
violent rhetoric amounted, in their opinion, to harassment. At
last, Angelica returned to her remarkably well-furnished tent
and proclaimed to the crowd of sympathetic onlookers gathered around the flapping entrance that if the College did not
put out a statement—and, a *proper* statement, mind you, full of
the right words approved by the right list of international lawyers—then she would have no choice but to begin inquiries into
where, exactly, the College's financial endowment was invested.
At 4:36 P.M. that day, the College put out a statement.

Edward, for his part, spent most of his week hidden away in
the Annexe. Someone who referred to herself as the 'disabilities
co-ordinator' had offered him a full suite in the main college on
account of his broken leg—three rooms, plus an entranceway
with a handrail and a little cord he could pull at any time he
liked to summon an anxious junior dean to his staircase. He
declined: by now, it was the highlight of his day to knock on
Rachel's door each evening, and be welcomed into the soft yellow light, the rugs, the posters from the galleries in Berlin they

had visited together. She would greet him with a kiss on the cheek, or the lips, and usher him inside, and suddenly everything would be all right, everything in the world.

This evening, however, Rachel was subdued. She was perched on her duvet, cross-legged, the posture she always assumed when hard at work. Quietly, Edward pulled the armchair a little closer. She was wearing a T-shirt and her hair was down, ready for bed. Every so often, she would bring a curled forefinger to her lips, hold it there for a few seconds, exhale.

'I can feel you watching me,' she said.

'Oh.' Edward rubbed the back of his neck, 'Sorry.'

'*I'm* sorry. I probably look a mess.'

'You definitely don't.'

'It's my fault I suppose,' she said, still typing, but less determinedly, a smile playing on her lips. 'You know I used to spend *ages* getting ready for our tutorials last year? I used to plan out my outfits and everything. How ridiculous. I've set myself up to disappoint you.'

'You are the least disappointing thing I have ever seen.'

'You're sweet. I'll be done soon, I promise.'

'What are you working on?'

'You won't like it.'

'The speech?'

She nodded.

'Isn't your thesis draft due in next week?'

"Yes, I know. It's probably not wise.'

'It definitely isn't wise. Why don't you give it a rest?'

'If I don't do this then I just keep *thinking* about it, and it goes round and round in my head and I can't do the thesis anyway.'

Edward lifted himself out of the armchair and settled on the bed next to her. 'Listen, Rachel. Can you stop typing a second?' She stopped typing and trained her dark brown eyes on him. 'I know this is probably not going to go down well, but I do feel like I should remind you, once again, that *you do not actually need to do this*. You can just stop. We could do anything.'

'The day's almost over.'

'I could make you dinner. You've barely eaten.'

'It's 9 P.M.'

'I don't mind.'

'Edward. Edward, listen . . .' Gently, Rachel laid a hand on his. 'I admire your efforts in trying to get me to stop. But I actually want to keep going, okay?'

'Just think about it?'

'I have thought about it. I do think about it.'

'It's getting worse, you know. Did you see the most recent email?'

'From Angelica? No, Edward, I try not to read those things.'

'You should take a look at it. Seriously, look. There . . .'

Reluctantly, Rachel opened the email. She shook her head and frowned. 'I don't get it.'

'It's getting worse, Rachel.'

Rachel was reading through the email a second time now. With her cursor, he noticed, she had highlighted a single word: *violence*. 'I mean, it's just so obviously *false*: that's what I can't stand. The way people talk. It's like they're possessed.'

'I know. I keep telling you this.'

'Why is everyone going on about being "unsafe" all of a sudden?'

'Maybe they feel it.'

'They don't feel it.'

'People feel all kinds of things, if they try hard enough.'

'You know what, Edward? I know this is probably an unpopular opinion, but I don't actually think that's true. I think "I feel unsafe" is just something people have learned to say because it gets the grown-ups to notice them. Most of the *Jewish* students who say they feel unsafe just say it because it's the only way they can make their case without everyone calling them a fascist. Don't look at me like that: it's true.'

'You mean you've never once felt unsafe here? Have you not heard Angelica recently?'

'No, actually, I really haven't felt unsafe. I've felt *angry*, sometimes. And upset. And frustrated, obviously, because goodness knows no one knows how to listen anymore. But there's something so awful and disingenuous about pretending that I'm under a *real* threat—about waiting for the University to pat me on the back and tell me how much they care about me and ask me if I want extra time in my exams.' She sighed, navigated back to her speech, and deleted a few words. 'And of course, when people *start* talking like that, it just makes everyone quietly hate them. Jews especially—yes, Edward, I mean it. It makes people think we're all liars, or hysterical, or neurotic, or whatever. Which will of course be *excellent* for us in the long run. You know my friend Deborah, from J-Soc turned to me the other day and said she "felt assaulted." *Felt assaulted.* What does that *mean*? Is that my English? Is this something that makes any sense at all?'

'It's not your English'

'Honestly, I don't understand why it's so hard for everyone to just say *what they actually believe.* I don't understand why it's so impossible among my Jewish friends to admit there might be a few Jews who *might* be being a *tiny* bit dishonest about this—because Jews, despite what a number of people in this city seem to think, are people too. And no, actually it isn't me being self-hating, or guilty, or whatever because I'm also not sure why among my non-Jewish friends—who it must be said are dwindling in number all of a sudden—it's so impossible to suggest that some of the *Muslim* students might be doing the same thing. Like when they all go and demand a new scholarship reserved just for "people who identify as Muslims," whatever that means. Because that'll help! That'll solve everything!' She had begun to nod to herself and was navigating her way down to the bottom of the document. 'You know what, Edward. Thank you. You've actually given me some ideas.'

'Rachel.'

'Hmm?' She was typing again.

'Rachel listen to me. You can't say that.'

Still typing: 'Why not?'

'You can't say anything like it.'

'I have to say *something* like it.'

'And you think *that* will help? Rachel, please stop typing just for a second. Can you close the laptop?'

'I'm closing it.'

'With extreme reluctance, it seems.'

'Look, I've done it.' She frowned up at him. 'Do we really need to have this fight again?'

'Yes. Because I have a terrible feeling that this makes a lot of sense in your head and will make absolutely no sense to anyone listening to you. And they will *punish* you for it.'

'I think you've managed to let them convince you that *you're* unsafe.'

'What are you even going to say in this speech that matters so much?'

'Oh, so *now* you care about my opinions all of a sudden . . .'

'Yes, I do care. I want to know what my girlfriend is going to say when she stands up in front of the most deranged people I have ever met and talks about the most controversial issue of the last two thousand years.

'Why are you so nervous about this?'

'You're avoiding the question.'

'You really want to know?'

'*Yes.*'

Rachel took a deep breath and opened up her laptop. 'You know when people say "us"?'

'Us?'

'Us. Gather themselves up into one big comforting unified thing. When Youssef says "us" to you. Or one of my Jewish friends says "us" to me. Or when Angelica tells me she doesn't approve of what "we" are doing in the Middle East.'

'I know the procedure, yes.'

'Well I'm trying to find a way of saying something which, just for a second, might break up that "us." Not forever, not with all us-es. Just something that will get through to people, even if only for a second. Sometimes I think that if all the writing in the world managed only that, then it wouldn't have entirely failed.'

Edward stared at her. She looked very beautiful, flushed with purpose in the lamplight. 'And you think that's worth ruining your life in Oxford for?' he said.

'Yes, I do, actually.'

'And *my* life? What about you and me, what about that "us"?'

Rachel sighed. 'I have to try this, Edward. I have to. I know it might not make any sense to you, but you could at least try and appreciate that it does to me.'

'Are you at least going to say something about what's going on?'

'What do you mean?'

'What's going on. What's been happening to people. Over there. People have been killed.'

'I think people know that's going on, Edward.'

'But couldn't you, I don't know, condemn it? Make a statement, just so people know you don't . . .'

'You sound like Angelica.'

'Well maybe she's right about this. Look, I don't want to pick sides here, but I just think that it might be worth making clear what you actually *do* believe at the outset. Just reminding everyone, you know?'

Rachel's expression had grown stony. 'Right,' she said. 'Let me guess. You want me to say that I categorically condemn the violence on both sides, and make it clear that I'm a good Jew who does not identify in any way with this foreign government I have no civic connection to. Maybe I could show them my German passport, too, just to make it clear?'

'Rachel . . .'

'In fact, maybe then I could, by way of balance, say something like "but we must also acknowledge that there is no place for antisemitism in this institution?" Maybe I could say something about how "we must strive to make this a fair, safe and inclusive environment for all students?" Everyone would clap, congratulate me. Maybe they would congratulate you, too. Would you like that, Edward?'

'You're being unfair.'

'*You're* being unfair. You want me to speak like them, because you want an easy life. No, don't protest. You do.'

'You're acting like there's only one thing that matters in the world, and it's *Oxford*. But maybe—no, listen for a second, I know this might be hard to hear but it's true—maybe what we do here doesn't really matter much. Maybe we do have to put things in context.'

'What are you talking about?'

'Come on, Rachel. Think about it. Imagine your talk goes as well as you could possibly hope for—which it obviously won't, but let's forget that for now. Suppose it goes perfectly. So what? Will it save lives? Will it help anyone at all? Or has what's going on, perhaps, got literally nothing to do with the way we talk about it in a fancy room in West Oxford with red leather seats?'

'I know my talk won't save lives, Edward.'

'Have you even seen the pictures?

At that, Rachel's face fell. When she replied, her voice was very cold. 'Of course I've seen the pictures.'

'Have you actually *looked* at them, though?'

'I've seen the pictures, Edward.'

'And?'

'And what?'

'Doesn't that change things? Doesn't it make you think that maybe this fear you seem to have of *putting things in context* isn't actually all that important?'

Rachel stood and paced over to the window. Outside, the light was dipping, and there were a couple of geese on the grey water. In a very soft voice, she said, 'Is that what you think of me?'

'I can't hear you. Can you turn around?'

'I said is that what you *think* of me?' Something in her voice made him flinch—not even the volume of it, but the tone, drained of all affection. 'Do you think I don't *know?* Do you think that I hold the opinions I do *because* I don't know? Because I do, actually, Edward. I do know. I think about it every day. Because you *do* think about things like this every day, when they're being done in your name. And yes, sometimes—because I'm *such* a bad person and I'm nowhere near as spiritually in touch with all the sufferings of the world as Angelica—sometimes I do force myself to forget these things. Maybe I shouldn't. Maybe I'm wrong.'

'Rachel. Listen . . .'

Rachel wiped her eyes with the back of her hand. 'Yes, look at me. Look at the Jewish girl crying her eyes out when there are so many other people so much worse off than her. How irritating.'

'Rachel. Please . . .' He began to rise from the bed.

'Stay where you are.'

'Rachel, look at me.'

With a thumb, she rubbed the corner of her eye.

'I'm sorry,' he said. 'I didn't . . .'

'No you're not sorry. You're sorry that I'm crying and you feel embarrassed.'

'I'm sorry that you're upset. I don't think you need to be. I don't think you've done anything wrong, actually.'

'I'm upset because you don't get it. I'm upset because I'm

trying to do something that I think might help, and all you do is tell me that I'm mistaken, and I'm making everything difficult for you.'

'I don't think that's fair.'

'But that's what you want, isn't it? You want me to stand around and look pretty and not make a fuss.'

'Honestly this is so far from the truth.'

'Is it? You get cross at me whenever you catch me working on this. You like me, right up until such time as I begin to have thoughts of my own.'

'I love you, Rachel.'

'What?'

'I love you. I don't want you to shut up, I want to be with you more than I've ever wanted to be with anyone, and I'm *trying* to get through to you.'

'No. No, no. You can't do that Edward.'

'What can't I do?'

'You can't just tell me you love me because you want me to stop. That's not fair.'

'I can't believe you think that's what I'm doing. Did you not hear me?'

'Isn't it? Why now then?'

'What?'

'Why now? Why not in the botanical garden, or the Annexe courtyard? That night in Berlin, why not then?'

'This is ridiculous. You know, Rachel, astonishing as it might seem, not everything I say is about this speech and my campaign to prevent you from giving it. That encampment is not about your speech, and those dead children are not about your speech, and me telling you I love you is not, I promise you this, about the speech. Maybe Angelica was right.'

'Oh, thanks.'

'Maybe she was. Maybe you *are* selfish, and obsessed with Israel, and Judaism—because honestly, Rachel, a normal person wouldn't listen to someone tell her he *loves* her and interpret it as evidence of one giant conspiracy against her.'

'What are you talking about?'

Edward began to gather up his crutches. 'This is exactly what Youssef warned me about. Look, this isn't going to work if every time I have any opinion ever it's evidence of . . . Don't shake your head: it's true. It's . . . It's . . .'

'Go on, I'm listening. Say your piece.'

'It's massively oversensitive, and neurotic, and just *unfair*. And I . . . What are you doing now?'

'I'm done with this Edward. You can go.'

'I'm talking to you.'

'Well I'm not talking to you.'

'I thought you believed in people talking things out. Isn't that the point of your speech? Dialogue? Communication?'

'Well, I guess you've convinced me to the contrary, Edward. Well done you.'

'Don't be like this.'

'I mean it. You've won. Turns out that, with some people, it's simply not worth trying.'

Rather than going back to his room, Edward swept through the Annexe's iron gate and out towards the river, head full of turbulent, half-formed thoughts. He could feel the summer wind on his face, the day's heat radiating up at him off the pavements. What was she *thinking*? Why did it mean so much to her, this stupid ethnic squabble? Hadn't she heard what he *said*? The crutches had begun to cut into his arms, but he didn't mind; he swung himself up the ramp and over the footbridge, throwing himself carelessly into each long, weightless step. By the time he had reached the other side of the bridge he realised how exhausted he was. There was a small bench overlooking the black water, and he sat down, letting the lap of wavelets against the concrete soothe him, feeling the moss-covered wood cool against his back.

He must have been there for nearly half an hour when his

phone made a noise. He reached for it at once, expecting it would be Rachel: *Message from Angelica*, it read. He glanced over his shoulder, and opened the message.

— *Is everything O.K.?*

He typed his response quickly.

— *?*

    What do you mean?

    why wouldn't it be

Her message came in at once.

— *I heard.*

— *What did you hear?*

— *Relax*

    am not spying on you

    it's just that obviously Tabitha's room is right above Rachel's . . .

— *Oh, good, so you have spies in the Annexe too . . .*

— *You know Edward I actually just wanted to check you were OK.*

    She said it sounded like you were fighting about something?

— *I'm fine.*

    We're fine.

— *Wow you really don't trust me at all do you?*

— *Last time I saw you it sounded like you never wanted to hear from me again*

— *I was upset*

— *Well I'm upset now*

— *What were you fighting about?*

— *You really want to know?*

— *Yes, obviously*

— *The Chamber. Her speech*

    which you're thrilled about no doubt

— *I'm sorry, Edward*

He took a deep breath and looked around. Once his eyes had readjusted to the dark, he could see that the path was empty, except for the geese huddled at the foot of the pontoon. His phone buzzed again.

— *where are you now?*
— *The riverbank*
  I needed a walk
— *Which side are you on?*
— *What?*
— *Which side*
  Of the river
  College or annexe?
— *Oh*
  College
— *Want to come over?*
— *?*
— *Do. You. Want. To. Come. Over.*
— *Like now?*
  Why?
— *Well first because I thought you might want to talk to someone*
  (and believe it or not we did use to talk about things)
  and second because I can actually help with this
— *How can you help?*
— *Well it sounds from what Tabitha was saying that you couldn't change her mind*
  which means if you do want to help her
  and personally Edward I don't think you should bother
  but if you do want to help her, you need to make sure that the people in charge of drafting statements and staging protests don't decide to focus their energies on Rachel. And I can help with this.
— *You'd do that?*
— *Look Edward I'm trying to be magnanimous but if it's really that hard to believe then I shall stop offering*
— *Fine*

— Fine? I'm not forcing you, Edward.
— I'll come
    When?
— Any time you like

Edward spent most of the route to Angelica's red-carpeted, mahogany-trimmed staircase wondering what, exactly, had prompted this lull in her otherwise uninterrupted disdain. Perhaps she had 'been thinking.' She had often declared herself to have 'been thinking' when she couldn't be bothered to string out a fight any longer; despite her vehemence, she was not averse to the occasional climb-down or retreat, and saw confessions of past error as an opportunity to announce her own personal growth. Yes, that was probably it. Briefly, as he stepped through the empty lodge and into the windless front quad, he felt rise within him the familiar, warm sense of having risen in Angelica's estimation: he thought guiltily of Rachel, but quickly reasoned that he was here on official peacemaking business. She would understand, if she knew. It wasn't Angelica he was after, he reminded himself, but her blessing.

When he arrived at her staircase, the door to her room was already ajar. The bedroom was empty, the bed neatly made, and the assemblage of lamps and fairy lights combining to flood the whole room in their soft, inviting glow. There was a scented candle burning, though such things, he knew, were against the college rules. Above the music that was playing quietly from Angelica's laptop, he could hear the shower running. In fact, the door to the bathroom was slightly ajar too; through it he could smell the floral steam—the mingled scents of her shampoo, her body wash, the expensive creams she rubbed up and down her legs.

He pulled the door shut behind him.

'Angelica?'

No answer.

'*Angelica.*'

The sound of the water stopped. 'I'll be one minute,' she called.

When she emerged, she was wearing a silk robe—a black one he had never seen before, fringed with little patterns of lace. In her hand was a clean white towel, which she used to dab at her neck, the top of her chest. Her skin looked very soft from the steam.

'You got in the shower?'

'What?' Angelica wrung her hair absently with the towel. 'Yes, Edward. I got in the shower. Well deduced.'

'You knew I was coming over, but you got in the shower anyway?'

'Yes.' A pause. Angelica was still dabbing at herself, lips pressed together in faint amusement. 'You were just taking so *long*. I'm very busy tomorrow. And now I feel more comfortable.'

Edward turned towards the door: 'Look, I don't know what you think this is . . .'

'For goodness' sake, Edward. What have I done wrong now?'

'You invite me up to your room. At night.'

'It's nine forty-five. It's hardly *night*.'

'And you *have* to have a shower?'

'It's warm evening. It's the warmest evening of the year so far.'

'And the robe?'

'What about the robe?'

'You had to wear that too?'

'You have very strong opinions about what I'm wearing suddenly, don't you? Shall I cover up?' She rolled her eyes and chuckled. 'I thought you had seen it all before, anyway.'

'You don't need to laugh at me.'

Angelica hung the towel on the back of the door and made her way over to the bed. She sat, leaning back, legs crossed. 'Maybe I'm being extremely presumptuous, but I'd have thought I'd have been a *little* more memorable than that.'

'Angelica . . .'

'You're allowed to remember what it was like, you know. You're allowed to think about it.'

'I know that, but . . .'

'You're allowed to think about *me*.'

'Can we drop this?'

'It's actually something of a poor reward, for all the effort I put in. Don't look at me like that. I *did* make an effort.'

'I never said you didn't make an effort.'

'I liked the way you look at me. You can sit down by the way, if you're tired.' She glanced at the space next to her bed.

'I'll stand.' Edward re-balanced his weight awkwardly on his crutches.

'You don't need to keep all your sightlines clear, you know, as if you'll need to make a speedy getaway. Are you worried I'll kidnap you? Pounce on you?'

'Don't you think Saïd would want to know I'm here?'

'We're just talking. This is just a conversation. Anyway,' she continued briskly, adjusting the sash that held the robe together at her waist, 'Saïd wouldn't mind.'

'Are you sure about that?

She nodded thoughtfully, uncrossed and re-crossed her legs. 'He's very different from you.'

'Right. Good.'

Angelica had begun to smile mischievously. 'Ah, *there* it is,' she said. 'You want to know, how, don't you. How he's different from you. How you and he match up.'

'No, not really.'

'You do.' She nodded smugly to herself. 'Don't worry, Edward. I didn't say *better*. Just different.'

Edward swallowed. 'Different how?'

Angelica brought a finger to her lips, as though thinking very hard. 'He's very strong, obviously. *Very* strong.'

'Obviously . . .'

'And very . . . I don't know. Grown-up. And *passionate*. He likes to tell me about what it was like growing up, in Ramallah. He's travelled so much you know. For his activism. I mean he really *cares* about these things, in a way so few people manage in Oxford. It's really very admirable.'

'How enjoyable. I think I should go . . .'

'But still, it *is* different, with him. It's like . . . I don't know. It's like when I'm with Saïd, I find myself guided into some mould, and it's all very exciting, and flattering—but sometimes I'm not sure I *entirely* identify with it.'

'Goodness, I wonder what that must feel like. I can only imagine.'

'Why don't you come to the event at the Chamber with me? Next week.'

'I'm going to support Rachel.'

'Of course, but think about it. She'll be rehearsing beforehand. She'll be busy. She's probably been quite distracted lately. You could come with me. I could get us very good seats...'

'Aren't you going with Saïd?'

'Oh for goodness' sake, Edward. It's just Saïd all the time with you, isn't it? Saïd, Saïd, Saïd. What if I don't want to be the person I am with Saïd when I go to the talk? What if I want to be someone different?'

"What are you talking about?"

Angelica pushed herself up from the bed and padded over to the chest of drawers in the corner of her room. 'You know what I realised the other day? I had just got out of the shower, right here by this chest of drawers. And I opened the top drawer, and slipped off my robe. And I realised that, whenever I know I'm going to see Saïd that day, I choose white underwear. Every time. White, and lacy. Little bows—innocent. Isn't that funny?'

'Hilarious. I'm in stitches.'

'Do you remember what I wore with you?'

'No.'

'Of course you do.'

'I don't really want to talk about this.'

Angelica turned to face him, leaning carelessly against the chest of drawers. 'You know, Edward, just because you remember things it doesn't mean you're cheating on her. It's safe, to remember. It won't make it happen again. It won't make my robe fall off.' She took a step forward, so that her bare feet were on the rug. 'Tell me what colour underwear I wore when we were together.'

'You wore black, but . . .'

'See? It's like unconsciously, I wanted to broadcast something very different with you.' She pressed her lips together in thought. 'Black. I wonder what that was meant to convey?'

'I don't know. Listen, Angelica. Angelica, no, stay there. I thought we were here because you were offering to help me . . .'

'I will help you. I can help you.'

'This isn't helping.'

'I only mentioned it because I'm trying to tell you that's in the past now. What I'm *trying* to say is that I've been dressing up for everyone in my life as long as I can remember. Certainly every man, anyway.' She was playing vaguely with the lapel of her robe now, not looking at him. 'So yesterday, Edward, I decided to do something different. I caught the train down to London—the Burlington Arcade, do you know it? No?—and I bought a new set. Just for me, to match the dress I'm going to wear later this week in the Chamber.' She stepped forward again, eyeing him with interest. 'Do you want to know what colour it was? Can you guess?'

'No.'

'Bright, bright red. Scarlet, really. It's beautiful, very finely made, and the material is very light. French. *Very* expensive.' She shook her head, as if puzzled by something. 'Red,' she said to herself. 'I wonder what that means.'

'Danger, traditionally.'

'Perhaps.' She nodded thoughtfully. 'Which one would you choose, Edward? If you could do it all again. Imagine we've just met. Imagine this is the first time you've ever been to my room, and I'm here, fresh out of the shower, staring up at you. You can't believe your luck, obviously.'

'Obviously.'

'Which one would you choose? When I slip off my robe, in this imaginary scenario, which one would you like me to be wearing underneath? Black, or white, or red? I'm interested to know.'

'Look all I wanted was to talk about the speech . . .'

'We both know that's not why you came here.'

Her voice was surprisingly firm. For a while, she sat there in silence, appraising him.

'It was, actually,' he said.

'No, Edward. It may have been what you told yourself. But it wasn't why.' She stepped forward again, close enough for him to smell the shampoo in her wet hair.

'Can you stay where you are, please?'

'I'm, just standing here, Edward. I'm not touching you.' She gazed up at him, her face unusually fresh and naked, without the customary, careful make-up. 'She won't know, you do realise that. It would be exactly the same. You could walk around tomorrow like nothing ever happened.' She nodded to herself. 'You could lean forward, and kiss me—and do whatever you liked with me, in fact—and then this Friday, in the Chamber you could give me a polite, cold smile, and walk straight past me. And no one would know. Rachel wouldn't know.'

'Angelica, this is ridiculous.'

'Is it? It doesn't sound so ridiculous to me.'

'Well, it is.'

'You know I was doing some reading the other day. About Judaism, as it happens. Yes, don't look so surprised. I wanted to know more. And as I was doing my reading, I realised something.

The thing about Judaism, Edward, is that it really doesn't matter how you *feel* about things. It doesn't matter what's in your heart.'

'I don't understand how this is relevant.'

'It's much more practical than that. It's really about the outer rituals. What you *do*, and *profess*. They have all these little loopholes and workarounds, for everything. If you go through the motions, you can carry all kinds of little secrets without it much mattering or anyone seeming to care. No one has to know anything. Isn't that interesting?'

'Is that even true?'

'It made me think of you too—no, not because of Rachel, don't shake your head like you're offended. Because of your *name*. *Zahir*. Za-*heer*. Did I say it right this time? I've been practising.'

'I should leave.'

'You don't want to leave. I can tell. You're actually blushing.'

Edward reached down for his crutches.

'Come here, Edward.'

'I'm leaving, Angelica.'

'Don't be silly, Edward.'

Edward turned towards the door.

'*Edward.*' Something very hard had crept into Angelica's voice. 'Don't you dare leave. If you leave that's it.'

'That's it? It's already "it," Angelica. It was "it" a long time ago.'

'Edward. Look at me. If you're going to turn me down, you can at least look at me.' She began to undo the sash of her robe. 'Look at me and tell me you don't want to be with me any more.'

'Angelica, please . . .'

'No one will know.'

'I can't.'

'You can.'

'I don't want to.'

Angelica stiffened. 'If you leave, Edward, it really will be over. I won't help you, and I *certainly* won't help Rachel, and the next time you want someone who has a bit of sway in this college to put in a good word for you, secure you some funding, a nicer room, whatever—well, I'm afraid you'll be on your own.' She folded her arms across the loosely-tied robe. 'Well, Edward?'

Edward said nothing. He simply turned on his heel and strode out along the corridor, eyes fixed on the carpet, not even bothering to stop at the various friends and minions of Angelica who already leaning inquisitively out of their doorways. He did not ask them what they had seen, or what they had heard—or what they thought they had seen, or thought they thought they had heard.

The day of the Symposium dawned bright and warm. As he set out from the Annexe, Edward could feel the heat of the late spring lancing into the riverbank; on the verges of the roads that led up to College, a few flowers had sprung up overnight. The hours in the library passed slowly. By the time he arrived at the Chamber at 5 P.M., the building was teeming. There were buttoned-up posh girls and buttoned-down posh boys already drinking gin and tonics, and cocktail waiters mopping up after them like nannies; there were earnest Student Union people angling for votes, and cawing young conservatives in their thousand shades of beige; there were people with clipboards, and notebooks, and large, professional-looking cameras; there were students bussed in from a local school for their own edification, looking bemused; there was Iqbal, in full, white robe, peering intently at a felt notice board to which the words *Israel—Palestine: A Comradely Symposium* had been optimistically tacked; there were five or six tall Arab men, wearing the same long, white garments, standing around him in a pious-looking ring and glaring over at another group of men, identical in composition except for the skullcaps they wore on their heads; there was the security guard, thumbs twitching over his utility belt; there was Monty in a tuxedo, halfway through a teary rapprochement with Giles, in a tracksuit; and, in the centre of it all, there was Liberty—standing at the foot of the foyer staircase, a few steps higher than the rest, scanning the crowd fascinatedly, a look of remote, regal amusement playing on her immaculately made-up face.

Edward, for his part, tried to avoid catching anyone's eye. Most people gave him a wide berth thanks to his crutches, which he now needed mainly for balance. He had come alone: he hadn't spoken to Rachel since their argument—they would discuss whatever they needed to discuss afterwards, he decided, and he would apologise—and Youssef had not replied to any of his messages for several weeks. The only person in College he had discussed the Symposium with, in fact, was Conrad—who *was* going, he assured him, but almost definitely would spend the entire event making inappropriate comments, possibly in the form of heckles, and was only really subjecting himself to the arduous 500-metre trudge to the Chamber because somewhere, deep in his voyeuristic little soul, he was hoping it was all going to kick off.

'Edward?'

He sensed Angelica even before she even uttered his name. It was that voice again—the famous, grown-up voice, echoing through the Chamber's foyer.

She cut briskly into his path. 'Edward? Edward. What are you doing?'

She really did look beautiful. She was wearing a bright red dress, almost a ballgown really, satin, with a long slit up one side so he could see the smoothness of her leg. Her hair was perfect. Everything about her was perfect in fact, except for the Amerindian backpack sagging incongruously from her shoulder. She looked him up and down disapprovingly.

'Angelica tutted. 'I've been looking for you. Here, you can't get through that way—look at the *state* of you.' She ushered him round, away from the entrance.

'Look, Angelica, I . . .'

'Is something wrong?'

'Of course something's wrong. The other night . . .'

'I don't know what you're talking about, Edward.'

'You invited me to your room, and . . .'

Angelica glanced around her. 'Can you keep your voice down please? I think you're misremembering, anyway. You've always had such a wonderful imagination.'

'You know I'm here for Rachel, right?'

'Of course I know that, Edward. I'm not stupid.'

'Not for you. Not for whatever it is you and Liberty probably have planned.'

Angelica chuckled. 'I don't have anything planned, Edward. I'm not going to stop you from going in, either. Watch her, applaud her if you like. Wave a little Israeli flag in the air, if you must. It's okay. I don't mind.'

'What are you planning? I can tell you're planning something.'

'Oh for goodness' sake. What is it that's making you so suspicious?'

'Why do you keep shifting your weight like that?'

'It's the dress. It's uncomfortable.'

'What's in the bag?'

'Are you interrogating me now? You're interrogating me, aren't you? You've lost it, Edward. You've finally lost it, and turned into a conspiracy theorist. A *philo*semitic conspiracy theorist, in fact—how terribly modern.'

'What's in the bag, Angelica?'

'My things, Edward. My camera. My purse. My eye-shadow. My lipstick. Do you really remember *nothing* about me?'

'You threatened me yesterday. You threatened Rachel.'

'Do you want to look inside? Is that it? You don't want to have me as your girlfriend, or kiss me, or touch me, or look at me, but you want to go through my bags? After all you were telling me about what it's like for you at airports? I'll unzip it—here . . .'

'Leave it, Angelica.'

'Are you sure? Here, look . . .'

'I said leave it.'

Slowly, smugly, Angelica shrugged the backpack up on to her shoulder. For a few seconds, she was overcome with the small victory; then, some dam of resolve in her broke, and she shook her head in pity.

'This isn't why I came up to you, you know,' she said.

'Why *did* you come up to me?'

'I wanted to say I was sorry. About the other night.'

'Right. Of course you did.'

'I mean it Edward.' She leaned in, close. 'I'm sorry, okay? I'm sorry.'

Edward stared at her. 'You're really sorry?'

'I was upset, and humiliated, and believe it or not, I *don't* want to be your enemy. I really did like you, you know.' She gave his wrist a small, almost imperceptible squeeze, and stared at him, just for a moment, with something approaching sadness. Then she brightened: 'Now, come in this way—it's much more accessible—and for goodness' sake, don't break another bone while doing it.'

And with that, Angelica trafficked him through the foyer and over to a small door in the corner marked NO ENTRY TO THE GENERAL PUBLIC. At the sight of them, the security guard bristled. Angelica gestured at Edward's crutches.

'Look, Terry. Look at him. It's me, anyway. You know me. Are we going to have to have another scandal?'

The security guard shot one more glance at Edward, and nodded them through. Angelica held open the door and Edward found himself in a small passageway, scarcely wide enough for the pair of them. To their left was a narrow staircase, with an emergency exit sign glowing above the door at the end.

'It's just through there.'

'That way?'

'That's it. At the end. Just make your way through and sit down,' whispered Angelica impatiently. 'There's space at the end of the row.'

'Aren't you coming?'

'I'm . . . I have something I need to do first. But don't worry, I'll be along in a second. You go.'

Edward stared at her. She seemed strangely agitated: heel tapping the floor arrhythmically, hand massaging the nape of her neck.

'What do you need to do?'

'I have a friend . . . they're waiting for me in the gallery. Go and sit.' Her gaze twitched up towards the stairs. 'Please, Edward. Don't mess this up.'

Reluctantly, Edward obeyed. He took his seat, only to realise he could see Rachel, on the foremost pew, drawing nervous little circles in the air with the ball of her foot. On the seat next to his was a programme. He picked it up. Rachel would be second to speak—after Iqbal, who was already on his feet and deep into his grand, public musings.

'. . . Now I know, of course, some of you affect a certain . . . *commitment* to the cause,' he was saying. 'Because this is what people *do* here, I'm afraid, amid the decadence that has crept into this place of learning. They *affect*—put on little performances, take on little roles. Yet all the while, our vast, cruel, complicated world keeps . . .'

Edward glanced back over his shoulder, towards the doorway and the narrow gallery stairs. Still no Angelica. What was she *doing* up there? *I have a friend . . . they're waiting for me in the gallery. Something I need to do . . .* And then he realised. It tore through him like a sudden distension of muscle: he hadn't seen Saïd once—not in the foyer, not here in the auditorium. Why didn't he notice before? Saïd the Palestinian, Saïd the Muslim, who was not on the speaking list, who was scarcely seen without Angelica these days, and who he was sure, now—yes, absolutely sure—would do anything in his power to wrench him and Rachel apart. He scanned the gallery, but a banner emblazoned with the words ISRAEL—PALESTINE: A COMRADELY SYMPOSIUM obscured everything. What were they *planning* up there?

He took one more look at Rachel, then scooped up his crutches, and, whispering an apology to the faces next to him in the row, hobbled towards the door. Back in the hallway, the staircase looked formidable, only a few feet wide, and steep, doubling back on itself, a line of brass rings, the remnants of an old rope bannister, climbing the left-hand wall. He tried to place both crutches on the first stair, it was too narrow; he tried again, and again the crutch slipped. After two or three more attempts, he decided to abandon them in the corridor and steady himself with his arms alone—the brass rings on one side, the wall on the other.

He was about a quarter of the way up the first flight when he heard her. Her voice seemed thin, hesitant. For a few seconds, it made him stop right where he was. 'Good evening everyone,' she said:

'To tell the truth I . . . I don't quite know where to begin. Something about this evening has forced extremity, hasn't it? Forced us to be adversarial.' A small, hesitant laugh. *'Don't worry, I'm not going to stand up here and ask imploringly why we can't all just get along, why we can't all just be friends. You heard from Iqbal why that's not an option. But still . . .'*

The sound was coming from both directions now, through the gallery above as well as through the corridor below. He began once more to pull himself up the stairs.

'Still, we have to wonder why it's this *conflict,* this *bloodshed, that exerts such a hold over us. Why this ancient shibboleth has to be revived here, has to be continually reborn, in this safe little corner of the world—and why it is that people who ordinarily are the first ones to point out that a people is not quite the same as*

its government, or its self-appointed spokespeople, and would be horrified, just horrified, if someone told them that they were identical to the tiny groups of men who claim to represent them—why do these people make an exception for this conflict? People like to expand complicity—cast the net wider and wider until everyone on the planet is involved. That's what we do nowadays, how we show how sophisticated we are. But if everyone is involved, no one is responsible. There's no room any more to stand up and say no—no this was not, is not, me. A pause, a few rustles from the audience. *I wasn't born in Israel, and I really don't consider myself from Israel, but I have family there, whom I have visited. Whom I do visit.* A few murmurs. *Yes, I know, I know, how terrible of me. And I've noticed that there is something about that place that strives towards the universal. Wherever you are on the planet, the Holy Land, the Promised Land, Al-Ard Al-Muqaddasah, whatever you want to call it, has sway. It's not just we Jews who feel we have a stake in it. It's a billion Muslims, and a billion Christians. Perhaps Disraeli was right: "The history of Jerusalem is the history of the world."'*

There she was. Edward spotted her as he rounded the stairway's hairpin: Angelica, in a conspiratorial huddle—yes, now he was sure of it, she was definitely with someone else—at the far end of the gallery. The brass rings were biting into his fingers, leaving little, smarting grooves, but he pushed on.

*'I don't know if any of my fellow speakers have noticed this, but there's no neutral territory in Jerusalem, or in Israel. Not any more—not after all this time, not after all that history. Every shrine is the Temple. Every garden shed a tabernacle. Every swimming pool is an Arab bathhouse, and every gymnasium is a slice of Rome. "Jerusalem Syndrome," they sometimes call it. Every meal is a sacrament; every time you cross a threshold you plant a flag. Everything refers to everything else, every part to the whole. It's like art—like a poem, or a novel. In fact, it began as a novel—*The Jewish State—*a novel by Theodor Herzl, published*

just at the turn of the century. Israel is what happens when novels come true.'

He could make out Angelica's face now. She was crouching, her hair wild and mussed, the hem of her dress pooled at her ankles. The backpack was leaning against her flank, half-unzipped. And behind her . . . Edward stopped. The highest stair was level with his shoulders, and he reached out desperately, steadying himself on the kickplate. He could almost laugh. Something Burgess once said: 'Gender confusion: how Shakespearean.' Squatting next to Angelica, peering over the bag, wasn't Saïd at all, but a young, slender woman.

'. . . But what I want to know—and what I would like you all to ask yourselves this evening—is can we really live like that? Can we really hold the world to the standards of art? I mean, what kind of life is that, where each individual represents the group, where a part represents the whole? If there is one thing I want to argue this evening, it's that, maybe, we've become a little bit too keen to perform that procedure. Maybe it's because we all study so hard here, comb old texts for the tiniest resonances to magnify into an essay, a thesis, a whole degree. I certainly do it. But when we start to do this with people . . . well, what then? We're all just symbols, or ciphers, for whatever is convenient for everyone else. We're characters in some other person's novel. We're scapegoats, waiting our turn to be driven out into the desert.'

Minka was on her feet now next to Angelica, dungarees rustling, stooped low behind the banner to avoid detection. She had positioned herself directly above the speakers; with an audible hiss, she jerked her head toward Edward. Angelica looked startled: she tugged at the zip on her backpack, but it kept catching on fabric.

And then it made sense. The backpack, Angelica loitering at the food truck, over the box marked Sarapatel. He felt sick. Minka had completely taken over now, tearing at the zip with her fingers, holding the precious cargo up to the light. Against the floor, the plastic bags looked dull and black, but under the fierce halogen bulbs they flared to their true colour—the same bright, shimmering red, in fact, as Angelica's dress.

He was about to shout something—'Wait,' or 'Stop,' or 'Please, somebody . . . ,' or anything really—but realized that if he did, Minka would not wait to unpack the rest of the bag's contents and tip out what she had unloaded on the audience below. He had to tell Rachel, get her out of range, at least; after that it wouldn't matter. Nothing would matter. Ignoring the bolts of pain that streaked up into his hip, he turned back towards the stairs, looping his finger once again into the brass rings. Too *slow*: he tried taking them two at a time, the pain coursing through him with every impact. He could see the crutches lying helplessly at the base of the stairs. And he could hear her, louder now, a new, earnest energy in her voice:

'I tried telling this to a friend—someone I care about very much. Someone who's never quite felt at home anywhere, who's always struggled to understand where he comes from. He's emblematic, I think. We're all so obsessed with roots here—with private histories and family trees, precisely because we know how inadequate they are to explain us, or anything about us. And those of us who do feel those roots, those ties—who've been told that their every breath propagates a tradition—well, I promise you we know it better than anyone. There's an aphorism from Kafka he brought to my attention, that friend of mine. I'd forgotten it, but I think it's worth repeating. Who is "we," I wonder? Humanity? The Jews? The lines lying sleekly on the page? And why "for"? From what does this follow? Perhaps I'm not making any sense. Perhaps nothing makes any sense. But I'll read it anyway. I'll read it to you, just in case it does.'

He was almost at the bottom of the stairs. Curling his finger agonisingly into the final brass bracket, he reached forward and scooped up his crutches. He started out into the corridor, stumbling in his haste. Ten yards away now, eight, six . . .

'. . . *For we are like tree trunks in the snow. In appearance they lie smoothly and a little push should be enough to set them rolling . . .*'

He could hear it in her voice—a knowingness. He imagined her casting her eye around the Chamber searching for him, seeking him out.

'*No, it can't be done, for they are firmly wedded to the ground. But see, even that . . .*'

And then she fell silent. Edward was a few paces from the door now; as he crossed the space, he heard the noise build: the whispers, then the murmurs, then the shouts. He banged open the door with his shoulder, not minding the pain any more, crutches trailing impotently behind him, and began to shout: 'Stop! Stop it!' And for a few seconds he scarcely realised what was happening—not until the security guard grabbed a fistful of the skin on his shoulder and marched him out towards the main entrance—he didn't realise that it was *him* they were staring at, pointing and shouting; that *he* was the vessel into which all the anger, all the outrage—the weeks of provocation from Liberty, the flyers, the rallies—had begun to pour. He opened his mouth to protest, to explain himself. Check *upstairs*, he wanted to scream—the gallery, Angelica. But nothing came out. Nothing. Not a single word: not when he saw the new banner unfurled from the balustrade, the word MURDERERS! looming over them in crude, red daubs. Not when he saw Rachel staring back at him, eyes wide and dark and shining with disappointment. Not when he saw the blood on her face, on her chest, on her hands.

CHAPTER 17

I didn't do it.'

'Ladies and gentleman and Minkas of the jury,' said Youssef, grandly. 'You are asked to accept that this pasty, broken, shell of a man—a Muslim no less, former paramour of known Hamas fighter Angelica Mountbatten-Jones, and long-time associate of an incredibly handsome Egyptian formerly apprehended for terrorist activities in the porter's lodge—you are asked to believe that this man, Edward, is innocent.'

'I didn't *know,* Youssef. I didn't know about Minka, or the blood. I thought Angelica had forgiven me.'

Youssef heaved himself out of the Annexe-issue swivel chair. He paced over to Edward's window, faintly amused, eyeing with interest the shoppers who trudged past along the embankment, funnelled between the tips of willows that frisked over the water and dark, brimming clouds. The visit was unexpected and, at least to begin with, unwelcome. Edward had spent the last two days sequestered in his room. He hadn't seen anyone since the Chamber. He hadn't *wanted* to see anyone since the Chamber, but when the knock came, and he saw Youssef propped jauntily in the doorway, bottle of calvados dangling from his hand, he had to admit it felt good to have him at his side.

'You didn't *know,*' said Youssef, 'But you played your role all the same. And rather well from what I'm told. A pure heart in a guilty body. I mean, let us be honest, she wouldn't have got past that security guard if she didn't have your pathetic Vitamin D-deficient little skeleton to act as her skeleton key.'

'She tricked me. Angelica tricked me.'

'Let us consider the facts Edward. You had just had a fight, loud enough for Angelica's gargoyles to hear, with your Israeli girlfriend about the crimes of her people—excellent performance on that front, by the way. I'm glad you finally saw sense.'

'That wasn't what the fight was about, Youssef. And as I've said before, and not that it matters, she's not actually . . .'

'Please stop speaking. Why are you still speaking? You have this terrible fight, a battle for the ages, and then you trundle up to Angelica's room on your crutches and do goodness knows what with and to her by way of consolation.'

'I didn't *do* anything with her. Or "to" her. This is the point.'

'It was very late at night.'

'It wasn't that late.'

'Witnesses on her corridor observed that she was wearing extremely little clothing.'

'It was a robe. And it's not like I asked her to wear it.'

'I am not criticising you, Edward. You are only human, after all. And barely even that—listen, I know I always say this, but you really do look *extremely* withered and feeble today. When was the last time you ate a large bowl of mashed fava beans? This is a time-honoured Egyptian restorative.'

'What? No. There is nothing *to* criticise, Youssef. I went to talk about Rachel. Angelica and I fought. I left.'

'Izzy K has been hinting to the contrary. Izzy K has been saying that Angelica confided in her several weeks ago that you and Angelica had been growing close and cosy and intimate again.'

'Izzy K has been lying.'

'The two of them went to Burlington arcade to buy new, complicated, highly technologically advanced underwear *with you in mind*—congratulations, by the way—and Izzy K kept the receipt as proof. There is also, you may be interested to know, video footage of you leaving Angelica's room. But listen, Edward. I am not judging, or blaming, or even accusing. Whether or not you did anything untoward is for Allah and his angels to decide, and maybe some kind of civil court. All *I* am saying is that, given the profusion of such suspicious factors, and given your insistence that you just *happened* to be up in that gallery by accident at the *precise* moment all that horrible pigs' blood was thrown, you can see why a number of people in College are finding all this to be a rather improbable coincidence.'

Edward watched Youssef in the alcove. He seemed very cheerful, swivelling happily on his chair and scanning the décor of Edward's room with horrified interest. Outside the window, it had begun to rain—an intense summer rain that sounded like a roll of drums against the Annexe's corrugated metal roof.

'Have you heard from her?' Edward asked. 'Angelica, I mean. Not Izzy.'

'Gone I'm afraid. Immediate North London hegira.' Youssef sighed. 'The thing is, Edward, I believe you. I do. But Angelica and Minka . . . they, I'm afraid, would have the world believe otherwise. And to be fair to them . . .'

'To be *fair*?'

'You have spent a whole year going on and on about how Muslim you were. Even *Liberty* had started to believe you, had she not?'

'But no one believes me now?'

'Calm, Edward. You haven't killed anyone. You haven't molested anyone like dear old Lawrence Pfister.'

'It's illegal, Youssef. You can't just . . .'

'*Calm,* Edward. It's all *internal* here, unofficial. Haven't you noticed? The University does not want any snakes in its precious garden. And of course,' he continued thoughtfully, 'to them, you're a Muslim, lest we forget. You're the huddled masses, the swarm of the oppressed. You must remember this, when they summon you. You have the right to be outraged.'

'I'm *not* a Muslim.'

Youssef just grinned. 'You are now,' he said. 'Now, Edward. I want you to listen. It will be difficult for you, given your irritating habit of answering back and asking stupid questions, but you must try. For once in your life, you must sit still, shut up, and listen to Youssef Chamakh very carefully.'

Edward listened defeatedly as Youssef ran him through the protocol he had worked out for how he was to weather the inevitable storm he would be subjected to by the College, the University and above all Liberty. What was the use in resisting, anyway? Liberty, he said, had begun a rapid reorientation—new pivots, new triangulations, a swift breach with Angelica, the acquisition of a gently oblivious boyfriend called Shmuel—and led the charge of official censure so swiftly that anything Edward could say would, he knew, be only half the story by the time it left his lips. She had penned think-pieces, open letters; she had recorded several interminable video-monologues and sent volleys of them flying round the College. Youssef brandished his phone and forced Edward to sit through three or four minutes of careful, lawyer-approved expostulation: of course we can disagree, indeed we *must* disagree and discuss in any free society; but we must still respect each other's religions and beliefs, and strive, if nothing else, for balance: she, for example, had always championed honest and open debate in her presidency at the Chamber, and was shocked to see it threatened by—and yes, she wasn't afraid to use the word—violent extremism. That was why, for her forthcoming electoral slate, she was announcing that, alongside the suite of Diversitas workshops that were already mandatory for members of the JCR, she would be recommending that freshers undertake a new workshop, on 'Seeing Both Sides,' organised by a very exciting new company called 'Agora.'

'But you must not worry about her too much, Edward,' continued Youssef, with just a shade of imam-voice. 'She is running for office, after all . . .' He waved his hand dismissively. 'You must trust me—I have been seeing *plenty* of Liberty Vanderbilt-Jackson in recent days. And I can assure you with a good deal of reliability that, secretly she wishes she'd done it herself.'

'Since when were you friendly with Liberty?'

'Oh, I am in demand now, Edward. Thanks to you. What does *Youssef* think of all this? What would *Youssef* recommend? Youssef Chamakh: the good Muslim. The Muslim who *didn't.*' He straightened his cuff with a dignified little jerk. 'Everyone loves Youssef now. The tutors. The porters. Lolly has been extremely solicitous. I am starting to regard her as a distinctly rosy prospect. Did you know she recently secured a highly prestigious management consultancy internship? And you'll never guess where she has a tattoo . . .'

'Lolly is being nice to you because I told her you liked her last term, and that the unstable, disrespectful and frankly insane way you've been treating her is the result of what happened with the night porter.'

'What?'

'That's why she's being nice to you. It's not because you're *fashionable* all of a sudden. It's your obsession with being fashionable all the time that has got me into this, Youssef.'

Youssef snorted. 'Oh of course. So I'm the villain in all this? Youssef Chamakh. I was trying to help you, Edward.'

'I'm not saying you're a villain.'

'What *are* you saying?

'I'm saying that something awful has happened, and it's actually very upsetting, and someone has been hurt, and it might be worth remembering that this is not just some opportunity for a few Muslims in Oxford to improve their social standing.'

'This is a fatal dereliction of duty, Edward. Listen to yourself.'

'Listen to *yourself*, Youssef. Listen to the things you say about Rachel, and Jews. All the time.'

'Where is this coming from? Have you been drinking? Have

you checked the water pipes in this horrible stable you call a "room"? You might have lead poisoning. It has happened before.'

'Can't you see, Youssef? There's something *wrong*. Wrong among Muslims, in this country—wrong with *us*, if you like. Why can't you see it? It *keeps* happening. These little comments, little remarks—you, Iqbal, Saïd. And the more I think back to some of the things my family have said, the more I . . .'

'There is no "us," Edward. You know what I think? I think you've finally lost it.' He began to nod. 'Yes, that's it. I didn't want to say it, as you seemed very happy reading your stories about cockroaches and moles and tree surgery and so forth, but you've lost it. This is literature for you. You have finally started seeing things that aren't there.'

'I've not *lost* it, Youssef. Maybe there is no "us." Maybe I'm not a part of this thing at all. But there is a problem, in Oxford, when it comes to Jews. And you're a part of it, aren't you? No, don't shake your head. It's there. You *know* it's there.'

After Youssef left, he sent Rachel what must have been the twentieth or thirtieth message since the Chamber. She didn't reply. She didn't even open it. Before leaving the Annexe for college, he knocked on her door, called out for her, but if she was home, she gave no indication. Once in College, he sat for a while at the edge of the empty green, now fleeced with young dandelions, overlooking the chapel. He wasn't sure what made him stand and go inside: he scarcely ever thought about the chapel, which sat there innocuously at the edge of the quad, the tower short and unassuming, ivy muffling the walls. He pushed open the heavy wooden door. It was very quiet, and gloomy, with shafts of sun cutting across the nave so that the dust blazed up in thick bands from window to window. The pews were nearly empty, but not quite. Farther up the aisle, features hard to make out through the sunlight that streamed down from the windows along the nave, was a figure, stooped as though praying, muttering to himself. As he drew closer, Edward saw him reach back behind his neck and unhook a string of beads, one which looked remarkably familiar.

'Saïd?'

Saïd glanced back at Edward, and nodded politely when he saw him, then resumed his prayer clicking the beads one by one over a curled forefinger, like a fishing line over a reel. He was muttering to himself, slow and incantatory:*'Yah Wahleedahtah Allah, sahlee lee ăz'leenah nahaa'noo ha'tah'ah alen wah fee sah'ahtee mahooteenah.'* A long pause. *'Ameen.'*

Edward cleared his throat. 'I'm . . . I'm sorry. I didn't mean to interrupt.'

'You're not interrupting.'

'I didn't know you came here.'

'I ought to come more often than I do.'

'I don't want to intrude. Sorry. I can go . . .'

'You can join, if you like.'

'Oh, no. I'm not actually . . .'

'I believe the chaplain is very liberal about such matters, if this is what you're worried about.' Saïd patted the pew next to him gently with his palm. 'Sit,' he said. 'I can say the next one in English.'

One by one, the beads begin to tick over Saïd's fingers. 'Hail Mary, full of grace, the Lord is with thee. Blessed art thou amongst women, and blessed is the fruit of thy womb, Jesus . . .'

It took him a moment to realise what he was hearing. 'Wait,' he said. 'You're . . . ?'

'I am, yes.'

'I thought . . .'

'You thought I was a Muslim?'

'I don't know—it's just people said . . .'

'People say a lot of things, Edward. But very few actually asked.'

Edward glanced at the prayer beads. 'But the prayer beads? Aren't they Sufi beads? Youssef said . . .'

'A rosary.' Saïd unfurled his hand to reveal a small, silver cross. 'And I'm afraid Youssef says a lot of things.'

'He said you thought you were "more Muslim than the rest of us."'

Saïd frowned. 'Are you sure he was being quite serious? Youssef makes a lot of jokes, you know. It seems to be his way of being sincere.'

'I . . . I don't know. I thought so at the time.'

They were quiet a while, staring up together at the vacant bank of pews opposite. 'Why did you ask Rachel to speak at the Symposium?' said Edward.

'I didn't ask her to speak.'

'She said she talked to you about it.'

'She did. And I told her she had to decide for herself. This was all.'

'That was it?'

'Are you asking me if I knew about Angelica?'

'*Did* you know about Angelica?'

'Of course I didn't know.' Saïd sighed, and clicked together the beads absent-mindedly. 'Listen, Edward, I know that the rumours might suggest the contrary, but I am afraid I don't even know Angelica very well at all. I have the impression she wants to be *seen* with me. This is the extent of it.'

'But that night by the Annexe. She called you "Darling" . . .'

'I know. I found this odd, too. I assumed she was doing this to upset you.'

'It did upset me.'

'I'm sorry, Edward. I was under the impression you had treated her appallingly. I think in some ways, you *did* treat her appallingly.'

'You only heard her side of it.'

'True. But as injustices go, Edward, this seems a small one.'

'So you really were never going out with her?'

'No. We had dinner together twice. In college. She asked me if I wanted to protest outside the Chamber a few times, and I said no, that the Chamber thrives on people like me getting very angry outside it and attracting attention on its behalf. And this was the extent of it.'

'So you *did* know she was planning something.'

'Yes. Outside. In the street. Where she has every right to protest, and where actually, Edward, in the great scheme of things, a little noise and disruption in the interests of helping people who are dying might not be the worst thing. In fact, I do wonder if a street protest, a few chants, some bloodstained placards, wasn't the *only* thing she was planning, until you came along with your crutches and gave her a bright new idea.'

'She would have done it whether I was there or not.'

'She couldn't get in that gallery without you.'

'But my leg. She wouldn't have just *used* it like that. I mean all those workshops on disability. Those pamphlets . . .'

'Short of the old line in Exodus about lambs with broken bones being unfit for sacrifice, I see no earthly reason why she would not use your injury for whatever purposes she saw fit.'

'She's trying to frame me for it, you know.'

'She won't succeed.'

'You don't know that. I've somehow managed to lose or alienate all the people who care what happens to me.'

Saïd exhaled slowly, took one last look at the rosary beads, and stowed them in his pocket. 'Edward, he said, listen. Listen a second. Why are you saying this to me now?'

'Because you're here. Because you asked.'

'But what does it achieve?'

'Maybe you can convince Liberty that I'm telling the truth. Or convince Angelica to tell the truth herself.'

Saïd chuckled 'You really think a good word from *me* would help? Now? Under the circumstances?'

'Liberty still respects you. She would listen.'

'I promise you she would not listen. Honestly, Edward, I think you may have mistaken Liberty and Angelica's temporary fascination with me, and the people of Palestine, and the abstract idea that they and I might have suffered, with popularity.'

'People in Oxford *love* you, Saïd. They spend time with you. They invite you to things.'

'All this could be said of you, too.'

'It's different, with me.'

'No, Edward. It just looks different from the inside.' Saïd shook his head and turned on the pew to face Edward. 'Before I came here I thought if I can just make people aware of *my* issue, the problem that matters to *me*—if I can convince enough people in Oxford, which is full of the people who decide how the world works—then that would be it. Awareness would be raised, and plans would be formulated, and policies would be carried out, and, as if by magic, if I worked very hard and wrote good essays and got a good job for the right international organisation, Palestine would be free. And I could go home, Edward. I could go home, to a country that doesn't even exist yet.' He laughed bitterly. 'But I have been here for several years now. And I can tell you with some confidence that, whatever the problem is here, it is not a lack of *caring*. There's an old joke people tell in the West Bank. I had a taxi driver tell me it when I was at that conference in Ramallah. We were driving down this road—a terrible road, just rocks really—and trying to avoid all the new roadblocks and checkpoints. Because there are new ones every year, Edward. New borders to take into account new settlements, so if you want to get anywhere you have to take detours—this is why I had the driver. And at one point, we were totally, totally lost. The roads had started to look all the same, and the light was running out. The driver glanced back at me, and smiled, and said: "God, how I long for the days before we had peace. Things were *so* much easier."' He smiled sadly. 'It's a joke. You understand?'

'I get the joke.'

'What I am saying is that in all the world, all the great wide world full of wars and suicide-bombings and factions of people that hate each other, *hate* each other like nothing you could imagine—and really, Edward, you couldn't even *begin* to imagine—in all the world there is nothing so dangerous as a bright young man, or woman, who went to Oxford and thinks it's his job to fix it.'

Most of the birds outside the Business School's window were pigeons. The males were strutting up and down, cooing, ruffling and unruffling their iridescent necks. The females sat quietly atop the guttering, watching.

'Shall we begin?'

Edward turned his attention from the window. Liberty was at the head of the conference table chair, swivelling gently from side to side; behind her, the red digital clock blinked its way into the next hour. She was wearing a simple, black and white business suit, and her hair had been stripped of all its beads. She looked like someone the Business School might put on one of its posters.

'There's still one missing, but I think we should press on anyway.' Liberty glanced behind her at the clock. 'Shall we begin, Edward? Everyone? Okay. Let's begin.'

He didn't feel particularly nervous. He had been sleeping rather well, curiously enough doing his work diligently; his hair was combed, his shirt crisp. He had received his summons only yesterday: the Business School, 10 A.M. by the power vested in Diversitas, and had made his way slowly over after breakfast, over the freshly mowed quad and through the centre of town, which was already opening itself up to one of those perfect May mornings, the birds singing, the spires and cobbles warming under the sun.

'Now, you know why you're here, so I won't bore you.' Slowly, enjoying each moment, Liberty unscrewed the cap from one of the bottles of mineral water on the desk and poured herself a glass. She had gathered her most trusted associates: Oscar, a few more replacement-Angelicas whose names he didn't know, Riz. To her right, in pride of place, was Izzy K.

'By way of an opening statement,' continued Liberty, 'I want to remind you that technically, this tribunal has no powers. But between you and me . . .' She leaned forward. 'We know that the University takes what we have to say seriously. Like, really seriously. So for your own sake, Edward, I suggest you take today really seriously too.' With her finger, she squared the papers on her desk, then imperiously cleared her throat: 'First of all, we want to check that you have no objection to the Committee.'

'Objection?'

'About its makeup. It's *composition*. You think it's representative enough, balanced enough, et cetera. We were hoping for one more member from one of the approved list of diverse groups. But it doesn't look like they're going to show . . .'

Edward scanned the conference table. The chair to his left— the one furthest from Liberty—stood empty. 'Who's missing?'

'Actually, I don't think that needs to concern you. The charter allows us to proceed with a quorum whether or not . . .'

'I'd like to know, Liberty.'

Liberty grinned, her lip retracting over the edges of her teeth, with their minute serrations. 'Someone we brought in *specially*,' she said. 'Someone who knows you well enough, and occupies a position of authority in your . . . your *community*.'

'Wait.' Edward sat up. It's not . . .'

'Excuse me Edward?'

'It's not Iqbal, is it?' It all made sense now. The empty chair, the statement. Iqbal had been at the forefront of official censure, putting out a generous statement on behalf of the Muslim Association calling for *ecumenicism* and *interfaith dialogue*— emphasising, seven or eight times, that he'd been splashed too.

'I'm afraid I'm not at liberty to say Edward. The charter is very clear . . .'

'I'm not stupid, Liberty.'

'So you say.'

He glanced around in disbelief. Oscar was writing something down in a pale green exercise book; Izzy was still gazing adoringly to her left. 'So what?' he said. 'This whole thing is just for show?'

'The Committee has yet to make up its mind.'

'With all respect, Liberty, I don't think that's true at all. The Committee knows full well what it plans on doing, and there is nothing I can say, nothing I can do, to change its recommendation.' He shrugged: 'I don't care. I don't care about any of it.'

'Perhaps we should stay on topic.'

'Yes, perhaps we should.'

Liberty glanced down at a typewritten agenda, whose contents Edward could not see. 'So,' she said, 'you have no formal objections?'

'I object to the whole thing. I object to you acting like you own the place. Who *are* you? The President? The president of what?'

'Right. Under which *section* of the charter would you like to lodge it, this objection of yours?'

'Under every section. Or none of them. An objection of spirit. You've heard of the spirit of the law, haven't you? From all those classes on *The Merchant of Venice*?'

'I'm afraid the Committee doesn't recognise this distinction, Edward. There are by-laws. There's a constitution.'

'Oh, come *on*. You know what I'm talking about. The difference between Christians and Jews in Shakespeare. We *did* have tutorials remember? Years ago, before I was a Muslim and before you were an anti-Semite.'

'Slandering me isn't going to help you, Edward.'

'Remember when you told me that you *know Jews*? Remember that? Well, you were lying.'

'Actually,' Liberty glanced to her side. 'This might be relevant.

Make a note, Oscar.' She turned back to face him. 'Go on, Edward. Why not tell us. What is the difference, in your opinion, between a Jew and a Christian?'

Edward shrugged. They had already made up their minds anyway. 'It's about law, isn't it?' he said. For Jews, the law is identical to the letter, the statute—if you want to escape punishment, you have to find a loophole. For Christians, it's about the *spirit* of the law. You can choose to suspend the law if you think it's right to do so. You can be merciful.'

Liberty raised an eyebrow. She had begun to scribble things down too.

'Think about it,' continued Edward. 'Shylock loses his case because the Christians find a loophole in his contract. They beat him at his own Jewish game.'

'Right, Edward, I suggest you not pursue this topic; I assure you, it's only prejudicing . . .'

'That's what he means,' said Edward, 'when he says "I am content." He means that they've adhered to the contract. He's not being ironic. It's true.'

Liberty cleared her throat. 'Thank you for the tutorial, Edward. But to the matter at hand. The Committee has already heard testimony from Ms. Angelica Mountbatten-Jones, and one Minka Gunn, who prefers to go without a gendered title. The testimony they supplied implicated the subject of the current inquiry . . .' She peered over the lip of the table, 'that's you, Edward . . . in a severe transgression of the Student Code of Conduct, the University Undergraduate Handbook, the Student Union Code of Ethics . . .'

'Won't *they* be appearing today?'

'That wouldn't be appropriate.'

It was all he could do not to laugh. 'So I don't even get to see my accuser. Brilliant. Wonderful.'

'I remind you, Edward, that this is not a trial but an independent inquiry. Do you understand the difference?'

'Not really, no.'

'Listen, Edward. If you feel it's appropriate, then I can read the charter to you in full. There are twelve items. I believe it would take about fifteen minutes. Would you like me to read it to you?'

'No. I would rather die.'

'Well then. May I proceed?'

Edward nodded.

'On 15 May, in the debating hall known colloquially by students as "The Chamber", four bags of pigs' blood were released from the galleries overlooking the speakers, most of whom were Jewish . . .' Liberty pulled a pen out of the spine of her notepad, and brought it to her lips as she searched for the word. 'Of Jewish *extraction*. Now, the Jewish Students' Association liaison has informed us that, according to the laws of something called *kashrut* . . .'

'I know all this, Liberty.'

'Very well. I suppose you do, don't you? You've had enough experience.' Liberty flicked though a few more of her papers, clearly annoyed, as though robbed of the pleasure of ceremony. 'Ms. Mountbatten-Jones alleges that you were part of the plan. That it was your injury that allowed the pair of them to access the gallery, and that you yourself went up to the gallery to check on them.'

'That's it? Those are the charges?'

'That is what is alleged.'

He nodded slowly. It was useless anyway. It would have happened one way or another, from the moment he stood up to her in the Chamber. 'Well then,' he said. 'I don't wish to take up any more of the Committee's time. I won't dispute the allegations.'

'Excuse me?'

'I won't dispute them. Write up whatever you need to write up, and we can all be going.'

Liberty looked slightly flustered. She leaned over to Oscar, murmuring something behind her hand, then repeated the process with Izzy K on the other side. 'Are you sure that's all you want to contribute, Edward? I must say that I had expected some disagreement between you and the version put to the Committee yesterday.'

Edward shook his head. 'I make no dispute.'

'How about some words of extenuation? We on this committee are all fully aware of how sensitive an issue this is. And we have plenty of sympathy for your politics, of course . . .'

'I have no politics.'

'Now, Edward, let's not be *too* hasty.'

Oscar piped up, his narrow, rodent-like face suddenly bunched up in thought: 'Perhaps, Edward, if you just gave an informal statement about your state of mind, the Committee could write a letter to the University explaining that you weren't fully in control of your actions. Diversitas could then put in a request to undertake mediation . . .'

'I don't want a mediation, and I don't want to say anything in my defence.'

Oscar looked startled. 'That's okay. We can find you an advocate. Or religious representative, if you prefer.'

'I don't want an advocate. Or a religious representative.'

'An advocate might seriously improve . . .'

'All I want,' said Edward, voice beginning to rise now, 'is for this to be over. I can deal with whatever consequences the powers that be impose.'

Liberty said nothing. Then Izzy raised a hand, tremoring with ill-suppressed energy. 'Liberty, if I may . . .'

'Yes, Isabella.' She said it without taking her eyes off Edward once.

Izzy cleared her throat: 'I believe Edward is being deliberately . . . deliberately *evasive*. The role of this committee is to consider the different competing perspectives that surround the event, and then make a recommendation to the University accordingly. By refusing to co-operate, he's kind of . . . I don't know. He's implying that we don't have any authority. He's *mocking* us, Liberty.'

'How have I refused to co-operate? I've co-operated fully. I've told you to pass down whatever judgement you please. I won't dispute it. That *is* co-operation. Surely.'

'Liberty . . .' Izzy had swivelled to her left, completely ignoring Edward now, a strange, pleading detectable in the corners of her eyes. 'Edward knows exactly what he's doing. He knows that in a case . . .' She glanced back at Edward, then lowered her voice: 'in a case as *politically* sensitive as this one . . .'

'I can actually hear you, you know. And politics has nothing to do with whether or not I'm guilty.'

Izzy didn't appear to have noticed: 'It would be hugely beneficial for the wider community to understand the political sensitivities that contributed to this . . . this episode. Especially seeing as Edward has a family connection. I mean, we all have our own opinions, don't we? He has every reason to feel . . .'

Edward stood abruptly: 'Is the Committee now testifying on my behalf?'

Izzy took a deep breath, and took out a handkerchief to blot out the little splashes of mineral water that had lapped over the sides of the glass when she had nudged the table during her speech. 'I for one,' she said, still not meeting Edward's eye, 'think it's entirely obvious what Edward is doing, and would recommend the University impose the harshest possible sentence on him as a result. He is patently refusing to co-operate with the tribunal. By doing so, he . . . he . . .'

'I think there's someone at the door,' said Oscar.

'Can't they wait?'

There was a knock.

'If they're late, they can't just barge in,' said Izzy.

Liberty thought for a few seconds. 'Let them in, Oscar,' she said.

Oscar scurried over to the door and pulled it ajar. He peered round for a few seconds before he opened it, whispering something to whoever had knocked. Once satisfied, he stepped back.

'Our missing Committee-member,' he said.

There, standing on the threshold where the pale wood of the conference room met the dark, geometrical carpet of the hallway, his white robe still fluttering round his ankles, his hair faintly dishevelled beneath the grey *kufi*, was Youssef.

'Sorry I'm late, everyone.' He stroked his beard, now as dense and coiled as Edward had ever seen it. His voice, Edward noticed, was deep and authoritative—rather like his imam voice, but less of a pastiche and more like the real thing. 'Now,' he said. 'What did I miss? What did this well-meaning little moron say? Did he mention how much he loves Jews? This is an important feature of his makeup.'

'I think the Committee had actually almost finished, Youssef,' said Liberty. We undertook our duties without you, as the charter permits. I'm afraid Edward was refusing to co-operate.'

Youssef glared at Edward. 'He was, was he?'

'He was *threatening*,' chipped in Izzy, 'to bring the Committee into disrepute.'

'I see.' Youssef drew himself up to his full, majestic height, and proceeded over to the empty chair. 'Liberty, if I may?'

She nodded her assent, and he sat.

'Perhaps,' he continued, 'the Committee could permit us a short adjournment. There is provision for it in the charter, I take it? I have read it. Section thirty-three? Paragraph four? With the spelling mistakes?'

Liberty pursed her lips. 'There is, but . . .'

'Now Liberty,' says Youssef, spreading his arms out wide. Edward could swear that a new, Arabic lilt had crept into the plumminess of his voice. 'Surely you wouldn't mind. I'm certain if Edward and I could talk alone—informally, as it were, Muslim to Muslim—then some sort of agreement could be reached. It's been an emotionally demanding few days for all of us. But especially for those . . . How should I put it? For those of us with skin in the game.'

Liberty stared at him for a long time. 'Very well,' she said at last. 'You talk to him. You see if you can get through.'

One by one, they filed out of the conference room. Youssef pushed himself up from the table and ambled over to the broad picture window; he made no attempt to capture Edward's attention, just stared out alongside him, involving him, as though to let him know that that this, at least they had in common: this view, this greyness. Most of the birds had already flown away.

'So this is the plan, is it?'

'What is?'

'This. Going down with the ship. Adding yourself to the great list of Muslim martyrs, along with Sumayya and Yasir and the gentlemen who used to sell kebabs with Abdul. Are you experiencing a thrill? Has a great winged horse descended to usher you to the higher realm? Or might you, perhaps, be being a *tiny* bit overdramatic.'

'I'm not giving them what they want, Youssef. I won't do it.'

'Calm, Edward, I'm on your side. Not Liberty's. I'm a Muslim again now, not African, keep up. But I do wish to figure out what my dear, lost little friend is doing.'

'I'm taking some responsibility. For what happened, for once in my life.'

Youssef gazed through the window. It had begun to rain: broad, violent stripes that hit the glass at strange angles and pooled thickly in the stiles; unusual rain, rain from a closer set of heavens. 'You're not guilty, though,' he said at last.

'Am I not?'

'Not of this.'

Youssef turned from the window. 'Listen, Edward. There's a very easy way out of this. You write a letter to Liberty explaining

356 · THOMAS PEERMOHAMED LAMBERT

that you've chosen to go through me, since you feel we have a certain rapport. Culturally speaking.'

'You mean we're friends? Because recently I've not really been able to tell.'

'Better not say *that*. It might prejudice them. Though yes we are friends, and you know it really, and you are being so extremely slow I worry you might have sustained some head injury in your little collision the other day.' He sighed. 'Now, once we have written said letter, I write up a report to Liberty, explaining how, given your ancestry, your religious conversion, you were bound to get caught up in the IsraelPalestine controversy. I mean, it *is* the great issue, isn't it? The great shibboleth. The one question on which neutrality is not an option. You got swept up, because you are excitable and poorly educated and have an extremely weak character. Everyone will believe it, I'm sure.' He nodded to himself, the skeleton of a plan forming in his mind. 'And *then* we can dispute Angelica's version of events—say you weren't even a major participant, that you were basically tricked, that you were possessed by an evil djinn, that a Jew ran over your family dog when you were five, et cetera, et cetera. If this even necessary.'

'You mean I give in? You know your plan seems very similar to Liberty's, Youssef.'

'You tell the *truth*, Edward. Or at least the version of it that will stop you from getting kicked out of this place.'

'I never converted, you know. I'm *not* a Muslim, and if I get out of this by telling everyone I am one, then that'll be a lie. Another lie, to add to all the others.'

'You came along to a lot of events with me, you know. In my humble Egyptian opinion, that counts as a start.' Youssef pulled his chair closer and placed a hand on Edward's shoulder. Something about the warmth of it, its weight and surety, made Edward feel very sad.

'You should have seen her. On her face, all the blood.' He

wiped his eyes with the hem of his sleeve. 'She didn't deserve it. Of all the people . . .'

'I know.'

'That's not what you said last term. You kept talking about "the crimes of her people," from what I remember.'

'I was upset.'

'But you do think that, don't you? On some level, that's what you think.'

Youssef stared at him for a long time, his eyes mobile, searching. 'Listen, Edward. I don't have an answer for you. All I can give you is advice. You are extremely stupid, you do realise this?'

'Wow, thank you, this is excellent advice.'

'What I'm trying to say is that it's never going to be there, this security you want. You will never be your authentic self. Think about it. You want to be told what you are, and you want to be free of it. You want to be told what to think, and you want to feel belief spring up of its own accord in your soul. You want to be innocent, and you want to be guilty. You want Rachel to love you, and for some reason you appear to want her to hate you, perhaps in the hope that it might count as some kind of penance. You want to be exotic and you want to fit in. And I understand it, Edward. Really, I do. But this kind of thinking is, at its core, stupid, English, sun-cream-wearing, un-Islamic drivel. Drivel.' He shook his head. 'This is not the *way*, Edward—punishing yourself, turning your back on everything. Come now. Leave the self-flagellation to the Shi'ites. Come and be a Muslim with me. Choose *life*.'

'I should talk to Rachel.'

'Of course you should talk to Rachel my weird little friend. How are you only just realising this? Come now, that's good, get up. That's the spirit.'

Edward let himself be ushered to his feet. 'What if she doesn't believe me, Youssef?'

'Of course she'll believe you. She's crazy about you, for some unfathomable reason. She wants to be with you, and she's *looking* for an excuse to be with you, and if you look in her eyes and you tell her the truth, that you were tricked, and you are sorry you fought, and that you love her so much that you are willing to forego even *my* scintillating presence to be with her, then trust me on this, she'll believe you.'

'She hasn't replied to any of my messages. She doesn't answer when I knock on her door.'

'I'm sure she just needed time.'

'You don't know that.'

Youssef strolled over to the window. For several seconds, he stared out through the rain, at the glassy pavement and down at the traffic on the roadway; then he broke out into a grin. 'Say, Edward,' he said. 'When was the last time you corresponded with her?'

'A few days ago. Why?'

'I see.' Youssef began to laugh.

'What are you doing? What's so funny? *Youssef.*'

'A few days ago?'

'Yes, I just said that.'

'Did you tell her you were coming here? To the Business School?'

'What? Yes. I knew she would find out about the hearing and I just wanted to pre-empt whatever lies Liberty came out with.'

'And did you give her the date and time?'

'Yes, I think so.'

Youssef began to chuckle. 'Well then,' he said. 'I *really* wouldn't worry. Come to the window, Edward.'

'What? Why?'

'Come to the window. Either I have fallen victim to strange, un-Islamic visions, or, well . . . Why don't you just look for yourself?'

Acknowledgements

Writing a book can sometimes be a lonely endeavour, but it cannot be done without the help of others. In particular, I would like to thank Christopher Potter for his exceptional editorial guidance, and Anna Webber, for supporting this novel even in its infancy. I am also deeply grateful to Daniela Petracco, Michael Reynolds, Michael Kerrigan, Leonella Basiglini, Millie Guille, Patricia Chido, Ginevra Rapisardi, Eva Ferri, and everyone else at Europa and beyond who has helped see this book through to publication.

In addition, I would like to thank Joe Mead, Connor Haseley, Max Lambert, Jamie Lambert, and Merv Lambert for their invaluable input on the manuscript, and my parents, for their patience and support. Most of all, I want to thank Wanda, this book's dedicatee, who has been an inexhaustible source of inspiration, humour, and encouragement. Without her, *Shibboleth* simply could not have existed.

ABOUT THE AUTHOR

Thomas Peermohamed Lambert is a writer who divides his time between London and Oxford. In 2022, he was selected as a London Library Emerging Writer, and he is currently a Clarendon Scholar at the University of Oxford. *Shibboleth* is his first novel.